They all knew that, as a boy, Matt had often romanticized about his mysterious parents. Connie herself had suspected that he might be her father's illegitimate son. But if so, why had her mother agreed to take him into the family and bring him up? Surely that was the last thing a betrayed wife would contemplate — unless she was a saint, and Mother had had as many faults as anyone else. She had also had her virtues, but Connie had never felt that unstinting forgiveness was one of them. Her determination grew as she sipped her tea. Matt would know what it felt like to be humiliated. She would write him a letter, spelling out the facts, and she would spare him nothing. His life would be ruined; his confidence would be shattered, and nothing and nobody would be able to save him. It was a cruel step to take, but Connie had been hurt once too often and now she felt desperate enough to take it.

The Butterfly Box

PAMELA OLDFIELD

WARNER BOOKS

A *Warner* Book

First published in Great Britain in 1996
by Michael Joseph Ltd
This edition published by Warner Books in 1997

Copyright © Pamela Oldfield 1996

The moral right of the author has been asserted.

A CIP catalogue record for this book
is available from the British Library.

ISBN 0 7515 1647 3

Typeset by Palimpsest Book Production Limited
Printed and bound in Great Britain by
Clays Ltd, St Ives plc

Warner Books
A Division of
Little, Brown and Company (UK)
Brettenham House
Lancaster Place
London WC2E 7EN

TO JOSEPH
WITH LOVE

Chapter One

WHEN THE PHONE RANG, FRAN, curled up on the sofa, glanced up from the manuscript she had just started to read. In the notebook on the coffee table she had written only the date, January 3rd, 1938 and a name, Paul Hallam. She waited for Annie to answer the phone, but as it still rang she moved the manuscript from her lap, preparing to answer it herself.

Dot asked eagerly, 'Shall I, Fran?'

'What?' Fran rolled her eyes humorously. 'And disturb poor old Fritz?'

'Fritz? Oh, yes!' Dot looked down at the small dog on her lap and bit her lip guiltily. 'I mustn't, must I, Fritz?'

A small snore from the elderly dachshund set her giggling and Fran experienced the familiar pang of regret that her sister, born when Fran was five, would never live a full life.

Fran went into the hall and picked up the receiver. 'Maidhurst 344.'

'Fran, it's me.'

Shocked, Fran stared at the receiver.

'Fran! It's me. Connie. And please don't—'

Fran hung up.

Annie appeared from the kitchen, wiping her hands on a teacloth. Once their nanny, she was now the housekeeper.

'I had flour all over my hands . . .' she began, then frowned. 'Is anything wrong? You look as white as a sheet.'

Fran swallowed. 'Wrong number,' she said.

Annie eyed her suspiciously. 'Wrong number?'

'Yes.'

Fran turned away and walked back into the sitting room. Connie! Her throat felt dry and her heart was racing as the familiar pain flared. How dared she ring up out of the blue like that!

Dot asked, 'Wasn't it anybody?'

'No.' Fran sat down and picked up the bulky manuscript, but she did not read it; instead she stared into the fire, despising herself for being so vulnerable after all this time. She reminded herself that she had vowed never to spare another thought for either of them, yet here she was, undeniably shaken by the sound of Connie's voice.

Dot said, 'How did it ring if it wasn't anybody?' Her pale face wore an expression of deep disappointment and her blue eyes reproached Fran. Her gold-red hair was worn long and this added to her childlike appearance.

'It was a wrong number.' Fran hoped her sister would accept the lie, but at that moment the phone rang again.

Dot brightened; the telephone fascinated her. 'There it goes again,' she said hopefully.

Hearing Annie's footsteps in the hall, Fran waited, her heart thumping. If Connie insisted on speaking to her it could be for only one reason – she wanted to renew their friendship. Fran doubted that she would ever be ready for that.

Annie put her head round the door, said, 'It's the office,' and withdrew. Relieved, Fran jumped to her feet and hurried into the hall.

'Fran, it's Marjory here. Just to check that you've received the Paul Hallam manuscript?'

'I have, thanks. In fact I've just started reading it. The title's rather good, I thought – *The Granite Cloud.* Intriguing.'

2

'Possibly. I thought it too obscure. The reader's report was tentative, but as it came via Peter Westrop, Mr Starr seemed to think you should read it. You know what chums they are – same club and all that.'

Fran detected the touch of frost in Marjory's tone and could visualize the little shrug Marjory would give as she spoke; she knew that Marjory found Fran's own privileged status hard to accept. She asked, 'Have you read it?'

'I wasn't overly impressed, to be honest. But give it a try, just to keep Kenneth happy.' When 'Mr Starr' became 'Kenneth' Fran knew that Marjory was annoyed – doubtless because she objected to the fact that he wanted a second opinion.

'There's no letter with it,' said Fran. 'No details at all. Do we know anything about Hallam?'

'Only that it's his first novel. Peter Westrop is never very forthcoming about his authors.'

'I'll read it and let you know. If I've finished it by tomorrow I'll bring it in with me.'

'Will you be at the meeting in the afternoon?'

'That's the idea.'

'I'll see you then.'

'Bye.'

Fran returned to the manuscript, intrigued but also slightly exasperated. Office politics were something she had never enjoyed, but as a member of the Massey family it was often hard to avoid being drawn into the conflicts of interest which arose from time to time. Her grandfather had founded Massey & Co. but later, when times were hard, they had been forced to merge with Starr Publishing to become Massey and Starr Ltd. Later still, after a board-room battle, the Starrs had seized control and now they were Starr Massey Ltd with Kenneth Starr as managing director. As the only remaining member of the Massey family, Fran was one of the senior editors and Marjory Evans still jibbed at the disparity between them. For this reason Fran was glad that she need not spend all her working week in the office. Reading and editing manuscripts could be done at home, and this also allowed her to spend time with Dot. An accident when Dot was seven had caused significant and irreparable brain damage, so that at twenty-one she had the mind of a ten-year-old. She did, however, have a real talent for drawing and watercolours and she divided her time quite happily between this hobby and the dog, Fritz.

Now Fran told her, 'It was Marjory on the telephone, about this.' She indicated the manuscript.

'Is it a good story?'

'Maybe. I'll let you know when I've finished it. The author's name is Paul Hallam.'

'Nice name.'

'Yes. I suppose it is.'

Marjory's call had distracted Fran's thoughts from Connie but now, as she settled back to work, the anguished memories threatened to overwhelm her and she had to make a conscious effort to blot them out. She bent over the page, her brown eyes intent on the words, her slim shoulders hunched protectively. Like most members of the Massey family, Fran's hair held reddish tints, but hers was a deep auburn, worn in soft waves close to the head in the fashion of the thirties. She was twenty-six and unmarried. As a child Fran had been painfully plain and Connie, eldest and prettiest of the four girls, had been their father's favourite, a fact he had made no attempt to disguise.

Fritz snorted suddenly and woke up. He at once slithered from Dot's restraining hands and padded out of the room on his stumpy legs.

Fran watched him go. 'He's getting rather deaf,' she remarked. 'He didn't hear the telephone ring.'

'He was asleep.' Dot was immediately defensive of her pet.

'I only meant we should bear it in mind – when we

4

call him and when he's with us in the street. He may not always be aware of the traffic. We mustn't assume he can hear everything we can hear.'

'He's an old dog, isn't he?'

'Fairly elderly, I suppose. He was born just after—' She stopped.

Dot finished the sentence for her. 'Just after Connie and Matt went away. So that makes him ... um ...' She wrinkled her forehead, struggling with the arithmetic. 'Um ...' She looked hopefully at Fran. 'Nine? Ten?'

'Something like that.' Fran took a deep breath. Was it really ten years since their quarrel? She checked the calculation. Yes, it was more than ten years ago. Mary had bought the puppy for Fran, in one of her familiar gestures of sympathy, but eleven-year-old Dot had immediately commandeered him. Seeing the instant rapport between them, Fran had surrendered her pet willingly and Dot and Fritz had been inseparable ever since.

Dot looked anxious. 'Will he die?' she asked. 'Will Fritz die, like Father did, and be buried?'

'One day – but not yet. Maybe not for a long time. Don't worry about it, Dot.'

The phone shrilled and Fran jumped at the sound.

'Marjory!' cried Dot triumphantly.

But Fran feared the worst. It could be Connie again, determined to say whatever was on her mind. Speaking to her would bring it all back, and the heartache would begin all over again. Suddenly Fran made up her mind. She would not be intimidated in this way; she would tell Connie, quite firmly, that she had nothing to say to her, and ask her not to call again. She would not lose her temper, would not be goaded into an undignified exchange. She stood up and went out into the hall and Annie, seeing her approach, went back into the kitchen.

'Maidhurst 344,' Fran said and was annoyed to hear the telltale shake in her voice.

For a moment there was a silence at the other end of the line, then she heard Connie's voice.

'Mother's dead.'

It was Fran's turn to fall silent. The words rang in her mind as she tried to grasp their meaning. It seemed impossible that their mother had died. She had gone to France as usual to escape the winter, and had seemed well enough considering.

'Fran! Did you hear me? I said Mother's dead. *Dead*!'

'I heard you.'

'Then say something, for God's sake.'

Fran said, 'Who told you? How? When did she die?' She sat down on the chair beside the telephone, her legs weak. Her mother was *dead*? Surely there must be some mistake.

'She died in her sleep, which was a blessing. But it was a terrible shock for Violet and Alice. Poor Alice found her dead in bed. As she said, we all knew it was coming, even Mother. You don't live with TB without knowing your days are numbered, but she's been frail for so long. A creaking gate. I suppose we began to think she would last for ever.'

Fran struggled to keep the awful truth at bay. Instead she focused resentfully on the thought that it was just like Connie to know everything first. Typical of her. Without knowing why, she asked, 'Why did they tell you and not me?'

Connie's voice was even sharper than she remembered. 'Because I'm the eldest one in the family, that's why. Alice didn't want to phone all of us so she—'

Fran cut her short. 'Yes, I see.' In her heart she recognized that it was perfectly logical, yet stubbornly she clung to the idea that she felt mortified. Mother had died and she had to hear about it from Connie, of all people. It made the news so much worse somehow.

Connie went on, 'I've left a message for Henry at his college, and I've told Mary—'

'So I'm last on your list.'

'Yes, you are, if you must know.'

'Thanks!' Even as she spoke she knew that she was carping, and that to do so at such a time was entirely unacceptable. But being annoyed was so much easier to bear than the grief which threatened her. Mother was gone from them and none of them had been able to say, 'Goodbye'. Or, 'I love you'. Or anything.

'What did you expect?' Connie snapped. Fran could imagine her sister's expression. 'Think about it, Fran. I was hardly looking forward to speaking to you after all these years. Don't flatter yourself. Yes, I left you until last, and you can take offence if you want to.'

'You could have asked one of the others to pass on the message.' Fran knew that she was being childish but the words tumbled out. The old rivalries were still there and always would be. She felt confused by the conflict of her emotions; she wanted to feel grief but instead was experiencing this overwhelming bitterness. She blamed Connie for that, too.

Connie said, 'I've arranged for her body to be brought back to England. We don't want—'

'*You've* decided! What about the rest of us?' Fran's voice shook with indignation. 'She was our mother, too.'

There was a silence. Fran noticed that Dot had come out into the hall and was listening with an expression of deep alarm.

Connie said, 'For heaven's sake! I'm the eldest, therefore I'm expected to make the arrangements. Arranging a funeral is not exactly easy.'

Fran was silent.

'Trying to consult everybody would take too much time, so you can all sit back and let me do the work. All I want you to do is to break the news to Dot as gently as you can. I suppose I can trust you to do that, can I?'

Fran's eyes had filled with tears as the knowledge of their mother's death finally dawned. She struggled to hide them from Dot until she could talk to her calmly. 'I'll do that,' she said. Damn Connie and her domineering ways! Damn her for everything! She closed her eyes and felt two large tears roll down her cheeks. Her mother was dead. She had known it would happen but this news had taken her completely by surprise.

She said, 'Write to me. Put it in a letter. Dot's here. She's getting upset.'

'Oh, God! Trust you!'

'Will it be from here – the funeral?'

'Of course it will. That's her home. I'll get the undertakers to call on you. They'll do everything that's necessary.'

Fran hesitated. 'You will be here, I take it?' She longed for Connie to say 'No', but it was a forlorn hope.

'Of course I will. We'll all be there. Don't be ridiculous.'

'Even Matt?' Fran forced herself to ask.

'I think not,' Connie said briskly.

Fran caught the vindictiveness behind the words. 'Has he said he won't be coming?' She waited but there was no answer. 'Connie? Does he *know*? About Mother?'

'I haven't told him. I don't know where he is. We don't want him there. *I* don't want him there. Don't meddle, Fran.'

'He has a right to know. I can find his address; Mother has it somewhere.' Fran felt a little better. So Connie didn't want him there. That meant *she* was still hurting. Fran was not the only one still to bear the scars.

'I tell you he's not to be invited!' Connie's voice was shrill.

'After what happened . . . Can't you see how impossible it will be?'

'Impossible for you or him? Or me – or hadn't you considered me?'

'God, you're spiteful! I had forgotten how much I disliked you.'

Fran said, 'I'll see that Matt knows that . . .' She stopped, aware of Dot's presence. Then, rephrasing her sentence, she said, 'I'll let him know what's happened. He'll want to come, I'm sure.'

Dot put a timid hand on Fran's arm and whispered, 'Who is it? What's happened?'

Fran put an arm round her and whispered, 'I'm just going to explain.' To Connie she said 'I must go.' The tears welled up once more. 'Poor—' She bit back the word.

Connie said, 'For the last time, Fran, I don't want Matt there. Mother didn't love him—'

'She did! At least, she tried to love him, and we are the only family he has. He loved her – at least I always thought he did – and that's what matters.'

'I tell you, she—'

'Goodbye.' Once again Fran cut the conversation short by hanging up on her sister. She turned to Dot and took her by the hand. 'I've something to tell you, Dot,' she said, 'but first we'll find Fritz because he will want to know, too. I'll ask Annie to make us some tea.'

*

When Fritz was once more ensconced on Dot's lap and the tea had been poured, Fran took a deep breath. Somehow she had to explain their mutual loss without breaking down. She kept thinking about her mother, trying to come to terms with the fact that they would never speak to each other again. Trying to accept that her mother now lay in her coffin, entirely separate from the world. Her father, Geoffrey, had died five years earlier and in a way that had been easier to bear. He had always been Connie's champion; Fran had mourned him, but the ache of loss had not been so intense.

Dot, sipping her tea, watched Fran unhappily.

'Is it Mother?' she asked, propelling Fran into the conversation. 'Is she ill again?'

'Very ill, Dot. Very, very ill.' Fran hesitated, not wanting to rush the explanation. She wanted to break it as gently as possible. When her father had died, it was her mother who had dealt with Dot. Now it was going to be Fran's responsibility. She waited for Dot to cope with the idea of severe illness.

Dot put down her cup. She stared down at Fritz and began to fiddle with his collar. Avoiding Fran's eyes she asked, 'Like last time?'

A previous collapse had meant that their mother spent a few weeks in a sanatorium.

'Not quite like that. No. This time . . .' She leaned forward and took hold of Dot's hand. 'This time we don't think she's going to get better.'

Dot withdrew her hand and began to stroke Fritz. 'Why not?'

'The doctors can't always make people better.'

'But she will get better, won't she?'

'I'm afraid not. Not this time.'

'Not ever?'

'No.' Hurriedly Fran brushed away tears from her eyes and swallowed hard.

Dot's eyes were troubled. 'When Father died – well, is Mother like that?'

'Yes, Dot,' Fran admitted shakily. 'Poor Mother is dead, and we will all miss her dreadfully.' As she said this her own grief broke through the fragile barrier and she began

10

to sob. After a moment she was aware of Dot kneeling beside her, with her arms around her.

'Don't cry, Fran. Please don't cry,' she whispered. 'You've still got me.'

'Yes, I have,' Fran stammered. 'And you've got me, Dot.' She was trying desperately to stem the flow of her tears but they came faster, scalding her cheeks, and she was angry with herself for her lack of self-control. She had meant to break the news carefully to Dot and instead it was Dot who was comforting *her*. 'I'm sorry,' she sobbed.

Dot patted her shoulder. 'It's not your fault,' she said. 'I expect Jesus wanted her. Annie says that's why Father died. I know all about it – and the angels and everything.'

Fran fumbled for a handkerchief, wiped her eyes and blew her nose. She put her arm around Dot and kissed her. 'You are such a dear,' she said. 'I'm so lucky.'

Dot sat back on her heels and inspected Fran's face. 'Your eyes have gone all red.'

'It doesn't matter.'

'Will I cry?'

'Maybe. Probably. Everyone cries when they're feeling sad. Come to me when you feel like crying and I'll hug you.'

Dot's eyes gleamed suddenly. 'Will there be flowers again? All those flowers like crosses and circles and things?'

'Yes. Lots of flowers.'

'And things to eat?'

'Of course. You could help Annie. You make lovely jam tarts and fruit buns.'

'And shall I wear my black dress and my black coat and hat?'

Fran smiled faintly. 'You rather fancied yourself in that

11

outfit, didn't you? Yes, we shall all wear black to the funeral.'

'And will Matt come?'

Fran looked at her. She had said she would invite him, and of course she would. But did she want to see him after all these years? He had not attended her father's funeral because it had been August and he had been on holiday, cycling in the Lake District, his landlady had said. Now it was January. In spite of her defiant words to Connie, she found herself hoping that he would stay away.

'Will he come?' Dot insisted.

'He might,' said Fran, and prayed that if he did she would not make a fool of herself. The past was over and Matt no longer had a place in her life. She had made a fresh start and her career with Starr Massey promised to be a long and successful one. Probably she would never marry, but she would never be lonely. Dot needed her and Annie appeared indestructible. The family home was spacious and comfortable and would suit them all well enough. The money her uncle had left would ensure that they were never in need financially.

Dot said, 'Fritz wants to go for a walk.'

Fritz, who looked remarkably comfortable stretched out in front of the fire, opened his eyes and then hastily closed them again.

Fran laughed. She knew that Fritz always wanted what Dot wanted. 'He looks rather settled to me.' She glanced out into the garden where a cold January wind hurled the dead leaves in a crazy dance. 'Are you sure he does?'

'Oh, yes!' Dot scrambled to her feet. 'We'll wrap up warm. I'll wear the new scarf that Annie knitted for me, and we could walk as far as the station.'

Apologizing silently to the hapless Paul Hallam whose novel would now have to wait, Fran put the temporarily abandoned manuscript back into its folder. Probably Dot was right. A walk would give them both some much needed exercise and the chance to digest the information about their mother's death. As Fran made her way to her room to collect a coat and stout shoes, she had no idea that the tragedy would set in motion a series of events that would lead to far darker tragedies.

*

Friday dawned with huge lowering clouds which brought heavy rain by lunchtime, when the mourners gathered round the open grave where five years earlier they had laid Geoffrey Massey to rest. Dark umbrellas sprouted like sinister mushrooms, adding greatly to the general misery. Fran, with one arm round Dot, struggled against the wind to keep a black umbrella over their heads. The rain pounded relentlessly on the wooden lid of the coffin as it was lowered into the muddy earth. Some of the flowery wreaths were already bedraggled, their petals battered by the force of the downpour. Fran wondered what her mother would think if she could see this sad little group of family and friends who had met to say a last goodbye. Could she, Fran wondered, see into the hearts of her children? And if she could, what would she find? Love, certainly, but maybe some less chari- table feelings too. Indifference? Or resentment? Looking back over the years, Fran was forced to admit that the Masseys were hardly a united family and the even tenor of family life had rarely triumphed for long. Small and not-so-small arguments had developed with depressing regularity. Some had collapsed into obscurity, while others survived to fester in their memories. Would her mother consider her time on earth worth while, Fran wondered unhappily. Maybe the good outweighed the bad. She hoped so.

Putting the past behind her with an effort, she tried to keep her eyes on the coffin and her mind on the words of the funeral service. Rebelliously, however, her thoughts reverted to the man who stood opposite them – the man who had caused her mother the greatest grief. Against her better judgement, Fran glanced across at him. Matt had come into the church at the last moment and had seated himself right at the back. Now he was huddled into his dark overcoat and had turned up the collar to give himself more protection from the rain. His hat was pulled well down and she could see very little of his face, but she remembered the smooth brown hair which fell softly across the large grey eyes. She would have recognized him anywhere, she told herself, and the slight figure and rounded shoulders touched her soul. Poor Matt. She had always thought of him that way and probably always would. Matt, the cuckoo in the nest. The outsider whose past was hidden behind an impenetrable wall of secrecy, broken only by the occasional enigmatic remark made by her mother or father. As a baby Matt had been taken into the family soon after Connie was born but, for reasons the children had never understood, he had never been formally adopted. Fran had always been especially kind to him to compensate for her parents' obvious dislike. His gratitude for her affection had created a strong but disastrous bond between them.

Dot shivered. 'Is Mother buried now?' she asked, making no effort to lower her voice.

'Nearly.'

'I'm glad I'm not dead. Aren't you?'

'Yes, I am.' Fran kept her own voice low, but saw from the corner of her eye that Connie was casting disapproving looks in their direction.

'Shall we do any more singing, Fran?'

14

'Not today. The singing part's over.'

Dot stamped her feet. 'I'm cold. Fritz wants me to go home.'

'It won't be much longer now. It will soon be over.'

Fran risked a quick look at Connie, who was standing beside the vicar holding a single yellow rose. A man whom Fran did not recognize stood beside her, holding an umbrella over their heads. They had been sitting together in the church, so presumably he was a friend of Connie's. Fran regarded him surreptitiously, aware of an unwilling admiration. He was not particularly tall, but slim and with a relaxed stance. His face wore a good-natured expression and even among a crowd of mourning strangers, he appeared totally relaxed. His hair was hidden by his hat, but even from this distance Fran could see that his eyes were exceptionally blue. In contrast, Connie's back was ramrod straight, her expression grim, a fact which caused Fran some unease. Connie and her friend had gone directly to the church so that she and Fran still had not met. Inside the church, Connie had sat with him in the front pew with Fran, Dot, Mary and Henry in the pew behind her. She had not once turned her head to acknowledge any of the family. A black veil hid her freckled face and light brown eyes and a hat covered her auburn hair. Fran felt an unexpected pang of compassion for her. Connie had never lived up to her childhood prettiness but had grown heavier and less attractive as the years passed. The indulgence shown her by her father had allowed her to become opinionated and headstrong and had not prepared her for the rough and tumble of the real world. Fran knew that her sister found it difficult to co-exist with colleagues, and after only one year with the family firm she had been firmly edged out. A friend of her mother's had found her a job as a trainee librarian in Maidstone where she was able to put her considerable talents to good use. Fran sighed. Seeing her sister again after all these years was doing nothing to heal the rift between them.

Dot plucked at her coat. 'I want to go *home*.'

'Very soon,' Fran promised. 'Look, the vicar has closed his book.'

She looked at Henry, caught his eye and smiled encouragement. He was the youngest member of the family and the only boy. At eighteen he had just gone up to Cambridge, studying English Literature. Everyone expected him to follow Fran into Starr Massey as soon as he had qualified, and he was eager to become a part of the team. Henry was rather like Connie to look at, with the same colouring, but none of her ways. Friendly and outgoing, he loved everyone and assumed that he was loved in return. His arrival in the Massey family in 1920 had proved a further difficulty for Matt, who until then had been the only boy and secretly hoped to be offered a place with Starr Massey. To his dismay Henry had become 'heir' to that particular throne and Matt had not been sent to university. Even Henry had protested at this unfair treatment, but their father's decision had not wavered. Henry had always idolized 'big brother Matt' and had been devastated by the tumultuous events which later led to his banishment.

Connie and the vicar now conferred and, at a signal, the gravedigger stepped forward and tossed a spadeful of wet earth on to the coffin. Connie threw in the rose and they all murmured the last 'Amen'. As Fran and Dot moved thankfully towards the cars, Mary fell into step beside them. Her eyes were red with weeping and she looked utterly miserable.

Dot said, 'We can go home now, Mary.'

Mary swallowed hard. 'It's so awful, this rain,' she said. 'Mother hated the wet weather. And it's spoiling all the flowers.'

Mary was pretty but extremely shy. She was the only

girl with grey eyes, but these were never seen to best advantage because she wore glasses to correct poor sight. At twenty-three she was three years younger than Fran, and for the past two years had been teaching French in a boys' boarding school. She had always been wary of Connie and, occasionally, frightened of Matt, but now she slid an arm through Fran's and clung to her as the three of them stumbled awkwardly across the sodden grass towards the path.

Mary glanced up at Fran nervously and said, 'I see Matt's turned up. Connie doesn't look too happy about it. I do hope they won't start quarrelling again. Mother did so hate upsets.'

Fran tightened her lips. 'Connie will have to like it or lump it.'

Dot looked startled. 'Will she, Fran?'

Fran forced a smile. 'She'll behave herself,' she said. 'Don't worry.'

Mary said, 'She's brought a man with her, so perhaps she will be on her best behaviour. Let's hope so. He looks rather nice. I wonder how she met him?'

They reached the road where the rest of the mourners were shaking the wet from their umbrellas and climbing into their respective cars. Dot and Mary sat in the back of the first car and Fran slid into the seat beside the driver. He said, 'Nasty weather, madam.'

'Yes, it is.'

He checked his rear-view mirror, waiting for the rest of the cortège. They moved forward at last and Fran cast a guilty backward glance towards the churchyard. It felt like a betrayal, to be leaving her mother in that cold, silent place, yet her father was there also. Perhaps, in that other world, they were able to comfort each other.

Dot said, 'Fritz wants one of those cakes with little wing things.'

Mary dabbed at her eyes. 'You mean butterfly cakes.'

17

'Yes. Those. I had one this morning. Annie said it didn't matter; she said Mother wouldn't mind.'

'Of course she wouldn't.'

Fran sighed. She had been up half the night comforting Dot, who had woken in the early hours to the realization of her mother's death. At least Dot had given way to her grief and for that Fran was thankful. Tears, in her opinion, were there to be shed when circumstances decreed, and there was nothing worse than an unexpressed sorrow. At two-thirty in the morning a glass of warm milk and honey had finally coaxed Dot back to sleep, but she had woken again just before five from a nightmare.

Now Fran was desperately tired, but knew that sleep was a luxury to be denied her for many hours. Still, at least she could look forward to a comforting meal, for Annie had worked hard to prepare hot soup followed by a cooked ham and salads. Connie had brought an extra guest, but he could be accommodated quite easily. That was no problem. The problem, Fran acknowledged, was that for the first time in years the entire family would be under one roof, a potentially dangerous situation. She herself would try to behave as though nothing untoward had ever happened. Dot posed no threat unless, inadvertently, she said something tactless. Henry would ignore the past and enjoy himself, and Mary would not make any provocative comments.

Matt and Connie were the unknown quantities. Matt was in a position to take the high ground, but Connie might seize the moment to air personal grievances. Fran felt a wave of panic and struggled to suppress it. As Mary had said, the presence of Connie's companion might make a difference. If so, it was just possible they could avoid a family row. Fran crossed her fingers. It would take more than a little luck to steer them through the next few hours, she thought.

*

Annie, back early from the church, scurried to and fro with plates, glasses and baskets of bread as Connie came face to face with Matt in the hallway where he was taking off his coat. He handed it to Dot, who was acting as cloakroom attendant, and turned to find Connie smiling thinly at him while her eyes remained cold and hard.

'Connie!' he exclaimed. 'After all these years.' Reluctantly he held out his hand and, after a moment's hesitation, she touched it briefly.

A man was standing beside her and she clutched his arm suddenly with a proprietorial gesture and leaned close to him. 'Let me introduce you two,' she said. 'Matt Massey, Del Farrar.' As the two men shook hands she went on quickly, 'Del was kind enough to drive me here in his car. I was so grateful. Wasn't it sweet of him?' She gave him a bright smile.

'It's no big deal,' he said with a good-natured shrug.

'Oh, but it is!' she insisted. 'Del is from the United States,' she told Matt. 'He's written a novel and I'm so proud of him. It's going to be a winner.'

Del said, 'Hey! Not so fast, Connie! I wouldn't like to bet my last dollar on it.'

Fran appeared just then and Connie turned to her with the same brittle smile. 'Fran! I want you to meet a very dear friend of mine. Del Farrar, my sister Fran.'

Del's handshake was warm and firm and Fran was suddenly grateful for his presence. The sight of Connie and Matt being polite to each other gave her grounds for cautious optimism. 'Nice to meet you, Mr Farrar,' she said.

'Call me Del. Everyone does. My condolences on the death of your mother. You'll miss her.'

'Thank you. Yes, we will. She was so much part of our lives here. Just Mother, Dot and me. It's hard to believe that Mother won't be coming back as usual from her winter break.'

Connie said, 'It's so much worse for you. Poor Fran! You never did manage to move out.' To Del she went on, 'I cut the apron strings years ago and made a life for myself. I like to be in charge of my own destiny.' She laughed lightly, waiting for his appreciation.

Refusing to be drawn, Fran let the remark pass, but Del smiled at her.

'Connie said your mother had been ailing for some years. She must have been glad to have you around.'

Stung by this obvious reproof, Connie struggled to retrieve the situation. 'It's the English way,' she told Del. 'A throwback to Victorian days when the dutiful daughter stayed at home to care for the aged parents. You could call it a British tradition.'

Del merely smiled. Fran found it hard to take her eyes from him. His eyes really were astonishingly blue, his voice was warm and his tan spoke of warmer climes. He must realize that he was attractive to women (*she* found him tremendously so), yet he showed none of the arrogance that frequently afflicts such people. His smile was generous, and unwillingly Fran found herself envying Connie and wondering where her sister had met him.

Connie went on hurriedly, changing the subject. 'Del is a writer and *tremendously* promising. I've taken him under my wing and I'm doing what I can to help him find a really good publisher.'

She gave a little smirk in Fran's direction and Fran recognized the snub for what it was. So Connie had *not* suggested that Del Farrar submit his novel to Starr Massey? Fran bit back a sharp reply.

Matt, however, understanding also, smiled at Del. 'Have you tried Starr Massey, Mr Farrar? The family firm. Fran is a senior editor. Worth a try, although I say it myself.'

Del looked at Connie with raised eyebrows and she had the grace to colour slightly.

'Good lord, no!' she exclaimed. 'I didn't even suggest it. That would hardly be appropriate.' She smiled up at Del. 'That agent I found you will know the right editor for you. That's what agents are for.'

'I guess so,' he said. 'If not, I shall certainly remember Starr Massey. Thanks for the tip.'

Fran spoke to Matt. 'How are things with you, Matt? You haven't changed.'

But as he turned to her, she realized for the first time just how much he *had* changed. His eyes had darkened somehow and his face was thin – not gaunt exactly, but she could see his cheekbones more clearly. Studying him, she felt a deep sense of disappointment that she no longer felt the urge to comfort him. She had not wanted to relive the hurt, yet discovering that he no longer had the power to move her was somehow worse.

For a moment he didn't speak but seemed almost to devour her with his eyes and she found herself floundering for words to cover the awkward moment. 'That is, you *have* changed, Matt. Of course. We all have. You – you've lost a little weight, but it suits you.'

She was suddenly aware that Del Farrar was watching her, his eyes shrewd. What on earth was he making of the Massey family, she wondered.

Matt said, 'You've turned into a swan, Fran. You were always the ugly duckling.' He turned to Del. 'Connie was the pretty one, *then*. Father's little favourite.' He laughed lightly as though the words were simply those of a brother teasing a well-loved sister, but Fran's heart immediately skipped a beat. Perhaps she had been too optimistic. The old grudges *might* be given another airing.

Del, however, appeared quite unmoved by the undercurrents. He said easily, 'Families!' and shook his head with

21

mock exasperation. 'I guess they're the same the world over.' He turned to smile at Dot who had joined them, the dog tucked under her arm.

Connie, ignoring her, shot a look of pure hate in Matt's direction and then turned back to Del. 'How right you are! But Matt isn't quite family. He had no home when my father took him in, but he's never been officially adopted into the Massey family.'

'It's something I've always been thankful for!' said Matt and he turned on his heel and walked away.

Fran felt her face stiffen with embarrassment and she dared not meet Connie's eyes. Dot, however, was oblivious to the tension. 'Connie and Matt ran away together,' she told Del, 'but Mother said they didn't like each other after all so then they . . .' She screwed up her eyes in concentration. 'They decided to separate.'

Fran felt herself redden as her mother's carefully chosen words returned to haunt them, but Dot, unaware of the various emotions evoked by this revelation, had lost interest in the subject. 'This is my dog. His name's Fritz. That's a German name because he's a dachshund and they come from Germany. He won't bite you, he never does. Not even the postman.'

While Del was admiring the dog Connie moved closer to Fran and whispered, 'I swear I'll swing for Matt one of these days! "Father's little favourite!" I *told* you not to invite him. He's going to cause trouble, you wait and see.'

Fran said, 'Well, you *were* his favourite, weren't you? His "little princess", his "pearl," his "bonny lass".' Dismayed, she realized that the childhood disappointments still rankled.

'Oh, God!' cried Connie. 'You're as bad as Matt. Two peas in a pod! You were made for each other!'

'A pity that you interfered then.' Fran regretted the bitter

22

words as soon as she had uttered them, but there was no going back.

Connie's face flushed angrily. 'Me?' she hissed. 'It was Matt who seduced me, remember.'

'That's not the way I understood it.'

Connie's eyes narrowed furiously but she struggled to keep her voice down. 'Then you heard lies! It was Matt who forced himself on me. It was Matt—'

'I heard that you were drunk and that you—'

'Me? That's a damn lie. Who told you all this?'

'Matt wrote to me.'

'Wrote to you? The bastard!' For a moment her face crumpled but then anger overcame grief. 'Well, he would, wouldn't he? My God, that's so like him. If you only knew what I went through with that man—'

Annie appeared suddenly and said, 'Excuse me but—'

Connie rounded on her fiercely. 'Can't you see we're talking?'

Unabashed, Annie tossed her head and addressed herself pointedly to Fran. 'It's all ready now. Should we start before the soup gets cold?'

Fran choked down her own anger, intensely grateful for the timely interruption whether intentional or not. Annie knew them all well enough to scent trouble and might well have seen the need for intervention. 'Thank you, Annie.' She was ashamed of her spiteful outburst and annoyed with herself for such lamentable lack of control. This was her mother's funeral, and Fran had promised herself that she would behave impeccably. Yet here she was brawling with Connie before they had been in the house together for ten minutes. 'We'll start, Annie. Shoo them all into the dining room, will you? I expect everyone's starving.'

Connie, who was obviously struggling with her own emotions, closed her eyes and took a deep breath. Then she said, 'I'm sorry, Fran.'

Fran thought the words lacked conviction, but she gave her a small nod by way of acknowledgement and made up her mind to sit as far away from Connie as possible.

Dot said, 'Would you like to sit next to me, Del? I helped Annie make the soup. I pushed the potatoes through a sieve and I chopped the carrots and I—'

Connie interrupted her. 'Del is *my* visitor, Dot dear, but you can sit on one side of him. I'll sit on the other and then we can both look after him.'

Del caught Fran's eye and said, 'I guess I'll go to the bathroom first.'

'The bath—? Oh, yes. Sorry. I'll show you the way.' She led the way upstairs. 'I'm sorry about – well, we are a rather disunited family. And Dot can be devastatingly honest.' She laughed awkwardly.

He said, 'It's I who should be apologizing, intruding like this, but your sister wanted me to come.'

His smile was reassuring. There was something about him that comforted her and she studied him, vaguely disconcerted. It was a long time since any man had made such a good impression on her. Hiding her confusion, she indicated the correct door and went quickly downstairs. As she did so she made a determined effort to calm down, and by the time she reached the hall she was feeling a little more in control of her feelings. 'Just a few hours,' she told herself, 'and then they will all be gone and it will be over. I can surely be civil for a few hours.'

She waited for Del at the bottom of the stairs, unwilling to leave him to find his way into the dining room alone. When he reappeared he smiled. 'You have a fine house, Fran. Very English.' He stood beside her, looking round, his hands thrust casually into his pockets.

Once again Fran found herself wondering about his relationship with Connie. Were they really as close as she

24

suggested, or was it a business relationship connected with her work in the library?

He said, 'Connie kept me in the dark about Starr Massey. I'd like to know more about it some time.'

'It's a long, rather sad, story.' She led the way into the dining room. 'It once belonged to our family, but over the years we've lost control, for one reason and another. But you must tell me about your book some time.'

Before he could answer Connie waved to him imperiously. 'We've saved you a seat here, Del. Dot has quite taken a shine to you.'

'I'm flattered!' he laughed and, with a half rueful grin for Fran, made his way to sit between them.

For a while Fran busied herself helping Annie to serve everyone, and by the time she sat down at the table harmony appeared to reign as people chatted amicably, comforted by the hot vegetable soup. Matt sat on the other side of Dot and was charm personified, although he did not once address Connie directly. Connie gave her full attention to Del, laughing at all his jokes. Henry was his usual bubbly self and even Mary looked relaxed as the wine worked its magic. Fran began to think that the family reunion would pass off without further incident; when Annie caught her eye and winked, she was able to smile back. Her mother was dead, but at least her unruly offspring were all met together under one roof and, for the moment at least, managing to celebrate her life without rancour.

*

Matt was listening to Henry, who was talking with great animation about life at Cambridge and Caius in particular. He smiled as Henry described the social activities, but beneath the smile he simmered with envy. Henry Massey went to university and 'larked about a bit'. Matt Massey had had no such luck. The idea of Cambridge had never been

25

seriously considered when Matt was growing up. It had been made painfully clear to him that he 'was not considered university material'. The realization that no money would be spent furthering his education had changed Matt from a reasonable scholar into a sullen, uncooperative dullard, and his school reports had documented the disastrous collapse of his standards.

'Matthew no longer shows any interest in the French language . . .'; His grasp of geometry seems to be slipping away . . .'; 'A disappointing examination result . . .'; Matthew's attention span is lamentable. . . .'

Matt forced his wandering attention back to Henry who was talking about his fellow undergraduates and one in particular. 'Barrett, of course, is an absolute *fool*!' He grinned. 'He has to be seen to be believed. He wears this extraordinary waistcoat all day and every day – a sort of paisley design in the brightest colours you can imagine, with a bit of gold thread thrown in for good luck.' He laughed engagingly at the memory and his listeners laughed with him. 'He does no work at all and says he wants to be a politician! One night he shinned up the flagpole – God knows how – and stuck a jerry on the top. There was the most awful rumpus!' Delighted by the memory, Henry's eyes met Matt's. 'You'd like him, Matt. He's such a character.'

Matt, who thought he would definitely detest the boy, forced a smile. 'Sounds as though he'd make a good prime minister!' he suggested and the idea produced another wave of laughter. Inwardly he seethed. So that's how the students spent their time. Precocious little brats! He told himself that he was thankful he had never been to Cambridge. A fate worse than death, by all accounts, where all you learned was how to make a silly ass of yourself.

Innocently Henry rushed on. 'I was out with him one evening in a punt and these girls were watching us from the bank.' He took another gulp of wine. 'Barrett has to ask them to join us, of course, and they clamber in, giggling and finding it all a bit of a lark, and we've only gone about a hundred yards when Barrett takes us too near the bank and this enormous bough scoops him off the boat and drops him in the water!' His eyes sparkled. 'I'll never forget his face! Never! Poor old Barrett!'

Dot, flushed and excited, squealed with laughter and Matt saw Fran cast an anxious glance in their direction. Mother bloody hen! She'd be worse than ever now that Mother was gone. Deliberately ignoring Fran's warning shake of the head, he reached for the bottle and refilled Dot's glass. Damn Fran! Once he had loved her, but jealous Connie had come between them. He'd written to Fran, begging forgiveness, laying bare his very soul, but she had never answered his letter. He still regretted those four pages over which he had agonized for an entire day. Since then there had been no contact until today, and he was relieved to discover that he felt so little for her now. He wasn't sure why; she was still a very attractive woman and it was obvious that the American was smitten. And that was getting up Connie's freckled nose!

He swallowed hard. Connie. The bitch! He could not look at her without distaste. The so-called 'elopement' had been a complete fiasco and he would never forgive her. She had used him to score over Fran and, in doing so, had brought about his alienation from the rest of the family. Father had been delighted at the chance to say 'I told you so' to anyone who would listen. His stupid behaviour with Connie had served to justify the worst predictions anyone had ever made about him. Father had seized the opportunity to sever all connections with him, and Matt had been too proud even to plead his case.

Suddenly Dot leaned towards him. 'Tell me what you do, Matt. I want to know what you do.'

She looked at him with adoring eyes and he felt the slightest stirring of compunction. Poor Dot. It must always be Dot and never Dottie – he had once used that name and Father had flown into a temper. 'She is not dotty!' he had shouted, refusing to believe that Matt had used the word as an endearment. It had earned him a good hiding and the injustice still smouldered. But Dot was not to blame for her father, and he had been sensible enough to understand that.

Connie, sensing his reluctance, urged, 'Yes, do tell, Matt.'

He saw the mocking gaze. She knew; she could tell.

'I'm a representative,' he told Dot, keeping his voice steady with an effort. 'I drive all round the country selling—'

'A rep!' cried Connie. 'What a hoot! A rep for what? Not ladies' underwear, I hope! Oh, not that!'

Matt felt a wave of anger sweep through him. 'For Foreland Weave, the big stationery firm.'

Del looked interested. 'Foreland? They operate in the States, too. That's one hell of a corporation.'

'What is stationery?' asked Dot, peering up into Matt's face.

He could see the love in her eyes and felt a rush of anguished affection. He, Matt, had been the indirect cause of the accident that changed her life so dramatically. Impulsively he put an arm around her shoulder.

'Stationery, my dear Dot, is things that they sell in stationers' shops. Envelopes, notepaper, notebooks—'

'Like in Mr Everett's shop? He sells notebooks and pencils and rubbers and elastic bands and newspapers. Do you sell newspapers, Matt?' She looked at him, wide-eyed, ready to be impressed.

'Not newspapers, no. But all the other things like diaries, confetti, doilies . . .'

28

Dot frowned hazily. 'What is confetti?'

Connie's mouth tightened. 'When people are foolish enough to get married other people are stupid enough to throw small scraps of coloured paper over them. Don't ask me why.'

Dot turned to her. 'But you wanted to get married, Connie, don't you remember? You told me that day at the picnic. You said you wanted to have lots of children. And you're not stupid.'

'That's a matter of opinion!' said Matt to nobody in particular. He saw Connie stiffen and hoped she would retaliate. He wanted her to show herself in her true colours so that the American boy-friend would see the *real* Connie. If Connie thought she could put him, Matt, down and get away with it she had another think coming! He could give as good as he got.

But Dot had lost interest in the idea of marriage. 'But where do you live now, Matt?'

'I have a very nice flat in Crouch End, in north London,' he told her. 'It overlooks a park. And I have a little car. A Ford. It's a good little motor. Nice runner, as they say in the trade. Brown, with yellow wheels. So what do you think of all that, eh?' He gave Dot's nose a playful tweak and she giggled with delight. 'You're a bit of a minx, Miss Dorothy,' he told her. 'Did you know that?'

'Am I? What is a minx?'

'A very cheeky person.'

She looked a little dubious.

Del said, 'It's a compliment, Dot.'

Matt wished he would stay out of the conversation, but Americans were known for their brash ways. They were famous for it. He saw no reason for Del Farrar to be present but no doubt Connie had twisted his arm. Matt knew to his cost just how persistent she could be and felt a flash of pity for the man. If Connie ever got

29

her claws into him, God help him! He would live to regret it.

Dot said, 'Yellow wheels! How lovely!' Her blue eyes were wide with excitement and his heart ached for the future that would never be hers. She would never marry, never have a family. He swallowed hard. Perhaps she was well out of it. Relationships were a minefield; he had been blown up once and nothing would induce him to try again.

Mary leaned forward to catch his eye. 'You'll have to give us all a ride, Matt,' she suggested shyly, her face a little flushed from the wine.

Connie said, 'In this weather? No, thank you!'

Matt ignored her. 'Next year I shall get something a bit newer – probably.' He immediately regretted the last word. Why shouldn't he exaggerate a little? What did they care anyway? He could live in a slum or a palace, and none of the Masseys would give a twopenny damn. 'I'm due for some promotion, too,' he invented. 'Probably make sales manager by the summer. It's on the cards.' He grinned with a confidence he did not feel. The truth was that the firm had no intention of promoting him, and the car would have to last another year at least. It was a swine of a car, very temperamental, and he frequently chose to travel by train instead. His 'very nice flat' was a large bed-sit in a house overlooking a school playground.

Henry said, 'Sales manager? Wow! Congratulations, Matt!'

Del nodded warmly. 'Nice going, Matt! You should come over to the States some time. Some of the newer models will amaze you! The Auburn 851's a beauty. Hydraulic brakes on all four wheels and an eight-cylinder engine. It's out of my league, but she's really something! I drive an old Bentley, would you believe. A friend had it shipped over from England a few years back.'

Connie looked at him, her right hand resting lightly on his sleeve. 'They say that everyone in America has a car because of the long distances they have to travel from A to B. Is that true, Del?'

'Not quite,' he laughed, 'but I guess we do have a love affair with the motor car!'

Fran tapped on the table with her fork and said, 'If you've all finished, we'll move into the sitting room. A little later we'll have tea and cakes. Annie's been working so hard to do Mother justice. But before we leave the table I think we should spare a thought for Mother, God rest her. Without her none of us would be here – with the exception of Del . . .'

'And Matt,' put in Connie.

The sudden silence showed her that she had gone too far and she flushed guiltily. Serve her right, though Matt. He said, 'How very charming!' and was delighted with her fall from grace.

Fran, momentarily thrown by the interruptions, continued. 'And – and we are all that's left of her – of her and Father, that is. I don't want to make a speech, but I will say that I hope it is not too long before we all meet again.' She smiled wryly. 'For once we've managed not to fall out – at least not seriously – and if Mother's looking down on us I think she would approve.'

Matt bit back a caustic comment. She was papering over the cracks, he told himself irritably.

As though she could read his thoughts, Fran threw him a look of entreaty and then raised her glass. 'A toast to absent friends!'

There was a self-conscious murmur of assent and a clinking of glasses. This was quickly followed by a shuffling of chairs and throwing down of table napkins as everyone rose to leave the table. With interest, Matt saw Del rise quickly and move to the other end of the table where he talked earnestly to Fran. Connie's look of chagrin warmed Matt's heart and he was aware of a small triumph. He

31

caught her eye and whispered, 'It looks as though Fran is going to steal Del right from under your nose! I rather hope she does. A perfect example of the biter bit, eh?'

Connie gave him a look of such intense hatred that for a second or two he was taken aback, afraid that she might hit him. Her face worked and her nostrils flared. 'I'll make you sorry for that, Matt,' she said. 'And don't imagine that I can't. I'll make you so sorry you'll wish you'd never been born!'

Chapter Two

FRAN AWOKE THE FOLLOWING MORNING with a deep sense of relief. The funeral was over and, although there had been the occasional bitter clash, the major eruption of hostility which she had dreaded had miraculously been averted. Probably due to Del Farrar's presence, she reflected. She had seen off the last person with a heartfelt sigh, and now looked forward to her life resuming its normal pattern of work and more work. But first she was going to follow up a suggestion which Del had made – that they submit some of Dot's watercolours to a publisher. Her flowers, he felt, were good enough to be used as illustrations for a book on English flora. And he was probably right. It was a brilliant idea, for not only would it give Dot a small income, it would make her more independent. The thought that she *worked* might help her to see herself as an adult instead of a child. In fact, Fran felt distinctly remiss for never having thought of it herself, especially as a member of a publishing family.

She pushed back the bedclothes and swung her legs out of bed, deciding that she would gather some of the paintings together and submit them secretly. That way Dot need not risk the disappointment of rejection. Half-way to the bathroom, Fran reconsidered this. If, as she suspected, Del was tactfully suggesting that Dot could feel more in control of her life, then protecting her was not the answer.

'We'll talk it over,' she said firmly. If the idea met with her approval, Dot herself must write the accompanying letter, and she must also learn to deal with the possibility of rejection. For a moment Fran smiled, thinking that Del would approve of her new way of thinking.

As she cleaned her teeth it occurred to her that if one of the family had made the suggestion she would almost certainly have felt annoyed at the inference that Mother had not known what was best for Dot; might have been over-protective. Coming from *Connie*, Fran might well have resented the idea as a partial reflection on her own wisdom. So why did Del's idea seem so entirely acceptable? The answer was obvious – because Del Farrar had no particular axe to grind. As she ran the bath she recalled the way his good-natured face lit up when he smiled. And she liked the easy way he moved, with a natural grace ... and the way he had tried to smooth her path, refusing to be put out by the family's petty jealousies. Del Farrar was assured and confident and she liked him tremendously. He had impressed her, there was no denying that – but he was *Connie's* friend. Fran's smile faltered. Del was the first man in whom she had felt any interest during the ten years since Connie and Matt had broken her heart. Fate could be very unkind sometimes.

The bath-water was not very hot, which meant that the geyser had not been lit early enough. No doubt Annie had slept a little late, but that was hardly surprising. There had been a lot of washing-up to do yesterday and Annie, Fran and Dot had worked until nearly ten trying to restore the kitchen to some kind of order. Shivering, she towelled herself dry and tried to remember what Del had told her about himself. It was surprisingly little as there had been no time for lengthy conversation. He came originally from Virginia where his family had owned a horse farm, but now he was a lawyer in New York. Connie had said he was thirty-five. He was an only child. Fran wondered whether or not he was married but Connie, if she knew, had kept that information to herself. Surely, if he had a wife, he would have brought her to England with him? So Fran argued, but this was because she hoped he was single. Why? Why could it matter to her? She shrugged as she pulled on her clothes. She could not admit to herself that she was more than interested in him. She hardly knew him and would almost certainly never see him again. Connie would see to that!

'So stop thinking about him!' she told herself and made an effort to do just that as she went downstairs.

When Dot joined her twenty minutes later, Fran at once broached the subject of the watercolours.

'Del Farrar thought they were so good!' she told her. 'He thought they were good enough to be in a book about flowers.'

Dot's toast was arrested half-way to her mouth as she flushed with pleasure. 'He said *that*!' she said. 'Del said *that*! Oh Fran! Wasn't he a nice man!'

'Yes, he was. Very nice.' Fran hastily busied herself with a second cup of tea. 'So why don't you look through your paintings and choose the best ones, maybe a dozen, and I could help you write a letter to Alan Platt? He's the art director at Starr Massey. Then tomorrow I can take them in with me when . . .'

'Tomorrow's Sunday.'

'Oh, yes. So it is. The funeral has got me all mixed up. Monday, then. So what do you think, Dot?'

'Yesterday was Friday. Today is Saturday and tomor-row—'

'Yes. But what about the idea – about your paintings? Shall we do it?'

Dot looked at her a little anxiously and Fran relented a little. Having to make a decision unaided was probably pushing her sister to the limit too quickly. She began to explain what would be involved.

'If they use your paintings, Dot, to illustrate a book, they will *pay* you something,' Fran told her. 'You'd be earning, just like me and Connie and Mary.'

'And Matt?'

'And Matt.'

'And Henry?'

'No. Henry isn't earning yet. He's studying; that's different.'

Dot frowned. 'Do you like Matt, Fran?'

'Of course I do.'

'But he never comes to see us, except yesterday.'

Fran groaned inwardly. They had never discussed this, and Fran's first instinct was to deny that there was a problem. Her mother had always insisted that Dot should be spared the harsher aspects of life. It was certainly easier than the lengthy explanations that might be required to make Dot understand the frailties of human relationships, but was it fair to her? Once again she was beginning to doubt the wisdom of her mother's policy. She took a deep breath. 'He doesn't come to see us because Matt and I had a – a sort of quarrel once. A long time ago.'

'I see.'

No, you don't, thought Fran with a sinking heart.

Dot's stare was disconcerting. '*And* you quarrelled with Connie, didn't you?'

'Yes, I'm afraid so. It was a long time ago and you probably don't remember it. We didn't say anything to you because Mother thought we shouldn't upset you.'

'Poor Mother. She's dead now.'

Fran nodded.

'Why did you?' Dot asked. 'Quarrel, I mean. Why?'

Fran hesitated briefly. This might be the wrong thing to do, but there was only one way to find out. 'I loved Matt, like a brother, I mean, and he . . . he said he loved me.'

'Like getting married, you mean?'

'No, not quite that. A different kind of love. Matt and I were *special* friends. We told each other all our secrets. He was my best friend.'

'I wish I had a best friend.' Dot's tone was wistful.

Fran pressed on. 'Then suddenly . . .' She heard her voice shake. '. . . suddenly Matt and Connie . . .'

She stared helplessly at Dot, who said quickly, 'It doesn't matter, Fran. You needn't tell me if you don't want to.'

'But I do want to. Just give me a minute.' She swallowed hard. 'You were only eleven at the time and . . .' Fran fell silent. How stupid she had been to trust Connie. Fran's special feeling for Matt had never been expressed until one fateful day when she was barely sixteen. In a moment's weakness, she had confided in Connie; had told her that Matt liked her best. Twenty-year-old Connie had said very little except to mock the idea of a special friendship, but she had gone out of her way to attract him. To Fran's astonishment, she had begun to *flirt* with him and, not long after, she and Matt suddenly ran away together.

Fran forced herself to continue. 'Mother and Father were furious, but they didn't know where they'd gone. A week later Connie wrote to say they were going to "stay together."'

Dot's eyes widened. 'Poor Fran!' she said softly. 'Was Mother *very* cross?'

'Yes, she was. And so was I, but mostly I was unhappy.'

'You kept on crying. I heard you. And Mother said you had a bad headache and I was to stop fussing. And then Mary bought Fritz for you, and you said I could have him because he loved me the most.'

Fran stared at her, astonished by the clarity of Dot's memory. 'That's right,' she said slowly. 'Mary bought me the puppy to cheer me up.'

And to give me something to love, she thought with a rush of remorse. It was such a loving gesture, so like kind-hearted Mary, yet at the time Fran had been too bitter to accept it as such. She had given the puppy to Dot, scorning her sister's attempt to ease her hurt. Wounded by loss and diminished by Matt's betrayal, Fran had been half out of her mind with grief, wanting only to die and refusing to be comforted by anyone. Looking back after all this time it was hard to imagine that she had been driven to such extreme behaviour. She had hoped that her suffering would somehow punish Matt and Connie for the pain they had inflicted, and would cast a shadow over their happiness. It was a time of desperate confusion.

Dot asked, 'Are you friends again now?'

A good question and Fran thought about it, trying to be objective. 'I'm not sure,' she said. 'I don't hate them, but I still can't quite seem to forgive them.'

'But they didn't stay together, did they?'

'No, that's true.'

'Didn't they like each other after all?'

'No, I suppose not. I don't know why they separated. If Mother knew, she certainly didn't tell me.' It was only when Connie left Matt that Fran had begun to heal. To her it was an admission that they had made a mistake, but in fact it did not change anything except the way she felt. Matt had disappeared for a while and nobody had looked for him. Mother, angry and upset, had muttered about him, and Father had said that it confirmed his suspicion that the boy was unstable and 'a thoroughly bad lot'. Matt had finally made contact when their father died and the family put a notice in *The Times*. He had sent some flowers, but had stayed away from the funeral.

Fran sighed. 'They stopped liking each other,' she explained. 'Living with someone isn't always easy. I expect being married is difficult.'

'Oh, it is,' Dot told her earnestly 'I know because Mother told me. She said I was lucky because I'm not the marrying kind. Are you the marrying kind, Fran?'

Fran smiled shakily. 'Apparently not.'

'Did anyone ask you?'

'No!'

'And Connie isn't, is she? She lives all by herself.'

'Yes. Connie's – just Connie.'

'Connie's funny. She doesn't like the snow, she hates it. She told Matt. He said he reckons we're in for a white Christmas, deep and crisp and even like the carol, and he laughed and Connie said, "Trust you to say that. You really are a bastard "'

'Dot!' Fran was shaken. Her sister seemed to miss very little.

'And then I said that I like snow because of the snowmen and everything and she said—'

Fran looked at her with dismay. 'When was all this? Yesterday? At the funeral?'

'You were in the kitchen with Annie – and Connie said wasn't I a bit old for snowmen and it was time I grew up, and Matt said, "Leave her alone, for God's sake. At least her heart's in the right place." Isn't Connie's heart in the right place?' She looked worried.

'Of course it is. Matt meant that Connie isn't very kind. It's just a saying.' She hesitated. Correcting Dot made her feel like her mother, but since Mother was dead presumably someone would have to act as mentor. 'Actually, Dot, "bastard" is a rather unpleasant word. It's not very polite to—'

Dot looked indignant. 'But Father said it. And Mother said, "Don't use that word. You know it offends me," and

39

Father said it was the truth. I heard them. They were talking about Matt.'

'You shouldn't listen to other people's conversation,' Fran said, with an attempt at severity. She wondered uneasily what else Dot had squirrelled away in her memory.

'I couldn't help it. They were shouting. My bedroom is next to theirs. Why *doesn't* Connie like snowmen?'

Her abrupt change of subject came as a relief and Fran said, 'She had a bad fright once, when she was a child. We were tobogganing, and she and Matt wouldn't come home with the rest of us. Somehow Connie crashed into a tree and fell into a big snowdrift. She knocked herself out. When she came round it was dark, and she couldn't find the way home. She might have died if Matt hadn't found her.'

'Good old Matt!' said Dot.

'Some say!' To forestall another question, Fran said, 'But we're all happy now. Mary at her school and Henry at Cambridge . . .'

'Connie at Maidstone and Matt with his car . . .'

'And *we're* quite happy here, aren't we? You and me and Annie.'

She expected a whole-hearted 'Yes' but to her surprise Dot was silent. She looked at Fran with an expression that was hard to interpret. After a long silence she gave a small sigh and tried to return Fran's smile. 'I think I'll go and look for my best flower paintings,' she said.

As Fran watched her go, she was aware of a nagging doubt. Had she upset Dot in some way? Wasn't she happy? Perhaps, where Dot was concerned, Mother had been right and honesty was not the best policy after all.

*

Monday morning was always hectic, but on this particular Monday Fran sank into her seat with a grateful sigh and stared round at the familiar office. After the traumas of the past week she was glad to be one step removed from her domestic situation. It was easy here to throw herself into her work and forget those members of her family who had the power to hurt her. She had a collection of Dot's watercolours in a folder, and later she would take them along to the art department and hand them over to Alan Platt.

She tossed her clutch bag on to the shelf behind her and stared with dismay at a pile of unopened letters which had accumulated during her absence. A youngish man with blond hair came into the room and, as usual, leaned against the door jamb.

'Fran! You're back. So sorry about your mother. Did everything go OK?'

'Hullo, Stuart. Thanks and yes. Reasonably OK. Apart from a few squabbles – but my family is like that.'

'Aren't all families? I dread Christmas when all my aunts and uncles get together.'

She laughed ruefully. 'And the weather, of course. It teemed down. Still, poor Mother was well out of it. No more cold, wet days for her, bless her. I still can't believe it. I keep wanting to tell her things and then I remember . . .' Her voice shook a little. 'I remember that I'll never be able to tell her anything again.'

'Poor Fran. My mother died when I was six and the little brother they'd promised me died with her. But I can still remember it. Everyone in black and the awful gloomy music. I was terrified.'

'Six!' She was appalled, imagining her colleague as a small fair-headed boy. 'How perfectly dreadful for you. Who brought you up?'

'An aunt. A spinster aunt on my father's side. Can you imagine it from *her* point of view? She knew nothing about children at all, but she *volunteered*. My father was too dazed

41

even to think clearly, but she moved right in and took over the housekeeping. And me, of course. She was a brick. Still is, although she's nearly eighty.'

'She's done a good job.'

He grinned. 'Thanks! I'll polish the halo later!' He pushed himself away from the door jamb. 'Anyway, it's good to see you back. I missed you.'

'Anything world-shattering happen while I was away?'

'World-shattering? Let me think ... Oh, Wragg threatened to leave, but that's par for the course ... La Marjory gave me a slight talking-to. Didn't like the tone of one of my memos ...' He mimicked her voice. '"Rather too flippant, if I may say so, Mr Starr ..."'

Fran laughed with him.

He went on, 'And Westrop rang, but Marjory hedged, saying the manuscript was with you. Any good, is it?'

'Shall we say "distinct possibility" although to be frank I haven't read all of it. I stayed up until two this morning, but then my eyes wouldn't stay open. A few more chapters to go. I'll read it in my lunch hour.'

'Not another Dickens, then?'

'No-o, but promising. And different. If I *do* want to recommend it I'm going to have to push for it. Marjory's not keen on it.'

'The best of luck, then, my love!' He took out his watch, glanced at it and groaned. 'Well, duty calls!' He gave her a mock salute. 'Bye for now!'

He went off whistling down the corridor and Fran turned to the large diary on the wall beside her, seeing with relief that she had no engagement pencilled in. For a moment she allowed her gaze to wander round the small room which was her second home. Starr Massey spread itself across one floor of a large house in Bedford Square. The more spacious rooms were inhabited by the art director and his small team, and the managing director and his secretary. The rest of them were accommodated in smaller rooms known affectionately as 'broom cupboards'. They were, in fact, sufficient, and Fran was quite content with hers: it contained a large mahogany desk with a telephone, a Victorian inkstand, a stack of manuscripts and a tray full of papers which should have been filed weeks ago. The inkstand had belonged to her grandfather, the firm's founder. A fern in a glazed pot languished on the windowsill, and the walls were half hidden by an untidy assortment of shelves which supported more manuscripts and folders. One shelf had been reserved for a display of books which were currently being published and which stood, face out, displaying their jacket designs. 'To reassure me,' she thought with a smile, 'that out of this organized chaos a few books do get published.'

'Good morning, Frances.' Marjory's smile was scarcely warm. She was small and bustling and reminded Fran of Mrs Tiggywinkle. It was rumoured that in her younger, prettier days she had been the favourite of Stuart's father and that they had enjoyed a discreet affair for many years. His death in 1935 had left her alone and vulnerable. 'What did you think of the Hallam novel?' she now asked. 'Hardly our kind of title, I thought.'

'I liked it actually.' Fran reached down into her briefcase and produced the manuscript. 'In fact I thought it extremely promising.' She looked at Marjory who, predictably, was raising her eyebrows in disbelief.

'Promising? In what way?'

Fran pointed politely to the spare chair but Marjory ignored the invitation. Not a good sign, thought Fran, suppressing a sigh.

'In several ways. I thought it had originality and a distinctive voice. The story-line holds together well and . . .'

'It lacked pace.'

'True, but that can be easily remedied with some judicious

pruning. The characters were well rounded, entirely credible, I thought. Especially the main one – Pritchard.'

'Pritchard? But he was a crook. The main character should be someone the reader can identify with. You can't identify with a crook.'

'Oh, but you *could* in this novel. That was one of the ways in which it was original. It's an interesting idea and I thought he managed it rather well. He is a beginner, after all. It's his first book.'

'And it shows.'

Fran refused to be ruffled. 'OK, so there are weaknesses. But shouldn't we be encouraging him? It could be pulled together; he only needs some guidance. The novel has a powerful message. Pritchard is a sort of – well, a *flawed* hero if you like.'

Marjory tightened her lips, annoyed. 'And some of the language leaves much to be desired.'

'It's gritty, I admit, but it rings true. It's convincing.'

'Gritty?' Marjory protested. 'I think it's taking realism a bit too far.'

'It could be toned down a shade if it was really necessary. It seems to me that if Mr Starr thought it worth—'

'Oh, you and Starr! I suppose you've got it all sewn up between you.' She was obviously finding it difficult to hide her resentment. 'Well, I shall have my say at the meeting and I certainly hope that this is one we don't take on. I've thought about it a lot, and I just can't believe it's our sort of book. But there you are.'

Fran was tempted to say, 'It's called progress', but thought better of it. Instead she said mildly, 'I was wondering if perhaps we could have him in and talk to him – Paul Hallam, that is. See how far he'd go along with us. Find out how amenable he is to some advice on fine tuning. Some people can take criticism, some can't.'

'Why go to all that bother if it's not our kind of book?'

'It just might be. I have a feeling about this one.'

Marjory pushed impatient fingers through her dark hair. 'Feelings don't sell books. I was taught to look for sound qualities and commercial possibilities, not to rely on feelings.' She held out her hand imperiously, but Fran held on to the manuscript. 'I'll send it along later,' she said lightly, hoping to have time to finish it before the meeting.

Marjory opened her mouth, changed her mind and abruptly closed it. Fran smiled pleasantly, found a letter opener and began to open her mail, putting some on one side for urgent consideration, others in the tray to await a less crowded timetable.

Marjory said, 'Sad about your mother.'

'Yes. We shall miss her dreadfully.'

'I thought that with the funeral and everything, you probably wouldn't get round to the manuscript.'

No doubt hoping I wouldn't, Fran thought uncharitably. 'I read it yesterday when it was all over.'

The phone rang.

'I'll leave you to it, then.' She departed as Fran reached for the telephone.

'Peter Westrop here.' The agent's voice was warm and friendly.

'Peter! Nice to hear from you. How are things going?'

'Fine. I heard your mother died. I'm so sorry.'

He actually *sounded* sorry, she thought, touched. 'Thank you. We knew it was coming, she's been in failing health for so many years, but it's still a blow.'

'I hate funerals at the best of times, but especially in the winter. They're so cold and depressing and watching the coffin go down – ugh!'

'We have to bury the dead,' she protested.

'Do we, though? I'm all for the new-fangled cremation, myself. Then they can scatter my ashes and that'll be me gone. I don't want to stay around cluttering up the place.'

'Cremation! That's a dreadful idea.'

'It'll come, you'll see. They've done it in India for centuries. Very civilized, the Indians. But I haven't rung to depress you. Any news on the Hallam script? I sent it to the big cheese and he said he'd pass it on to Marjory. I know I'm pushing a bit but I liked it a lot. I was expecting an excited phone call but, so far, nothing. A resounding silence.'

Briefly Fran explained the position. 'Great possibilities, I feel. Mr Starr, senior, seems keen, too.'

'Ah!' She heard him laugh. 'That means Marjory isn't. I doubted she would be. It's tough and – well, raw, I suppose, but I couldn't put it down.'

'We've a meeting this afternoon. No doubt someone will get back to you. For what it's worth you'll have my vote.'

They chatted for a moment and then he rang off. Free at last, Fran buzzed Sophie, the secretary she shared with Marjory and Stuart, but discovered she would be tied up with the latter for about twenty minutes. She was reading through her mail when Derek, the youngest of the three Starr brothers, arrived, his overcoat spattered with raindrops. As he took it off he said cheerfully, 'I missed you. Did it all go off all right? I was so sorry.'

Derek was small and wiry with smooth dark hair, good-looking in a feminine way with long eyelashes and a rosebud mouth. He liked to play the fool, but Fran knew he had a shrewd brain and was much cleverer than he looked. He hung his coat over the door and sat down.

'As well as funerals ever do,' she said in answer to his question. 'Poor Mother.'

'But she's at peace now, Fran. Cling on to that thought.

Nothing at all can harm her. That's what my mother said when my sister died. It's corny but true – and it's a comforting thought.'

'You're right. Thanks, Derek.'

'So how shall I cheer you up? I know. We'll go out to dinner tonight. Or tomorrow night. Or we'll go to the theatre. Or better still the ballet.'

'Give me a bit of time, Derek. I need to pull myself together and I've so much reading to catch up on.'

'The opera, then. Covent Garden.'

'And I must be with Dot for a while. Until she's over the worst.'

'If only you'd marry me I could see you every day and we need never go anywhere!'

She laughed. 'You're impossible.' Derek had been proposing to her for years but, although they sometimes went to the theatre together or out for a meal, there was nothing serious between them. Fran liked him, but that was all there was to it.

'Impossible? I'm not impossible. That's not the word. The word is *"eligible"*! I'm what's known as an eligible bachelor, and you should snap me up. I'm that desirable property, a deb's delight. You're making a big mistake, Fran.'

'And you're wasting my time, Derek. I've so much work to do.'

'Work?' He looked puzzled. 'Oh! *Work*! I knew there was something at the back of my mind.' He stood up. 'Maybe next week?'

'Maybe.'

She grinned at his retreating back. Then the phone rang again, and this time it was Del Farrar.

'Del? Good heavens! This is a nice surprise.' Ridiculously her heart leaped at the sound of his voice, and she prayed her excitement was not evident in her reply.

'It could get a whole lot better!' he told her. 'I'm free for lunch and I wondered if you'd join me? We could meet at the Cumberland, Marble Arch, but I won't have too much time. I'm tied up here until one, and I'm meeting an old friend of my father's at his club at two. I'd have about an hour.'

Fran closed her eyes, trying hard not to read anything important into this invitation. It was perfectly logical. Del probably didn't know many people in London and was feeling lonely. True, she hardly knew him, but Americans were known for their casual hospitality.

He said, 'Fran? Are you still there? Have I said something dumb?'

'No, of course not,' she said hastily. 'I'd love to see you.' Her heart was suddenly racing.

'Say one o'clock?'

Fran resisted the urge to cheer. 'I'd love to. Shall I see you in the foyer, then? At one.'

'You got it!'

Slightly dazed, Fran replaced the receiver and stared ahead. She was beaming with delighted anticipation, but as the seconds ticked by her elation was gradually tempered by a question that suddenly loomed large. Was Del *married*? No one had referred to his marital status but that didn't mean he was single. Was it possible that such an attractive man could have avoided matrimony all this time? But even if he was, she argued, did it matter for this one occasion? A lunch was hardly in the same category as dinner in the evening when the atmosphere might possibly be romantic. A candle-lit supper was hardly the same as a hurried lunchtime scramble in broad daylight, surrounded by businessmen doing deals or housewives resting after a morning's shopping in Oxford Street. And even if he did have a wife, would she object to her husband lunching with a friend? The answer was a resounding 'Yes' and Fran knew it. But she also knew that, come one o'clock, wild horses would not drag her away from the Cumberland Hotel.

*

The rest of the morning passed so slowly that Fran wanted to scream with frustration. An author rang to complain about the jacket design of his latest thriller, and an agent rang to turn down an offer Starr Massey had made for her client's fourth romantic novel. Fran then had a long conversation with the sales representative for the south-east, and dealt with a call from an irate journalist who wanted an address that she was not at liberty to reveal. She drank three cups of tea and ate five Garibaldi biscuits and found it extremely difficult to concentrate her mind on her work.

When at last she was able to leave the office it was already a quarter to one and, knowing how dense the traffic was in the West End, Fran decided to go by underground rather than by taxi. The train had been travelling for only a few moments when it came to a grinding halt mid-way between two stations. Nobody commented until they had been stationary for about five minutes, and then the muttering began.

The woman next to Fran hugged a small suitcase protectively to her and said, 'Something ought to be done about these blooming trains. They're a disgrace. Look at the dirt!'

Fran murmured something non-committal, trying not to be drawn into a conversation. She wanted to think about her coming meeting with Del Farrar, and was wondering if she dare invite him to dinner one evening. They had a shared interest in books and writing which might give her an excuse. There was always the risk, however, that Connie would somehow hear of it. The question was, did she herself care what Connie thought? She stared ahead, busy with her thoughts, minding her own business.

The door at the end of the carriage opened and the guard hurried through, making his way to the front of the train.

'What's happened?' someone asked.

Another shouted, 'How much longer?'

He muttered something about 'a bit of a delay' and 'an accident'.

'What sort of accident?'

The woman with the suitcase told him, 'I've got a train to catch, I have. You're going to make me miss it!'

As a hand reached out to pluck at his sleeve, the guard turned angrily. 'If you must know,' he said, 'some poor devil's fallen under the bloody train! Now pipe down and let me get on with it.'

When the immediate horror of the situation had left Fran's mind, she realized with dismay that Del would be sitting in the foyer at the Cumberland, waiting for her. Fuming with impatience, she noticed a man opposite consulting his watch.

'Quarter past one already,' he told her irritably. 'And I'm afraid we could be here for some time.'

He was right. When the train was re-started it crawled through the tunnel, and when it stopped at the next station everyone was asked to get off. On the platform there was an unnatural hush as passengers stood around in small groups, conversing in low shocked voices. A policeman was taking a statement from the train driver, who looked very shaken, and several bystanders were also being questioned. A body wrapped in a red blanket was being taken away on a stretcher. Fran rushed to the escalator, wishing that she had chosen to go by taxi in the first place. When she reached the street, however, she saw that dozens of other train passengers had had the same idea and were standing along the edge of the pavement two and three deep, waving and whistling to the few empty taxis that came along. As

50

she waited impatiently her thoughts reverted momentarily to the unfortunate soul who had just died beneath the train. Was it an accident, she wondered, or was it suicide? Or could it have been deliberate? Had someone *pushed* him? Or her? The newspapers were full of violence of one sort or another. Assassinations, wars, murders. Her own life might be sheltered but out there, it seemed, death and destruction were everywhere.

Her reverie was rudely disturbed by a middle-aged man in a bowler hat pushing her roughly aside in order to take the first taxi that had stopped nearby. She cursed him under her breath, becoming increasingly desperate. This was impossible. Abandoning the chance of getting a taxi she began to walk, pushing her way through the crowds of wet and disgruntled shoppers that thronged the pavement. It seemed to take for ever but at last she reached the hotel, hot and flustered and horribly anxious. A quick look around the foyer confirmed her worst suspicions. It was too late. She had missed him!

'Oh, Del!' she whispered, wanting to cry with frustration.

An enquiry at the desk elicited the information that there was a message for her. A Mr Farrar could not wait any longer and expressed his regrets.

For a few moments Fran felt positively ill with disappointment. Then, with an effort, she rallied.

'For God's sake!' she told herself furiously. It wasn't the end of the world, although it certainly felt rather similar. 'It doesn't *matter*!' she muttered, but it did. Whatever would he think, she wondered miserably. And, worse, would she ever see him again? The possibility that he would return to America without their meeting filled her with anguish. Then another thought struck her. Presumably he had waited so long that he had missed his own lunch? And she would miss hers.

'Hell and damnation!' It was easier to be angry than to allow the self-pity to take hold of her. On a sudden impulse she went to the nearest telephone, dialled Connie at the library and blurted out the pathetic little story. 'So could you please let me have his telephone number?'

There was an ominous silence. Already Fran was regretting her hasty action, but it was too late. The silence lengthened. 'Connie? Are you there?'

Connie's voice was cold. 'Well, you've got a nerve, Fran! Asking *me* for his number. If he'd wanted you to have it I'm sure he'd have given it to you.'

Fran struggled to keep her voice steady. 'If you don't have it, just say so.'

'Of course I have it.' The triumph positively crackled through the air waves. 'But I don't think it's the thing to do to hand out other people's numbers. If, as you say, you've stood him up, then he may not relish a call from you.'

One up to Connie, thought Fran. 'Oh, well, perhaps you're right,' she said. 'When he rings I'll explain that I wanted to reach him but that you didn't feel able to pass on the number. I'm sure he'll understand.'

Fran hung up, afraid she would burst into tears. The call to Connie had been a mistake, she could see that now. She drew a deep breath and let it out slowly. She must be sensible. There was no need to panic. If Del wanted to see her again he would make contact. If not . . . but she would not think about that. She stared round her and saw a young man and woman run to greet each other, their eyes blazing with love. A terrible envy seized her as their arms went round each other. She wanted suddenly to be in love and to be loved in return. A great hunger for affection almost overwhelmed her. Del Farrar had come into her life and had interrupted the smooth, uneventful lifestyle she had created for herself. Now she knew with a shattering certainty that without him, it would never again be enough.

Chapter Three

C ONNIE STARED AT THE RECEIVER and then hung up, shaken and furious. Damn Fran! How like her to twist the truth like that. Around her the library hummed with quiet efficiency, but Connie stared at the familiar scene with growing bitterness. Timid Miss Silk, the senior librarian, had no doubt hidden herself away in her office as usual. Subscribers, uncomfortably hot in their outdoor clothes, browsed slowly among the bookshelves – like so many sheep, she thought disparagingly. The junior staff whispered amongst themselves behind the front desk, exchanging the small confidences which she, Connie, was never allowed to share. Not that she cared. She had never craved popularity. At the large wooden table a middle-aged man in a motheaten pullover consulted several volumes and wrote furiously in an exercise book. Who did he think was impressed by that? He pretended to be an author doing research, but she had her doubts about that.

'Damn you, Fran!' she mouthed silently. If Fran told Del that she had been unhelpful, he would know at once why. He would understand that Connie was jealous. Her mouth felt dry and she wished the conversation had gone differently. She wished she had simply given Fran the number, sounding totally disinterested. But how could she? She *was* interested.

Del Farrar was a very attractive man and Connie had had high hopes of more than friendship. Matt's words came back to her: 'The biter bit'! Oh, God! Was it a judgement on her? Her face felt frozen in a mask of despair.

Sally, the trainee, stood on a pair of steps, carefully replacing books on the top shelf. Connie gazed at her with unseeing eyes, listening to the fierce beating of her heart. She put her left hand protectively against her chest. Del Farrar and Fran! So now *he* had betrayed her. They were all the same. Trusting a man was a recipe for disaster, and she should know. How *could* he do this to her, she asked herself passionately. Hadn't she done all she could to help him? To be supportive? She had read his damned novel and said all the right things about it. Hadn't she found him a literary agent, for God's sake? She had gone out of her way to study American politics, had expressed an interest when Joseph Kennedy was made ambassador to Britain, and had 'tutted' disapprovingly when the Duke of Windsor cancelled his trip to the States. So why did he turn to Fran and ask *her* out to lunch? It was so patently unfair. Men! She hated them all – except Henry, of course, though he would probably break some poor girl's heart before he was much older. Hell! Why was fate so unkind? They would carve 'Failed Happiness' on her tombstone; it would be her epitaph.

'Miss?'

She became aware that someone was standing beside her table, an elderly lady with an anxious look on her face.

'Yes. What is it?' she asked tersely, unable to keep the tension from her voice. She longed to say, 'Go away and leave me in peace', but that was out of the question. She needed this job. The tontine money alone would not cover all her needs, although it was a welcome addition to her salary.

'If it's not too much trouble, Miss, I'd like a bit of advice.'

The tone was querulous and the eyes a faded blue. Connie made a great effort to pay attention; that was what she was paid for. 'How can I help?'

The woman hesitated. 'Forgive me for asking, my dear, but are you quite well?'

With a start Connie realized that her hand was still pressed against her heart and hastily lowered it. Feeling rather foolish she said, 'Yes, I am, thank you. Tell me how I can help you.' She indicated a nearby chair. The woman sat down gratefully and began a long and meandering story about some diaries which had come her way which had once belonged to an uncle in the cavalry. She wanted to make them into a book and needed some background information on Egypt in the late nineteenth century. Connie tried to concentrate, but her thoughts were not so easily contained and visions of Del and Fran intruded frequently. She was tormented by the thought of them lunching together and, no doubt, talking about her, Connie. Fran would make her into a kind of ogre and Del would find it all amusing in that relaxed way of his. Now she saw that taking him to the funeral had been unwise, but at the time she had wanted to show Matt and Fran that other men found her attractive. Del had been surprised by her invitation because they really did not know each other as well as she had pretended. Perhaps he had only accepted out of politeness. The truth was that she had rushed the friendship, using him as a prop for her self-confidence. It simply had not occurred to her that he would latch on to Fran. She should never have taken such a calculated risk. Matt had said Fran had grown into a swan and unfortunately Connie could not argue with that. Fran *was* attractive, although Connie would never admit it.

'Of course, I shall only deal with the facts in a light way,' the woman continued earnestly, 'because I don't think people are terribly interested in politics. There were some wonderful old photographs, too, and where possible I shall compose a few lines of explanatory text to go with each one. If you'd care to see them, I have them here.'

As she fumbled eagerly in her handbag Connie quickly forestalled her. 'Some other time, perhaps,' she said. 'I'm terribly busy today, but I'll find you a couple of books which may help.'

She did so with her usual efficiency, which this morning gave her no pleasure. Del had never taken her out to lunch; had never even suggested that they meet outside the confines of the library, but she had toyed with the idea of inviting him to dinner when the time was ripe. Now, thanks to Fran, it probably never would be.

At the front desk she stamped the books and smiled 'Goodbye', her mouth stiff, her mind in turmoil beneath the calm exterior.

Sally, the trainee, looked at her sharply. 'You feeling OK, Miss Massey?'

'Why do you ask?'

'You look a bit pale.'

'I'm perfectly all right.' Walking quickly back to her table, she sat down. She was not all right; she was more upset than she would admit. She was trying to hate Del, but it was difficult. Deep down she knew that betrayal was too harsh a word. In all honesty he was blameless, and in a way that made her feel worse. She had caused all this heartbreak herself by her precipitous behaviour. There! At last she had admitted it. Mortified, she felt her cheeks burn and covered her face with her hands. 'Father's little favourite.' The ridiculous phrase would not leave her. And 'Connie used to be the pretty one.' *Used* to be! Matt certainly knew how to wound, but then he always had. Unaware of time passing, Connie remained gripped by despair.

'A cup of tea?'

Sally offered her a small tray on which was a cup of tea with two digestive biscuits in the saucer. It was not time for the mid-morning break, and Connie could not hide her surprise.

'But why?' she asked, taking the tray with hands that trembled.

'Miss Silk thought you looked a little unwell.'

So Miss Silk had ventured out. 'That's very kind.' Connie forced out the platitude. The last thing she wanted was pity. To explain her obvious discomfiture she added, 'I'm rather shivery, actually. I may have a bit of a chill. It's so cold out.'

Sally smiled. 'Like the North Pole! But my mother likes the cold. She says her arthritis is worse in the summer. Funny, isn't it?'

Connie gave her a bleak look. The tea would help her pull herself together and the biscuits were a bonus.

'Mum says we'll have snow if the temperature goes up a bit. Too cold at the moment.'

Connie mumbled something and sipped her tea. Her least favourite word: snow. It never failed to send a shudder through her, although she was at pains to hide her fear. The fearful memories of that dreadful day lay buried in her subconscious for most of the year, but as winter approached they always resurfaced. Even now, in the warmth and security of the library, she was helpless to resist the images that crowded her mind with such appalling clarity. Once more she felt her panic as she had regained consciousness and found herself entombed in snow. She felt the numbing cold of her hands as she clawed her way out and the terror that had gripped her as she found herself alone in a silent, white landscape, lit only by a pale moon that occasionally emerged from behind the clouds. Stumbling desperately through the deep snow for what seemed like hours, she had shouted hysterically until she fell to the ground, sobbing, with the certain knowledge that unless she was found she would die before morning.

The rattle of the cup in the saucer was becoming noticeable. She saw that her hands were shaking and hastily put the cup and saucer on a corner of her table. Sally was looking at her with concern and Connie felt a flash of irritation.

'You'd better get back to your work,' she said sharply.

'Oh! Right, then.'

Connie cursed her stupidity. The girl was offended. Why had she snapped at her? She called, 'And thank you for the tea!' but Sally pretended not to hear. Oh, well! It was the story of her life, she thought with resignation. No one except her father had ever understood or appreciated her.

She picked up a list and stared at it for a moment. Ah, yes! The names of subscribers whose books were overdue. She reached for a pile of pre-printed postcards and began to scribble addresses with a shaking hand. Perhaps if she concentrated on her work she could keep other, less charitable, thoughts at bay. She had written five cards when it dawned on her that she had written the same one twice.

'What the hell am I doing?' she asked herself as she tore the unwanted card into two and threw the halves into the waste-paper basket.

Suddenly she knew what she would do. The idea had been in her mind ever since the funeral. She would punish Matt for all his cruelties, she would revenge herself for the humiliations he had heaped on her while they were together. As soon as the decision was taken, she felt stronger and less vulnerable. Why shouldn't she strike back? Matt was the enemy and she had suffered enough at his hands. True, *she* had left *him*, but they could never have stayed together. He had never loved her and had been at pains to let her know. And after her mother's visit there was nothing else she could do. Carefully picking up her tea she tried once more to drink it, and this time there was no giveaway rattle. With a slow, deep breath she told herself that she would fight back. Connie smiled mirthlessly. She would use the only weapon at her disposal – the information her mother had passed on to her. Mother had begged Connie not to tell Matt and Connie had respected her wishes. Now, however, Mother was dead and only Connie knew the truth, a truth that would prove devastating to Matt.

They all knew that, as a boy, Matt had often romanticized about his mysterious parents. Connie herself had suspected that he might be her father's illegitimate son. But if so, why had her mother agreed to take him into the family and bring him up? Surely that was the last thing a betrayed wife would contemplate – unless she was a saint, and Mother had had as many faults as anyone else. She had also had her virtues, but Connie had never felt that unstinting forgiveness was one of them. Her determination grew as she sipped her tea. Matt would know what it felt like to be humiliated. She would write him a letter, spelling out the facts, and she would spare him nothing. His life would be ruined; his confidence would be shattered, and nothing and nobody would be able to save him. It was a cruel step to take, but Connie had been hurt once too often and now she felt desperate enough to take it.

*

Monday, 10th January, 1938

Dear Matt,

You may have thought that you could make a fool of me in front of everyone at Mother's funeral, but I am not the complaisant creature I once was, thanks to you. You did your best to humiliate me and I am honest enough to admit that you succeeded. I am also honest enough to think that it is time you had a taste of your own medicine. So how about the following? You are Violet's son. That's right, Matt. Poor Aunt Violet, who nobody talks about. Hidden away in St Maxime's with Mother's sister. Bit of a shock, is it? Well, serve you damn well right! I for one am cheering!

Don't raise your hopes, Matt. This is not some horrible, tasteless joke I'm playing on you. It's the truth, exactly as Mother told it to me the day before I left you. You see, Matt, she was afraid that I would marry you. Little did she know how unlikely that was after the few miserable weeks we had spent together. But she was not to know what a selfish pig you could be, nor how bad-tempered you were. Since we are so closely related, she had to stop us marrying, but she still wanted the unpalatable truth kept from you. Touching, isn't it? Well, now she's dead and I've decided to tell you.

And did you know about the tontine, Matt? I don't think anyone ever bothered to mention it to you. We were all too busy gloating. Uncle Alex, who disappeared into the blue, finally became a very rich man. He died with no family of his own, so he left his money to us – that is, me, Fran, Dot, Mary and Henry. In fact, he left it to Father's *legitimate* heirs and you weren't one of them. He left it by way of a tontine, which is a kind of codicil to a will. It means that when one of us dies the remains of their share is divided out among the others. That way it stays in the family and our share of Starr Massey is assured. Terribly decent of him, wasn't it?

So now you know everything. Or nearly everything. I don't know who your father is. If Mother ever knew, she didn't tell me. Maybe you should ask Aunt Violet. If she's not totally mad she might just remember!

Don't try to contact me, Matt. I never want to set eyes on you again. Let's just say that with this letter, we're quits, and leave it at that.

Connie.

As soon as the letter fell into the pillarbox Connie regretted it – not because she didn't want to hurt Matt, but because suddenly she feared how he might react. Once or twice during their time together she had witnessed Matt's temper and knew how very easily he could lose control. Not that he had ever laid so much as a finger on her, but he had come very near to it. She also knew the way his mind worked. Even as a child he had been sly and devious. She had always suspected that, after she was knocked unconscious, it was Matt who walled her up in the snow, but she had never put the idea into words. It was Matt who had 'found' her and, for once, he had been the hero of the hour. No doubt the adult Matt could be equally cold and calculating. A shiver of apprehension ran through her as she imagined him reading the letter. She had made a bad mistake, an error of judgement. Had it been possible, she would have withdrawn the letter from the ministrations of the Royal Mail, but it was too late. As she turned homeward, her anger was evaporating and in its place she was aware of a growing feeling of compunction. Certainly she had wanted to punish him, but the anguish he would now suffer was rather more than he deserved; a little excessive for the 'crime' he had committed. Glancing up into the cold, grey sky, Connie hoped her mother was not aware of the way her oldest daughter had abused her trust.

A gust of icy wind whipped up a few dead leaves and sent them fluttering against her legs. She drew a deep breath and tried to resist the feeling of unease which now held her. Mother was dead and she, Connie, was a grown woman with a mind of her own. She must be allowed to make her own mistakes. Drawing up the collar of her coat, she told herself not to be foolish. Tomorrow morning Matt would read the letter and his agony would begin. It was no less than he deserved. If he rang her it would have to be at the library and she would warn the staff that she was 'not available'. If he wrote to her she would tear up the letter without reading it.

62

'Serve you right, Matt!' she muttered. 'From now on, just stay out of my life!'

*

The following morning, which was Tuesday, Fran came downstairs to find Dot in the hallway talking to a girl she had never seen before. Fritz was there, too, wagging his tail somewhat doubtfully. Annie, on her knees, was buckling him into a smart tartan coat which Fran had bought for him the previous Christmas. She looked up with a nod in the girl's direction.

'This is Amy, my sister's grand-daughter. You remember? You said she could come for a few days.'

'Hullo, Amy.' Vaguely Fran remembered something about – what was it? A grand-niece?

The girl stared up at Fran with a serious expression in her large blue eyes. 'My mummy's in St Mary's Hospital, but she's coming out again as soon as she's better.'

Fran smiled at her. She was a plain Jane, she decided, saved by large blue eyes. Her brown hair was held back severely in two long plaits tied with crumpled red ribbons. Her mouth was large and her chin a little too pointed.

Amy went on, 'You must be Frances, but everyone calls you Fran. I think Frances is much nicer, but I suppose it's too late for you to change it now.'

Dot said eagerly, 'Yes. I like Frances better.'

She smiled at Amy, and Fran realized with pleasure that the child would be company for Dot and might help her through the first few weeks of being without her mother.

'Fritz wants us to take him for a walk. He likes Amy.'

Fran smiled at them both. 'Well, I hope he keeps you two in order!'

Dot laughed, but Amy seemed to be considering whether Fran's remark was intended as a joke.

Annie said to her, 'Make the most of it, young Amy. You're only having this one day at home. Tomorrow you'll be at school.' She explained to Fran, 'My niece, Ellen, is most emphatic that she shouldn't miss any schooling, and thank goodness the village school here found a place for her. I hope it won't be for too long, and it's good of you to let her stay here. I'll see to it she doesn't make a nuisance of herself. I'll put her in the end bedroom.'

'She'll be fine, I'm sure. But is that little bedroom warm enough? It faces east and it's so cold at the moment.'

'I lit a bit of a fire in there this morning just to air it, and I'll put a hot-water-bottle in the bed.'

Dot was struggling into her winter coat and Amy was pulling on a navy-blue mackintosh which was obviously part of a school uniform.

Dot told Fran, 'We'll go as far as the station. Are there any letters to post?'

'Not today. Haven't you got any? I thought you were going to write to Mary.'

Dot put a hand to her mouth guiltily. 'I'll do it this afternoon. Poor Mary.' To Amy she said, 'Mary's one of my sisters. I'll tell you about all my brothers and sisters as we go along. I've got four.'

'I haven't got any,' said Amy. 'Mummy always says that one was quite enough, thank you. I suppose I was a bit difficult when I was younger.'

At last all the gloves and scarves were in place and, dressed to withstand the winter cold, they declared themselves ready. Annie opened the front door for them and Fritz braced himself against the icy wind that immediately found its way into the house.

Fran said, 'Say "Hullo" to the station-master for me. I

hope his lumbago's a bit better,' and she and Annie watched them go.

Closing the door, Annie said, 'She's a funny little thing. Old-fashioned as they come.'

Fran smiled. 'Was she difficult when she was younger?'

'Very. Wouldn't eat. Wouldn't sleep. Terribly active and easily bored. Ellen said it was the reading that saved her sanity. As soon as Amy learned to read she could amuse herself. Proper little bookworm, apparently, but then an only child has to amuse herself. You wouldn't appreciate that, with your lot!'

Fran shrugged. 'All we seemed to do was squabble with each other!' She smiled. 'And still do, unfortunately!'

*

Maidhurst station was nearly a mile away, through a lane which twisted and turned and was flanked on each side by a ditch and ragged hawthorn trees. On either side of them the fields stretched away at a gentle slope – bare brown earth, ridged for spring, glinting with frost in the thin sunshine. A solitary wood pigeon murmured from the shelter of a small copse of trees, leafless beech and chestnut amongst them. The fallen leaves whirled crazily as the wind seized them and Fritz rushed after them, barking with excitement.

As Dot described the members of her family, she was pleased to see that Amy listened intently.

'Connie is my oldest sister,' she told her, 'but we don't see her very often. She lives in Maidstone, which isn't far, but she's cross with Fran so she stays away from us.'

'Why is she cross?' Amy threw a stick for Fritz, who ignored it and pounced instead on a dead starling which was lying by the side of the road.

Dot screamed at him to 'Leave it!' but he picked it up

and hurried ahead, keeping a safe distance between himself and his companions.

Dot, who would normally have chased after him, decided that she would rather continue her conversation with Amy. 'Why is Connie cross? I think it's because Connie stole Matt from Fran. Matt's always lived with us, but he's not really our brother; he's an orphan, so we all had to be kind to him.'

'Was he kind to you?'

'Sometimes. Once he was horrid to me. He shut me in the coal cellar and I had to climb up the big chute where the coal comes in. Luckily the doors don't shut properly so I could get out. It was dark and I got covered in coal-dust, and it went into my eyes and made them sore. Father gave him a good hiding and Matt blamed me.'

'He sounds awful.'

Dot thought about this, a small frown on her face. 'He's not awful, not really. It's all because of him being an orphan. I write lots of letters, but I can't write to him because none of us do. Fran wouldn't like it. But I knitted him a scarf once. It was red and white and blue stripes. Mother said it was very patriotic.'

'Patriotic? What's that?'

'I don't know. But it was. It was a Christmas present. He loved it and he said he would wear it all year round, even in the summer!' She giggled.

'In the summer?'

'It was only a joke. But I write to my brother Henry and to Mary, my other sister. I write every week. She's a school-teacher and she likes me, too.'

'Is she married?'

'Not yet. She's a bit shy. But when she does marry I shall be a bridesmaid.'

'Lucky thing!' Amy sighed deeply.

'And I shall be a bridesmaid again when Henry gets

married, although he's only eighteen.' Dot glanced at Amy and saw that she was impressed.

'I shall get married as soon as I'm old enough,' Amy confided. 'And I shall have five or six children and we'll all live happily ever after!' She laughed and made an unsuccessful run at Fritz, who neatly sidestepped and ran away again. 'That bird's disgusting,' she said. 'I hate dead things.'

Dot's expression changed. 'You don't hate my mother and father, do you?'

'Of course not, silly. I meant *that* sort of dead thing.' She made a sudden spring at Fritz, who growled a mild warning and nearly tripped over his dead bird.

Dot breathed a sigh of relief. '*We* don't live happily ever after,' she said, reverting to the previous subject which seemed safer. 'Connie doesn't like anybody, and Fran doesn't like Connie or Matt, and Matt – well, nobody knows what Matt likes. I like them all, but what I like doesn't count really. So I write letters, even to Connie.'

'Does she answer? Do the rest of them answer?'

'Oh, yes! I get lots of letters. Sometimes I answer the telephone, but it's never for me. I'm not supposed to, though.'

'Why not?'

Dot hesitated. 'I get a bit mixed up with the messages.'

'When I get married I shall marry a rich man and we'll probably have a telephone. You could ring us.'

'Could I really?'

'Why not?'

They stopped to look over a farm gate and Dot pointed to a house in the distance. 'That's the vicarage and further over, that's the church.'

Amy looked around. 'Not many houses,' she objected. 'At home there's houses everywhere. And people. There's nobody around here.'

'That's because it's the country' Dot explained. 'It's – well, it's *isolated*. The country always is.'

'I'm a townie.'

Dot stifled a pang of envy. A townie! It must be wonderful to be surrounded by houses and people. She saw that Fritz had deserted the dead starling and was trying to wriggle under the gate that led into the field. With a little scream she grabbed his collar, hauled him back and gave him a token slap. 'He mustn't go into fields in case he chases the sheep.'

'What sheep?'

'In the spring there'll be sheep with their lambs.'

Amy frowned. 'But there's no grass. What will they eat?'

'It will grow, the grass. You'll see.'

'I won't be here.' She investigated the dead starling, then kicked it to one side. 'Are you courting?' she asked suddenly, 'because if you are I know all about it. A girl at school told me.'

Dot hesitated. This, she had learned, was a delicate subject. Her mother had told her frequently that she need not bother her head about it. 'I don't think so,' she said.

'Don't *think* so?' Amy laughed. 'You must know if you have a young man. An admirer. Someone who wants to marry you.'

'Well, then, I don't.' For a moment Dot thought wistfully that it might be rather nice. 'It's not for me. That sort of thing is not for me.' Her mother had explained that some people were the marrying kind and others were not.

'I am.' Amy looked up at her. 'If you solemnly swear on your dead mother's grave that you won't tell a soul, I'll tell you his name.' Without waiting for the oath she went on, 'It's Terry, and you must never tell. He gave me this.' She held up her left hand on which a red stone sparkled. 'He got it from a cracker. It's an engagement ring; it's a ruby.'

'It's pretty.'

Gazing at the ring, Dot was overcome with a deep sense of inadequacy. In case this showed in her eyes she knelt quickly to fuss over Fritz, pretending to straighten his tartan coat. Lucky, *lucky* Amy! She was wildly envious and wanted a ring just like hers. When she could bear it she stood up and rejoined her new friend who had wandered on and was now staring over the gate at the small station platform.

'That plant's dead,' she said accusingly, pointing to a frozen geranium in an oversized plant pot.

Dot felt it necessary to defend the station-master, who was their friend. 'It always dies in the winter. Mr Walker puts a new one in each year.' She put Fritz's lead on, although the chance of a train at this particular time in the morning was small. Those travelling to London to work had gone several hours earlier and the stopping train was not due until midday. Fritz sat down and thrust his long snout through the gate.

Amy said, 'I flirt with Terry. I wink at him . . .' She demonstrated. 'Sometimes I roll my eyes like this – and sometimes I let him kiss me. It tastes a bit horrible because he's always sucking peppermints. Ugh!'

'Don't you like peppermints? I do.'

'Then you'd like flirting with Terry.'

A cat strolled past the gate on the other side and Fritz began to bark hysterically. Amy watched him for a moment and then said, 'His legs are too short. And he hasn't got any knees.'

For the second time Dot experienced a deep anxiety. With a sinking feeling in her stomach she knelt down to examine her beloved pet, but could find nothing wrong. 'It's because he's German,' she suggested.

But Amy had already lost interest. 'He put his arm round me once – Terry, I mean. I had to put a stop to that. You never know where that could lead.'

'No, I suppose not.' Dot wondered where it *could* lead. It sounded harmless enough.

Amy was leaning over the gate, but there was no sign of the station-master.

'I expect he's brewing up,' said Dot.

'What's that?'

Dot smiled, pleased to know something that Amy didn't know. 'It's making a pot of tea.'

'Oh, *that* sort of brewing.'

The cat sprang up on to the top of a low shed and Fritz suddenly fell silent, exhausted by his efforts.

Dot said, 'We can look in the waiting room if you like. There's a fire and—'

'No, thanks.'

Dot felt vaguely dissatisfied as they turned for home. The lack of an admirer had never worried her before, but now she began to consider all the men in her life in case any of them might be adapted for the role.

She said, 'Matt loves me.'

'Has he given you a ring?'

'No-o. Not yet.'

'He's not in love with you then.'

'Oh, I see. He gave me a pencil once with a tassel on the end.'

'It's not the same.' Amy held out her hand. 'Can I take him for a bit?'

Dot surrendered the lead absentmindedly. Perhaps Mother was wrong about marrying?

Amy glanced at her. 'D'you want to marry Matt?'

'I don't think so.' Did she? It was all rather sudden, and she would have to think about it. 'Del admired my flowers,' she said, brightening. 'I do watercolours of flowers and he thinks they are *very* good. He said—'

'It's not quite the same thing. It's not love and kissing. It's not *romantic*, not like me and Terry.'

No, of course not. How silly of her. Dot began to feel flustered and irritable. It really wasn't fair. Amy had everything – lots of houses and people and an admirer and a ring. And a mother who wasn't dead. For a moment tears pricked at her eyes but she blinked them back. There must be something . . .

'Have you got a dog?' she asked, as casually as she could.

'No.' Amy pursed her lips. 'Mummy won't let me have one because they shed hairs.'

Dot recognized the regret behind the words and felt agreeably privileged. She, Dot, had her very own dog. Poor Amy had nothing.

She watched proudly as Fritz trotted ahead of them at the end of his lead. The mile-long walk to the station was quite enough for him and she could see that he was getting tired. She told herself that if she had to choose between a dog and an admirer, the dog would win. She wanted to say so, but a quick glance at Amy's downcast face made her change her mind. Amy was her friend and Dot would keep that comforting knowledge to herself.

*

Matt walked up Bayfield Road, his head full of problems. The job with the stationery firm was not working out and before long he suspected that he would have no job at all. The orders he gained were small, and the regional manager was snapping at his heels, demanding better results. There were targets to be met and he was not meeting them. Matt had just returned from three days in the Berkshire area and had very little to show for all his efforts. The last client had been downright rude to him, and the exchange still rankled.

'Oh, it's you again! It's not three months, is it, since you were here last?'

71

'It is actually, Mr Graver. Exactly three months to the day.'

'Well, I don't want anything. Haven't sold the last lot yet. See for yourself!'

'The notebooks have gone.'

'Had to practically give 'em away. Special price. Didn't make more than twopence on each one. I want no more of those. I want no more of anything, so there's no point in—'

'But you must see the new birthday cards we're doing. We've commissioned a team of young artists—'

'Sorry. Not interested.'

'But do just take a look – for future reference.'

'Not interested means exactly that, Mr Massey. Save your breath . . .'

Matt hated the man, from his bulging eyes and waistline to the long strands of thinning hair he brushed across the top of his almost bald head. Ignorant pig. The world was full of them, he reflected bitterly. If there was any justice in the world someone would set fire to his damned shop!

The boys from the school were going home and one of them kicked a football which narrowly missed him.

'Watch it!' he shouted.

'Sorry!'

Slightly mollified by the apology, he turned in at the gate of No. 25 and fumbled for his key. The evening loomed ahead, promising nothing, and he sighed as he mounted the stairs. He would tackle the hated paperwork and cook himself something simple. It would be scrambled eggs, probably – he thought there were three left – or there might be a tin of sardines left in the cupboard. He had invented a tasty way with sardines: mash them with salt, pepper and a dash of vinegar and spread the mixture on hot toast or a slice of fried bread. Not that the fried bread was very popular with Poppy Parfitt, his landlady. She always complained when he fried anything on the grounds that the smell of frying 'permeated' the house. 'Permeated'. She liked long words. Stupid cow! And what a name – Poppy! It didn't suit her and he knew it wasn't her real name; he had seen envelopes addressed to Mrs Brenda Parfitt! Scowling, he unlocked the door to his room and went inside with the usual feeling of despondency. It faced north and had been decorated and furnished with no attempt at style. Everything was secondhand and looked it.

He looked around and said, 'Welcome home, darling. Had a good day?'

The familiar joke did nothing to lighten his mood. Who was he kidding? Even during his few weeks with Connie, she had never said that. Connie had never said, 'Welcome home, darling.' *Never*. He felt a rush of self-pity and his stomach rumbled uneasily, reminding him of his hunger. Perhaps he would just make a pot of tea and stuff himself with biscuits? Easy but filling. He had eaten an early lunch in a small café – sausages, mash, gravy and peas. The woman who served him had been friendly enough and had given him an extra spoonful of mashed potatoes. There were still a few decent people in the world, he reflected, although they were few and far between.

He picked up the few letters which had been pushed under the door and wondered, not for the first time, whether nosy Poppy had steamed them open and resealed them. Once she had made a reference to his mother being away in France, and Matt was sure he hadn't told her although she insisted that he must have done. She was a sly one.

He put the letters on the table and knelt to turn on the small gas-fire. It lit with a 'pop' and for a moment he crouched in front of it. One of these days, when he was desperate enough, he would turn on the gas and gently float away. Then they would all be sorry. But not just yet. He glanced at the envelopes and suddenly recognized Connie's familiar handwriting. And it was postmarked 'Maidstone'! *Connie* was writing to him? His heart began to pound with anxiety. He had regretted his unkindness at the funeral and had toyed with the idea of writing briefly to apologize. He should never have made those caustic comments – at least, not on such a sad occasion. If Mother had been listening it would have confirmed her opinion of him as an insensitive lout; he had heard her one night when he crept downstairs to eavesdrop on one of their rows. So perhaps she was right. He had never thought of himself that way, but anything was possible. Not that he cared any more. She had never loved him and now she was dead.

'So, Connie,' he said to the unopened letter. 'What have you got to say, I wonder? What is important enough to persuade you to write to me, blackguard that I am?'

So was he a blackguard also? Wasn't there anything admirable about him? If there was, no one seemed to be aware of it. Except maybe Dot, and she was hardly the best judge in the world. As always when he thought of Dot he saw, with a flash of unbearable hindsight, the small figure dangling helplessly from a tree. The rope, tight around her throat, had starved her brain of oxygen. He should never have allowed her to follow him in that harebrained escapade but she had begged and pleaded and he had finally relented. He had helped her up into the branches where he was 'mountaineering' with a rope around his waist and long nails which he was knocking into the tree trunk to provide footholds. Before he knew what had happened she had somehow twisted the rope and then, in her panic, she fell. He had been well thrashed for his part in the tragedy. Poor, sweet Dot! He would never forgive himself for what had happened.

He turned Connie's letter over and over in his fingers, reluctant to read its contents. He had had enough for one day. Mr Graver and an empty cupboard were depressing him. A letter from Connie could only make him feel worse. Perhaps he would burn it unread. Connie . . . in the snow. Now that was a different kettle of fish altogether. He *had* meant to frighten Connie and had deliberately sent her down that steep slope hoping that she might hit the trees at the bottom. When in fact she was knocked unconscious he had thought her dead; he had entombed her in the snow and then gone home. Interrogated, he said Connie had gone off in a huff and he didn't know where she was. When they set out in search of her he had known where to look and had hurried ahead. He had been desperately relieved to see her staggering about, half dead from cold and shock. For finding her he had been fêted as a hero. Life was funny that way.

He opened the letter and began to read. As the words danced before his eyes, his bare cupboard and his brush with Mr Graver paled into insignificance. Aunt Violet – his *mother*? A tontine? . . . For a moment or two he was too shocked to feel anything, and then a wild confusion protected him from the worst of it. Eventually, however, he became aware of a terrible coldness as fear and then horror gripped him.

'I don't believe it . . . I don't believe it . . .' he muttered. 'Oh, God, no! No!' As he reached the end of the letter the paper slipped from his fingers. 'It can't be true,' he whispered and his voice shook. 'Not Aunt Violet!'

Violet, the mysterious skeleton in the Massey cupboard, had been a source of fun for the children when they were younger. 'Crazy Aunt Violet' had featured in their secret amateur theatricals and was always portrayed as mad or evil. The bogey-man; not the sort of character anyone would want to own as a mother. 'Christ, *no*!' he shouted and reached again for the offending letter. This was something Connie had invented to pay him back for his little unkindness. Oh, how he wished he had kept his stupid mouth shut. This loathsome idea was Connie's way of punishing him, but it could not, *must not* be true. If Father had truly been his father as he had always suspected, then he could not have – would never have . . .

'She was your *sister*, for Christ's sake!'

No, it was impossible. Unless Violet was his mother and Father was *not* his father. He sank further into the armchair and covered his face with his hands. He had always known that he was illegitimate and had pretended not to care, but deep in his heart he had cherished the hope that his conception had been the result of a love match. A respectable but unacceptable love match between Father and an unknown woman. *Respectable*. Aunt Violet was impossible; it simply could not be true.

'Jesus Christ, Connie. I could kill you for this.' Tears pressed at his eyelids and the terrible conviction grew that Connie was telling the truth. If this were not true, Connie would never have risked his anger. He knew her too well to suppose otherwise. If, *if*, this were true and Violet *was* his mother, then who was his father? He found a handkerchief and blew his nose. He must pull himself together and think it out sensibly, and must *never* let Connie know what this letter had done to him. She must never have that satisfaction. It came to him suddenly that perhaps he could ignore it, pretending that he had burnt it unread. He felt a small return of control. There were things he could do to rob Connie of her triumph. He could mention to Dot when he answered her letter that he had burnt a letter from Connie. Dot would show the letter to Fran and Fran might tell Connie. A fresh thought struck him. Did the others know? If, as she said, Connie was the only one who knew about Violet, then there was always the chance that she would tell them too. Matt felt utterly degraded by the mere idea of such a catastrophe. He felt sick and his head ached; his appetite had deserted him.

'Oh, Connie!' he muttered. 'You cold-hearted bitch!'

Suddenly he re-read the latter half of the letter. The paragraph about the tontine had been obscured by the more devastating information about his mother. A tontine? Codicil to a will? As he read it his despair gave way to anger. Uncle Alex had become rich and had left all his money to be shared among the Massey children. *With the exception of Matt*. Because he was not legitimate.

He felt a great need to express his growing anger, but words were not enough. He wanted to throw something, scream and shout, hurt someone. He wanted to return the pain with interest. If he could do that he might feel better.

'I'll get you for this!' he told the absent Connie. He would punish them all for their sins against him. They had inherited wealth and had kept the secret from him, no doubt laughing at his ignorance.

'You smug bastards!' The word struck him as incongruous. *He* was the bastard who had not inherited a penny; who had suffered the ultimate humiliation of being Violet's son.

He stood up restlessly, fuelled by his anger, and began to stride about the room until a knock on the door interrupted his thoughts. Then he felt a moment's panic, as though the shame he was feeling might be there on his face for all to see.

'Yes?' He made no move to open the door.

'It's me, Mr Massey. Poppy.'

Who else could it be, he thought savagely. The woman was an idiot. 'I'm busy.'

'It won't take a minute.'

Damn her! Some women couldn't take 'No' for an answer. Their minds were unreadable. Never trust a woman, he told himself.

She said, 'You're not in the altogether, I hope,' and giggled like a schoolgirl.

77

He had an almost overwhelming desire to drag her into the room and beat her into a pulp. He was facing the worst crisis of his life and she had to come barging in. Closing his eyes he counted to ten, then said, 'Just a moment.'

When he opened the door he saw that she carried a tray with a cloth over it. She said, 'I thought perhaps you'd got a young lady up here. You know I wouldn't like that.'

'That makes two of us, then.' He glared at her, hating her. She was obviously over forty, probably nearer fifty, and her once-thin body was now scrawny. Her face might once have been pretty in a common way, but now it was slack and the heavily applied make-up did nothing to improve its appearance. She had once confided in Matt that she had lost her husband to another woman many years before and had frequently dropped hints about her lonely existence – hints which made him wary of allowing her into his room. Once she had screamed for help and he had gone rushing downstairs to find nothing worse than a large moth fluttering round a table lamp. Two days later, by way of thanks, she had given him a handkerchief on which she had embroidered the letter 'M' in white silk. It had crossed his mind that she might have designs on his body, perish the thought, and he had tried ever since to keep out of her way.

She laughed. 'I thought you'd like a bit of suet pud for your afters, Mr Massey. I made such a big one, and it's never the same the next day.' She whipped off the cloth and the suet pudding looked entirely appetizing. To his surprise, Matt's appetite returned instantly and he felt ravenous.

'Thanks very much.'

He was standing in the doorway, barring her way, but she looked past him. 'Busy, are you? We never get a chance to chat, do we?' She gave him a glance from beneath her lashes. 'Never have a chance to get to know each other.'

Matt looked at her, startled and then deeply offended. This horrible creature with her painted face and shapeless

78

body thought he might want to get to know her! It was positively disgusting. Did he really look that desperate? His already battered self-esteem fell even further.

He took the tray and said, 'Some other time perhaps. I'm desperately behind. Paperwork and more paperwork.'

'It's what makes the world go round.'

'I suppose so. Well, thanks anyway.'

To his relief she took the hint and made her way downstairs. 'Good riddance, you old bat,' he whispered, but the suet pudding was delicious and he gobbled it down in huge mouthfuls, desperate for comfort of any kind. Afterwards he made himself a pot of tea and drank three cupfuls as hot and as sweet as he could bear it. Then he sat back. He tried to imagine himself in bed with Poppy and shuddered. There had been one or two women in his life since he left Connie, but no one lasted more than a week or two. What women had to offer no longer seemed to interest him. He wondered suddenly about Violet and the man who fathered him. Had that been a long, emotional involvement or a sordid affair, a 'quickie' up against a wall in a dark alley? He tried to remember whether any of the world's famous men had been born to unsuitable mothers. Napoleon, perhaps? Shakespeare? Or even, coming closer to home, a British politician – or a famous actor? The warm carbohydrate mass inside his stomach was soothing him. As time passed a little of the tension left him and the nightmare of Connie's revelations faded slightly.

He began to think about Violet in a less critical way. Tentatively he said, 'Violet.' Then, 'My mother, Violet.'

It was a pretty name; that was something. He had never seen a photograph of her, so she might have been a beautiful woman. The Massey women were a handsome lot, by and large, so he might have had a beautiful mother. Could she have been attacked and raped? His heart thudded. A beautiful *wronged* woman? Could he bear that? Was she still beautiful in a sad, faded way? It puzzled him that she had known where he was all these years and had never made contact. Never even sent him a birthday card. Had they prevented her from doing so? His eyes widened at the thought. Had she sent things to him, sad little gifts, which Mother and Father had kept from him? He was beginning to feel much better. A new idea struck him. Perhaps he could go after the man who had wronged his mother and – and do what? For a moment he hesitated. And *kill* him?

'Why not?' he muttered.

In his present mood, the idea of killing the cause of his anguish seemed a reasonable one. Perhaps then the family would appreciate him for what he was and not condemn him for the accident of his birth. He had a wonderful vision of himself tramping the world in relentless pursuit of the man who had ruined his mother. He *liked* the idea. He liked the idea of killing him too. He liked the idea of killing *someone*. He felt that he was strong enough and capable enough to kill and get away with it.

Abruptly he sat up, astonished. Of course! He had the answer to it all. He would go to St Maxime and he would talk to his mother. No one would expect that. Connie would be stunned. Instead of being crushed by her spiteful letter he would be uplifted by it; it would prove to be the turning point in his life. He would become an altogether different person – the *real* Matthew Massey: strong, resourceful, relentless. The Mr Gravers of this world would not recognize him.

'But can I do it?' he asked himself. He imagined Violet, a frail but still beautiful recluse, shut away from her only child, grieving in dignified silence all these years. In his mind's eye he pictured their reunion, which would be touching in the extreme. Of course, Mother's sister Alice would be there, but she would be the only witness. Violet would tell him the name of his father and his search would begin. When he found the wretch he would reveal the fact that he, Matt, was

80

his son. Then he would kill him! He conjured up a picture of the man begging for mercy, but Matt would be remorseless; he would put his hands round the man's throat and strangle him. It occurred to him that he had never known exactly where Alice and Aunt Violet lived, simply because he had never been interested. But presumably Fran would have the address. Mother had spent so many winters there that Fran must surely have written to her at some stage? Not that Fran must know what he was about. No one must know. He would find a way of discovering the address without revealing his true purpose. The more he thought about it, the more confident he became.

'I'll do it!' he cried. He could almost feel the adrenalin surge. He could kill, he *knew* it.

Or perhaps he would slit the man's scrawny throat – and then stand back while he bled to death. Or he would put a bullet through his brain. He would stare down into those wide, terrified eyes and he would pull the trigger. Whichever way he did it, he would make it clear who he was and why he was doing it. There must be no doubt in the man's mind that Matt was his son, the son he had disowned.

As his imagination went to work Matt became more excited. The idea of a terrible retribution appealed to something basic in his nature. He could not wait to put the plan into action and suddenly it seemed imperative that he make a start. He searched through his pockets for small change, then rushed down the stairs and out of the house, banging the door behind him. He almost ran down the road towards the telephone box at the corner; fortunately there was no one using it. He tugged open the door and, as he picked up the receiver, he realized that he was shaking. Having dialled the number of his regional office, he pretended to be Henry and told the secretary to cancel Matt's calls for at least a few days as his brother had been taken seriously ill. The secretary accepted everything he said; it was so easy. When he finished the call Matt stepped out of the phone-box and thrust his hands into his pockets.

For the first time in his life he felt eight feet tall.

Chapter Four

F RAN SETTLED HERSELF ON THE chair beside the telephone and searched her notebook for the agent's number. While it was ringing Dot came into the hall and said, 'Fritz wants me to give him a bath. Shall I?'

'A bath?' Fran regarded the dog with raised eyebrows. 'He looks clean enough to me.'

'But he smells. Yesterday evening he rolled in something nasty and Amy said it must have been a fox's dirt or else a cowpat or—'

'Amy said? What does she know about it? I thought you said she was a townie?'

'She is, but she knows about everything. She knows about getting married and flirting and kissing and cuddling and things like that. She knows about dying and going to heaven and being an angel. She knows about—'

Fran smiled. 'She's a mine of information!'

'Yes, she is. So can I give Fritz a bath?'

'You can if you want to, but you'll have to keep him in the house until he's quite dry. If he goes outside damp in this weather he'll catch pneumonia.'

'Will he? Pneumonia? Oh, dear!' She looked at Fran anxiously.

'He'll be all right if you keep him in.'

'Shall I ask Annie to help me?'

'If she's not too busy. I should bath him in the kitchen where it's warm.' She looked at Fritz, who was regarding them intently. 'Poor old Fritz!'

Dot said quickly, 'He likes it really. He just pretends he doesn't.'

Fran frowned at the telephone. 'He's not answering. That's odd. What day is it today? It is Friday, isn't it?'

'Friday, yes. The fourteenth. Who's not answering?'

Fran hung up. 'Peter Westrop, the agent.' She glanced at the clock on the wall. 'I'm a bit too early, I suppose. He doesn't usually arrive until ten, but Mrs Garner should be there.'

Dot said, 'Come on, Fritz.'

'Nice bath, Fritz?' Fran teased, bending to pat the smooth, dark head.

His tail stopped wagging abruptly and his ears went back.

'Don't *tell* him,' Dot protested. 'You know how he hates it.'

'You said he *wanted* a bath!' Fran reminded her. 'Well, it won't do him any harm, but try not to get soapy water all over the kitchen floor.'

'If it does, *I'll* wipe it up.'

'Annie will make sure that you do!'

Fran drummed her fingers on the hall table and glanced again at the clock. She was up early every morning now, trying to keep busy. The aim was to prevent herself from thinking about her mother, or about Del who had not been in touch since Monday when she had failed to meet him at the Cumberland. She would not admit, even to herself, how disappointed she was. Every time the phone rang her hopes soared, but each time so far she had found herself speaking to someone else.

Even as she thought this, it rang and she snatched

the receiver from its hook. The operator's voice was as impersonal as ever. 'I have a call for you.'

Fran muttered, 'It won't be him. It *won't*,' in a desperate effort to save herself the agony of disappointment. In fact it was Mary.

'Oh hullo,' said Fran as brightly as she could. 'Nice to hear from you. Is everything all right?'

'Yes. I just . . . I wanted to hear your voice, that's all. I'm just being silly.'

'Of course you're not.' She had a vision of Mary, tense and unhappy. 'It's because of Mother, isn't it?'

There was a pause. 'Yes. How did you know?'

'I miss her too, you know. We all do.'

'I miss her so much it *hurts*, Fran. In my throat. It aches unbearably. I mean, I know I didn't see her very often, but I always knew she was there. And now she isn't and never will be . . . And I had a letter from Dot, and she said how sad *she* was and I . . . I thought about the house with just you and Dot and Annie and no Mother and . . .' Her voice shook.

'Oh, Mary! I'm so sorry, dear. I know how you feel. It's dreadfully sad, for all of us.'

'I just thought if I rang you – I mean, I needed to hear your voice.' There was another long pause. 'You sound a bit like Mother.'

Fran swallowed hard. 'Do I?' The idea pleased her. 'I'm glad. I'll always be here, Mary. You know that. You're not alone and you mustn't think that way.'

'I know. I'm just – I couldn't sleep last night for thinking about her. I was thinking about when I started school and how scared I was, even though I had you and Connie and Matt. Mother bought me Bun, that tiny furry rabbit, to have in my pocket. And she said it was a sort of magic rabbit that would stop me feeling miserable. Whenever I felt scared or shy I was to touch the rabbit.'

'I remember.' Fran found herself smiling.

'And it worked. I've still got him. His fur's all worn away but . . . I've got him in my pocket now to remind me of Mother.' She cleared her throat. 'How's Dot bearing up?'

Fran was grateful for the change of subject. Her own feelings of grief and loss were never far below the surface and she was finding it difficult to suppress them. 'I think she's OK. You can't always tell with Dot, of course. She's giving poor old Fritz a bath this morning.' She heard Mary's shaky laugh at the other end of the line. 'And I've taken a few of her watercolours to a chap in the art department. Del suggested that they might be good enough to use in a book. Del Farrar – d'you remember him?'

'The man who came with Connie to—'

'Yes. So Dot is quite thrilled about that. And she's got a young companion for a week or two: Annie's great-niece.'

'That's nice for her. I envy you all together.'

'Poor Mary. But look on the bright side. It won't be too long before it's half-term, and then you'll be home again.'

'It won't be the same, though, will it, without Mother?'

'No, it won't.' Fran tried to think of something comforting to say, but nothing sprang to mind. She always worried about Mary. She was such a lonely soul, her shyness such a barrier to possible friendships with either sex. Would she ever marry, Fran wondered suddenly, and have a family of her own? 'We'll have a good, long talk when you come home,' she promised.

The silence grew intolerable. 'Mary?'

'I feel as though I shall never be happy again.'

'Oh, *Mary*! Don't say such things. Of course you will.'

'Fran, I keep thinking about Matt at the funeral. He looked so – so down. I mean, poor and sad and . . . so unkempt. Did you think so?'

'He did look a bit down on his luck.' Fran spoke reluctantly, unwilling to think about him.

'I know you don't like him because of what happened with Connie but – do you think we should care about him? What I really mean is, should we ever forgive people like Matt and give him a second chance? I felt so bad, thinking about Uncle Alex's tontine. And poor Matt not getting any money; not even *knowing* about it. He looked so dilapidated and if we could share the money out again so that he got some it might make all the difference. Is it possible? Would the others agree?'

'It's not legally possible, Mary; Mother did make enquiries at the time. The trouble is that legally he is not one of our family; he's lived with us since he was a baby, but Father never adopted him. The tontine was specifically designed to keep the money in the Massey family, to ensure the continuation of the firm.'

'Oh, I see … Well, if I write to him would you mind?'

'Of course not. But I hope you won't tell him about the tontine. I think he would feel much worse about everything if he knew.'

'I won't mention it. I just keep thinking that if he feels as sad as I do about Mother and nobody writes to him, he'll be so alone. You and Connie won't write – I understand that. And Henry won't bother. Dot is sweet but she may not understand.'

'It's very thoughtful of you. Write to him, Mary. I'm sure he'll appreciate it. I'll send you his address. It's somewhere around.'

'I must go. I've got form 3A now, little darlings!' She forced a laugh. 'Bye for now, Fran.'

'Bye, dear.'

Fran replaced the receiver and felt horribly guilty. She'd been so obsessed with Del Farrar that she hadn't spared a thought for Mary. They had once been quite close with only four years between their ages, but since Mary went to college they had drifted apart. Now Mary's post as French teacher at the school was a residential one. Fran frowned, wondering if Mary was as happy at the school as she claimed to be. She seemed to like the other members of staff and she certainly loved some of her young charges, for her occasional letters to Dot were full of their exploits. Shaking her head, Fran sighed and told herself that Mary was a grown woman and could look after herself. So why was Fran concerned? Was Mother's mantle somehow falling on to her own shoulders? She drew a deep breath and let it out slowly, thrusting the idea from her. She mustn't fuss, but when half-term arrived she would see that Mary had some fun. A little bit of excitement would not come amiss, either. She would give a dinner party, and maybe arrange a trip to London to the theatre. If *only* Mary could find a nice young man! A little romance might help.

Fran sat for a moment, thinking about Mary, and was so engrossed that when the phone rang it startled her.

'Hold the line, please. I have a call for you.'

Fran waited impatiently for the operator to connect them, her fingers crossed. This time she was sure it would be Del, but to her surprise it was Matt. She almost said, 'Talk about the devil!'

'It was good to see you again, Fran. Sad occasion, but I *was* pleased to see you.'

Fran, taken aback by the unexpected warmth in his voice, mumbled something suitable.

He went on, 'How are you bearing up?'

'We're all right, Matt. Well, as much as we'll ever be without her. I was thankful there were no family fireworks. Funerals, wedding and christenings are always potentially explosive, especially with our family.' She hesitated. 'I didn't get much chance to talk to you, Matt. Are you really OK? You've lost a little weight.'

'It goes with the territory. Dashing around the country, snatching meals when and if – you can imagine.'

She felt a sudden compassion. 'You must look after yourself, Matt.'

'Well, nobody else will!'

She was silent, knowing she must not start feeling sorry for him.

After a moment or two he said, 'Seeing you all again made me realize what a rat I was.'

She felt a rush of nervousness. 'Matt, I don't want to talk about it.'

'But I must, Fran. Mother dying has made me stop and take stock. I've made mistakes and I've been a bit of a louse in the past, but – I'm not all bad. At least I don't think so.'

She said nothing encouraging, wondering where this was leading.

'Fran, I'd like to take you out to dinner one evening. I'd like us at least to be friends again – hopefully, even good friends. You were always special to me, you know that.'

She mustn't listen to him; he had such a way with words. 'It wouldn't work, Matt. It's too late. I'm sorry.' Despite her brave words she was aware of a tightening in her throat as she remembered the deep affection she had once felt for him. She had been a plain, awkward child – the ugly duckling of the family – and knowing that she was special to Matt had been important to her self-esteem. But things happen and people change. She had moved on; she had finally found her own identity without his help, and she was not willing to risk losing it again. 'Too much water under the bridge, Matt,' she told him, as briskly as she could. 'Hackneyed but true. I think in your heart you know that I'm right.'

Confused, Fran tried to keep control of her emotions. She didn't totally believe in his 'change of heart' but, with Mary's words still in her mind, she did wonder if his experience of the funeral had made him feel isolated. Maybe he was hoping to ease his way back into the family but if so, she suspected it was a lost cause.

He said, 'You could be wrong, Fran. You could be making a mistake.'

'I don't think so. You hurt too many people, Matt.'

'I never had a chance to explain, Fran. There was never an opportunity. I'd like you to know. If you'd just listen – you owe me that much.'

'Do I?' Did she owe him anything, she thought? Surely it was the other way round. And did she want to know how it had happened? In all these years she had never been offered an explanation for Matt's abrupt departure with Connie. At the time she had been too unhappy to demand one; too vulnerable to risk further humiliation. Months had turned into years. She hesitated too long and Matt, it seemed, took her silence to mean assent.

'That night, Fran, when you and Mother took Dot to the hospital. She'd swallowed something. I forget now. Berries, wasn't it?'

'Deadly nightshade. She thought they were elderberries.' Fran remembered it well. There was still time to stop him, but now curiosity overcame her reluctance. Perhaps once she knew exactly what had happened she would be able to put the past to rest.

'I was alone with Connie,' he told her, 'and suddenly she began to – to give me the eye. I thought she was joking at first, and then she produced a bottle of red wine. God knows where she got it from; Father always kept the cellar locked. We went up to my bedroom so that Annie wouldn't see us.'

'Whose bright idea was that?' Fran heard the spite in

her voice and bit her lip. She had known it would be painful.

'Hers.'

He would say that, thought Fran.

'We drank all the wine and Connie told me that I was her favourite and that she'd always loved me. At first I couldn't believe her, but then she tried to convince me. Of course I wanted to believe it – my vanity was touched!'

'I can imagine.'

'We got plastered—'

'On one bottle of red wine?'

'Connie went downstairs and got some cooking sherry from the kitchen. When she came back upstairs she said we were alone in the house and could do whatever we liked. She said Annie had gone for a walk.'

'And you believed that?'

'I was too drunk to care, really. Then later she invited me to—' He paused. 'We got into bed and . . . you can imagine the rest.'

'You didn't – surely you . . .' Fran fought down a desire to scream at him. He and Connie were almost brother and sister! She managed to say nothing. I'll give him enough rope, she thought, and he'll hang himself.

He went on slowly, picking his words with care. 'Two weeks later she told me she was pregnant.'

'Pregnant? Oh, God!' Fran had not expected that and she was shocked into silence.

There was a long pause. 'She said I'd be turned out of the house in disgrace, and she was probably right. Father couldn't have had a better excuse. She said she'd stand by me but we'd have to run away together and I must help her get rid of the baby, and then we could come home again. Fran? Say something.'

'It's horrible!'

'I know. But at the time – it wasn't anything I'd planned.

Don't you see that? It all just happened. At the time I believed her. I panicked. I thought if I refused she might blame it all on to me – pretend that I raped her, maybe. So away we went. And of course, she wasn't having a baby. She went to a doctor – or said she did – and then said there *was* no baby.'

Fran tried to breathe normally but her chest seemed to be constricted. Questions hurtled around in her mind, making her dizzy. Was Matt telling the truth? Was that really how it had happened? And had Connie ever loved Matt? Fran had always thought Connie had acted out of jealousy rather than affection. Even now she found the story barely credible, and wondered how much was Matt's invention. He was putting all the blame on Connie, but he might well have been a willing partner – especially after all that alcohol. He must have guessed how it might end.

She said, 'You were nineteen, Matt. Hardly a child. Old enough to know what was going on.'

'Too stupid to say "No"! I'm not proud of myself.'

Fran struggled with an urge to strike back at him, but the truth was she no longer had the need to retaliate. Nor, she was surprised to discover, was she utterly heartbroken. Supposing, that is, that he wished to pursue the relationship. Thinking of Del made her feel whole again and suddenly she could not be bothered with recriminations. The past was done.

'Let's let it die, Matt,' she suggested. 'I'm glad you told me, but there's no point in saying any more. We are two different people.'

After a long silence he said, 'There's someone else! There *is*!'

'No.' She hoped she sounded convincing. She *hoped* there might be someone else, but unless Del phoned her there was no one.

'There is!' he said again.

'If there was someone else, Matt, it would be my business, not yours.'

'Ouch! My God, Fran, you certainly are a different person.'

She swallowed hard. 'If there's nothing else, Matt, I've got a lot of work to do so if you don't mind . . .'

'There *is* something. I thought I might write to Aunt Alice.' He said it casually, but immediately Fran froze. All that talk about letting bygones be bygones and here was the *real* reason for the call. There was a sudden tension in his voice that told her this was important to him.

'I want to thank her,' he explained 'for all she did for Mother. And to say I'm sorry she wasn't at the funeral. She was Mother's sister, after all. I thought it was odd. Violet, well, I can see why she wouldn't come.'

Surprised, Fran said, 'Can you?'

'A bit crazy, wasn't she? That's what we all thought.'

'I suppose so. No one ever talked about her. We just assumed . . .' Fran frowned. What *did* they know about Father's sister? None of the children had ever seen her. Mother and Father never spoke of her, and she had never sent cards for birthdays or at Christmas. Had the children *invented* her madness? Had she perhaps been merely eccentric? An embarrassment of some kind? She shrugged. Violet had been and still was a mystery figure, but Alice was Mother's elder sister. If Matt wanted to write to Alice, who was Fran to stop him? 'I can find her address if you wait a moment.' She hurried into the dining room and found the old notebook in which such details were kept; then returning to the phone, she gave Matt the address.

'Villa Maris, Gulf of St Tropez!' repeated Matt. 'Sounds rather nice, doesn't it? Strange that in all these years we children were never invited. Only Mother.'

'I think that was the idea. She needed a break from all of us. Six children must have been a bit of a handful. And then lately the climate was kinder for her lungs. But why do you say that, Matt? Do you think there is something ominous about the fact that we weren't invited?'

'Ominous? Hardly. Odd? Yes, perhaps. Anyway, I'll drop her a card. Alice, I mean.'

'Right.' Fran was aware of a growing unease. He was up to something. He had used the desire to get back together again as a cover for his real purpose – which was to ask for the address in St Maxime. But *why*?

As though reading her mind he said quickly, 'Well, I'm sorry you feel that way, Fran, about you and me. I had hoped we might both be a little sadder and wiser by now and—'

'I *am* wiser, Matt, and that's why I say "No". A reluctant "No", because you were special to me. And what you did caused me terrible heartache.' How trite that sounded, she thought with a flash of anger. He would never know how completely her confidence had been shattered. She had suffered a loss of innocence and trust, and her image of herself had been distorted. But crushing Matt now would do neither of them any good. 'I'll always have a small corner in my heart for you,' she said, 'but that's as far as it goes. I'm sorry, Matt.'

A few seconds passed and he said, 'Your loss!'

This time she was sure she detected no trace of real regret. So he had never expected a reconciliation; that was merely an excuse for the phone call. She wondered what he would have said if she had accepted the belated olive branch. Damn him!

'Well, that's it then,' he said. 'Dot OK?'

'Yes, I think so.'

He didn't know how to make his exit, she thought, and smiled. She would help him.

'Goodbye, then. Look after yourself!' She hung up.

From the kitchen she could hear shrieks of laughter

from Dot, and then Annie was shouting a warning. There was a crash and a slithering sound and Fritz appeared in the kitchen doorway. He was covered in soapsuds which flew in all directions as he scampered determinedly down the passage. Dot came flying after him with a towel in her hand.

'Stop him!' she cried, but Fran held up her hands in a gesture of surrender, deciding that this particular situation called for discretionary action.

'I've got work to do,' she told Dot and, temporarily abandoning her call to Peter Westrop, she gathered up her notes and made good her escape.

*

At three o'clock Fran arrived at the offices which Peter Westrop shared with his three partners. She was greeted by Mrs Garner, the receptionist, a plump, kindly soul who had been there for as long as Fran had been in publishing.

'Miss Massey! How nice to see you.' She beamed at Fran. 'Mr Westrop has just got back from lunch and knows you are coming. I'll tell him you're here.'

Fran waited impatiently. She had made several unsuccessful phone calls during the morning, only to be told by the operator that the line was engaged. When she finally did get through she learned that the agent was 'in a meeting' with a client and was then going out to lunch. Frustrated, she had decided it would be easier to jump on a train and visit in person.

Mrs Garner came back into the reception area and held open the door to her employer's office. 'Mr Westrop will see you now.'

Peter Westrop was a short man with a round face, a jovial nature and a cheerful expression which rarely wavered. He stood up now and welcomed Fran with a vigorous handshake accompanied by a broad smile.

'Good to see you, my dear,' he said, subsiding heavily into his chair. 'The treasure is bringing us a tray of tea.'

Fran thanked him and sat down in the chair facing him across the vast oak desk, a family heirloom of which he was immensely proud. The desk itself was a riot of papers and files from beneath which a lower layer of books and manuscripts occasionally protruded. The office itself was large, with a high ceiling, and framed book-jackets covered most of the walls. There was a Persian carpet in the middle of the floor, half hidden by the desk, and an aspidistra stood on a plinth in one of the windows. As always there was a smell of lavender wax polish lovingly applied, and the deep sash window sparkled.

'I'm glad you could spare me a half-hour,' she began. 'I must say right away that I am not supposed to be here. My colleagues have no idea that this meeting is taking place, and I hope we can keep it that way for the time being.'

He raised his eyebrows. 'Very mysterious!'

'I'd like to speak to you confidentially about *The Granite Cloud*—'

'Ah! Hallam's novel! Well, as I told you, I'm surprised by the rather disappointing noises from your firm's direction. Mrs Evans was distinctly chilly when I mentioned it.'

'She wasn't impressed, I know. I like it tremendously, but I'm a bit of a lone voice in the wilderness at the moment.'

The tea arrived and Mrs Garner poured two cups for them before withdrawing. Fran took a digestive biscuit and nibbled it absentmindedly. 'The trouble is, like all first novels, it needs a lot of work to do it justice, and I don't think anyone is prepared to spend that much time on it.

I have to say that we are at the moment being offered some very good stuff by well-established authors. Also, of course, there is quite a bit from the States. I can see their argument, actually, but I would like to work on this one.'

'You feel that strongly about it?'

'Yes, I do. Has anyone else seen it? Faber, perhaps, or Hodder and Stoughton?'

'The former, yes. The latter, no, though they were next on the list in fact. I thought it might be Barry Fitt's sort of novel.' He blew on his tea and sipped it noisily. 'Always digestives,' he remarked, shaking his head at the plate of biscuits. 'Have you noticed? I think Mrs Garner likes them. I certainly don't. I've tried telling her and she humours me for a while, and then suddenly I notice that we're back to the digestives again.'

Fran was not taken in by this apparent lack of interest on his part. Peter Westrop was one of London's best agents and his casual manner concealed a sharp mind. She knew he was giving himself time to think.

She laughed. 'At least they're not as boring as *Neece* biscuits.'

'Hmm!'

After a moment or two she asked, 'Do you think Paul Hallam would be willing to accept criticism? That's the big question. And spend the time necessary for the amendments? I don't have time to do the alterations myself, but I could show him what's needed and set him on the right track. The point is, Mr Westrop, I think this could be a breakthrough novel for Hallam. If I invest time and effort on the book, could you guarantee us first refusal at a reasonable price? That way I might be able to persuade them to take him on. If, as I expect, the novel earns out and reprints everyone would be happy. If necessary, I could give him some guidance on his second novel – for which we'd have the option, of course. He does have one, I hope?'

Tilting his chair back, the agent stared at the ceiling with pursed lips. 'He's working on something else, yes,' he said at last. 'He's not short of ideas. And yes, I think he would accept criticism. He has the right attitude. I liked him from the start; I wouldn't have taken him on otherwise. Mind you, it wasn't right for the US market, and that's a shame. Too outlandish for them, I suspect. They wouldn't know what to make of him. He doesn't fit neatly into any accepted genre. I don't know what you mean by "reasonable price". It would have to be a totally fair price.'

'Fair in view of the amount of effort I shall put into it.' She leaned forward earnestly. 'Without all the improvements you might never sell it – or might have to let it go cheaply.'

'But you do like it?'

'I do. I think it has a wonderfully original tone, although the language might need to be toned down a bit for our readers. It's too slow, but the pace can be adjusted with some judicious cutting. But it will have to be done well. We mustn't spoil it. I'm suggesting that Mr Hallam and I work on it together secretly, then you submit it to us again saying simply that it's been reworked at your instigation. I'll see that we read it again. I'm sure I could then persuade our managing director to take it on. Then if they know I helped him, it won't matter.'

He laughed, rocking back in his chair. 'You're a devious woman, Miss Massey; you take after your father, God rest his soul, but I'll put it to my client.'

'He mustn't come to the office. We can talk over lunch at home.'

'I'll talk to him later and get him to phone you.' He smiled, pleased. 'Splendid. I have a feeling this man will be good for Starr Massey.'

'And we'll be good for him.'

He poured her a second cup of tea. 'Now that the business is done, let me say again how sorry I was to hear about your mother. Condolences and all that.'

'Thank you,' said Fran.

She drank the second cup of tea and they talked generally about the publishing business and various mutual acquaintances. Fran was struggling to hide her elation. Paul Hallam was 'in the bag' – or very nearly – and she felt more certain than ever that he was going to be a star in their small firmament.

*

The staff room at Marlham Preparatory School for Boys was at the front of the building facing south-west, so by late afternoon it caught the sun. It was furnished comfortably, but the furniture was shabby and the rug faded. There was never any suggestion that the room should be refurbished because money was never available for such luxuries. The school, like many small units, was always struggling to survive. Sometimes they made a modest profit, but that was a rare event. It was owned by Samuel Harper, assisted by his wife Doreen, who was the matron. Samuel was a tall, spare man with stooped shoulders, while his wife had been nicknamed 'Roly-Poly' for reasons that were obvious. The school thrived under Samuel's stewardship and their reputation was sound. Marlham combined academic success with a less sparkling sporting record.

With her arms full of exercise books, Mary edged open the staff-room door and, as always, found the sunlit room a comforting place after the chilly north-facing classroom which she shared with the twenty boys who made up 3A. Lettie Crewe, the young geography teacher, was already hard at work, her dark head bent over a similar pile of books,

99

her red pencil hovering energetically above the blotched attempt of one of the first-year boys.

Mary said 'Is it really only Wednesday? I can't believe the week is going so slowly.' She slumped into an armchair and set the books down on the adjacent coffee table.

Lettie gave a short laugh. 'The whole *term* is going slowly.'

John Witcombe looked up from his bible. He was a thin, academic-looking man with sandy hair and steel-rimmed glasses.

'My entire *life* is going slowly,' he told them. 'At a snail's pace, to be exact. By the time my brother was my age he was a fully-fledged vicar with a decent parish, and I'm stuck here with the monsters in 2B and no prospects whatsoever!'

His subject was scripture, and Mary found him rather pious and thoroughly harmless. Not like Dan Forbes, who taught games and liked to make suggestive remarks. Fortunately Dan was engrossed in one of his favourite detective novels, his long legs dangling carelessly over the stuffed arm of the chair in which he sat. Mary tried never to be alone with him.

Mary glanced at the clock above the mantelpiece. Nearly five o'clock. Tea was at five-thirty, and she was always hungry, although some of Annie's gingerbread waited in her room in case she was ever overcome with sudden hunger between meals. Annie always sent her back to school with a cake tin containing a substantial cake and a packet of chocolate or dates – it was a family joke. Thinking about it made Mary smile. Mother had called it 'Mary's tuck-box', she reflected with a faint smile, trying not to think of her in the dark coffin.

She blinked rapidly and hoped that the other two would not notice as she brushed tears from her eyes. They had all been so kind since the funeral – almost too kind. Their consideration had undermined her efforts to cope with the grief. Determined to appear cheerful, she began to whistle tunelessly as she opened the first exercise book.

'J'aime promenader au jardin . . . Je n'aime pas promenader au jardin . . .'

Apart from her grief for Mother, Mary was also worrying about the letter she had written to Matt. Fran had said it was a good idea, but had the letter been a little too friendly, she wondered nervously? What would Matt think? She had tried to be kind and sisterly, but Matt was difficult to understand and he might misunderstand her intentions. Deeply uneasy, she suspected that the letter had been a mistake, but it was too late now. He would have received it and read it and – and what? Would he answer it? She didn't know what to hope for. He might ignore it, and in some ways that would be a relief.

Lettie threw down her pencil and groaned. 'Listen to this, for heaven's sake! Would you believe it? Quote: "The Limpopo River runs through the middle of India from north to south!" *India*! What on earth am I doing here?'

Mary said mildly, 'Maybe they've moved it!'

Only John laughed.

'"The middle of *India*"!' Lottie grumbled. 'Is he deaf or something?' The pencil snaked across the page and then she shut the book with an irritable snort. 'I need some fresh air. Anybody coming with me?'

Mary shook her head. 'Sorry, Lettie, but I'd better not,'

John said, 'Count me out! I'm not the hardy type and it's freezing out there.'

Dan glanced up. 'Enough to freeze a monkey's—'

John said quickly, '*Thank* you, Mr Forbes. There are ladies present.'

Dan snorted and returned to his book. Enough to freeze a monkey's *what*, Mary wondered.

101

When Lettie had gone, John said, 'India! She must be the world's worst teacher!'

'Oh, don't say that!' said Mary.

'But it's true,' he insisted. 'You know what they say — you can take a horse to water, etc. etc. But every teacher with poor results should ask herself whether—'

'Or *himself*!' Dan suggested.

'What?' John frowned. 'All right then. Should ask himself or herself if they are failing to get the facts across.'

Mary thought about it. 'But sometimes they just don't listen,' she suggested. 'The children. Sometimes they're ill or unhappy and they can't take it in. They're not receptive.'

'But why not? If we are making it interesting enough, they *should* be receptive.'

Mary hated it when John rode this particular hobby-horse because she always suspected that the argument was a subtle criticism of her own teaching skills. She shrugged and bent her head over her books.

At that moment there was a knock on the door and a small boy held out a letter. 'This is for Miss Massey.'

John said, 'What about an "excuse me"? Where are your manners?'

The boy looked puzzled and Mary quickly took the letter from him. 'Thank you, Simon.' She smiled at him and, with a sideways look at the scripture teacher, the boy hurried away.

Mary looked at the letter and recognized Matt's handwriting. Her hand shook a little with an anticipation that was not entirely pleasurable.

'It must have come by second post,' she said. 'I looked this morning and there was nothing for me.' She stared at it.

'Aren't you going to open it?'

'Oh! Yes, of course.' Tearing the flap of the envelope, she took out the folded sheet and began to read.

'My very dear Mary . . .' She caught her breath. *Very dear?* '. . . How sweet of you to write to me. Nobody else bothered, although I expect I shall hear from Dot. I am off to France for a day or two on personal business, but when I come back I would like to come and see you . . .'

Excitement surged through her, but with it came a frisson of anxiety. Matt had ruined Connie's life, so Mother had said on more than one occasion, and he had made Fran unhappy. In a way she was consorting with the enemy, and she felt sure Mother would have disapproved of a meeting between her and Matt. But poor Mother was dead. So unless she was actually looking down from heaven, she would never know.

'. . . I have a little car, as I told you, and I will bring a picnic . . .'

A picnic? In winter? Mary smiled.

'. . . We can drive somewhere pretty and relax and talk . . .'

Talk? Abruptly, Mary's anxiety deepened. What was there to talk about? Was he going to tell her his version of the trouble between him and Connie and Fran? Would he try to persuade her to take his side against theirs?

'. . . I shall be thinking of you and will telephone when I get back to England. Your loving Matt . . .'

The words danced before her eyes 'Your loving Matt!' Was he loving? Was he *her* Matt? She stared at the letter as though hypnotized. Was this some kind of *love letter*? She had never had a letter like this from a man, and she wanted to be happy but instead she felt a terrible disquiet.

Dan asked, 'Love letter, is it?' in a voice which suggested that this was highly unlikely.

'Sort of!' she told him defiantly. 'Someone wants to take me for a drive and — and out for a meal. A . . . family friend.'

John said, 'Aha! A *male* family friend?'

Mary smiled at him. 'Could be!' It was rather nice to tease them all just a little. She wouldn't say who it was, and she certainly wouldn't tell them he was her brother – because Matt wasn't a real brother, although she had always thought of him that way. Until he had run off with Connie, of course, and then she had been forced to re-think the relationship. Perhaps the letter would set the tongues wagging? She knew what they thought of her. Poor, shy little Mary Massey. On the shelf. The wallflower. It would be wonderful to see the look in their eyes as she jumped into Matt's car and they drove off together. Slowly she began to see herself in a different light. She imagined herself returning from the outing with flushed cheeks and a happy smile. An enigmatic smile. Perhaps Matt would kiss her again. Once, when they were children, he had kissed her under the mistletoe . . .

'An *admirer*?' John persisted.

Impulsively Mary folded the letter, put it to her lips and gave him what she hoped was a mysterious smile. 'I think you could say that.' It really was quite fun to drop these exciting hints. And anyway she wasn't lying exactly, just maybe embroidering the truth a little, but she didn't care. And suddenly she didn't care what Mother or Connie or Fran would say if they knew. She would go with Matt in his car, and she would share his picnic. She imagined a bottle of champagne and a cold chicken with salad, then remembered that it was January and cold enough for snow. Well, maybe he would bring hot soup in a flask with crusty bread wrapped in a warm cloth? They would follow it with cheese and grapes. It would have to be something simple, because at the funeral poor Matt had seemed to be rather hard up. Of course he had pretended, the way he always did, that things were fine and getting better all the time. All that about promotion. She hadn't really believed it, but that didn't mean she should turn down his offer. Whatever it was she would enjoy herself. It would be an experience and she would write to Fran afterwards and tell her all about it. Smiling to herself, she made up her mind. She would *live* a little.

Chapter Five

THE GULF OF ST TROPEZ was grey, with dark clouds threatening rain as Matt stared unseeingly across the bay. However, it was several degrees warmer than it would have been in England, and there was no wind. These facts gave Matt no comfort as he wandered along the promenade, trying to summon the courage to visit the mother he had never seen.

A part of him longed to see her, the other part dreaded the disillusionment it might bring. He stood hunched into his overcoat, watching four hardy souls playing boule. A stray dog, waving his feathery tail like a banner, invaded their pitch but was eventually discouraged by shouts and threats. Matt envied the players their apparently normal lives. During his short crossing on the ferry and the long train journey, he had almost convinced himself that St Maxime would be the scene of an emotional reunion which would set him on the path towards a happier future. Now that he was so near, this rosy vision was fading and in its place he saw embarrassment, resentment and revelations that might have a totally damaging effect on his life. This visit might prove to be the worst mistake he had ever made, but he had come so far and felt unable to leave without seeing the woman he had always known as Aunt Violet. He still found it difficult to think of her as his mother, but in Connie's spiteful letter he had recognized the awful ring of truth.

'Go now!' he told himself. 'Do it!'

But he remained on the promenade, looking out over the sullen sea where a small yacht was making slow headway in the windless air. To his right a small kiosk advertised 'crêpes' but it was closed. To his left three elderly women shared a wooden seat, huddled together for warmth, while their canine pets scurried among the shrubs with their leads trailing.

Matt had spent a mainly sleepless night in a shabby room in a third-rate hotel and the continental breakfast, eaten in solitary splendour, had not satisfied his hunger. He wondered what his mother was doing at quarter-past nine in the morning. Eating warm croissants and sipping fragrant coffee, perhaps, and reading a day-old English newspaper. He imagined her in a wicker chair beside a window, her head bent gracefully over *The Times*. Presumably she was still interested in all things English? A faint smile touched his cold lips. Edward VIII's abdication must have come as a shock, but then he and Mrs Simpson were now living in France, and that might please his mother.

'Go and see her!' he told himself again, and this time he turned from the sea and crossed the road. He began to walk slowly eastwards, glancing from time to time into the windows of the shops on his left, dodging the tables and chairs outside the cafés. He had already asked for directions and knew the exact location of the house. He walked with his hands thrust into the pockets of his overcoat, shoulders hunched, head forward as though forcing himself into a high wind. Passing the church on his right, he turned up a narrow hill, somehow forcing himself to go on although every instinct now urged him to abandon the visit. He turned right and his steps slowed as he glanced at the names of the houses on his left. The Villa Maris had a garden, he had been told; he would recognize it easily. An old man wobbled past on an ancient bicycle. From an overhead window the sound of music reached him and he recognized the melody without being able to put a name to it.

The tall detached house with its whitewashed walls was unmistakable. He stood clutching the high wrought-iron gates like a prisoner desperate for freedom. A gravelled path led straight to a front door between well-kept lawns edged with a variety of shrubs. The remains of a climbing plant draped over the door and straggled upwards over the first-floor balcony. The house was built in the old symmetrical style and the downstairs shutters were green. A few small conifer trees, planted at random, threw soft shadows across the grass.

He whispered 'Oh, God!' and, lifting the metal latch, pushed open the gate. The few yards to the front door seemed endless, but at last he was pressing the bell. As he heard it peal within the house he resisted the urge to turn and run. His stomach rumbled ominously and he stiffened. Whatever happened he must not make a fool of himself. Whatever he found, whatever she said . . .

The door was opened by a large woman in a flannel housecoat. She was elderly, with greying hair and faded blue eyes. She said, 'Oui?'

For a second or two the foreign word threw him but, of course, they would not be expecting a strange Englishman to arrive on their doorstep uninvited. He stared at the woman and swallowed hard. Was this his mother?

'Je suis—' he began, then corrected himself. 'I'm – I'm a friend of – that is, I'd like to . . .'

Her expression was distinctly suspicious and he made a big effort to remember what he had planned to say by way of introduction. He searched her face for a likeness, but found none.

'You're English?' The door opened a fraction more. 'What do you want?'

'I'd like to speak with Violet Massey, if I may. Are you—'

From somewhere in the gloom behind her another voice called out, 'Who is it?'

'I don't know, but he's English.' Turning back to Matt, she asked, 'Who are you? What do you want with her?'

So was this or wasn't it his mother? Matt felt a sweat break out on his skin. 'I just want to see her, to – to talk to her and—'

'Who *are* you?'

'I'm – I'm Matthew Massey.' He swallowed hard. 'Her son.'

There! It was out; he had said it. If this was his mother, he would see the shock in her eyes and maybe something more. A glimmer of joy, perhaps? Perhaps not.

He watched the face closely and saw shocked disbelief followed by an unwilling acceptance.

'Her *son*?'

He nodded. The woman seemed about to speak, changed her mind and abruptly closed the door in his face. Matt stared at the flaking blue paint, shattered by the rejection. He stood there, frozen into immobility. An immediate and deep sense of loss overwhelmed him, but it was quickly replaced by one of anger. He had come this far and he would not be treated this way. He leaned forward and pressed his finger on the bell, letting it ring and ring. After a while it was opened again and the same woman appeared, now dressed in a tweed skirt and twin-set. There was, Matt realized, a similarity between this woman's voice and Mother's. So presumably this was Alice.

'There's no need for that,' she told him, with a glance at the bell. 'You'd better come in.' He followed her into the gloomy interior and found himself in a large living room

109

with doors leading off. There was a smell of coffee and he felt vaguely comforted by its familiarity.

'I'm Alice,' the woman said. 'Your mother's getting dressed.'

Just like that, thought Matt, as though it were the most normal thing in the world for a long-lost son to turn up on the doorstep.

'Vi doesn't usually get up this early. She sleeps badly – always has done. When she has the nightmares neither of us gets any sleep.' She indicated a chair for him and sat down herself. 'So you're Matthew. You aren't how I imagined. You look too thin in the face. We've seen photographs of you, obviously, and Winifred used to bring us news. Did *she* tell you? About whose son you are?'

'No, it was Connie.'

'Hmm. A flighty one, that, from all accounts, and you were no better. Oh, yes, we heard all about it. Running off together! Vi was not at all pleased.'

Matt stammered, 'Since Moth – I mean, since *Winifred's* death I've—'

'Sorry I couldn't get to the funeral. I couldn't leave Vi and she couldn't come, so that was that.' She shook her head. 'Nasty business, Winifred going like that. Nice and quick for her but a shock for us.'

'Yes, I suppose so.'

'So here you are, Matthew, after all this time.'

'Yes. Is my mother . . . ill?'

'Ill?' Alice's mouth tightened. 'You could say that. She's got a problem; she drinks too much, and she can't really take it with her constitution. But who can blame her after what she's been through.' It wasn't a question. 'Not that she will hear a word against him. That's loyalty for you.' She shrugged. 'I daresay you'd like some coffee. Anything to eat? We probably have some bread or' – her eyes brightened – 'you can pop out for some croissants.'

110

'I'm not hungry.' If he went out to buy croissants he doubted if he would come back. His palms were damp now and he could hardly breathe. 'A cup of coffee would be nice.'

She heaved herself out of the chair and made her way into a room at the back of the house which Matt supposed was the kitchen. The clinking of crockery confirmed this. As he waited he could hear sounds from another room which was obviously a bedroom. A drawer was pulled open and closed; a door opened, probably a wardrobe. He tried to calm his feverish thoughts, still longing illogically to escape from the situation he had created. His mother drank too much. Was that why they had hidden her away? And if so, could she be cured? On the far side of that door his mother – his real mother – was dressing, and he wondered what was going through her mind. Was she also in a state of panic, alternating between hope and despair? If she felt the way *he* felt, then Matt pitied her.

Alice returned with cups and saucers and said carefully, 'You mustn't expect too much, Matt. Your mother has had a very sad life and sorrow leaves scars. She's been tremendously brave, and I have always admired her. She wanted so desperately to keep you, you know, but the family were against it. That's why I offered her a home here in St Maxime. Your father wanted to send her to a convent but I said "No". She was entitled to some life and we've managed here pretty well. We rub along, as they say, although I'm not pretending it's always been easy. And she could have married, you know. Oh, yes, she was very attractive. But she always loved your father and she wouldn't even look at another man. She might have found happiness. Who can tell?' She sighed. 'Of course, Vi loved it when Winifred came to stay because then she would get up-to-date news and a chance to talk about you . . .' She glanced towards the bedroom and called, 'Oh,

111

do hurry up, Vi! Stop titivating! The boy's waiting to say "Hello".'

As Matt held his breath the bedroom door opened and his mother came into the room. He suddenly felt tremendously weak; his heart fluttered painfully within his chest. With a tremendous effort he rose slowly to his feet and found himself staring at a petite woman with straggling white hair pinned up on top of her head so that a few strands curled around her face.

He stammered, 'Oh, Mother!' and hardly recognized the hoarse, anguished voice as his own. He was immediately lost for words. She looked so frail, like an elderly porcelain doll. Her pale face had been made up with too much rouge and her powder had been applied a little too generously. Her hands were thin, with long fingers, and her neck was scrawny. Only her eyes saved her. They were large and still a deep blue.

She said, 'Matthew! Oh, my dear!' and there were tears in her eyes.

Tactfully Alice withdrew to the kitchen and closed the door.

'I hope you didn't mind,' Matt began, his voice trembling with mixed emotions.

Her fragility disconcerted him. He wondered whether she would expect him to kiss her, and then felt a pang of anguish that she had not rushed to hug him. She was wearing a pair of slacks and a frilly blouse beneath a velvet waistcoat, and Matt found the effect a trifle theatrical. All she needed was a long cigarette holder, he thought, and was instantly ashamed of his criticism.

'I expect you're angry with me,' she said. Her voice was husky and she sat down carefully as though she expected the chair might collapse under her non-existent weight.

'No. At least – yes, I have sometimes been angry. I have sometimes . . .' He swallowed. 'I have wondered why.'

'I'm sure you have. So have I. Many, many times.'

Her eyes were fixed on his face in an unwavering stare and he desperately hoped she would like what she saw. He sat down, struggling to breathe normally as the fluttering in his chest persisted.

She shrugged her thin shoulders. 'Why, I asked myself, didn't I just up and run away? Say "To hell with them" and disappear? But I didn't have the guts, I suppose. I'm such a coward.' Before he could argue the point she went on, 'I had no money, no home, no husband and no job. I *could* have run away with you, but we might have both starved within the first month. You were born here, did you know that? In that bedroom.'

He shook his head, hardly listening. She hadn't kissed him. Was it an oversight or didn't she want to kiss him? The question was beginning to distract him.

Alice brought in a jug of coffee, poured them each a cup and muttered something about the washing-up. She went back to the kitchen but glanced round to say, 'And remember what I told you, Vi. Don't volunteer.'

As the kitchen door closed, Violet said, 'She's probably got her ear to the keyhole. She hates to miss anything!' She began to laugh and it turned into a cough.

'What did she mean?' Matt asked. 'Don't volunteer for what?'

She gave him a long, calculating look. 'She told me before she let you in that I mustn't volunteer any information. "Just answer his questions. That's enough," she said. I once said that if ever you came to see me – I thought you might possibly arrive at my deathbed – I would tell you everything. *Everything*. She said I was a fool, that some things are better left unsaid. What do you think?' She raised her cup to her lips and sipped thoughtfully.

'I agree with you,' he said eagerly, pleased that they saw eye to eye on something. Perhaps it was a good

113

omen. 'Honesty should be the best policy. Shouldn't it?'

He was beginning slowly to recover his confidence. She was bearable. Not exactly a disappointment. She might drink too much, but she was hardly mad. And Alice said that she had loved his father, so she had not been raped. He could see, too, that she had once been beautiful and presumably that was why his father had fallen in love with her. To gain time, he too began to drink his coffee.

'So ... you think honesty. I wonder.' She shook her head.

Matt watched her with growing astonishment and admiration. How calm she was! Her son had appeared out of the blue and she was chatting to him as though it were the most natural situation. She was either remarkably cool under fire or she was a consummate actress. He had *known* he was going to confront her and yet he was confused, a mass of conflicting emotions. As he watched her his mood swung further and he was suddenly consumed with happiness. It was happening at last! Now. He was here with his mother, and she was just another human being. No longer someone to be whispered about. Certainly not the skeleton in the cupboard which he had been led to expect. In fact nothing mad or bad at all – just a woman who had made a mistake which society could not overlook. He found himself smiling broadly, but could not find the words to express his relief.

Seeing his smile she said sadly, 'I wish you could stay happy, Matthew. I really do.'

He gathered his courage and said, 'I don't even know my father's name.'

After a brief hesitation she said, 'Alexander. We called him Alex, of course. There was never another man in my life, and never will be.' She shook her head and sighed. 'We might have been happy together but – Ah! There I go.

114

I'm volunteering! Alice will be cross if she's eavesdropping, although I daresay she's right.'

Alexander. Matt thought the name had quite a noble ring to it. He hesitated to probe further for fear of causing Violet distress, but he was desperate to know. He had found a mother who, though not actually affectionate towards him, had not rejected him. She had said she regretted not keeping him, and that knowledge rang celebratory bells in his brain. Now he needed to know a little about his father. He thought how furious Connie would be when she learned that he had searched out the truth and that her unkind words had lost all power to wound him; had, in fact, set him on the road to peace of mind. Gradually his thoughts were clearing, and the first rush of adrenalin had eased.

Violet warmed her thin hands round the cup. 'I suppose they told you I drink? Well, I do, but only to dull the pain. Only to ease the loneliness. I don't go out any more because I see happy families and I've grown to hate them. Fathers with children riding on their shoulders, and mothers with babies in their arms. They all have something I missed and I don't want to be reminded.' She frowned down at the cup in her hands and muttered, 'Anyway, I don't need to go out.'

So she *was* a recluse. Matt searched for words of comfort and found none. Instead he asked, 'What did he do, my father? I mean, what was his profession?'

'He was in publishing for a while. Later . . . He went abroad before you were born; he never knew that he had a son. You must realize that, Matthew. We didn't know where he was for years, until he died.'

'He's *dead*?' Matthew felt as though he had been struck a severe blow. His father was dead. Now they could never meet; never reconcile the past with the present or make up for all the wasted years. He felt a moment of unbearable loss. 'Where is he buried?' At least he could visit the grave, he thought.

There was a long silence and her expression made Matt nervous. Why had Alice advised her not to volunteer any information? Presumably because there was something he wouldn't wish to be told. His mood swung again, this time from relief to apprehension. He would have to ask the right questions. Deep inside him a small voice urged him to leave well alone, to be satisfied with what he had. It was enough. Perversely, something else within him insisted that he knew it all. The fact that Alice wished to keep certain facts hidden angered him suddenly. What right had *she* to decide what he should and shouldn't know?

Violet said, 'Somewhere in Australia.' The cup rattled suddenly against the saucer and she quickly put it down on the table and stared at the tiled floor.

'Australia? Was he a publisher in Australia?'

'No.'

'Then what?' He sensed that she was choosing her words and his anger deepened. He had a right to know about his roots. 'What did he do in Australia?'

Suddenly there was a loud clatter of pans from the kitchen and Violet glanced towards the kitchen door, her mouth a tight line.

'She's listening!' she said. 'I knew she would.'

Matt thought he detected a change of subject and raised his voice a little. 'What did he do?'

'He ran sheep; he made a great deal of money. He *married*.'

A second blow, much worse than the first. Matt had an instant picture of his father with a smiling wife and children leading a different lifestyle, and was filled with bitterness. He had half-brothers and sisters and they had known a father's love. His own father had given to them what he, Matt, had been denied.

As though reading his thoughts, she said, 'He had no

116

children. His wife died giving birth to a stillborn child. A girl. I was *glad*!'

Her tone startled Matt, but then he thought he could sympathize with her. Her lover had chosen to marry someone else and her anger was hardly surprising. He had died a wealthy man while she had been left to struggle on alone. He had allowed her to suffer all kinds of humiliations and had . . . With an effort Matt reined in his thoughts. He must not allow himself to be turned against his father. Who had his father left his wealth to, if not to the mother of his only child? He wondered if that question would be one too many. It might sound mercenary. While he was debating the possibility of asking it, she spoke again.

'So now you know it all, Matthew, are you satisfied?'

She drank the last of her coffee and waited patiently for his answer. Once again Matt's attention was held by the strange expression on her face. There was something in her eyes – almost a challenge, he thought uneasily. Was she daring him to press for further revelations and, if so, did he want to comply?

Without having made a conscious decision he heard himself ask 'So how did you meet my father?'

There was a long, still moment and further bangings came from the kitchen. His mother did not meet his eyes.

Matt said, 'I *must* know!' although now that the question hung between them he didn't want to know.

She drew a deep breath and said, 'I'll tell you, Matt, on one condition – that you promise to forgive me.' Suddenly he was ice-cold and could not say a word. Forgive her? The fluttering in his chest began again and he could hardly breathe. *Forgive her for what?*

He muttered 'Oh, God!' and wanted to run from the place.

She said calmly, 'He was my brother: your uncle Alex.'

For a moment he imagined he saw a flicker of malice in the blue eyes, but then it was gone.

'My – my *uncle*?' he stammered. Violet and *her brother*? But that was . . . Uncle Alex!? He waited for the dreadful words to register in his brain, to mean something, but for a while he was too shocked to feel anything. The silence lengthened unbearably and as it did he was aware of a sick feeling in his stomach and a roaring in his ears. He was going to faint. He clutched at the table with both hands. His mother *and her brother*! It was horrible. Disgusting. Unnatural – and what did that make *him*? Some kind of monster?

Finally the black horror overwhelmed him and he slumped forward, semi-conscious, his head on the table. He heard a cry from his mother and then a door opened and he was vaguely aware that Alice had joined them.

'I warned you . . . I warned you . . .' Her triumphant voice rang in his ears. He clung to the three words in an attempt to ward off a loss of consciousness, but they proved insufficient and he slid into a merciful oblivion . . .

'Matthew! *Matthew*!'

Someone was shaking him and a wet cloth was being pressed to his face. With a loud groan he regained consciousness and opened his eyes. Seeing his mother and aunt surveying him anxiously, he wished he had remained oblivious. The faces appeared grotesque and the voices said meaningless things until gradually his wits returned and he could see things in perspective once more. Then the memory of what he had learned hit him again like a blow in the chest and he doubled up, clutching himself protectively as though he could physically save himself from the terrible truth. He was the child of an incestuous relationship! He felt defiled, degraded, experienced an urge to throw himself into water and scrub himself all over.

'I don't believe it!' he gasped, but they all recognized the lie. 'I don't want . . . I can't—' He held up his hands as though to ward off any contact with his mother. 'Don't come near me!'

Since his recovery, Violet had made no move to do so, but now she moved from his side and sat down in a rocking-chair about four yards away from him.

'I told you not to tell it all,' Alice grumbled, 'but you wouldn't listen. So sure of yourself, Vi. So sure you know best. Never willing to listen to advice. You've always been the same. Always.'

'How was I to know—' She sounded sulky, like a petulant child.

'Because I *told* you! That's how. I warned you what would happen.'

She bent over Matthew, her hand on his shoulder. 'Are you feeling a bit better now, Matthew?'

Better? Stupid fool! They had ruined his life and she asked if he felt *better*! Matthew wanted to slap her hard and keep slapping her until she cried. Or died! He would never feel *better*. The outrage he felt grew within him, almost an ache.

'Matthew!' cried Violet, but he would not look at her. He *dared* not look at the woman who had slept with her own brother; he could not trust himself to speak or to move. He wanted to kill them both, and for one glorious moment he actually considered the possibility. Killing them might restore his sanity. He would do it willingly. Did anyone know he was here at St Maxime? Yes, dammit! He had asked Fran for the address. The thought of killing them filled his mind and he let his imagination run with the idea. He saw himself with his hands around Violet's throat. Her blue eyes would bulge from their sockets and she would struggle feebly; then she would collapse and he would let her fall to the floor like the disgusting creature she was. He breathed deeply, fighting to think rationally. If he did that, Alice would know and she would be

119

running for help. He would be caught and arrested within minutes.

'Oh, God!' he whispered despairingly. Perhaps instead he would kill himself, for what was left for him now? How could he live the rest of his life if he didn't avenge this terrible wrong? He thought of Connie and her letter and it suddenly came to him that *Connie didn't know the whole truth*. If she had known, she would have told it. And only Connie knew *any* of it. So perhaps if he could silence her . . .

'Another cup of coffee,' Alice was saying, and she hurried out into the kitchen.

Violet said, 'I'm sorry, Matthew, but—'

'Shut up!' he said. 'I don't want to know any more!'

'I did love him,' she insisted. 'He didn't force himself on me.'

'I don't want to hear it.' Did she think that made him feel better? Oh, God! If he hadn't forced her, then she had willingly . . . He shuddered, wanting to rush from the house but feeling too weak and vulnerable even to move from the chair in which he sat.

Violet's hands were clasped in front of her chest. She was determined to tell him what he dreaded hearing.

'He loved me, Matthew. We wanted to be together always. We didn't know what to do—'

'But you soon found out!' Matt told her harshly. It suited his mood to be as coarse as possible, to return tenfold the pain she had inflicted on him. Let her suffer, he thought furiously. 'You disgust me! You and him!'

Tears filled the blue eyes and her hands bunched into fists which she pressed against her eyes. He heard her crying and was pleased.

'Winifred always maintained—' Violet began but Matthew interrupted sharply.

'Leave my *mother* out of this!'

The deliberate insult drew further sobs from Violet

120

and he felt a deep satisfaction. Serve her damn well right!

'You're disgusting, do you hear!' He heard his voice shake and that made him angrier than ever. 'And I'm glad he's dead. D'you understand? If he's that sort of man, then I'm glad he's—' He stopped abruptly as another thought surfaced. Uncle Alex had been a wealthy man and – he closed his eyes in disbelief as the pieces in the jigsaw fell into place. His wealthy uncle *who was also his father* had left his money to Geoffrey's *legitimate* children. Connie had said that as he wasn't really one of the family, he had no share in the money. He drew in his breath sharply as the full irony of the situation dawned on him. Alexander – unaware that he had a son by his sister Violet – had left his wealth to his brother's children, while Matt himself had received nothing.

'Jesus!' he muttered. 'Jesus Christ!'

Alice had just set down the tray. In a fit of rage Matt snatched up the sugar bowl and hurled it across the room. It struck a mirror, cracked it and fell in pieces.

'Matthew!' cried Violet and her voice quivered ominously.

Alice said, 'There was no need for that.'

By way of reply Matthew threw the milk-jug and then pushed the tray off the table on to the floor. For a moment they all stared at the mess. Violet's sobs intensified and Alice rounded on her.

'Well, what did you expect, you silly woman! Of course the boy's upset!'

Fuelled by his anger, Matt stood up and instinctively they both drew back, frightened by his expression. 'You—' He searched for words bad enough to express his loathing. 'You filthy *hags*!'

With a little cry Violet jumped up, rushed into the bedroom and slammed the door behind her. Alice regarded

121

Matt fearfully. As he stepped towards her she paled and her eyes sought a line of escape, but she had backed towards the fireplace and now he was between her and either of the doors. As she retreated she snatched a brass candlestick from the mantelpiece and said, 'Don't you dare touch me, Matthew! I've done nothing wrong.'

He was tempted to strike her anyway. She had given Violet refuge all these years and that was now contemptible in his eyes. But he let his hand fall to his side. They weren't worth it. He turned away, still reluctant to leave, still unwilling to admit that what had happened all those years ago was his legacy. Nothing anyone could do or say could put matters right. Suffocating with the injustice and horror, he found himself tongue-tied.

'I'm going,' he said hopelessly, but still he didn't move. Illogically he felt that while he remained within Villa Maris his secret shame would be confined to those four walls. As soon as he stepped into the outside world he would be branded, a pitiable object, someone to be whispered about behind raised hands.

Alice said, 'I'm sorry, Matthew.'

He scarcely heard her and made no reply. As he stood there irresolute, a violent longing for revenge was beginning to force out all other feelings. Revenge was power, and power was infinitely more desirable than grief and shame.

Seeing that he no longer threatened her, Alice said, 'Don't go like this, Matthew. Let's try to be reasonable. Your mother deserves a little compassion. Let's at least try to part friends.'

'*Friends*?' He was astonished.

'These things happen,' she pleaded. 'It was a long time ago.'

Matthew ignored her. That way lay weakness and compromise. He could imagine the pleas for forgiveness and the tears. They were pathetic. He clung stubbornly to the idea of revenge. That way he might salvage a grain or two of self-respect. Somehow, someone was going to pay for his ordeal. If he couldn't be loved, at least he could be feared.

He looked into the puffy face and noticed the slack jaw and quivering mouth. They weren't worth the trouble, he told himself as he walked to the door, opened it and stepped outside. He would allow them to live on, wallowing in their squalid memories, hidden away from kith and kin. As he closed the door behind him he saw Violet's face at the window; he looked away quickly without acknowledging her, but he knew that her ravaged, tear-stained face would haunt his dreams. He went down the path and out of the gate. He had only himself to blame.

He turned right and began walking back into the town. She hadn't kissed him, and now he told himself that he was glad. His legs moved automatically, like a man on whom someone had passed a death sentence. And death, he thought wistfully, would be one way out of the nightmare. The possibility of a painless suicide was quite appealing and it was encouraging to know that he could, whenever he wished, put an end to the charade. But first he would punish someone. The wind was keen and he turned up the collar of his coat as he walked quickly; the exercise helped him and he felt as though he could walk for ever. He straightened his shoulders and felt an almost imperceptible lightening of his spirits. Fate had dealt him a devastating blow, but he would go down fighting. And he would take a few others with him . . .

*

Violet was sitting on the bed when Alice went in.

'I've cleared up the mess,' Alice told her. 'Proper little tantrum, that was.'

Violet twisted her handkerchief and sniffed miserably. 'It was my fault, not his. Blame me.'

123

'I *do*!'

'I wish I hadn't—' Violet began. 'You were right. Oh, Alice, I'm such a fool. What am I to do?'

Alice tutted irritably. 'Not a lot you *can* do,' she said with more truth than tact. She walked to the window and stared out. 'Quite nice-looking, wasn't he? His photographs didn't do him justice.'

'Lovely hair,' said Violet eagerly. 'Like mine.'

'And his father's.'

Violet ignored the jibe. 'Alex would have been so proud of him. If only Matt had stayed. We could have had a photograph taken, just the two of us. And one of the *three* of us,' she added hastily. After a long moment she said, 'Mind you, Winifred said he had a hasty temper. A short fuse, she used to say. Like Alex. The last time I saw *him* he was in a temper.' She sighed. 'I could write to him,' she suggested. 'Say how sorry I am.'

'You could.'

'But you don't think so?'

Alice shrugged. 'Why ask me? You never listen to me; you go blundering on and upset people. Of course he was shocked. It was a dreadful thing to find out, and you should have had more sense. He comes all this way and he was so pleased to find you, and then you have to ruin everything. Gab! Gab!' She made a yapping motion with her hand.

'I could apologize. Oh, Alice!' She covered her face with her hands.

Alice watched her with a mixture of compassion and irritation. The woman was such a fool. If only she hadn't upset him he might have stayed for a few days; it would have been fun to have a young man about the place.

'He might forgive me,' Violet said. 'He might come again. I'll apologize and beg him to forgive me. I'll write to him.'

Alice shook her head. 'Not yet, Vi. Give him time. You

didn't see the way he went off; you didn't see the look on his face. Murderous, he was. I thought he was going to hit me. I don't mind admitting he scared me. Shame, really, I rather liked him at the beginning. But there was something about him. I can't explain it but – he had such . . . such *haunted* eyes.'

'I thought I could send him my ring. The one Alex gave me before he left.'

Alice sat down next to her on the edge of the bed and looked at her uncertainly. 'Do you think you should? It's worth quite a bit, that ring, and you might need the money one day. That was a good one – eighteen-carat gold, and matched opals.'

'I don't care about the money, if he'll only forgive me. And Matt *is* his son. He ought to have it. After all, he got none of the money and he should have something. I'll tell him he can sell it. I think Alex would have wanted him to have it.'

'Please yourself, Vi, but I don't think you can buy his love. Not even with the Crown Jewels! At least not just yet. Maybe in a few years, when he's come to terms with it.'

'I may be dead by then!' Violet protested crossly. 'Trust you to spoil everything.'

'Well, that's rich coming from you. All I do is give my opinion when you ask for it. If I don't agree with you, you take offence. You always do.' She got up, annoyed. 'Well, I'm going to walk for ten minutes. Blow the cobwebs away. No good asking you if you'll come with me?'

'Not today.'

'You mean, "Not *any* day"!'

'I'm going to write to him. It can't make things any worse.'

Alice shook her head. 'Please yourself,' she said. She turned back at the bedroom door. 'And if you want my advice—'

'I don't!'

'*Don't* tell him it was his father's ring. He might accept it from you.' She waited for an answer. 'Are you listening, Vi?'

Violet slid from the bed and crossed to the table. She took a sheet of notepaper from the drawer and, with great deliberation, began to sharpen a pencil.

Alice longed to slap her. 'You'll be sorry,' she said. 'I mean it.' And with a loud snort of annoyance she went out of the room, slamming the door behind her.

Chapter Six

MARY GLANCED SIDEWAYS AT MATT and thought that he *was* handsome, in a funny sort of way. There was a fluttering sensation in her stomach and her face was flushed with excitement. True to his word, not a week after his letter Matt had turned up at the school unexpectedly, just as she was leaving the classroom at midday. He had sent one of the boys to find her, refusing to say who he was, making a great mystery of it all. He had insisted that he was taking her out to lunch – what he described jauntily as 'a winter picnic'. Her next lesson was at two and, she had told him she mustn't be late. Now they were driving along the road, heading for Fairlight Glen, in the chocolate-coloured motor car with its gleaming brass horn and yellow wheels. On the back seat was a wicker picnic hamper. She hardly ever rode in a motor and she was looking forward to describing the adventure to her colleagues when they gathered in the staff-room that evening. She had tried to memorize all he had told her about the Ford – double declutching (which apparently was an acquired art) and something called first and second gear.

Being alone with Matt under these circumstances was a novel experience, and one which she relished with all her heart. She was ridiculously proud to be seen with him and kept glancing sideways to look at his profile. He was wearing grey trousers, a white shirt and a rather worn Fair Isle pullover under his jacket. It was cold in the car and she marvelled that he did not feel it.

'I've got my love to keep me warm!' he had told her, and that had thrilled her more than she would admit. Maybe she would knit him a new pullover, as a surprise for Christmas. She was so happy she wanted to pinch herself. Here she was out in a motor, alone with a man for the first time in her life. If she had had more time she would have confided in Fran, who would have reassured her, but the invitation had come as a complete surprise which – as Matt had explained – was all part of the fun.

'A penny for them!' he teased.

'Oh! They're not worth it,' she protested. 'That is, I was just thinking how surprised Fran would be if she could see us now.'

'Wouldn't she! And how jealous!'

'Fran? Jealous?' Mary was startled. Was that why he had told her not to tell anyone who he was, and *not* to tell the family?

They turned off the main road.

'Well, look at you!' he laughed boyishly. 'Out with a young man – or maybe not so young! And if you thought that my turning up today was a surprise, you are in for quite a shock. I've something else for you.'

'Something else?' Her heart raced a little.

He slowed down to read the signpost. 'Turn right for Fairlight Glen! Right it is!'

Mary clasped her hands together and hoped he couldn't hear the sound of her heart which suddenly seemed ridiculously loud.

He said, 'I thought we might walk a little after we've eaten. There's a footpath, I'm told, that leads down to the Lovers' Seat.' He turned briefly and winked at her.

'You won't mind, will you? You won't be scared of me?'

'Of you? Oh, Matt, of course not!'

'Good.' He seemed to be in a particularly lively mood, she thought curiously. Perhaps it was her company that was working the miracle. Or perhaps she was flattering herself. It was as though he was suppressing a great piece of news.

'Have you been promoted?' she asked. 'Is this a celebration?'

'No.' He gave her a quick look and she saw that his smile had faded. The familiar guarded expression was back, and she was annoyed with herself. Why didn't she just wait and let him tell it in his own time? Whatever it was, she mustn't spoil it for him.

She said quickly, 'You're an awfully good driver. I thought I'd be a bit nervous.'

'Maybe you should be.'

Now what was that supposed to mean, she wondered with a flash of irritation. Matt hadn't changed. He had never been a restful person to be with, because it was never possible to be sure what he meant. Mary stifled a sigh. Annie had called him 'deep', and that summed him up beautifully.

He pulled up and stopped the motor. Around them the cliff-top was deserted, a wild landscape with clumps of gorse and a few stunted trees. Overhead sea-birds wheeled plaintively against a backdrop of scudding clouds.

'The perfect day for a picnic!' he mocked with a rueful lift of his eyebrows.

'Only Matt Massey would even *think* about a picnic in winter!'

She gave a little laugh to show that the words were kindly meant, but he ignored the comment and Mary turned to look at him, slightly embarrassed by their nearness. He was giving her a strange look, saying nothing, and she wondered for the first time whether she had been wise to accept his invitation. 'I mustn't be late, remember,' she said. 'I must be back by two or the children will be running riot!' When this picture failed to amuse him, she said, 'It's a lovely car, Matt. Marvellous. You are lucky.'

'Lucky? You think so?'

'Of course!' She glanced pointedly over her shoulder at the picnic hamper and said, 'Shouldn't we start?'

His smile appeared a trifle forced and she wondered if she was saying all the wrong things. Was she supposed to say something romantic, perhaps? He had said he'd got his love to keep him warm. Had he been *serious*?

Abruptly, he reached over to the back seat and produced a small velvet box, which he handed to her. 'Open it!' he told her. 'It's for you.'

She felt the colour drain from her face. Without opening it, she knew it contained a ring. 'Oh, no!' she cried.

'Oh, yes!' He opened the box for her and took out a lady's ring – a gold band set with opals!

'Oh, Matt, it's beautiful, but I couldn't possibly – I – I mean, it's very kind but—'

He took her left hand in his and, ignoring her struggles, tried it on several fingers until he found one which it fitted. The stone winked and sparkled and she felt a sudden tremor of apprehension.

'Oh, Matt!' she whispered. 'I can't! No!'

Before she could say more he had leaned across and was kissing her full on the mouth.

Totally confused she responded clumsily, but her thoughts were chaotic. This was impossible. She would have to tell him; she would write to him and send back the ring, explaining that it had all been a mistake. Better still, she would telephone Fran as soon as classes ended. Fran would tell her what to do. Maybe Fran would write to Matt and tell him, in a nice way, that Mary wasn't interested. Much as she loved Matt as a brother, she was never going to love him as a husband or lover. The very idea terrified her.

He drew back, giving her that same strange look. 'I won't rush you,' he said gently. 'I do understand that this has been a shock.'

He smiled suddenly and there was the boyish, charming Matt once again. She felt weak with relief. He understood; she had panicked for no good reason.

'I'm so sorry,' she stammered. 'I am fond of you, Matt, you know I am, but in a brotherly sort of way. I never thought – I mean . . .' Her voice trailed off and she stared at the ring. 'It's so beautiful, but I wish you hadn't bought it—'

'I didn't.' Matt picked up her hand and kissed it. 'It was my mother's,' he said. 'I wanted you to have it.'

'Your *mother's*?'

'The same. I knew you'd be surprised.'

She was staring at him, wide-eyed with astonishment. 'Your *real* mother?'

'Who else?' He laughed.

'You've found your real mother?' Mary reached for his hands and squeezed them affectionately. 'Oh, Matt, how wonderful for you. I'm so pleased. Where – and how? Don't shake your head like that, you wretch! You must tell me all about it.'

'First things first!'

He reached back into the hamper and produced a packet of sandwiches wrapped in greaseproof paper. 'Sandwiches first, followed by a special celebratory cake iced by yours truly and a bottle of bubbly!'

'You *iced a cake*?'

'I certainly did. Why not, for heaven's sake? All the best chefs are men – didn't you know that?' Unwrapping the sandwiches, he said, 'Fish paste: sardine and shrimp. I hope you like them. I was going to use smoked salmon or caviar but they're so *boring*!'

They both laughed and Mary took a sandwich. 'Bit of a doorstep!' she said but bit into it hungrily.

Matt asked, 'Don't they feed you at that place?'

'Of course they do, but I was too late for breakfast this morning. Aren't you having one? A sandwich?'

'Oh. Yes, I suppose so.' He took one and bit into it without enthusiasm.

Mary smiled. Poor Matt, he was too excited to eat. Now she understood the reason for his excitement and his strange mood. His childhood fantasy had become reality. He had discovered the identity of his real mother and she, Mary, was the first person he had told. It was a wonderful compliment. *And* he had given her the ring. 'How on earth did you find her?' she asked between mouthfuls of sardine and shrimp.

'Ah!' He tapped the side of his nose. 'All in good time. Suffice to say that I met my mother last week and she told me all about my father. It seems he was a major in the Army, barracked near where my mother lived.'

'A major! Good heavens! And he was married, I suppose?'

Matt hesitated fractionally, then agreed. 'But it was a love match, as they say.'

'How terribly sad for you. Does that mean you'll never meet him? If he's married, I mean.'

'Probably not. But my mother's awfully sweet. You'd like her, Mary. A pity you'll never meet her.'

Mary took a second sandwich and wondered when they would have the champagne to celebrate. Probably Matt would save that until last.

'I might meet them both,' she suggested, 'eventually. You never know, the wife might die and then he would be free to meet you – and us, of course. *And* to marry your mother!

132

Oh, Matt! It could be so wonderful!' Impulsively she leaned across and kissed him briefly on the cheek.

To her surprise he drew back sharply and said, 'Have you finished? I want to walk along the cliff and see the sea.'

'Well, I –' She was still hungry and they hadn't touched the iced cake, but maybe they would carry on when they got back from the walk. 'OK,' she said. 'Lead on, Macduff!'

He jumped out immediately and pulled an overcoat from the back seat. By the time Mary had climbed out he was already several yards away and striding along so that she had to run to catch up with him. It occurred to her suddenly that he might be going to propose and wanted to do it at the Lovers' Seat. She grabbed at his arm as she stumbled and nearly fell.

'Oops-a-daisy!' he said. 'Not drunk, are you?'

'Not yet,' she answered. As she clung to his arm she could imagine herself telling Lettie about the outing. The ring, the champagne, everything. She would make it sound as romantic and exciting as possible. And funny, of course. She would laugh it off as though she was in the habit of being given opal rings ... But whatever happened she mustn't encourage Matt to think about her in a romantic way – especially after what happened between him and Connie and Fran. She didn't love him that way, she was sure. But she glanced up at his face, wondering. There was no reason why she *shouldn't* think about him romantically, given time – although Connie would never forgive her, and that would be worrying. She would have to talk to Fran. Suddenly she was glad that her mother was dead and need not know. Mother had said some terrible things about Matt when he ran off with Connie.

They made their way along a narrow footpath which dipped and rose on its way to the sea – and then, there it was. The sea. Grey and forbidding, rolling and crashing against the beach below.

'What do you think?' Matt asked, as though he had personally arranged for it to be there.

'It's wonderful, Matt.'

'A few days ago I was looking at the Mediterranean.'

'Were you?'

'I had business in the south of France.'

'You do have an exciting life, Matt. I've never been anywhere.'

Another hundred yards or so brought them to the seat itself, a rather disappointing structure made of wood. They sat down and Matt put his arm around her shoulder.

'Not too cold, is it?'

It *was* too cold, but Mary would never have admitted it. The wind was keen and there were spots of rain in the air. Suddenly he stood up and went to the edge to look down. 'The tide's not in yet,' he remarked. Turning, he grinned. 'It's a long way down. Take a look.'

He held out his hand, but Mary shook her head. 'I'm no good with heights, Matt; you know that.' She patted the seat. 'Come back and sit with me. You were keeping me warm.'

After a slight hesitation he did as she suggested and they sat together in silence. There was no one to see them but the gulls which circled the cliff-face.

Mary glanced surreptitiously at the ring and thought how well it suited her slender hand.

'You like it?' Matt asked.

She nodded.

'It's yours — 'til death do us part!'

Again that unfathomable expression flitted across his face and Mary felt a small glimmer of unease. Suppose he lost his temper with her when she said she would have to think it over? He did have a temper.

He said again, 'A long way down.' Was he trying to scare her, she thought suddenly.

She shivered, exaggerating it. 'I'm getting cold,' she told him. 'Let's go back, shall we? I'd like a drink actually.' She smiled. 'To wash down all those sandwiches!'

He said 'Not yet. I brought you here specially. For a reason.' He did not look at her.

Mary waited, hardly knowing what to expect, torn between excitement and apprehension. But then Matt was a strange character, she reminded herself, and now, suddenly, he had discovered his parents and that must be tremendously unsettling.

Suddenly he said, 'What would you say if I told you I'd brought you here to kill you?'

For a few seconds she hardly registered what he had said. When she did, she protested, 'Oh, Matt! Don't spoil it. It's such a lovely outing and—'

'I nearly killed Dot, didn't I?'

'But that was an accident, Matt,' she protested. 'Don't talk like that. No one thought you meant to strangle her.'

'Father thought I did it on purpose, but I didn't. She *would* climb the tree. I didn't want her to.'

Mary put a hand on his knee. 'We didn't think you meant it,' she said. 'Honestly, Matt. We didn't.'

'And then there was Connie in the snow. She could have died. I nearly killed Connie.'

'But Matt! It was you who *found* her! Stop torturing yourself. It's all in the past.'

'Not for me it isn't.'

His voice had hardened and Mary's spirits plummeted. If they were in for one of Matt's bouts of self-pity, she would be late getting back to school.

He turned to her. 'I was the one who sent Connie down that slope; I knew she'd hit the tree. And I was the one who built the snow over her while she was unconscious. And I—'

'Stop it, Matt! I don't want to hear it!' She jumped to

135

her feet, but he grabbed at her arm and roughly pulled her down again to sit beside him. Tears pricked at her eyelids. Trust Matt to ruin everything with his stupid lies. Why did he do it? 'I think it's very mean of you,' she said shakily, 'to bring me here and then try to make me miserable.'

'I brought you here to kill you.'

'Don't be ridiculous! You did nothing of the sort.' She thrust out her left hand. 'Why would you give me this ring if you meant to kill me? You're just the same old Matt – for ever taunting. You can be so nice, Matt.' No, she thought regretfully. She could never marry Matt because she would never totally trust him. He was his own worst enemy. She looked at him earnestly. 'You can charm the birds off the trees if you want to, Matt, so why be so hateful to people who love you?' Tears started to run down her cheeks. Now they would quarrel and he would probably refuse to take her back to school. Suddenly the ring seemed an unlucky omen and she tried to pull it off.

'No!' He caught her hand and twisted her arm roughly, ignoring her cry of pain. 'You accepted my ring,' he said. 'My *mother's* ring. Given to her by my *father*!'

She fought against her tears and the pain in her arm. 'Just take me back to school, Matt. I mustn't be late.'

As soon as she stood up, Matt pulled her into his arms and kissed her. She struggled with him and suddenly found herself with her back to the cliff-edge. She felt the ground crumble under her shoes.

'Matt! For God's sake! Be careful!'

He laughed. 'What did I tell you? That I was going to—'

'Matt! Don't push me! I shall – oh, no!' It came to her like a lightning strike, fierce and terrible. He *was* going to kill her; it was what he had intended all along. She began to struggle desperately with him. 'If you push me, you'll come too!' she gasped, clinging on to him as he tried to disentangle himself. 'I won't let you go!' Surely he had not intended to kill himself, too. 'Help me!' she screamed at the top of her voice.

'Shut up!'

Matt was stronger than her but she was fighting for her life. 'Don't do this!' she pleaded frantically. 'Please don't, Matt. I'll do anything. I'll marry you if – oh God, Matt!' She slipped and now she was half over the edge, face to face with Matt on his knees while her hands clasped him around the neck.

He gripped her wrists so painfully that she screamed again and slowly he prised her hands apart until both her weight and her life were in his hands. She wanted to ask why, but she was paralysed with fear and could not utter a single word. Then Matt released her and she caught a last glimpse of his pale face as she fell backwards. The rush of air around her sucked from her throat the final scream and then she hit the sloping cliff on the way down. From then on she fell in a series of wild, slithering tumbles as grass, earth and rocks flashed past. She fell the last twenty feet on to the boulders and her shoulders and neck took the full impact. As she uttered Matt's name, the last thing she heard was the crunch of her bones. She had a brief glimpse of grey clouds and a moment's unbearable pain. Slipping into oblivion was a welcome release.

*

Matt looked down at Mary's body spreadeagled across the boulders only yards from the encroaching tide. He had expected her to look like a starfish, and was disappointed to see the twisted mass with one leg tucked under and an arm bent below her head. Awkward, he thought. But then Mary had been awkward in life, so he should have expected nothing else. He waited for a flash of remorse, but felt nothing but a cold satisfaction. She had taken his father's money and had said nothing. They had all conspired to keep him in ignorance all these years, so they deserved what was coming to them. Mary was number one. Suddenly he wished that he had told her *why* she was going to die. They ought to know. Next time he would remember.

He drew a deep breath and let it out slowly. Then he turned his face skywards in triumph. He had done it! He had hoped for a rush of elation, but this did not materialize. Again he looked down at the body, telling himself that he had the power to take life; the power and the will.

'Damn it!' he muttered, trying to shake off the feeling of anti-climax. 'I *murdered* her, for heaven's sake!'

She looked so small and uninteresting, like a piece of flotsam washed up by the tide. Still, he had taken the first step; he had made his first kill. Planned and executed it without any problems – a smooth and professional operation. Thousands of people who wanted to murder failed to do so, unable at the last moment to summon the necessary resolve. Or they bungled it. He, Matt Massey, had done it *and* he would get away with it. The tide was already coming in fast and in a few hours the light would fade and the body would be covered by the sea. It was unlikely, he thought, that anyone would choose to come to such a desolate place at this time of year. The tide would come in and hopefully the body would float away; it might be days before it was found. He smiled faintly as he stared down in fascination at his handiwork. She was no longer Mary but 'the body'. So at least that much had changed. She was no longer alive but dead so that, too, had changed. And he had brought about the changes. He was no longer 'poor Matt' for whom everything went wrong. He had the power to make things happen.

'The ring!' he exclaimed and, moving along the cliff-top, he searched for a safe place at which to climb down.

Ten minutes later he was standing beside Mary. Her head

rested at an awkward angle to her shoulders and Matt could see that she *was* dead. But just in case, he knelt down and listened for breathing. There was nothing and her chest was still. But he must take no chances, he reminded himself, impressed by his cool thinking at such a moment. Gingerly he took hold of her left wrist and felt for a pulse. Nothing. Her eyes stared upwards and he closed her eyelids. Blood from the back of her head was oozing out over the boulder and one of her legs had broken. He could see the white bone edge showing through her torn, brown stocking. Instinctively he crossed himself, then eased the ring from her finger.

'Married to Christ now,' he told her. He felt no rush of guilt, but still he longed for the expected thrill. 'Sorry you had to go first, but you were the easiest. I shall get cleverer as I go along!'

He glanced back up the cliff to make certain that there were no witnesses. If anyone *did* see him with the body, he would say he had seen her fall and rushed to see if she was still alive. He would claim not to know her, give a false name and then disappear. But there seemed to be no one else around. Carefully he climbed back up, the ring safely wrapped in a handkerchief and tucked into his coat pocket.

He began to walk back in the direction of the car, pleased to see himself alone as he moved through the bleak landscape. In his mind's eye he saw himself as a small but relentless figure painted against a rugged, hostile background.

'A force to be reckoned with!' he said, and a smile flickered and then spread across his face. Suddenly he felt ravenously hungry and he remembered the hamper – the 'winter picnic'! How gullible she had been. Poor Mary. So easy to fool. So *trusting*! At least there were a few more sandwiches. There was no champagne, no iced cake. He had made just enough sandwiches to dull Mary's suspicions, had she entertained any. He took a deep breath of the cold salt air and then another. Belatedly, adrenalin pumped through him and he finally experienced the beginnings of exhilaration. His heart thumped approvingly and he wanted to shout and sing. Some form of action was necessary and he broke into a run, forcing himself over the uneven ground, falling headlong but scrambling up again to pound on. The car was in sight now and soon he would be gone.

He had done it.

He had taken his first revenge.

*

The sound of the telephone ringing woke Fran from a deep sleep and it was a moment or two before she realized what was happening. She threw back the bedclothes, felt for her slippers and glanced at the bedside clock. Six thirty-five – on a Saturday? As she hurried down the stairs she found Fritz beside the telephone table, barking hysterically.

'Maidhurst 344.'

'One moment, please. I'm trying to connect you.'

The voice which spoke next, a man's voice, was unfamiliar and she felt a flicker of apprehension. Nobody that she knew would ring at this hour unless it was urgent.

'Miss Frances Massey? This is Samuel Harper of Marlham School.'

'Yes?' She frowned. What on earth was this about, she wondered? The school had never found it necessary to contact her before. Was Mary ill?

'I'm afraid I have some rather worrying news about your sister Mary. To put it bluntly, she appears to be missing.'

'Missing? But what—How do you mean, missing?' Fran sat down on the nearby chair and told herself not to panic.

'We really are most alarmed and we have just notified the police. They were willing to tell you, but I thought I should speak to you personally.'

140

'I appreciate that. Please go on.' Looking up, she saw that Annie was standing in her dressing gown half-way down the stairs, a look of anxiety on her face.

'It seems that a gentleman called yesterday and took her out. That was at lunch-time. She didn't return in time for her class at two o'clock, but we thought she was just late. The boy who carried the message to her claims that the man refused to give his name because he said his visit was to be a surprise and he was to tell no one but Miss Massey. By the evening when she hadn't returned we were getting worried, but we thought – that is my wife thought ... Well, this is rather indelicate but I hope you'll bear with me. She thought they might be spending the night together.'

'Mary? Spending the night with a strange man? I can't believe it.' She signalled to Annie, who joined her in the hall. 'Mary is missing!' she told her.

'Missing? Oh, no!' Her kindly face crumpled and she moved to sit on the third stair, clutching her dressing gown tightly around her neck as though to keep out bad news.

The headmaster continued, 'We didn't want a scandal, you see, and *certainly* we didn't want to besmirch your sister's reputation. We decided to wait until this morning in case she turned up, but—'

'But she hasn't?'

'I'm afraid not. I'm terribly sorry. The police have been informed and they were most attentive; they promised to do all they can, although officially she is not "missing" until she's been gone for twenty-four hours. We are hoping for the best – that maybe they have gone away together. Eloped, perhaps. Not that we want her to elope, but it would be better than being ... than having been—' Obviously deciding against that line of argument, he finished lamely, 'Well the truth is, we don't know what to think.'

Fran was trying to make sense out of the unexpected news. 'And did nobody know who this man might be?'

'Apparently she had a letter a little while ago; the geography teacher recalls her excitement. Mary said it was a letter from an admirer, and the staff were chaffing her about it. Miss Crewe says she was so pleased for her because she seems such a – well, not to put too fine a point on it, a solitary soul. Outside the school she had no friends of whom we were aware. That was what made it so exciting for her . . . But it's so unlike her to go off in this way, and it really is most awkward for us. The staff are co-operating splendidly, of course. We are doubling up some classes and I shall cancel the third-year games and—'

'I just can't believe it!' Fran said again. 'And there's no indication of an accident? You have rung the hospitals?'

'The police are doing all that.'

'They may have driven somewhere remote and broken down.' Even as she said it, Fran thought it unlikely, but it was a slim hope and she clung to it. 'I mean, they may have slept in the car all night . . .' She fell silent.

'We shall keep you informed, naturally, and you must please contact us at any time if you get any news or have any further ideas on the subject. The police will call on you later with further questions. By the way, we gave them a copy of a school photograph which included your sister, taken last summer. You might have something more recent. Do please try not to worry, Miss Massey. We shall pray for your sister at our morning assembly and I'm sure she will turn up safe and well.'

'Yes, of course she will. Thank you for your call. I'm sorry you, too, are having all this worry.'

'I have never expected life to be a bowl of cherries, Miss Massey. I simply pray for the strength to deal with whatever the Lord sends.'

'Of course.' Fran rolled her eyes at this homespun philosophy.

'I must go. The morning bell is ringing and there's work to be done.'

'Thank you again,' said Fran and hung up. She stared at Annie. 'What am I thanking them for? Mary is missing and I'm—'

Annie said, 'Missing? Mary?'

'Apparently.'

Briefly she told Annie what the headmaster had said and together they moved instinctively in the direction of the kitchen. Here a kettle was already steaming on the Aga and Annie made a pot of tea.

'We'll have to tell Dot,' said Fran. 'The police will be calling, and she'll guess something's wrong. Thank goodness it's the weekend. Amy will be around, and that will help to keep her occupied.' They regarded each other soberly over the teacup rims and Fran saw her own anxiety mirrored in Annie's eyes.

The old woman sighed. 'I'm glad your mother isn't alive. She'd be in a right old state with her daughter missing.' She screwed up her eyes, a trick she had when worried. 'I can't imagine Mary going off with a man. I mean, where would she meet one?'

'Someone connected with the school, I should think. A parent, maybe. It can't be another teacher.'

'What? The father of one of her pupils? Mary would never do such a thing.'

'Not necessarily a father. Maybe a younger uncle or a much older brother. I don't know. I'm only guessing.' She sighed deeply. 'I'm as much in the dark as everyone else, but we have to think of someone. A gardener, or someone like that?'

Annie shook her head without comment

'Oh, *Mary!*' cried Fran. 'Where on earth *are* you?' She finished her tea, put down the cup and steepled her fingers. 'A friend of Matt's, perhaps?'

'Does he have any friends?'

Fran shrugged and Annie said suddenly, 'Matt himself?'

'Hardly. Why should she make a secret out of a visit from her brother? It doesn't make sense. No, this person may have wanted to remain anonymous. *May* have. Oh, Lord, Annie! It doesn't look good.'

'You mean someone meant – meant something bad to happen to her? Oh, no! Never! Not Mary!' Annie's eyes were watery and for a moment she hid them behind her hand, sniffing loudly to discourage tears. 'I won't believe that anyone meant to hurt her,' she declared. 'An accident, yes. An elopement even, God help us! But not – the other.'

Fran rubbed her eyes tiredly. It was only ten to seven, but already she felt exhausted. 'I shall have to tell Connie,' she said reluctantly, 'and Henry, too. Damn!' She tutted quietly. 'They'll be praying for her at their assembly.'

'That's nice. A few prayers can't do any harm.'

Fran stood up. 'I suppose we'd better get dressed in case the police turn up early.' At the door she turned. 'She will be all right, won't she, Annie? They will find her?'

'Of course they'll find her,' Annie insisted. 'She'll turn up like a bad penny and we'll forget all about this little fright.' Suddenly she frowned. 'Isn't this Mr Whatsisname coming to lunch? The one who wrote the book? Will you still want to see him? I could phone him for you and put him off.'

'Paul Hallam. I'd forgotten.' Fran hesitated. 'I suppose I'd better get it over with. Things might get worse next week if they don't ... if Mary doesn't—' She ran agitated fingers through her uncombed hair and tried to remain calm. 'Let him come, Annie. It will help keep my mind off other things.'

As Fran turned left along the passage, Annie's voice followed her. 'It will be OK, Fran. You'll see.'

*

When Fran finally found the courage to telephone the library, Connie was obviously shocked. Fran listened impatiently as Connie blamed the school for not reporting Mary's disappearance earlier. In her own heart Fran agreed, but she saw no point in recriminations at this stage. She was willing herself to believe in Mary's safe return and determinedly pushed all other possibilities to the back of her mind.

'You'd better get down there,' Connie was saying. 'Find out for yourself. Ask around. Someone must know something.'

'The police are making enquiries,' Fran told her for the third time. 'I'd only get in the way. I think we should leave them to do their job.'

'Suppose she's in hospital with amnesia? If she's been in an accident—'

'They'll think of that; they'll cover every eventuality. I expect checking the hospitals is top of the list. I'll keep you informed.'

'I'll telephone this afternoon. D'you want me to come over to Maidhurst? I could stay a couple of nights.'

Fran could think of nothing worse but politely declined the offer. While she was speaking, she saw someone's shadow against the glass of the front door. 'I must go. Bye for now.'

It was a policeman. He was fair-haired and looked about thirty, with an eager expression and a generous moustache. He took off his bicycle clips and his helmet and followed Annie into the lounge, where he accepted her offer of tea and settled himself on the sofa with notebook and pencil.

He explained to Fran that so far none of the hospitals within a reasonable distance had dealt with anyone answering Mary's description, and certainly no one with amnesia. They were checking hotel registers and making enquiries at the nearby railway stations in case the 'young couple' had abandoned the car. They had also checked Gretna Green without success.

'Though, mind you,' he told her, 'they might be on their way. Takes time to get that far.'

Fran protested, 'But Mary hardly knew anyone. Why should they go to Gretna Green? She would never marry without talking to the family.'

'You know that, do you, madam? Quite certain?'

'Ninety-nine per cent certain. Yes.' But as soon as she said it she began to have doubts. Did she know Mary as well as she thought she did? Was she a dark horse? 'I don't *think* she would just go off like this.'

'People do funny things, madam. Take my word for it. The world's full of people acting out of character, as you might say. Now, if I may ask you a few routine questions.'

The questions were largely predictable and easily answered. Had Mary ever mentioned any men who were unknown to the family? Did she have a close friend to whom she might have confided the name of the mystery man? Had she ever done anything like this before? Had she any relatives with whom she might be staying or whom she might contact? Had she quarrelled with the family, or was she in trouble at her place of work? Had she any enemies?

Fran's stomach churned with fear at the implications of the last question.

'You don't mean that you think – that there's a possibility—' She was horrified. 'Not *Mary*? Why should anybody want to harm her? She's never had an unkind thought—'

'I'm sorry but we have to ask, madam. We have to consider every line of enquiry no matter how unpleasant. We'd be failing in our duty if we ignored the possibility that – let's just say that she might have been abducted. There are some very evil people in this world, and who knows why they think and do these terrible things?' He checked carefully through his notes and then looked up.

'And there's absolutely no one who could fit this boy's description of the man. Old, short with dark hair.'

Fran shook her head, then she said suddenly, 'How did he know the man was short if he was sitting in his car? A tall man looks short if he's sitting down, and to a young boy most men look old.'

He looked pained. 'I'm giving you the boy's description, madam, exactly as he said it. Of course we recognize its limitations. Dark hair might be black or dark brown, but at least we know he wasn't bald.'

'And the motor car?'

'As I told you, madam, we only know it had yellow wheels, but they're not at all unusual. It was . . .' He flipped over a few pages. 'Ah, yes! "a very dark car" – so most likely black.' He closed the notebook with a small flourish and tucked it away in his breast pocket with the pencil. 'We'll keep you informed, be assured of that.'

Fran saw him to the door, glad to see him go. He had depressed her unutterably and, impulsively, she went into the lounge and poured herself a large sherry. As she sat down her legs were shaking and her mind was dark with endless possibilities, none of them pleasant.

*

The policeman had only just gone when Amy and Dot returned with Fritz from their walk to the station. They were in a state of great excitement and Fran guessed the reason. There was no way she could hide the fact of Mary's disappearance.

'We saw a policeman,' Dot told her eagerly, 'coming from here. From our house! A policeman on a bicycle. Fritz wants to know what's going on.'

Fran put a hand on her arm. 'I've got something to tell you, Dot, and Amy might as well know too. Come into the sitting room with me and I'll tell you what's happened.'

147

Dot seated herself next to Amy and lifted Fritz on to her lap. They looked at Fran expectantly, and she wondered how she could tell them the worst without frightening them. Amy would not be troubled, of course, but Dot was prone to nightmares.

'Mary went out for a ride with a friend in his motor car,' she said carefully, 'and she hasn't come back yet. The headmaster at Marlham was a bit worried, so he asked the police to help them find her.'

Dot's mouth had fallen open.

Amy asked, 'And did they?'

'No, not yet. If their car broke down they are probably waiting for it to be repaired.'

The little girl's eyes widened. 'They may have had an accident!'

'If they're in hospital the police will let us know. So there's nothing to worry about.'

She looked at Dot, who had lifted Fritz up. Her face was pressed against the smooth dark fur of his back. Fran waited, allowing the information to register before she said any more.

Amy looked at Dot. 'Poor Mary.'

'Yes!' The voice was muffled, but Fran detected a little quiver of alarm.

'I'm sure she'll be back soon, and then she'll telephone and tell us what happened.'

Dot looked up at last and said, 'Poor Fritz. He's worrying.'

Fran managed a smile. 'Tell him not to,' she said. 'Mary will be fine. I know it.'

Dot asked, 'Was it Matt?'

'No. At least we don't think so. It was a man we don't know.' Fran looked at Dot uneasily, disturbed by the question. Why on earth had she assumed it was Matt?

Dot said to Amy, 'Matt ran away with Connie once – and scared everyone. But Connie was all right.'

Amy brightened. 'Let's go and search for her,' she suggested. 'We could take Fritz on his lead, a sort of tracker dog!'

'Oh, yes! That's a good idea.' Dot put the dog down and jumped to her feet. 'She might be hiding. Fritz could be a – a . . .' She looked at Fran. 'One of those dogs that can smell people.'

'A bloodhound.' Fran smiled, relieved. 'What a wonderful idea!' It would suit her very well if Dot was kept busy in her self-appointed search. Paul Hallam would arrive around eleven and they had a lot of talking to do.

Amy looked at Fritz dubiously. 'A bloodhound? His ears are about right, but his legs are too short. How can he be a bloodhound?'

Fran said quickly, 'It's the nose that's important. They should have a sharp nose. What do you think?'

They all studied Fritz's lean snout and Amy gave grudging approval, adding, 'The dog has to have something that belonged to the person who's lost. A glove or something. They sniff at it and off they go.'

Within minutes Dot, Amy and the shortlegged bloodhound had left the house, armed with one of Mary's scarves. Fran watched them go and then settled down for the next half hour, studying the notes she had made on the manuscript.

When she heard her visitor arrive at ten past eleven, she went out into the hall, a smile of welcome on her face. To her intense surprise and pleasure she found Del Farrar instead. Her delight was somewhat tempered by the timing of his visit, but at least he had made contact again and she found that immensely comforting.

'Del!' she cried and hurried forward to shake his hand.

Annie said, 'I was just explaining that you have another visitor this morning . . .'

Fran said, 'I do, I'm afraid, but it's so good to see you.' The sight of him moved her more than she had expected and with an effort she resisted the urge to hug him. He was a small, bright star in her presently clouded sky and she wanted desperately to persuade him to stay. However, she could hardly expect him to wait hours while she dealt with her author.

Del, however, appeared quite unmoved by her predicament. In fact he was smiling broadly. 'I have a confession to make,' he told her. 'I'm here under false pretences. You see, *I'm* Paul Hallam!'

Chapter Seven

D EL WENT ON WITH HIS confession. 'As soon as Westrop told me the name of the editor who was willing to help me with the manuscript, I decided to say nothing. At least, I told *him* of the coincidence but asked him not to tell you. I thought it would be fun to surprise you. I hope you don't mind.'

'Of course not. I'm delighted that it's you.' She smiled. Del could have no idea just *how* delighted! 'In fact, as it happens it's a huge relief. I'd been expecting to have to cope with a stranger and I'm not at my best this morning. But come into the sitting room and I'll explain.'

Annie, pleased with the unexpected turn of events, offered to make some tea.

'Could you make that coffee?' Del answered. 'We Americans don't function properly without it!'

With a nod she hurried away and Fran led Del into the sitting room. When they were comfortably seated she explained about Mary's disappearance and saw his expression change.

'You must be half out of your mind with worry!'

'I am, to be truthful.'

'You should have put me off. You can't feel much like work with something like that hanging over you.'

'I thought it would keep my mind occupied – keep the worst thoughts at bay.'

He reached across and took her hand in his. 'I'm so sorry, Fran. I know how fond you are of your sisters.'

Fran thought guiltily of Connie but said, 'The police will find her, I know they will. It's the waiting that's so difficult.'

'Are they pulling out all the stops?'

'I'm sure they are.' She did not meet his eyes. Were they? She assumed they must be. Passing the word around, issuing a description of Mary, questioning the staff at railways and bus depots. Someone, somewhere, must have seen her.

Annie arrived with a small jug of coffee and a pot of tea for Fran who busied herself pouring.

'English coffee!' she said as she handed him the cup. 'I hope it's up to American standards!' She sugared her tea, but made no attempt to drink it. 'And we don't have any doughnuts, I'm afraid. Only biscuits.'

'Doughnuts?'

'To dunk. Isn't that what Americans like to do?'

By way of answer he rolled his eyes humorously.

'I'm sorry,' she said. 'I'm being facetious. I don't know why – the shock, maybe. At least, that's my excuse.'

He sipped the coffee thoughtfully. 'How are the cops treating this? Missing persons?'

'I imagine so.' Her stomach churned a warning. She must not let other possibilities crowd in on her or she would panic. 'Of course it is. What else could it be? She's been gone less than twenty-four hours at the moment.'

'I guess so,' he said slowly. 'The trouble is – if you'll pardon me butting in – that back home, by the time they suspect a homicide time's passed and the scent's gone cold.'

Homicide! The word frightened her. 'Oh, Del! I don't want to even *think* like that! I'm sure nothing's happened to her. At least, it couldn't— She can't be dead.' She felt her lips tremble and put a hand to her mouth to hide her distress. Del moved to sit beside her and, to her surprise, his arm went around her shoulders.

'Hey! I'm sorry, Fran.' He tightened his grip and she found it wonderfully reassuring. 'I guess I spoke out of turn. Thinking aloud. It's a bad habit, but I meant what I said. I think it's a valid point.'

'Don't apologize. You simply put into words what I was afraid to think.' She drew a long breath. Del was right. She should face up to the facts and not try to fool herself that all would be well. Many 'missing persons' were never found.

He said briskly, 'I hope I'm not speaking out of turn here, but how about taking a run down? I have a rented car and we could ask around; do a little snooping. Just in case. Couldn't do any harm, could it?'

Glancing into his face Fran saw the genuine concern there and was slightly comforted. It was a tempting offer, but did she have the right to take up so much of his time, she wondered? 'But what about the book, Del?'

'It'll keep. Paul Hallam and his manuscript can wait. I think your sister has priority here. You'd feel better, too, doing something positive.'

She knew he was right, yet the shock had left her feeling lethargic and helpless. 'I don't know—' she said shakily. 'Maybe I should stay here in case they need to contact me.'

'Annie will take a message. And you should drink that tea kind of sweet. Good for shock.'

He added an extra spoonful of sugar and she accepted it thankfully. The hot, sweet liquid was comforting and as they drank in silence a little of her courage returned.

'Perhaps we should,' she agreed. 'Yes, we'll go down to the school. She might be there herself. She might have come back from wherever she's been.' She closed her eyes in a brief prayer. 'And then the nightmare will be over.' She finished her tea and stood up. 'Give me five minutes and I'll be ready.'

*

As they turned through the school gates and began the slow drive towards the house, Del whistled appreciatively. 'Some school!'

The red brick building was mellow in the thin January sunshine and the symmetry of its windows gave it an elegant appearance.

'Georgian,' Fran told him. 'It was once a private house, but the Harpers have had it for about fifteen years. The grounds are extensive.'

'They must keep the gardener busy! The lawn's like a pool table.'

Fran smiled, but her stomach was a knot of apprehension. On the drive down Del had done his best to blur her anxieties by talking about a variety of subjects. She had appreciated his efforts and the thinking behind them, but now the sight of the school brought the reason for their journey back into sharp focus. She attempted to think calmly in preparation for the interview ahead. Samuel Harper was teaching, his wife had explained on the telephone. Taking 3A, Mary's class, until a temporary replacement could be found. However she, as matron, was fully conversant with the problem and would make herself available to answer any questions.

They parked the car outside the imposing front door, watched suspiciously by a grey squirrel which was searching the front lawns for acorns. A blackbird landed too near it and Del laughed as, tail curled, the furious squirrel chased it away in a series of erratic leaps.

'Territory,' he said. 'The animal kingdom is all the same – and homo sapiens are the worst of all!'

At that moment they were admitted by a maid who was obviously expecting them. She led them up a broad oak staircase and along a wide passage. There was a smell of polish and chalk, and something else which might have been rubber-soled plimsolls. The maid tapped on a door marked 'Headmaster' and a woman called, 'Come in.'

Doreen Harper stood up from her seat behind her husband's desk and held out her hand. Comfortably built, with a round, cheerful face, she exuded confidence and looked every inch a matron, Fran thought fleetingly.

'My dear Miss Massey.' She nodded to Del and Fran introduced him as a friend of the family.

Two chairs had been placed in front of the desk and after the usual polite preliminaries, Fran and Del sat down.

'I can't tell you,' Doreen Harper began, 'how terribly sorry we are and how desperately worried. This is so out of character. Your sister is such a sweet girl and this sort of thing – disappearing like this – is not at all—'

Fran said sharply 'She didn't intend to disappear, Mrs Harper. I can assure you of that. Something has happened to her. We are all extremely apprehensive, and we feel the police might be expecting her to turn up and – and may not be doing very much just yet. To be frank, I wish very much that you had notified someone of her absence last night instead of waiting until this morning.'

Doreen Harper's expression changed. 'You don't mean, I hope, that you find *us* somehow to blame? I can assure you we had your sister's best interests at heart when we held back from notifying them.'

And those of the school, Fran thought, but let it pass. She must step warily; there was nothing to be gained from alienating anyone who might possibly help them trace Mary.

'I'm blaming nobody,' Fran told her. 'I'm simply trying to explain why we are here. If she didn't choose to go off, then something or some*one* has forced her. She may have had an accident, of course, or been persuaded against her will to do something out of character.'

Mrs Harper allowed herself to be mollified by Fran's words. Pursing her lips, she said slowly, 'I have to say this, Miss Massey, although it won't be easy for you — your sister was in a rather excited frame of mind when she left. Excited about the young man who had called to take her out. Lettie Crewe, who was probably her closest friend, described her as "almost radiant with excitement". That does rather suggest a matter of the heart. If she had been persuaded against her better judgement, or even with her full co-operation, to spend the night with this gentleman friend—'

'It's odd that she kept him such a secret,' said Fran. 'It's so unlike her. I cannot believe that she would do anything so inconsiderate, knowing how worried everyone would be. I know her better than anyone, Mrs Harper. Whatever has happened, I *know* she was not a willing partner.'

There was a long silence.

'My dear,' said Mrs Harper, 'you are making me very fearful for her safety.'

Del said quietly, 'May I suggest something?'

Fran said, 'Please.'

'Would it be an idea for us to see her room? If there were any clue, however small, Fran would be the most likely person to recognize it as such.'

Mrs Harper considered this. 'She left no note, if that's what you're thinking. The police asked about that and my husband and I did take a quick look. We found nothing.'

Fran seized on the idea eagerly. 'But I think we should have a look if you have no objection.'

'None at all. If you care to wait until lunch-time you can also talk to Miss Crewe. She may have something of use to tell you, although I have spoken to her already and she was unable to give us any leads.'

'What about the boy who took Mary the message?' Fran suggested. 'May we speak to him?'

'Certainly. I'll send for him at the end of the morning.'

'What about the other boys? Have they been questioned?'

'Well, no, but we didn't think it wise, at this stage, to alert the entire school to the fact that one of the teachers had disappeared. I think the parents would take a rather poor view of that – especially as we don't know for certain that she didn't go willingly. No school welcomes scandal, Miss Massey. If the police ever feel it necessary to take the investigation further – although we are hoping it won't come to that . . .' She left the sentence unfinished, shrugging plump shoulders. 'But as to the boy who took the message, he was in your sister's class last year and she was rather fond of him. A funny child.' She shook her head. 'But now I have some leaflets to prepare to send out to the parents. We put on a little play each year, as your sister may have told you. This year it's called "The Timid Ghost" – but listen to me! You won't be interested in that.'

Fran made no attempt to deny this, her mind on other things, but Del said, 'It sounds the sort of things kids love!'

Mrs Harper stood up, smiling as she did so. 'Oh, they do,' she agreed. 'Anything to do with giants, monsters, ghosts – you know what boys are!'

They followed her out of the room, along the passage and round a corner.

'All the female staff have bedrooms in this wing,' the matron explained. 'Now, this was – I mean *is*, your sister's room. I'll leave you to it, if you'll excuse me.'

Mary's room was small and modestly furnished, although in need of some attention. Fran had been here once before on the occasion of Mary's first 'Open Day' at the school. Then Mary had been there, her face flushed with excitement as she showed the family her room. The cushion cover she had worked in patchwork was still on the bed; the old pyjama case in the shape of a dog lay beside it, and seeing this brought a lump to Fran's throat. It was what Annie had made for one of Mary's birthdays many years earlier.

Seeing that Del also eyed the knitted dog, Fran explained. 'Mary was very unsophisticated; so trusting. She would never be able to cope with – with whatever evil had confronted her.' Now, with a tightening of her throat, Fran recognized the family photographs which stood on top of the chest of drawers. All five children at Camber Sands, the three girls each holding a bucket and spade.

'I remember that holiday well,' she told Del softly. 'Connie insisted that she was too old for a bucket and spade but then, at the last minute, she succumbed. It was fun, that holiday. There's Matt. Smiling for once. He hated having his photograph taken.' For a moment she stared at the likeness. Could Matt possibly be involved in Mary's disappearance? He looked so harmless as he stared out of the picture. 'He had weak ankles,' she said. 'He was supposed to wear special boots, but it was so hot Annie let him take them off.' She picked up the photograph and stared intently at her brother. 'The odd one out as usual. He bought himself a shrimping net and he did catch a few. He was so tremendously proud, but then he boiled them alive and none of us wanted to eat them. Poor Matt. That's Annie behind us, with Henry in her arms.'

Del was amused. 'Which one's you?' he asked.

'The one with the skinny legs,' Fran told him. She studied the four smiling faces; only Henry looked grim. 'Matt had just trampled on his sand castle,' she explained. 'He had built most of it for Henry, so he felt entitled to knock it down again. We were a funny lot. That's Mary.'

They both looked at the slim, laughing girl with the windswept hair and Fran said, 'She can't be – I mean, she must be safe. She *must!*'

Del picked up another photograph. This time the three

158

sisters were together in a studio. Fran's face was smug as she held a lavishly dressed doll, but Connie looked furious.

Fran smiled. 'I remember that day,' she told him. 'The photographer gave the doll to Connie and I made an awful scene. To silence me they took it away from her—'

'And gave it to you!'

Fran nodded. 'No wonder Connie hates me. I think I would in her shoes.'

'Hates you? Surely not!'

'Well, let's just say there's definitely no love lost between us.'

She sighed deeply, replaced the photograph and looked round the room. A few books on a shelf, pens and pencils on the writing desk by the window. So little that was Mary, Fran thought with a sigh. 'As a child, she used to keep a diary,' said Fran, 'but I daresay she gave it up later. That could have been enlightening.'

Half-heartedly she pulled open various drawers, but found nothing but neatly folded clothes.

Del went to the window. 'It looks out over the back of the property,' he said. 'She wouldn't have been able to see whoever it was if he pulled up at the front door. And neither would anybody else who happened to be in their room. Pity.'

Fran said nothing, unable to speak. There was a dark dread growing within her. Despite her intentions to think positively, the idea that she might never see her sister again was taking hold of her. The sight of the abandoned room chilled her and she shivered suddenly, swallowing hard to prevent tears.

'Fran!' Del had seen her stricken expression and put out a hand to take hers. 'Don't give up hope,' he urged.

Her lips trembled. 'It's just this room . . .' she stammered. 'There's so much of her here and yet there's nothing. It feels as though she's gone from it for ever.'

He pulled her close, his hand stroking her back. 'Don't let it get you down,' he murmured. 'You'll see. In a day or two – or even hours – she could be back and this could just be a bad dream.'

Fran looked into his face. In spite of the encouraging words, she could see the doubt in his eyes. He knew, she thought with a shudder; they both knew. 'Oh, God! Del!' she whispered. 'Sweet, dear Mary! She's never coming back! What are we to do?'

The tears spilled down her face and she felt his arms close round her protectively. His face was close to hers and his lips brushed her hair. He said nothing now; the time for false promises was over. She sobbed unashamedly, overcome by the conviction that another member of their family had been taken from them.

After a while he said, 'I shouldn't have brought you here. I'm sorry, it was a stupid idea. We can go now, if you like.'

She struggled free, reaching for a handkerchief, making a tremendous effort to stem the tears. She had come this far and she would carry on. Even if Mary . . . whatever had happened to Mary she needed to know the truth. If her sister *were* dead, then they must find her body.

There was a knock on the door and a young woman with a dark bob put her head round it. Seeing Fran's tearstained face, she looked surprised and hesitated.

'I'm sorry. I've chosen a bad time.'

'No, no,' Fran insisted. 'Please come in. I'll be fine in a minute. Are you Miss Crewe?'

'Lettie Crewe? Yes.' She came in and Fran introduced Del.

Lettie frowned slightly 'You're not worried, are you? I mean, seriously worried? We all think – well, to tell the truth, we *hope* – that she's eloped. For her sake, I mean. She was so excited and happy.'

She sat down on the bed and Fran sat in the armchair. Del stood beside Fran, one hand resting gently on her shoulder.

Fran said, 'Elope? Oh, she wouldn't. Not Mary.'

Lettie's smile was genuine. 'Oh, but that's just it. We all thought she was in love with this mysterious someone. We teased her about him, but she wouldn't say a word – just that it was an admirer. But her eyes shone when she talked about him. She—'

'What did she say about him?' Fran asked sharply. 'Did she say where he lived or where they met or anything? She must have said something.'

'Well, not really. She said they had a lot in common. I remember that because I said "Such as" and she laughed and said ... Oh, yes, she said she'd known him a long time but suddenly he was taking an interest in her ... She said she daren't tell you or Connie or Dot because you wouldn't approve. I suppose she was afraid you might not like him, and when you love someone you want all the world to love them.'

'So nobody ever saw him?'

'No.'

Fran took a deep breath and said carefully, 'Did you ever meet Matt? Do you remember him?'

'Her brother?'

'An adopted brother.'

'No, but she spoke of him sometimes the way she spoke of all of you. I was so envious, being an only child.'

Fran thought hard, pushing uncomfortable thoughts to the back of her mind. She mustn't jump to conclusions. 'Did she go out much on her own? What I'm wondering is where she could have met this man?'

Lettie shrugged. 'Hardly ever. She went into Rye once or twice, and into Hastings for bits of shopping.' She leaned forward earnestly. 'If she's met someone and they *have* eloped, I just wish her luck. All the luck in the world! I'd jump at the chance to get away from here. She found it pretty hard, you know. The Harpers are very impressive, but they're not easy to work for. The hours are much longer than you might think, and some of the boys are awful. Really difficult.'

Fran stared. 'Mary never spoke that way. We all thought she loved it here.'

'She had nowhere else to go, did she? She wanted to be married with a family. Please don't be too hard on her. If she's in love and this is what she wants—'

Fran said bleakly, 'I hope to God you're right. It would be such a relief, Miss Crewe.'

'Call me Lettie.'

'Lettie, then. If she's run off with someone she loves and he loves her—' She drew a long breath and let it out again, thinking furiously. She desperately wanted to be convinced, but try as she would the vision of a radiantly happy Mary on the arm of an adoring man did not materialize. Was it just possible she had been swept off her feet that way? Would she ever trust a stranger? But Lettie had said it was someone she had known for a long time. Matt fitted that description, but why on earth should Matt – no, it was impossible. After the débâcle with Connie, Mary would never allow herself to . . . to what? No. Rule out Matt. She became aware that Lettie was waiting for a further comment.

'The trouble is,' Fran said slowly, 'I don't think she is with a man she loves. I've got a terrible feeling here.' She put a hand over her heart. 'A sort of dread.' She looked up at Del in the vain hope that he might have been convinced by Lettie's theory, but he simply gave a slight shrug.

At that moment there was another tap on the door and Samuel Harper came in. One look at his face told them all that he was not the bearer of good news.

'There's been an unexpected development,' he said, and

at once Fran detected the slight tremor in his voice. He looked from Del to Fran. 'I must ask you to come to my study immediately.'

As they followed him silently along the passage and down the stairs, Fran was aware of a great emptiness. She was going to be told that Mary was dead; of that she was certain. The brief glimmer of hope offered by Lettie Crewe had been promptly snuffed out, and now she was to be faced with the truth.

There was a policeman waiting in the study, and the headmaster introduced him as Sergeant Hills. He was middle-aged, with thin fair hair, and he stood almost to attention, clutching his helmet. He had the look of a man with an unpleasant duty to perform and Fran felt a chill of apprehension.

'You'd best sit down, ma'am,' he said.

She shook her head. 'Tell me now,' she said faintly.

Del put a hand on her shoulder and whispered, 'Do as he says, Fran. Sit down.'

She obeyed. What did it matter?

The policeman took a deep breath and stared straight ahead. 'It is my painful duty to inform you, ma'am, that a body fitting the description of your—'

A body? *A body!* Fran put a trembling hand to her mouth.

'—sister has been washed ashore at Winchelsea Beach. We should be very grateful if you would attend the mortuary at the Stade, in the old part of Hastings, for the purposes of identification.'

Del's hand tightened on her shoulder in a mute expression of sympathy and support. The room seemed to swing in a dizzying arc and for a moment Fran could make no sound. She heard a chorus of voices and the word 'sorry' echoed painfully in her head. It had happened, the very worst thing she could imagine . . .

Mr Harper said, 'My wife is bringing you a brandy.'

'No!' she whispered.

Del said, 'Please drink it, Fran.'

She became aware that a plump hand was offering a small glass. Obediently she accepted it and swallowed the brandy in three gulps, then she leaned back and closed her eyes briefly, grateful for the momentary warmth it brought to her chilled body. When she reopened her eyes she asked, 'Mary *drowned*? How could that happen?'

The policeman pulled a notebook from his tunic pocket and consulted it carefully. He cleared his throat. 'The body was discovered by a woman collecting driftwood. There are bruises and other marks on the body which suggest a fall down the cliff. She was dead before the tide came in. There will, of course, be a post mortem, but at the moment it appears to be an accidental death. A fall, possibly from the nearby Fairlight cliffs. May I offer my condolences, ma'am.'

'A fall?' Fran tried to control her anguished thoughts. 'But how could she – I mean, surely the man she was with would have reported a fall?'

'Apparently not. Possibly he feared that he would be blamed . . . implicated in her death.'

'So he just drove away and *left* her?' Fran heard her voice rise hysterically and she put a hand to her forehead as a great surge of heat rose through her body. 'But he was supposed to be a friend, an admirer. Surely he would call an ambulance – fetch a doctor or something? How would he know that she *was* dead?'

There was a sudden hush in the room as though everyone present held their breath.

Samuel Harper exchanged looks with his wife and said quickly, 'You're surely not suggesting foul play, Miss Massey? That would be most unpleasant – for you and for the school. I really don't think we should go along that path.'

Fran felt a flash of resentment. He was fearful for the school; reluctant to allow a breath of scandal. Much nicer to agree to an accidental fall. 'But it doesn't make sense,' she protested. 'Just think about it.'

Del said, 'I must say Miss Massey has a point. It is rather extraordinary that—'

The policeman interrupted him with a little cough. 'There are really no indications that the victim was pushed. I suppose suicide might be a possibility—'

'Suicide?' Fran's voice was shrill.

'— but I imagine you know the young woman better than anyone.'

Doreen Harper suggested, 'A lovers' tiff, perhaps? They quarrel and he jilts her. He leaves her there and then she—'

Fran cried, 'No! Not Mary. She would never do such a thing.' She looked up at Del. 'She would *never* even consider taking her own life.' Returning her gaze to the policeman, she asked desperately, 'Are we sure it's Mary? Could there be any mistake?'

The headmaster shook his head. 'They gave us a description of the clothes and I very much fear they were attributable to your sister. A dark navy skirt with a striped blouse and a navy and white patterned cardigan she had knitted herself.'

Fran buried her face in her hands as she tried to imagine Mary jumping to her death. It was out of the question. She could have fallen, but why had she been abandoned by the man who took her out in his car?

The policeman pursed his lips. 'You'd be surprised how many people panic when an accident like that occurs. If they can see no way to prove their innocence, they think it's safer to leave the scene. Often people who discover victims of a crime decide not to get involved. Sometimes they are traced and then, of course, they look horribly guilty when in fact they're innocent. We see it all the time, ma'am. Understandable in a way.'

'Understandable?' She was beginning to tremble with a mixture of shock and frustration. The heat had drained away and she felt chilled through and unbearably weary.

The policeman continued his patient reconstruction. 'If she and her young man had parked the car on the cliff-top – and plenty of people do, even in winter – and then maybe they'd had a bit of an argument and she had run away from him in some distress and then *slipped* . . .' He shrugged. 'He wouldn't want to be accused of her murder, would he, ma'am?'

Fran hesitated, and Del knelt beside her, a deep compassion in his eyes, and took both her hands in his. 'This will get us nowhere, Fran. Let's go along with the sergeant and make quite sure that it is Mary. Know the worst. Then I'll take you home. We'll think it over carefully, and I'll be with you all the way.'

Suddenly Fran felt the last of her energy drain away. Del was right; this was no time for an argument. She nodded her head. She must satisfy herself that it was Mary before she did anything more. In her heart she longed to believe that if Mary was dead, it had been an accident. If anyone could convince her of that she would be eternally grateful. But somewhere deep within her was the dreadful knowledge that Mary had been killed. If that were so, then she would move heaven and earth to find her killer.

*

Mary's body lay on a table in the hospital morgue, covered by a white sheet. The assistant drew this back and Fran stared down at the face of her dead sister. There was a greyish bruise on her left temple and scratch marks across her chin; apart from these her face was pale and colourless, the lips bloodless. Mary's eyes were closed and Fran realized

166

with a lurch of the heart that she would never again see them open. She would never again see Mary smile, nor hear her voice nor exchange a sisterly hug. First her mother and now Mary! The double tragedy undermined her and she felt an urgent need to express her grief, but words eluded her. As she leaned forward to press a kiss on Mary's cold forehead, she fought down a sense of outrage that this lovely, gentle girl should have come to such an untimely end. Gently she stroked the still damp hair, searching for a sign that in death her sister was at peace, but she felt only shock and horror. And something akin to fear.

The policeman coughed discreetly, a reminder of the purpose of her visit.

'Yes,' said Fran. 'It's Mary.'

The attendant made a move to replace the sheet, but Fran shook her head.

'Not yet,' she begged.

Soon Mary would be laid out in her coffin, joining her parents in the family grave. Yet her time on earth had been so short that Fran did not want to let her go just yet. She touched her sister's cold hand, fighting down her despair. Two days ago she had been alive – a warm, sweet girl with years of life ahead of her. Now someone had taken that life from her. As Fran stared at her sister's face, the certainty grew within her that Mary's death had not been an accident, nor had it been a suicide.

The policeman said, 'Miss Massey . . .' but Del spoke firmly. 'Please! Leave her alone. There's no hurry.'

Fran leaned down and whispered, 'Who did this to you?'

The grey lips remained stubbornly closed, the expressionless face gave nothing away.

'I'm so sorry,' Fran told her. She wanted to scream and shout for vengeance, but that would achieve nothing. 'I'll find him!' she whispered and then, a little louder,

'Goodbye, dear.' She kissed her again, then slowly straightened up.

With obvious relief the attendant drew the sheet over Mary's face. The policeman led the way into the corridor and Fran was vaguely aware that Del was holding her hand.

She looked at the policeman. 'She was killed,' she said. 'My sister was *killed*. I have this feeling . . .'

The sergeant shook his head. 'Please, ma'am. You will only upset yourself. There is no firm evidence at this stage. None whatsoever.'

Del said, 'But there may be, when you have finished your enquiries.' His voice held an unfamiliar sharpness.

'We believe, sir, that it was most likely an accident, and that the gentleman in question panicked. We will attempt to trace him. You may rest assured, ma'am, that we will do all in our power—'

'Thank you.'

Fran turned to Del. 'Can we go now?'

'Of course.'

The policeman said, 'There is just the matter of the form to be signed . . .'

'Oh. Right.'

That formality completed, Fran, dazed and shivering, was led from the mortuary. She stood on the steps gulping in the cold sea air while overhead the gulls' plaintive cries echoed against the cliffs. For a few moments they walked in silence, past the black net sheds where one or two hardy fishermen worked on their nets.

'You need a hot drink,' Del told her.

'No,' she said. 'Let's walk a while.' Without waiting for an answer, she turned left and began to crunch over the shingle towards the sea. The sea was grey, whipped into thin white crests by the wind. The tide was nearly in and in her mind's eye she saw Mary's body floating among the waves and then stranded on the beach. With Del beside her, his arm across her shoulders, she walked amongst the tangled debris which the recent tide had brought in – seaweed, the husk of a coconut, spars of wood and a myriad seashells.

Fran stopped suddenly, picked up a pebble and threw it as far as she could into the water.

'I know she was killed!' she repeated. 'They *must* find him, Del. He *must* be punished.'

'I know.' The pressure on her shoulders tightened.

'I don't feel like turning the other cheek.'

'No.'

'I'm not as nice as you thought, am I?'

'Hey!' He moved to face her. 'I'm on your side, Fran. Don't you know that yet?'

He pulled her towards him and she leaned against him as his arms closed round her. Fate was so unkind, she thought. This was what she had longed for, yet the circumstances were all wrong. He was comforting her on the death of her sister.

'Oh, Del!' she murmured. 'I didn't want it to be like this.'

She saw compassion in his eyes as he looked down at her. 'This is tough, Fran. And it might get worse. But it *will* get better. And I want to help you, to be here for you.'

She nodded. Two boys ran past, shouting, pursued by an excited dog, and Fran remembered Fritz and then Dot and Annie. They would have to be told. Suddenly she longed to be at home; here she felt lost and afraid. 'Let's forget the hot drink and go home.'

'Home it is,' he agreed.

He settled her in the car with a rug around her knees and they drove back to Maidhurst in a thoughtful silence. Once or twice Fran caught him glancing sideways at her, but was grateful that he made no attempt at conversation. Her thoughts were chaotic and her emotions raw and she felt in danger of breaking apart. The natural resilience on which she had always prided herself had apparently deserted her. The immediate future and its problems loomed ahead, but overlying all these was the terrifying certainty that Mary had been murdered.

Chapter Eight

ONNIE WAS LISTENING TO THE six o'clock news as she waited for the toast. The scrambled eggs were keeping hot in the saucepan, and she had made a pot of tea. Not that the news was ever good, she reflected, but she had kept the wireless on all day to help keep the knowledge of Mary's disappearance from weighing on her thoughts.

The announcer's crisp tones filled the room. '. . . It is expected that other towns and cities will follow the example of Leicester and organize air raid precautions . . .'

She twisted the corners of her mouth disapprovingly. Scaremongering! England would never go to war again. She had learned a hard lesson in the trenches in France. Franco and his lot might choose to blow each other up, but they were foreigners.

'. . . There is speculation in the city—'

There was a knock at the front door and, turning off the grill, she went to answer it, grumbling at the interruption to her tea. Saturday's high tea was one of the best moments in her week and now the scrambled eggs would probably stick to the pan.

Through the frosted glass panes in the door she thought she recognized the uniform of the post office.

'Oh, no!' Not a telegram. They never brought good news.

'Massey?'

She took the orange envelope with a sinking heart. The boy hovered, presumably hoping for a reply and a tip, but Connie said, 'Wait here' and shut the door. She stood for a moment, turning the envelope in her fingers, unwilling to open it. When she did, the message was terse:

'NEWS OF MARY STOP PLEASE RING STOP FRAN'

'Oh, my godfathers!'

If it had been good news it would have been spelled out in the telegram. So it was *bad* news. Opening the door she said, 'No reply' and closed it again. Then she rushed into the kitchen, pulled the scrambled eggs from the top of the stove, threw on a coat and snatched up her handbag. She ran to the telephone box on the corner and dialled Fran's number with trembling fingers. Somewhere in the dark recesses of her mind the guilt still lurked. She should never have told Matt about his mother, this was God's way of punishing her for her meanness of spirit.

'Maidhurst—'

'Fran. It's me, Connie. What's happened?'

'Connie, it's Mary. I don't know how to soften the—'

'Oh, God! What's happened to her?'

'They don't know for sure, they think she fell. Connie ... she's dead. Mary's dead. I've just been to identify her body.'

'Dead? Mary? But ... Oh, Fran!' She stared at the black receiver which trembled in her hand. 'She *fell*? Fell where?'

'From a cliff at Fairlight – at least, that's what they're saying. Accidental death.'

Connie swayed suddenly and leaned against the door

of the booth, trying to marshall her thoughts. 'A cliff at Fairlight? But what was she doing there? It's January. And anyway she didn't like heights.'

'They think she was with this mystery man and that he may have panicked and . . .'

Fran's voice continued but Connie didn't hear any more. Mary was dead and a man was involved. Fear swamped her. She had a sudden picture of Mary struggling on the cliff edge *with Matt*. An overwhelming burden of guilt settled on her shoulders and her knees buckled momentarily. If a man had killed Mary . . . If the man was Matt, then this was her fault. But that was preposterous. Matt would never kill anybody. He might have a spiteful streak – in fact he did – but he would never *kill* anyone. And if he did then she, Connie, would be the prime target. She should never have sent that letter, she accepted that now and bitterly regretted what she had done. Beads of perspiration stood out on her forehead and she wiped them away with a trembling hand. But sending the letter was her only crime. And Matt would have found out one day. Somehow. She might have shattered his fantasies, but she could never have turned him into a murderer. Aunt Violet wasn't *that* bad, surely. She was better than no mother . . . presumably. She drew a deep breath and let it out slowly.

'Pull yourself together!' she whispered.

'Connie? Are you there?'

'Of course I am. I was thinking—' No, she would never accept that Matt could be involved with Mary's death. She must not allow herself to think that way. 'You say it was an accident?' she cried. 'They think it was?'

'Yes, but I'm not so sure. I know it's ridiculous, but I've got this terrible feeling that – that it was someone she knew.'

Connie thrust Matt's image from her. Stop being hysterical,

she told herself. It can't be true. It wasn't Matt. And even if it was, it must have been an accident.

Fran said, 'They also suggested Mary might have killed herself. Depressed by Mother's death.'

'That's nonsense! She never would.'

'That's what I said.'

Connie saw that an elderly man was now waiting to use the telephone. He was stamping his feet and clapping his hands in an effort to warm himself. As he peered into the booth she turned away, avoiding his eyes. She thought desperately, her mind confused and fearful.

'Connie? Are you all right?'

'Of course I'm not. You tell me Mary's been – that Mary's had an accident and – no, I'm far from all right.'

'Connie, one of us must tell Henry.'

'And I'm the eldest. Is that what you mean? So I get all the rotten jobs. The breaking of the bad news. Thank you very much!'

Fran's tone was reproachful. 'Look, Connie, I've just had to tell *you* and I've also broken the news to Dot and Annie. They're crying their eyes out.'

'Oh!' There were times when Connie hated herself. 'I'm sorry, Fran. But you know more than me about it.' To break the ensuing silence she asked, 'How did she look?'

There was a pause. 'Grey. Dull. It was Mary but it wasn't Mary, if you know what I mean. It was so awful.'

Her voice shook and Connie felt a moment's compassion. 'Poor you!' Reluctantly she added, 'I'll tell him, then. And the funeral?'

'I suppose there will be a post mortem – to see if there are any signs that it was not an accident. Oh, Connie, I just can't believe that she would kill herself, although she *was* upset. She phoned me earlier in the week; said she wanted to talk to me because I sound rather like Mother. My heart ached for her . . . But if she didn't jump, then either someone pushed her or she fell. And if she fell, why didn't the person with her – this man – why didn't he go for help? I can't believe any of it.'

Connie said quickly 'But why would anybody want to kill her? What possible motive could anyone have?'

The guilt flooded back. The idea of a post mortem terrified her. Would a post mortem shed any light on this type of accident?

'None,' said Fran. 'At least, none that we know of. If she had met a total stranger, maybe, but she told her friends at Marlham that she *knew* the man. That she had known him for a long time.'

'Well, I don't know.' Connie thought frantically. 'Maybe they're right. The police, I mean. An accident and – and the man panicked.' She wanted so much to believe this. If Matt had been with Mary and had upset her in some way, Mary might have panicked; she might have run. They might have been fooling around or chasing each other, and Mary could have slipped. It *must* have been an accident. 'No point in believing the worst, Fran,' she said. 'The police know best. They have experience in these matters and we don't.'

She crossed her fingers, willing Fran to accept this line of reasoning.

Fran said slowly, 'Listen, Connie. I keep thinking of what the boy at the school said – about the yellow wheels. Matt's car has yellow wheels. I know it's ridiculous, but I keep thinking that maybe – just *maybe* ...' She stopped.

Connie closed her eyes. 'That's a terrible thing to say, Fran.'

'I know it is.'

'It couldn't be him. Why should it be?'

'He's – he's rather unpredictable. We both know that.'

'He's not a killer.'

175

'No, it was just the coincidence. Then you don't think I should tell the police?'

'No, I don't.' Connie swallowed hard.

'I'm glad.'

'About what?'

'That you don't think it could be Matt. I didn't want to think it but . . . I've always been afraid of how he would react if he ever knew about the tontine.'

Connie drew a long, shuddering breath. This conversation was becoming unbearable and she said, 'I must go. I'm – I'm expecting someone this evening.'

'I'll keep you informed. And you'll tell Henry – and Matt, I suppose. I haven't told Matt.'

'*Matt*? Must I? I mean—' She stopped abruptly. Whatever happened, she mustn't make Fran suspicious. 'I'll tell them,' she said and slowly she replaced the receiver. She waited for a moment, unable to pull herself together, but when the elderly man knocked impatiently on the door she pushed it open and stepped out.

As she held the door open for him he muttered, 'About time, too!'

Connie felt an irrational surge of anger. 'Go to hell!' she snapped. 'Miserable old sod!' As though she didn't have enough troubles, she reflected bitterly. But her indignation quickly faded and she regretted the coarse word she had used. She had let herself down, and it was all Matt's fault. As she walked home the prospect of any contact with him made her sick with anxiety. She would telephone Henry at his college, later, when she felt stronger; when she had pulled herself together. But perhaps she would send Matt a telegram. Or perhaps that was too cruel. He would get a letter within a day or two, and he might be away on business anyway. She told herself there was no terrible urgency. If Matt had had nothing to do with Mary's death, it would be better to send a brief but

176

polite note. In it she would suggest that he contact Fran for further information. And poor Henry! He would be devastated by the loss of his sister so soon after losing his mother.

Maybe Matt had taken Mary out to make her and Fran jealous, and then there had been an accident. Then he might have feared to be implicated. God! *Please* let it have been something like that.

Tears sprang into her eyes as she finally turned the key in her own front door. Poor Mary, who had never hurt anyone in her life. Had someone killed her? She closed the door behind her and for the first time in her life, felt very alone and distinctly uneasy. If – and she really could not believe it – *if* it was Matt, why had he chosen Mary? And who might he choose next?

*

February 2nd 1938

Dear Fran,

I am so sorry I cannot be with you all today for Mary's funeral. I sent some flowers down on the train and hope they arrived in time. I had intended to be there, but I am suffering from the effects of a fall yesterday evening and can barely walk. I have had to miss a few days' work, but the doctor says there is no real damage so I shan't be on crutches all my life!

Matt smiled. It would have been a terrible risk, yet he *had* been tempted to attend just to see their faces – the faces of his future victims. He thought he could have carried it off rather well, looking hangdog and miserable and offering clumsy comfort. He liked the touch about the crutches. That might worry someone. He had meant to say that he was in bed with 'flu or a heavy cold, but at the last moment this had seemed too weak to excuse him from attending the funeral. Still, there was no way anyone could find him out in the lie, so what did it matter?

'Poor little Mary,' he wrote. 'It seems so terrible that her life is over, but I do believe that she was happy in her own way and we must cling to that . . .'

Matt had a momentary vision of her white face as she fell away from him, her mouth open, her eyes terrified. The image haunted his dreams and his waking moments alike. Poor, silly Mary. Stupid, gullible Mary. It had been almost too easy.

He went on, 'I am so pleased to hear the result of the post mortem. I was sure in my own mind that no one could have intended her any harm. She could have had no enemies. Accidental death certainly sounds more likely than suicide. It must have come as a great relief to you all . . .'

Damn! He crossed out the last sentence. It sounded as though he himself was not relieved. Now he would have to write a decent copy. After a pause for thought, he continued:

The verdict comes as a great relief, although I would like to get my hands on the blighter who deserted her. Cowardly bastard. (pardon my French!) Maybe there was nothing he could do and maybe he was scared, but there is no excuse for him to take off the way he did. Still, no doubt the police are still hoping to find him, and when they do we shall know exactly what happened . . .

But not if I have anything to do with it, he thought. She's gone, and no one is any the wiser. Only Connie might have suspected, but if she had she would have said something by now. Not that she has any real grounds for suspicion because she only knows the half of it. Nobody but Alice and Violet know the whole truth. And me, of course. Let's not forget poor bloody me.

'Oh, God!' He threw down the pen and stared at the letter. Suppose Connie *did* suspect something? Suppose she went to the police? Would they come here to check out his story? He must have an alibi ready – and another for today. Poppy might be interviewed and she could give the game away. Somehow he must make sure she would support him. He scowled as a horrible idea entered his head.

'Christ, no!' he snapped. Not Poppy!

'A fate worse than death!' he muttered. But he might need her. If he was going to carry on he would need all the help he could get. Mother's death was natural enough, and Mary's death had passed as an accident, but a second death in the same family would make it patently clear to everyone that the family had been targeted by a killer. There would be a murder investigation and then the enquiry into Mary's death would be reopened. A second death! That had a satisfying ring to it. It would have to be Connie. He had given the idea some serious thought and had come up with a simple plan. That was the secret, he thought. Most murderers tried to be too clever; he would keep it simple. He would go to the library one afternoon (when he had recovered from his 'fall') and would be sugary-sweet to Connie in front of her colleagues so that they would testify to his friendly intentions. Then he would go to her flat later and tell her how happy he had been to meet his real mother. He would sweet-talk her into letting him stay the night, and then he would smother her with a pillow. Later he could slip away in the middle of the night under cover of darkness. When questioned he would say that he hadn't stayed long because she had a date with someone. He would hint that it might have been Del Farrar. When he left her, she was alive and well. If he had intended to murder her, he would argue, would he have been

179

stupid enough to go to the library, thus announcing his presence?

> I do feel that at such an unhappy time we should draw closer together, Fran, and I hope you will give me credit for some brotherly feelings. I am as devastated as the rest of you, and surely I deserve some crumbs of comfort too ... Again my heartfelt sympathies,
>
> Your loving Matt.

He smiled at the last few lines. That would tear at Fran's heartstrings!

Ten minutes later he had completed the good copy and sealed it in its envelope. He addressed it with a confident hand and added a stamp, and as he did so another idea came to him. Assuming an expression of pain, he made his way awkwardly down the stairs and knocked on his landlady's kitchen door.

'Mr Massey! Come in!' Her face lit up with pleasure until he limped past her and then she was all concern. 'But what's happened to you? You're limping. Oh, you poor thing. Sit down – here!' She plumped up the cushion in an ancient wicker armchair and watched solicitously as he lowered himself carefully into it. Then she sat down opposite him, and he could see a stain on the front of her blouse. Gravy, probably, he thought. Mucky old thing!

'It's my leg,' he explained, letting out his breath in a whistle of discomfort. 'I took a nasty tumble yesterday as I was getting out of my car with an armful of stuff. Couldn't save myself, you see.'

'Poor old you!' said Poppy, leaning forward to pat his knee. 'Has the doctor seen it?'

Matt hesitated fractionally. Better not tell too many lies in case things hotted up. 'I haven't bothered him. I hate doctors – but I should have been at my sister's funeral today and—'

'Oh, yes! You told me. The one who fell down the cliff. Oh, dear! You are in the wars and no mistake!'

'So I doubt if I shall go to work tomorrow, but then it's the weekend and a good rest might do the trick.'

She put her head on one side and held up a forefinger. 'I know! A cup of tea! It never fails. I'll just put the kettle on. I could do with a cuppa myself.' She beamed at him, a smile which seemed to accentuate the powdered wrinkles around her mouth and eyes. 'Glad you popped down, Mr Massey! I was feeling a bit lonely.'

He held out the letter. 'I really came down to ask a favour. Would you post this for me? I'd be awfully grateful if you would; they'll be wondering why I didn't turn up.'

'Post it? Well, of course I will. Glad to help.' She sucked in her breath with a little shake of the head. 'Dear oh Lord! First your mother and then your sister. You really are a poor old thing, aren't you?'

'Not as old as you, you old bat!' thought Matt, but he smiled wistfully.

As she busied herself in the scullery he looked around him. It was a cheerful enough room, cheaply furnished but not uncomfortable and the fire, recently made up, was throwing out a good heat.

He watched her as she flapped around excitedly, keeping up a steady stream of conversation intended to either interest or impress him. Matt wondered just how far he would have to go with her to be sure of her support if it were ever necessary. The thought of her naked body filled him with repulsion, but he might be able to keep her loyal with a few kisses and the promise of more intimate delights. It all depended on how desperate she was.

She turned to place the tray on the table. 'The best china!' she told him with a little laugh. 'It was my mother's, and before that her mother's. Real Doulton, this is.' She lifted one cup and showed him the writing.

'I believe you,' he said. 'It's very pretty.'

'Not everyone gets the red carpet,' she told him.

'I'm honoured.'

'You certainly are.'

He grinned. 'Seems I did myself a bit of good on Tuesday, after all.'

'Tuesday? I thought you said it happened yesterday.'

Damn. She was quick. He shook his head in what he imagined was a bemused fashion. 'Must have banged my head as well!' he joked. 'It *was* yesterday. And today's Thursday. So it was Wednesday. Sorry.'

Well, at least his error had given him a chance to imprint the date on her memory. Still, he would have to be careful in future. She obviously wasn't as stupid as she looked. His thoughts raced as she chattered on while she poured the tea and produced a tin of biscuits. He must find a way to mention Mary, just by way of insurance. It would be useful to have someone to endorse his version of events.

Poppy handed him a cup of tea and the biscuits, and he chose a chocolate-covered wafer. She gave a little squeal of excitement. 'They're *my* favourites, too,' she told him and for a few moments they ate in a welcome silence.

Matt allowed his smile to fade and said, 'I can't believe she's gone. Poor Mary! I little guessed when I saw her at Mother's funeral that she would soon be dead herself. That was the last time I saw her, at Mother's funeral.' Better hammer the facts home, he told himself. 'She wrote me such a nice letter, too, and I said I would visit her at the school where she teaches. I never did. Poor Mary. I was her special favourite. Knowing Mary, she'd have been so looking forward to it. Now I could kick myself, of course.'

Poppy arranged her own features into a suitably sombre expression. 'You poor dear! It must be awful for you.'

'I was going to take her for a spin in the car – she would have loved that. She was a French teacher at a boys' prep school. Living-in at a rather dull boarding school. Poor Mary.'

Poppy shook her head sadly. 'But at least they know it was an accident. You thought earlier that she might have done herself in – that would have been dreadful.' She sipped her tea with her little finger delicately arched, peering at Matt over the rim of her cup, then said suddenly, 'I do wish I knew your first name. You know I'm Poppy, but—'

'It's Matt. Short for Matthew.' He smiled. 'You're right. We should be on first-name terms. Call me Matt.'

Her face lit up with pleasure. 'And you call me Poppy.'

'Right, Poppy!' They both laughed.

She held out the tin. 'Another biscuit, Mr – oh sorry! *Matt*!' She leaned forward confidingly. 'I think it's bad for you to be too much on your own. I mean, for anybody. You. Me. It's not natural, is it?'

Matt held his breath. Surely it wasn't going to be *that* easy?

'As bad for a man as for a woman,' she went on, nibbling round the edges of a ginger nut.

Matt looked at her throat and wondered how easily he could strangle her. Not that he wanted to, but if ever the need arose ... He imagined closing his hands round the scrawny flesh. One really tight squeeze and maybe a final jerk upwards. Vertebrae and a few muscles – oh, and the windpipe. He imagined her face growing purple and then he saw her collapse on to the floor. No blood. No witnesses. Death was so easy to arrange. You didn't need a university degree to murder. He felt a rush of adrenalin and had to lower his eyes for fear she read his thoughts. 'Calm down!' he told himself. 'Don't be sidetracked.' He took a deep breath and then another. For a moment there he had been almost tempted – but he needed her as an alibi.

'You all right? You look – well, a bit funny.'

'I'm – it's nothing.' He forced himself to look into her

eyes. 'I'm fine, Poppy. Just thinking about – you know – Mary and everything.'

She nodded sympathetically. 'You're all het up, that's your trouble. I'm the same. I get all knotted up inside. I get good days and bad days. Today's a bad day. My head's just bang, bang, bang. My husband used to say, "Relax, Poppy, for God's sake!", but I couldn't. The only thing that helped was . . . Now don't laugh, Matt. He used to brush my hair. Yes, he brushed my hair. Course it was long then, and very dark, but we were newlyweds and you know how daft you are. Well, maybe you don't. Were you ever married, Mr – Matt?'

'Never had that pleasure,' he said. 'Never found the right woman.'

She considered this for a moment and then patted her hair. 'Going a bit grey now, but then it was lovely.' She sighed for her past glories.

Matt regarded her lank curls. 'It's still very pretty.' The lie rolled off his tongue.

'Oh, it's not!' she protested, delighted by the compliment. 'I mean, do you really think so?'

'I mean it.' He swallowed hard. 'You know what they say: "Beauty is in the eye of the beholder."'

She looked at him with glowing eyes and a silence fell between them.

Matt smiled slowly, his eyes on hers with what he hoped was a meaningful expression. 'Let me brush your hair for you, Poppy. I'd like to. Truly I would.'

To his surprise tears sprang into her eyes. 'Oh, Matt! Would you really?'

He leaned forward and laid his right hand on her knee. 'There's nothing I'd like better,' he told her smoothly, and as he smiled gently he crossed the first two fingers of his left hand.

*

Amy and Dot sat either side of the lounge table, their expressions earnest, their attention fastened upon a vase of dried hydrangeas which stood midway between them. Dot had a set of paint brushes and a variety of tubes of paint. Amy was making do with a single brush and a paintbox which Dot had abandoned some years earlier. Fritz lay at Dot's feet, snoring rhythmically, and the only other sound in the room was the rain beating against the windows.

With a sudden gesture of impatience, Amy threw down her brush and stared critically at her half-finished painting. 'I knew I couldn't,' she said accusingly. 'I told you I couldn't, and you said I could. I'm going to throw it away.'

'Let me see,' Dot offered.

Amy wavered. 'It's no good,' she insisted. 'It's horrible.' But she passed it across the table for Dot's verdict.

Dot looked at the arrangement of shapeless blobs and inwardly agreed with her young friend's assessment. She smiled, however. 'It's not that bad,' she said kindly. 'You've got the colours exactly right and that's quite difficult.'

Amy brightened. 'Yes, I thought the colours were good – but it's the rest of it.'

Amy was torn between honesty and a desire to keep Amy at the table. 'Hydrangeas are awfully hard to do,' she said. 'Even for me. Mine's not very good either.'

Amy slipped from her chair and came to stand beside her. She looked at the delicate painting and sighed. 'No, it's not,' she agreed, 'but it's better than mine.'

'No, it's not,' Dot insisted. 'Look, that twig is the wrong length and – and I've made the leaves too green. They're really a sort of greeny-brown.'

Amy tutted. 'Well, except for the twig and the leaves it's better than mine.' She glanced down at Fritz and said 'I wish he'd stop snoring. I can't think properly when he snores. I'm just going to do a bit and then he snores and makes me go wrong.'

Dot looked pained by this criticism. 'He doesn't make me go wrong,' she said. 'I like to hear him snore. When I hear him I know he's near me.'

'Nobody *likes* to hear dogs snore. That's silly.' Amy returned to her chair, staring reproachfully at her painting. She looked at it for a moment and said, 'Is the colour *really* good? Brownies' honour?'

Not being a Brownie, Dot thought it safe to swear. 'Brownies' honour.'

Amy grinned. 'I knew it was. I was only teasing. My teacher says I'm good at drawing. Not this teacher, at this school. My teacher at home. Once I drew a Christmas tree being chopped down in the forest and there were tears coming from the tree. It was terribly sad. I got a big tick for it, and the teacher put it on the wall.'

Fritz grunted suddenly and woke himself up. He looked round cautiously and then yawned.

Amy looked down at him and laughed. 'You should put your paw in front of your mouth. That's manners, Fritz.' She dipped her brush in the water, sucked the end of it and applied it to the carmine red. 'I'm adding a few berries,' she told Dot, 'because this is such a boring plant.'

Dot let this heresy pass. She had a secret she was longing to share, but she was putting off the moment, waiting for exactly the right atmosphere. It was very important to her that Amy should make the right replies. There were times when her friend could be very scathing and Dot's secret was too vulnerable to be exposed to such a risk.

'I think Fran's got a – a young man,' she offered at last. 'I think she likes him.' Amy's immediate and undivided attention was very satisfying and Dot went on, 'She gets all pink in the face when the telephone rings and she doesn't wait now for Annie to answer it.'

Amy leaned forward, the berries forgotten. 'Is it Matt?'

'No.'

'I thought you said she loved Matt.'

'Not like that – not *exactly*. Not kissing.'

'You'll have to write and tell Matt that she's found someone else. It'll probably break his heart.'

'I might.' Dot felt unsure about this. Would Matt's heart be broken? 'I might not. But I do tell him things sometimes. I told him all about you.'

Amy appeared unimpressed by this news. 'Then who is it?'

'It's Del. Del Farrar. You know.'

Amy rolled her eyes. 'I thought you said a *young* man. Mr Farrar's old; his hair's silver.'

'It's not that sort of silver. Not *old* silver. Fran says it's silvery blond.' She wished now that she had waited a little longer. If Amy was going to say things like this it would spoil everything. But it was too late now. 'She kissed him and he kissed her back,' she said. 'I saw them but they didn't see me. I was looking out of the window upstairs and they were in the drive and he was getting into his car.'

Amy's face lit up. 'They *kissed*? Wow! Does anybody else know, or just you and me?'

'I told Fritz and he was very pleased. He wagged his tail, so I know he was. He likes Del.'

Amy put a hand over her mouth and giggled. 'They'll be flirting next,' she said gleefully. 'He'll be cuddling her and whispering into her ear. My boyfriend does that. It's delicious.'

Dot stared. 'Whispering what?'

'Things. Lovey-dovey things. It's nice, I think. I expect they'll be getting married next. I will, when I'm old enough. You have to be twenty-one, but it won't take long. Listen – this is a poem I got once, from a boy at school.'

'Your young man?'

'No, another boy.' She recited. 'You love me. I love you. You be good and I'll be true.'

187

Fritz began to scratch himself and Dot leaned over to stop him. She didn't want Amy to see how envious she was. Someone had written Amy a love poem but no one had ever written one for her. It was so unfair.

'What do you think?' Amy looked smug.

Dot hardened her heart. 'Nothing. Nothing much.'

'Why not?'

'I'm thinking about Fran, that's why.' She ignored Amy's scowl. 'I asked her if she liked Del and she said he was rather a dear. It's because she's so sad about Mary and Mother. He's being extra kind to us. I hope he does marry Fran.'

Amy shrugged. 'How can he? He's an American, he lives in America. Unless you want Fran to go and live in America without you.'

Dot was aware of a moment's panic but then she reasoned with herself. Amy was put out and she was just being horrible. Fran would never go to America – or if she did, they would *all* go. Impulsively she put down her brush. She was rather pleased with her efforts and would show it to Del next time he came.

'Fritz is bored,' she announced, surreptitiously disturbing him with the toe of her shoe. 'He wants to go for a walk to the station. D'you want to come?'

Amy rose eagerly, her bad temper at once dispelled by the prospect of a walk. 'We might see an express,' she suggested hopefully. 'We might see the Orient Express!'

'What's that?'

'I'll tell you as we go,' she promised and, friendly relations re-established, they abandoned the paints and brushes and dashed away in search of coats, scarves and gloves. Fritz, left to his own devices, seized the opportunity to enjoy a good scratch.

*

The station-master was in his office, but he came out for a

few moments to talk to them. Bob Hewlett, the porter, was sweeping the station platform. Despite the winter sunshine a cold breeze eddied around the various outbuildings, making his task more difficult than it should have been. Fritz leaped after a wayward paper-bag which had escaped his broom, nearly strangling himself as he reached the end of his lead. Dot bent to remonstrate with him while Amy engaged the station-master in conversation. In answer to his question about her future, she assured him she was going to marry and have a lot of children.

'Is that so?' He nodded approvingly. 'Lots of children, eh? That should keep you out of mischief.' He chuckled at his own joke while Amy regarded him suspiciously.

Dot called to her, anxious to show off her knowledge of the station and its workings. 'This is the ticket office,' she told her, 'and next to it, here, is the waiting room. Where you wait for the train – or for someone who's coming on the train. I wait here for Mary when she . . .' She faltered. 'I used to wait—' She fell silent.

Mr Walker shook his head. 'That was a sad business, Miss. Saw it in the local paper and could hardly believe my eyes. Not *our* Miss Massey, I said to the wife, but there. It was. We was all very upset – and so soon after your poor mother, God rest her soul. Poor Mrs Massey. She'll be sadly missed – but then at least she'd lived her life. Your poor sister –' He was lost for words.

Amy, unmoved by his remarks, followed Dot into the waiting room and looked around. The fireplace held a small but cheerful fire and beside it stood a brass coal-scuttle, newly polished. Mr Walker, following them in, saw Amy looking at it.

'Always clean and shining, that scuttle,' he told them. 'That's Hewlett's first job every morning – to polish that scuttle. The scuttle, the fireguard, door-handles where appropriate, window catches, anything brass. It's out with the Brasso and off he goes, come wind, come shine. Sets the tone, you see, for the entire station. We take a pride in this station, as you can—'

Amy said, 'Your plant's dead. The one in the pot outside.'

Dot looked up quickly. 'Mr Walker can't do much gardening because of his lumbago, and Mr Hewlett hasn't got green fingers.' She looked to the station-master for corroboration and was relieved to see him nod.

'You're right,' he said. 'There's some stations that can boast a pretty bit of garden in the summer. But *only* in the summer, you see? At Maidhurst we keep our brass polished *all year round*. That's the difference, young lady.'

Dot recognized the challenge in the station-master's voice and hurriedly distracted Amy's attention. 'This bench along the wall is for people to sit on, and this is the table—'

'I can see it's a table!'

Ignoring her interruption, Dot ploughed on determinedly. 'And these are the magazines for people to read while they're waiting. There's a mirror over the fireplace if you want to comb your hair.'

Mr Walker said, 'There's even a bit of shoe polish in case the gentlemen gets their shoes muddy, but that's kept in my office. Don't want that to walk. Not that I don't trust people – not my regulars, at any rate – but we do have the odd bit of thievery, I'm sorry to say. Have to empty the scuttle, too, at the end of the day, and lock away the magazines. Never would have dreamt of that at one time, but now it's all changed.' He took out his watch and glanced at it. 'Well, I can't stand here all day jawing, much as I'd like to. I'll leave you to it, but mind you're off the platform by eleven thirty-one when the express goes through. I don't trust that dog of yours. You'd best wait outside the gate where you can't come to any harm.'

As he limped away, Amy whispered, 'Silly old thing!'

190

Dot, shocked, said loyally, 'He's not silly. I like him.'

'You would. You like everybody. You shouldn't trust strangers, that's what my mum says.'

'But Mr Walker's not a stranger,' Dot began, but Amy turned to her suddenly with an exaggerated shiver.

'I wouldn't like to be here at midnight,' she said, wide-eyed. 'It would be ever so scary. All silent like the grave! All lonely and spooky and stuff.' She gave an exaggerated shudder. 'It's so lonely here. Miles from anywhere.' She rolled her eyes fearfully.

Dot felt a flicker of apprehension. 'But nobody would come here at midnight because there aren't any trains that late.'

'There might be *ghost trains! Trains full of skeletons!*'

'*Don't*, Amy!' Dot cried, her heart thumping and her imagination working overtime. At that moment Fritz, catching a glimpse of Bob Hewlett and his broom, began to bark fiercely. Dot took her chance to follow him into the sunshine outside.

'Fritz wants to go home now,' she announced.

Amy's face fell. 'But I thought we were going to watch the express go through.'

Dot shook her head. Although she wouldn't admit it, Amy's nonsense had frightened her and she needed a way to punish her. 'You can stay on your own,' she said firmly and set off, calling farewells to the station staff as she went.

Dot had taken a calculated risk. She did not really relish the walk home alone, but she was discovering a new confidence within herself. She walked briskly across the small forecourt, her head high, and willed Amy to follow her. She was soon rewarded by the sound of running feet and a plaintive, 'Wait for me!'

Chapter Nine

A S MATT WENT UP THE library steps he was looking forward to seeing the look on his sister's face
when she saw him. She would be panic-stricken
at the thought of an unseemly row in the hushed precincts
of her place of work. Hopefully his conciliatory tone would
keep her off guard long enough to allow him to work his
old magic. He pushed open the door and, affecting a slight
limp, crossed to the desk.

A young woman looked up and returned his smile.

'I'm looking for my sister, Connie Massey,' he told her
in the required whisper. 'It's a surprise visit. I'm Matthew,
her brother.' He grinned. 'The good-looking one!'

She laughed. 'I'll tell her you're here. I think she's in
the office.'

While he waited he glanced around at the shelves of
books and listened to the squeak of shoes on the polished
floor. It was a dull day and the overhead lights were on,
casting small pools of brightness. Outwardly he was calm,
but his drumming fingers hinted at the inner excitement. He
was controlling this with a supreme effort of will, of which
he was extremely proud. Only two days had passed since
Mary's funeral, but his impatience had overridden caution
and he had decided that Connie was to be next. She was the

one with the knowledge that could point towards a possible motive for Mary's death. As soon as she had gone he could breathe more easily. The irony was that she had brought the punishment upon herself by her spiteful letter. By rights, she should have been the first, but he had had to start with an easy target and Mary had fitted the bill perfectly. Connie would not be easy. She might already be suspicious; she would certainly be reluctant to change her opinion of him and she would be difficult to trap. That was the challenge. He had needed to find a way of making sure she would see him and had hit on the idea of the library, gambling on the fact that she would try to avoid an unpleasant scene. Tonight would be the first step. He had to ensure that the family knew that he and Connie were reconciled. It wouldn't be easy, but that didn't deter him. He also had to convince Connie that her revelations had not had the desired results, because then there was no reason for him to hate her. It would be like playing a large fish! Cunning was needed and 'Father' had told him many times that he had that in plenty.

The girl returned, looking flustered. 'Miss Massey says she's too busy to see anyone. I'm awfully sorry.'

He looked into her eyes, a deliberately intimate look. 'And *is* she? Busy?'

Her face flushed with embarrassment. 'We are rather understaffed at the moment because ...' The sentence trailed away and her downcast eyes gave the lie to her words. She looked around for help, but none of her colleagues were near enough to have overheard the conversation. 'I – I'm really awfully sorry. She suggested you might care to write—'

Matt leaned forward, adopting his eager, boyish expression. 'Please tell her that I have some good news. And that I can wait. I'll browse among the books until she's not so busy.'

The girl hesitated. 'She *was* quite emphatic—'

Somehow Matt kept the smile on his face. '*Tell her!*'

'Mr Massey, I really think you should go. She won't see you.'

His face was beginning to ache with the effort of maintaining the smile. 'And I say she will! Oh, dear! This is so like Connie.' He shrugged helplessly. 'It's so silly. She's my favourite sister. It was only a little tiff. Do you have sisters and brothers?'

'Actually only one sister, but—'

'And don't you sometimes fall out?'

'I suppose so.'

'I'm trying to make up.' He shook his head as though bemused. 'She does like to bear a grudge. It always has to be me that sues for peace. Give me a sheet of paper and a pencil. I'll give you a note for her.'

'Oh, but she—' Embarrassed, she bit back the end of the sentence.

Matt gave her a rueful smile. 'I can guess. She doesn't want anything to do with me; she told you to get rid of me. Am I right?'

'Something like that. I'm sorry.'

He could see that she meant it, that she was on his side. 'A sheet of paper, please,' he insisted gently.

Unwillingly, the girl produced a memo slip from beneath the desk counter. After a moment's thought, he wrote, 'Must talk to you. Exciting news. Please come. Matt.' As an afterthought he underlined 'Please', folded the note and offered it to the girl with a little mocking smile. 'She loves me really!' he told her, and wondered exactly what Connie had said about him. Perhaps they were all annoyed because he had missed Mary's funeral? That might have been a mistake. On reflection he probably could have carried it off quite well; he would have to be more confident next time. He smiled. He wouldn't

194

miss Connie's funeral, the bitch! Wild horses wouldn't keep him away.

The minutes ticked by and a small queue of people formed, waiting for someone to stamp the books they were borrowing. He smiled at them, his most charming smile. 'They won't be long. A bit short-staffed today.'

'Oh, are they? Well, I haven't got all day.' The elderly man at the head of the queue frowned.

The peppery colonel type, thought Matt, despising him. Pompous, overbearing stuffed shirt!

Matt said coldly, 'None of us have.'

'What?'

'I said that none of us have got all day, but I don't suppose a minute or two will be disastrous. Will it?'

While the man spluttered angrily the rest of the queue looked distinctly uneasy. They all brightened at the sight of the girl coming back to them and seeing the people waiting, she immediately stammered an apology. To Matt she said quietly, 'She said tonight at her flat. Seven o'clock.'

Matt grinned. 'I told you – she loves me really! Thank you. And you' – he put a hand lightly on her arm and whispered – 'are too pretty to work in a library!'

The blush inspired by this comment made Matt laugh and he was still laughing as he pushed through the swing door and ran down the street. Tonight at seven. His gamble had paid off.

*

Connie opened the door with a fiercely beating heart. After her letter, she had never expected to see him again – in fact she had rather hoped they would never meet. The note had puzzled her and curiosity had played a large part in her decision to see him. Now, although she had not wanted him to come at all, she had nevertheless taken pains with her appearance. Men were infrequent visitors to her flat and she had seized the opportunity to wear her new strapped shoes and a frilly blouse, telling herself that she must get some wear out of them. There was no way she could admit that, after all that had passed between them, she still wanted to impress Matt. Stammering a welcome of sorts, she was unprepared for the huge bouquet of flowers which he thrust into her arms. Confused, she pushed them away.

Matt said, 'They're for you, Connie. Don't you recognize an olive branch when you see one?' Once more he put them into her arms, and she regarded him with a mixture of anger and regret.

'I don't want your damn flowers—' she began but, taking her by surprise, he neatly sidestepped her and was in the hall.

'Matt! What the hell do you think—'

'I must talk to you,' he said. 'I told you. Exciting news – remember?'

'You're limping.'

'It's nothing much. I wrote saying I'd had a fall. Pulled a few muscles.'

He began pulling off his overcoat as though he owned the place and Connie swallowed hard. This was going to be harder than she had expected. 'You're not stopping, Matt, so get that into your head. I only said to come here to prevent you from embarrassing me at the library. And if you ever try anything like that again, I swear I'll—'

'You'll what?'

He was grinning, damn him! 'Matt, put your coat back on and—'

'Not yet, Connie. I have to tell you my news and I want to thank you. If you'll only listen to me—'

He hung his coat on the hallstand and she felt a flash of irritation. He had the cheek of the devil! But he had certainly caught her attention and she was intrigued in spite of herself.

'Thank me for what exactly?' This cheerful, smiling Matt was not at all what she had expected. He really was intolerable. She had dealt him a blow which should have reduced him to tears and here he was, grinning like an idiot and buying her flowers.

As if he had read her mind, he said, 'Don't take it out on the flowers. The poor things need water.'

Connie hesitated. She had made up her mind that she would not let him past the front door, but already he was in the hall and she was weakening, disconcerted by his manner. He had an air of repressed excitement and he looked just like the old Matt; the Matt she had both loved and hated all her life. It was this contradiction which had always fascinated her, and now she was about to be seduced by it again.

'No!' she said desperately. 'You must go, Matt. I don't want this. I can't bear it.' Furiously, she heard her voice shake. He was looking at her with that intense expression in his eyes. She had never been able to read him; had never been really close to him, the way Fran had. Theirs had always been such an easy rapport.

'Dear Connie! Please give me a chance. I need to talk to someone – to tell someone about my mother. I went to see her.'

For a moment Connie doubted that she had heard him correctly. 'You went to *see* her?'

He nodded cheerfully. 'I want to tell you about my real mother.'

'Your – you mean Aunt Violet?' This was the last thing she had expected to hear, that Matt had visited his mother. Her thoughts raced. He had seen his mother and he wanted to share the experience with her, Connie. Not Fran. For a moment she felt elated. Matt had chosen to talk to her rather than to Fran. But her satisfaction was short-lived. As yet Fran knew nothing about the relationship between Matt and Aunt Violet so Connie herself was the only possible confidante.

She stared at him, hiding her disappointment And why was he looking so damned smug? 'What about her?'

'Ask me in properly then and I'll tell you everything. Then I'll take you out to dinner as a way of saying "Thank you".' He took hold of her hand. 'Things have changed. We were never officially brother and sister, but now we're cousins. I'm family, Connie. Oh, come *on*! Relax, can't you! This isn't the real Connie. You're not really so cold and unforgiving.' With his right hand he gently tidied a stray lock of her hair and the small gesture moved her. Desperately she fought back tears of weakness. Damn and blast him!

'It's all such a game with you,' she said shakily. 'How can I trust you? After everything . . .' She stared down at the flowers, seeing them properly for the first time. Red roses and white lilies. She was astonished. What had she done to deserve such a tribute? 'They must have cost a fortune!'

'I told you, they're a "Thank you".' He glanced around the hall. 'Nice place. A lot better than mine.'

She bit her lip. He could always do it; could always say the one thing that threw her off balance. Now he was admitting that his own flat was not as good as he had pretended. No boasting now. He knew how little boasting worked with her and he was playing 'underdog'. She always fell for that. With a start she tried once more to harden her resolve and drew herself up tall. 'Say what you have to say, put on your coat and go.'

'No candlelit dinner?' He raised his eyebrows. 'Not just for old times' sake?'

The old bantering smile. She hesitated. 'Well, just for a few moments. Tell me about Aunt – about your mother.' She was longing to know what had happened about Aunt Violet.

'And then dinner? I hate to eat alone.'

'I'll see. Don't push me, Matt.'

It took him less than five minutes to establish himself comfortably in front of her small fire, legs outstretched

198

and a glass of her best sherry in his hand – the sherry she had bought for Del Farrar, Connie thought with regret. If it hadn't been for Fran, she and Del might have been sitting here, enjoying each other's company. She took a sip of her drink and let it warm her throat. Perhaps, after all, she *would* allow him to take her out to dinner. For all the heartache he had caused her over the years she would choose the most expensive dishes on the menu – and she would suggest champagne, since he was insisting it was a celebration. He had embarrassed her at the library, so she would return the compliment. Oh, yes, Matt! Two could play at that game. Hopefully he wouldn't have enough money to pay the bill and would have to borrow from her.

Matt said, 'You'd love her, Connie. She's a really sweet person. I felt so ashamed when I met her; when I remembered all the horrible jokes we'd made about her. We never really knew what we were talking about.'

'That's because Mother and Father discouraged questions,' Connie protested. 'How could we know? You can't blame us.'

Matt smiled patiently. 'I'm not blaming anybody – not even our parents. They're a different generation; they don't see things the way we do. In those days it was a great scandal, to have an illegitimate child.'

'But you liked her, Matt? You really *liked* her?'

'They were both very kind to me – tremendously kind – and *so* pleased to see me! Alice is on the large side, but my mother is rather frail. Like a bird. But they are both very quiet, very withdrawn people. I suppose that's because of the way they have had to live – with this so-called shame hanging over them.'

'Well . . .' She shrugged, lost for words.

'She asked me to call her Violet.'

Connie's sherry went down the wrong way and she coughed. Matt leaned across and patted her back. Then

199

his fingers strayed to her neck and she felt the familiar frisson as he touched her ear.

'Don't!' she said sharply.

'Because we're cousins? Or because you don't like it?'

'Both.' To hide her nervousness she fetched the sherry bottle and refilled their glasses. 'And what did you find out about your father?'

'Nothing really. That was the sad part. She has obviously been very badly hurt and she won't talk about him – except to say that he deserted her when she discovered she was pregnant. But there was a photograph of him which Alice showed me on the QT, and he was a handsome devil. The funny thing is I had always believed that Father was my father – if you see what I mean. I supposed he had had an affair with another woman, and that maybe she had died and so Mother had to agree to take me in. I thought that would explain why neither of them liked me very much. And now I find out that it wasn't Father after all.'

'Don't you even know his name? Or what he did for a living? Wouldn't she tell you anything?'

He hesitated and she was suddenly contrite, realizing she sounded like an inquisitor. 'Don't tell me if you don't want to.'

'His first name was Archie. She wouldn't say any more. He was a surveyor of some kind and he travelled a lot. Alice told me that.'

Connie felt a flash of inspiration. 'Maybe his second name was Matthews! So she called you Matthew. Archie Matthews. Rather nice.'

The doorbell rang and Connie frowned. 'I'm not expecting anyone,' she said, rising reluctantly to her feet. 'I do hope it isn't anyone from the library.'

Matt said, 'Get rid of them – whoever they are.'

Something in his tone made her glance at his face and, fleetingly, there was a harshness which disturbed her. It was gone almost immediately, to be replaced by a smile.

'Sorry, Connie. That was out of order. It's just that I wanted to have you all to myself. Selfish of me.'

As she went to the door she found herself wanting to believe him. How wonderful it would be to have Matt admiring her again. She would like that – as long as *she* was in control. Not like before, when she was desperate for his attention. She squirmed at the memory.

She opened the door and found herself face to face with Del Farrar. 'Del!'

He raised his eyebrows. 'That doesn't sound too welcoming. Is this a bad time to call? You said "any time at all" and I guess I took it at face value.'

She began to stammer, uncertain what to do. Matt would be furious if she allowed Del to join them, but on the other hand she had been longing for him to call round. 'Del! I – it's just that I have someone with me – my brother – at least he isn't . . .' If she took Del in, Matt might be rude to him. Probably *would* be. She couldn't risk that.

He shrugged lightly. 'It's no problem, Connie. I won't stay, I bought you these as a "Thank you".' He produced a large box of chocolates.

'For what?'

'For matching me up with Westrop. He's found me an editor who's very interested.' His smile broadened. 'I think you know her – it's your sister, Fran.'

Connie felt her face stiffen with shock. 'Fran? Your editor?'

'She hopes to be. It's early days, but she's already given me some help.'

She accepted the chocolates and stared down at the box. A picture of three kittens decorated the lid. Connie felt like crying. Here was a golden opportunity to spend time alone with Del and Matt had made it impossible. Inwardly she cursed Matt, the absent Violet and Fate.

He said, 'Fran certainly knows her stuff. What she says makes a lot of sense.'

Connie imagined a slight note of reproof. 'I didn't suggest Fran,' she began, 'because – well, because it seemed too obvious.' She searched around for a way to sound more convincing. 'I thought I should let Westrop decide. I knew, of course, that there was a very good chance he would send it to Starr Massey. I – I hoped he would . . .'

'That's OK. I'm real pleased.' He thrust his hands into his pockets and glanced down the street.

He was leaving and Connie panicked. She could imagine him with Fran, their heads close together over his wretched manuscript. How ironic that Westrop should have chosen Starr Massey! Against her better judgement she said, 'Look, do come in. Matt's only popped in for a quick chat. He'll be going soon and then we can talk. I could conjure up a bit of dinner—'

He hesitated. 'Are you sure I'm not interrupting anything? I could take us out for a meal – I guess Maidstone runs to a decent restaurant.'

She said a little too eagerly. 'There's the Star in the High Street.' A meal with Del was infinitely more appealing than one with Matt; she would risk a scene. 'Come in.' She held the door open, committed now to her course of action, wondering if she could possibly dismiss Matt. It would be too awful if Del decided to include Matt out of politeness – although dining out with *two* men would do her reputation no harm. She hung up Del's coat and led the way into the lounge where Matt was sitting forward in his chair. One glance at his face showed her that he had overheard everything.

'Matt,' she said with a cheerfulness she did not feel. 'You know Del Farrar, don't you? You met at Mother's funeral.'

Del said, 'Hi there!' and held out a hand which Matt pointedly ignored. 'I was sorry to hear about your sister Mary.'

Matt gave him a strange look. 'Mary? Yes. I couldn't get to the funeral.'

Connie said quickly, 'Poor Matt had a fall. He still has a bit of a limp.'

'That's tough.'

'Do sit down, Del.' She was still fearful that he would leave.

He hesitated and Connie looked at Matt with an unspoken appeal. 'Del has come round to talk about his novel. I said you were—'

Matt stood up. 'I heard what you said. I know when I'm not wanted.' He laughed to suggest that this was a joke, but Connie sensed his resentment. He looked at Del. 'She's doing rather well this evening. Flowers *and* chocolates.' He glanced meaningfully at the vase of carefully arranged flowers.

'They're terrific,' said Del. He was still standing, undecided.

Connie put in, 'Matt was just saying that he couldn't stay—'

'Was I?' He gave her an unfathomable look. 'I thought we were going out to dinner.'

Connie felt her face flame, but immediately Del held up both hands in a gesture of mock surrender. 'Hey, look. I'm not going to intrude.' To Connie he said, 'I'll drop by some other time and we'll have that dinner.' He smiled at Matt. 'I can see you two have things to say to each other. I'm sorry I barged in.' He moved towards the door and Connie was forced to follow him into the hall, her cheeks burning. Damn Matt! All her earlier, kindly emotions had been swept away, to be replaced by a familiar bitterness. She saw Del out and returned to face Matt who was still standing.

'There was no need for that—' she began.

'His trouble is he gives up too easily!'

'He was just being polite.'

'Or else he was glad for an excuse to back out.'

'That is so like you, Matt. Not content with spoiling my evening – he was going to take me to the Star.' She sat down heavily, defeated and near to tears.

'How do you know *I* wasn't going to take you there?'

'I don't *want* to go with you.' She knew she was being childish but couldn't help herself. Matt brought out the worst in her. 'You haven't changed at all, Matt, mother or no mother. I'd like you to go,' she said, her gaze fixed on her twisting fingers. 'I should have had more sense than to let you talk me round. Go, Matt. Just go.'

He seemed undecided, she thought miserably. She began to wish he'd taken offence and swept out, leaving her with Del Farrar. Then she could have explained away his bad behaviour and they could have dined out.

'I wanted us to be friends, Connie. I came here to try to convince you that that's possible. We can put the past behind us if only you'd let it happen.'

His words hardly registered as Connie struggled with her disappointment. 'It doesn't matter,' she said. 'I don't care about us.'

'It matters to me, Connie. All this bad feeling – it depresses me, if you must know. We're none of us getting any younger and—'

'Oh, for heaven's sake! That old chestnut!' She stared at him furiously. Now she would spend the evening alone, the way she always did.

He went on, ignoring her rudeness. 'I know you meant to hurt me with that letter but you didn't. Quite the reverse, in fact. When I explain about the visit you'll see why I'm willing to forgive and forget.'

She lifted her gaze to meet his, puzzled by his persistence. How could it matter so much to him?

'I wanted to be with *him*,' she muttered, 'not you.'

He refused to rise to the bait. 'Just imagine – a happy ending to all this bitterness.'

'Happy?' she challenged. 'How can any of us be happy with poor Mary hardly cold in her grave?'

That shocked him, she thought with grim satisfaction. That gave him pause for thought.

His eyes flickered briefly. 'Nothing will bring Mary back, Connie. It hurts me as much as it hurts the rest of you. Mary dying like that made me think how short life can be, and how suddenly it can end. It could happen to any one of us. Your life could be over by this time next year. Or mine. Or Fran's. Illness. Accident.'

'Very comforting!'

'I mean it. While we do still have time we could be a little happier; could become a little closer. Families need each other.'

Suddenly he crouched down in front of her, that unfathomable expression on his face again. 'Let's make a fresh start, Connie. Come out to dinner with me. What have you got to lose?'

Just for a moment Connie wavered. The Star beckoned with its soft carpets, intimate tables, small fringed wall-lights. She would have a decent meal. But afterwards? He would insist on seeing her home and would then want a nightcap and then what? He would probably ask to stay overnight and that would be fatal. He would be there in the morning and would see her at her worst. She couldn't bear that. No, she didn't want him in the flat again. True, she would then miss the intriguing details about his mother, but there was always a price to pay.

'Connie?'

Her mouth tightened. He had ruined her chance of an

evening with Del even though he knew how much it meant to her. Anyone else would have taken the hint, but that was so like Matt. The very least she could do was deny him her company.

'I'd rather not,' she told him. 'I think I'll have an early night. You'd better get a train back to London.' She avoided his eyes.

'So you're throwing me out?'

'If you like to put it that way – yes!'

'You'll be sorry,' he told her.

'I'll be the judge of that.'

Matt stood up. 'I'll see you soon,' he said and walked out of the room. After a moment she heard him slam the front door.

'No, you won't!' she said vehemently. 'Not if I see you first!'

*

The following day, in Bayfield Road, Poppy stood inside her bedroom, waiting for her lodger to come downstairs on his way to work. He came down slowly with an occasional grunt of pain. When he was nearly at the bottom she stepped out, allowing her negligée to swing open revealing the matching nightdress which clung to her a little more tightly than she would have wished.

'Matt!' she said breathily. 'I hoped I would catch you. I wanted to ask if I could hang some new curtains in your room while you're out. They're green and rather pretty. Floral. The old ones really are too shabby. I think you deserve better.' She smiled, her head on one side.

'Well . . .' He seemed unwilling. 'Couldn't it wait until I get home? Then I could help you with them.'

She shook her head. 'I put the last ones up all on my lonesome. I'm not helpless, you know. I was going to hang them for you, as a surprise, but then I thought, No, better ask him. It will only take ten minutes.'

'Fine, then. You'll have to excuse me.'

She blew him a kiss. He really was rather a sweetie, and with a little bit of luck she would soon have him eating out of her hand – and doing other things! But she must be sure he had no other women in his life, and to do that she needed to have a look round his room.

As soon as he had gone she washed and dressed and, taking her spare key, hurried up to his room with the green curtains over her arm. For days she had thought of nothing else except Matt Massey and had given her imagination full reign. It was seven years since she had had a man in her bed, but she had a good memory. If she played her cards right, Matt Massey was going to fill the void in her life. And he would do that exceptionally well. For a start, he was much younger than George had been. Not that she wanted to be unkind, but George had been bald and a bit on the tubby side – and hardly an adventurous lover. His idea of romance was a quick fumble under the blanket and then bang, bang! All over in a twinkling. Still, he had been generous. Had bought her the negligée and a crocodile handbag . . .

She stepped into her lodger's room and was taken aback to see how untidy it was. At least George had been a tidy man. The bed was unmade and she crossed the room and threw herself face down into it, inhaling deeply. Then she turned on to her back and reached up with her arms, pretending that Matt was lowering himself on to her.

'Darling!' she whispered, closing her eyes. He would be a better lover than George. Matt was the new generation and they had none of their father's inhibitions, if the reports in the newspapers were anything to go by. Sitting up, she noticed his paisley pyjamas and, with a smile, clutched them to her chest. Then she folded them carefully and put them under the pillow. He would know she had done it! A little reminder of what was on offer. Crossing to the dressing table, she examined herself in the tarnished glass of the swing mirror, allowing a naughty smile to play around her lips.

'Matt Massey, I *want* you!' she told him.

Better have a quick look in all the drawers; that's where most people kept their letters. And their *French letters*! She giggled. It would be reassuring to know he was prepared. If he had never had an older woman she would teach him a few tricks.

'Matt Massey,' she said, enjoying the sound of his name. 'Matthew Massey. Mr Matthew Massey.'

One by one she pulled open the various drawers and rummaged carefully amongst the clothes without disturbing them. Handkerchiefs with his initial on them. A couple of sleeveless pullovers, shirts, collars, cufflinks. Pants, long-sleeved vests, socks and ties. Terrible ties! Maybe she would give him a tie for his birthday, whenever that was. Come to think of it, she had two ties which George had left behind. She might give him those. Set the ball rolling, so to speak. The contents of the drawers were disappointing. Nothing very exciting. Not like George's dirty magazines. They had been *dreadful*! Still, some men seemed to need those sorts of things. And no French letters. That was a shame. Not that it mattered much at her age. Nearly fifty. She wasn't likely to fall now . . . She pulled open the drawer at the bottom of the wardrobe and was finally rewarded for her persistence. One letter from someone called Dot, and another from Mary. That must be the one who had jumped over a cliff or whatever. How did it go? Did she fall or was she pushed? There was also a small box containing an opal ring. Poppy felt a thrill of anticipation. She slipped the ring on to her finger and admired the effect.

'Oh, darling!' she whispered. 'I can't take it. I mustn't – oh well, then. If you insist!'

Giggling with delight, she returned to the mirror, moving

her beringed hand gracefully to and fro to see how it looked. Perhaps it had belonged to a wife – he had once hinted vaguely about a disastrous relationship. Certainly he never brought a woman to his room but he had explained this by insisting that his work left little time for women. Once bitten, he had said. Poor lamb! Still, if he played his cards right she would make it up to him. Reluctantly she replaced the ring in the box. She was not much older than him, really. Well, maybe ten years, give or take a few. He could be anything from thirty-five to forty-five. Anyway, some men preferred older women.

In the last drawer she found a sandalwood box. Wrapped in a scarf, it was pushed right to the back of the drawer. Lifting the tiny metal catch, she discovered rows of coloured butterflies pinned to a blue velvet base.

'Ugh!' She managed not to drop the box. She had an aversion to small things that fluttered and now fought down her initial distaste. They were beautiful and they no longer fluttered, but they were dead and the smell of sandalwood mixed with a hint of something else made her nostrils flare briefly. She had once watched her uncle killing some butterflies in his chloroform jar, gazing with horrified fascination as the poor creatures fluttered desperately to escape their death. She had begged him to let them go, but he had only laughed at her. He had murdered them, and she had never felt the same about him after that. As she stared at the butterflies she noticed a scrap of paper protruding slightly at one edge. Carefully she lifted out the velvet base and found a few cuttings from a newspaper about the sister who had died. Reading them with interest, she suddenly drew her brows together. Wasn't that the day . . . She stared at the cuttings. The twenty-ninth. Yes, that was the day Matt had gone to Birmingham on business. He'd been most emphatic about it. Going on about how he hated Birmingham and how bad the traffic was, and how there was nowhere to park a car. Funny how he had kept on about it. Go on the train, then, she'd told him, but he had some reason for needing the car. She particularly remembered because it was her birthday and she had wanted to invite him in for a drink, but he had said he'd be too late back. All the way to Birmingham in that tinpot car of his. 'It'll overheat,' she'd told him. Blow a gasket or whatever it was cars did. Just pulling his leg, really.

Replacing the cuttings and the velvet base, she returned the butterfly box to its hiding place. Then getting carefully to her feet, she stood up. Tom, her marmalade cat, had followed her upstairs and she shooed him out again. Disappointing. Nothing interesting. She had better get on with the curtains. Then she would go down and wash her hair and put in a few curlers. When he came home she wanted to dazzle him. Humming cheerfully she began to take down the old curtains. A labour of love, she told herself with a smile. She had set her sights on Matt Massey and he was not going to slip away.

Chapter Ten

FRAN LOOKED ACROSS THE SMALL table at her companion and hoped that her feelings were not blazingly obvious to every other diner in the restaurant. Del glanced up from his soup and smiled, the slow, heart-wrenching smile that she had already grown to love – to need, in fact.

'Not hungry?' he asked.

She smiled. How could she say that she would rather look at him than do anything else in the world? She would sound like a love-sick calf. So she smiled and began to spoon the delicious leek soup into her mouth. 'Antonio's' chef made the best leek soup she had ever tasted, but today she found it hard to appreciate anything but Del Farrar. And he had kissed her again. She clung to that thought even though it had been nothing more than a 'Thank you' kiss for the faith she had in his work. It had taken her by surprise and somehow she had resisted the urge to throw her arms around his neck and return the kiss with interest. Instead she had smiled shakily, speechless, afraid to assume too much. Maybe to an American a kiss was a more casual affair. Derek Starr had kissed her several times, but in each case she had known exactly what he meant: 'We could take this a stage further. We could have fun.' Unwilling to offer more, Fran had been careful not to encourage him, unwilling to lead him on. She liked Derek and enjoyed his company, but she had never been drawn to him physically. This he had never been able to accept, insisting that eventually she would succumb to his charms. Derek wanted no commitment from the women in his life. An affair, exciting but non-threatening, was what he preferred, and he believed that, with Fran, it was only a matter of time. The relationship had continued in a half-hearted way and lately Fran had heard rumours that he was seeing someone else, an idea which had caused her no concern.

Del Farrar had quite effortlessly swept her off her feet, and her joy was tempered only by the knowledge that his stay in England was temporary. She was also at a disadvantage because she knew so little about him. He had been married – maybe he still was. She had felt unable to ask him and he had volunteered very little. Connie might have been able to offer more information, but Fran shrank from the thought of confiding in her sister, who would immediately recognize the extent of Fran's interest.

She laid down her spoon and became aware that Del was regarding her with amusement.

'You're a million miles away,' he said. 'You didn't hear a word I said. Do I get to know what's going on in that pretty head of yours?'

The light-hearted compliment pleased her enormously, but she felt herself colouring. She was being given an opportunity and suddenly decided to take it. 'I was wondering about you. About – about what you are going home to in America . . . No!' She drew a sharp breath. 'No, that's not quite it, Del. I was wondering *who* is waiting for you.' She swallowed. 'There. I've said it.'

To her dismay the humour abruptly vanished from his eyes and he glanced down at his plate. Fran felt the room darken around her as her short-lived courage evaporated. She had blundered; she had jeopardized whatever was between them by her curiosity – or was it that he was married and didn't want to have to tell her? Desperately she searched for a way to limit the damage, but nothing would unsay the words. As the silence lengthened, the waiter appeared and whisked away the soup plates. She murmured, 'Very nice' in answer to his question and watched silently as he brought the braised beef and an assortment of vegetables. Afraid to look at Del, she accepted the food but wondered how on earth she was going to swallow any of it. Her throat felt dry and she was aware of a dull ache of misery.

When the waiter had left them to their own devices she suddenly saw Del's hand reaching across the tablecloth and, wonderingly, she clasped it as hope flared within her.

'I was putting off the moment,' he told her. 'Cowardly, I know, but I was so afraid – it's going to sound like a bad deal. I don't come out of it too well.' He indicated her plate. 'You eat, Fran. I'll talk.' He pursed his lips thoughtfully. 'I was married – still am. Her name's Lorna – but right from the start we weren't getting along too well. She was very ambitious – a secretary in a law firm, but with prospects. For a woman, she was doing exceptionally well, and I guess I was a little jealous. I could see she was wedded to the job, but I thought she'd be prepared to give it up and start a family. I was struggling in a small law firm but I wanted to write. Lorna persuaded me that if she carried on with her job I would be able to take a shot at writing. I took six months off and—' He threw up his hands despairingly. 'I wrote one hell of a bad story. A real stinker, as you British would say.'

'I'm so sorry,' she said, her throat dry. The words 'Still am' danced in her brain. He was married; she should have known. Somehow she went on eating, tasting nothing.

'I was shattered,' he admitted. 'I was so sure I could do it.' He met her eyes and went on, 'It's not a pretty story, my

213

life to date. Too many mistakes. Too much pride and anger.'
His grey eyes were dark with the admission of defeat.

'Del, we all make mistakes. That's how we learn, isn't it?
I've been less than perfect.'

'Not to me, Fran. I—' He stopped himself in mid-sentence. 'OK. You want the whole sad story?'

Did she, she wondered nervously. 'Only if you want to tell it.'

He ate another mouthful of food and said, 'This is good', but there was no real enthusiasm in his voice. 'OK . . . so I was pretty difficult to live with. I was a failure. But Lorna said to persevere and she would keep her job. I realized why she was so keen: she didn't fancy the earth mother bit. Then she got promotion. I took that badly, too.' His smile was a little twisted. 'Are you getting the picture, Fran?'

'Most men would have felt the same way. You're being very hard on yourself.'

'I tried another novel, but it didn't work. I tried some short stories – then Lorna told me she was . . . was expecting a child. She was furious and blamed me.'

Fran stared at her plate. So he was married with a child? She should have known it was too good to be true, but she felt sick with disappointment.

'Fran?'

She forced herself to meet his gaze. 'I'm listening.'

'We had a son. Robert D. Farrar.' He smiled briefly. 'We called him Rob.'

'And D for Delaware.'

'Right.' His face lit up at the thought of his son. 'I wish you could have known him. He'd be nearly seven if he'd lived.'

If he'd *lived*. Fran's throat contracted.

'He was some kid, Fran. Bright. Sassy. We both adored him. To my surprise Lorna suddenly abandoned the idea of a career and decided she wanted more children. So I was back in another law firm by this time. I'd given up on the writing. I guess we were happy for a while. Then, just before his sixth birthday, he died.'

'Died? Oh, God, Del!' She saw the pain in his eyes. 'How?'

'Diphtheria. The hospital did all they could but he was never a strong child. Never robust. They said his heart gave out.'

'Del!' She searched for words, knowing that there were none. 'I'm so sorry.'

'You know, Fran, it was so strange. It was as though he *knew*. A week before his birthday party was due he asked if he could have it that day – a week early, in fact. We tried to talk him out of it and then Lorna's mother winked at us. She said, "We'll have birthday number one today and birthday number two next week." She set to and baked cookies and stuff. Lorna invited a couple of the neighbours' kids and we had streamers and crackers. He was so thrilled.'

'But how *odd*!'

'Wasn't it just? Two days later he was running a fever and couldn't get his breath. He was taken into the hospital but they couldn't save him. He died the day before his birthday.'

'So he never would have had a birthday party.' Fran shook her head. 'That's incredible.'

He nodded, then sighed deeply. 'First his dying brought us together, but then gradually we drifted apart again. She said she didn't want another child – another "heartbreak", as she called it – and went back to work. Then in October last she told me she was pregnant again, but that I'm not the father; she's been having an affair with one of her colleagues. She moved back to live with her parents. He's determined to marry her, so . . .'

Fran thought she detected regret in his tone and felt a flash of unease. 'Do you want her to stay with you, then?'

'No – but if he'd deserted her I guess I'd have given it one more shot. It's all such a mess. There's this sense of failure. Why couldn't we make it work? Didn't we try hard enough?'

Fran sat silent, selfishly relieved for herself but sad for him.

'So . . . she's divorcing me.'

'Divorcing you? But you did nothing wrong. It's so unfair.'

He shrugged. 'That's the way the system works. I had to go through the usual farce – a private investigator, a strange woman in my room and a photographer waiting outside. It was utterly sordid, not to say stupid. Some day they'll have to change the law. In the meantime we're stuck with it. So we're in the middle of a divorce.' He regarded her soberly. 'Some story, huh?'

It was her turn to reach out a hand and he took it gratefully. 'Thank you for telling me, Del. I shouldn't have pushed you but I – it was important to me. Since it's the time for honesty – I wanted to know if there was any hope for us.'

'I'm not exactly a catch. An awkward S.O.B, according to my wife.'

'An S.O.B? What's that?'

'An awkward son of a bitch.'

'Oh!' She laughed. 'Well, I like you. A lot.'

'And I'm crazy about you!'

She caught her breath. 'Are you?'

Fran counted to ten, unable to believe what was happening. He *did* care about her. 'I have faults, too, you know, Del. Ask Connie. She'll be only too pleased to assassinate my character. And with good cause. I'm touchy, jealous, impatient, a bad loser—'

'Sounds good to me!' He rolled his eyes humorously.

Fran leaned forward earnestly. 'We've both had some

216

bad times. Maybe we're due for some good times. If only you weren't going back to America we could—'

'I have another few weeks. I'm going to Scotland to be best man at my godson's wedding. Top hat and tails stuff.' He grinned. 'Me – in a top hat and morning suit? I shall look like a penguin.'

'You'll look very smart, Del.' She kept her tone light, but Scotland was merely a reprieve. After that, presumably he would go home. She said, 'Maybe I'll come and see you off. I've always wanted to watch a big liner leave Southampton. I'll throw a few streamers and shed a few tears.'

'You could come with me.'

'To America?' She was shocked. America was the other side of the world. America was New York, another publishing industry, the destination of countless messages, numerous telephone calls and letters.

She tried to make the required leap. 'America!' she whispered. But then there was Dot . . . 'I couldn't,' she said reluctantly.

The waiter appeared beside them, looking reproachfully at the half-full plates. 'Was there something wrong?' His tone was accusing.

'No,' Del told him. 'We just aren't hungry.' He glanced at his wristwatch. 'Bring us a couple of coffees, will you? Thanks.'

Fran said, 'I think we failed the test.'

He grinned. 'Never going to get the good diner's badge!'

Fran gazed at him. 'Are we falling in love, do you think?'

'It's beginning to feel like it!'

'Oh, Del!' She felt a surge of unbelievable happiness. 'I can't believe it. Do we deserve to be so happy?'

'Why not? We're not so bad. And we're not hurting anybody.'

As they sipped their coffee Fran suddenly became serious once more. 'I just want to tell you something about me – about my shadowy past.'

'It's no good, Fran. You can't put me off now. It's too late.'

'No, seriously, Del. So that we have no secrets.'

'OK. Go ahead.'

She put down the cup and clasped her hands on the table in front of her. 'I was once in love with Matt. Yes, I know he's one of the family but we were never told who his real parents were. We still don't know. He was always my champion against Connie and the others, and as I grew older I thought I was in love with him. At least I thought I was special to him. Then one day, in a rash moment, I told Connie how I felt – and that I was his favourite. A few weeks later he and Connie suddenly ran away together. I was – I felt betrayed by both of them. In fact I hated them. I was only sixteen at the time. The worst year of my life – until this past year.'

'It's been tough.'

She nodded. 'My parents were frantic with worry. None of us dared mention either Connie or Matt. They set about searching for them, and after a few weeks they traced them to a small town in Dorset. Mother sent Connie a telegram; then Connie telephoned and Mother went flying off to wherever they were.' She frowned at the recollection. 'Mother came back, tight-lipped, and said it was all over. Father forbade us to talk about it, but of course we did. Connie never came home, though. She finally got the job at the library and has lived in Maidstone ever since. She's very good at what she does; she'll go as far as a woman can go in the job.'

'And Matt? Did he come home?'

'No. It was the end of the family – or it felt like it.'

'And do you still love Matt?'

After a slight hesitation she said, 'No. I want to – as a brother, I mean – but I can't. That's another of my faults: I bear a grudge. Hardly the forgiving type, although sometimes . . .' She shook her head. 'I think about Connie. Mother hinted that they'd quarrelled a lot – Connie and Matt, I mean. It must have been awful for her.'

'But why were they so set against Matt?'

She shrugged. 'I don't know. They had never really taken to him. They gave him a home, but they never took him to their hearts. And he was so difficult.' She weighed her words, trying to be fair. 'He wanted to be loved and yet he wasn't lovable. That's why I loved him, I suppose. To make up for the others.'

'Soft-hearted Hannah!'

'Now, of course, I think we're beyond all help of salvation. Matt blames Connie for seducing him and then deserting him. That isolated him from the family.'

'I noticed he didn't come to Mary's funeral.'

'I wondered about that. He claims he had hurt his leg, but that is rather a coincidence. I don't think he wanted to come, but that may be because he wasn't made exactly welcome when Mother was buried. He seems to be slipping further and further away from the Matt I knew as a boy. Maybe I can't see him clearly any more. What did you make of him, Del? As an outsider?'

'You really want to know?'

She nodded, surprised by his serious expression.

He watched her face. 'I see him as a bit of a maverick,' he said slowly. 'A loose cannon. I'm no expert but I'd say there was a lot of repressed anger deep down.

219

Understandable, from what you tell me. Perhaps "unstable" is the best word.'

Fran felt suddenly defensive. 'You obviously don't like him.'

He shrugged. 'I don't know the guy, Fran. Let's just say I'd treat him with kid gloves until I knew him better.'

'Connie claims he was impossible to live with.'

'She should know. Maybe you had a lucky escape.'

'Maybe so. So now you know the Massey family, for better or worse. Some of them, anyway.'

'I didn't get to say much to your brother Henry.'

'Henry's the nicest of us. Cheerful, trusting, totally open-minded, with a very good brain. He wants to join the family firm, of course. He'd be a fool not to.'

'You must miss him now he's at university.'

'Not really. He was away at boarding-school for years.'

He grinned. 'Ah, yes! The English do love their boarding-schools.'

'Henry loved it. Some boys hate it.'

'And Matt?'

'He wasn't sent. He wasn't clever enough – or so Father maintained. He went to school locally.' She fiddled with her table napkin. 'I suppose you think us a strange brood.'

'Not at all.' He laughed. 'I'd say you're a pretty average family! You know what they say – "Open any door"!' He raised his glass. 'A toast to the Massey family!'

Laughing, Fran joined touched her glass to his. 'And God bless all who sail in her!'

Suddenly she glanced at her watch. 'Good heavens! I've got a meeting at two. Monthly sales presentation. I'll have to get a taxi!' She stood up reluctantly. 'I hate to dash away,' she told him. The thought of leaving him, of being without him, was devastating.

He stood up. 'I understand. You go on. I'll finish my coffee and settle the bill.' Abruptly, he took hold of her hands and pulled her gently towards him. Then, in full view of everyone, he put his arms around her and kissed her. 'Oh, Fran!' he whispered. 'I think it just might turn out OK!'

*

The monthly sales meetings took place in the Starr Massey board-room and were important events in the company's calendar. The six sales representatives attended and the various books to be sold during the following month were presented to them. They were thus able to familiarize themselves with the merchandise they would carry to their respective customers, and would be able to talk about the books with reasonable confidence. Nobody underestimated the importance of the sales staff whose job it was to 'sell into' the bookshops. Competition among the different publishers was intense, and booksellers would allow only a small amount of time for each representative.

When Fran hurried into the room, nearly ten minutes late, all heads turned in her direction.

'This is not like you, Miss Massey!' said Marjory, obviously pleased by Fran's late arrival.

Fran looked at the managing director. 'I do apologize. I hope I haven't kept you all waiting.'

'We did wait,' he said, 'but never mind. As Mrs Evans pointed out, it's rare for you to be late.'

With a quick smile at those already seated around the table, Fran took her own seat, mentally reviewing the books that were on today's agenda. She herself was presenting a second novel by James Lucas, a little-known author from Sussex who wrote about an English family living in Portugal. Stuart, she knew, had a book about cricket, written by a former English coach. Marjory was an unknown quantity;

glancing at the typed agenda in front of her she saw that the words 'To be disclosed' had been pencilled in alongside Marjory's name. Derek had finally guided *This Sceptred Isle* (his brain-child) to completion after months of rewrites by its author, Diane Hammel.

With an effort Fran settled in her chair, adopting an air of keen interest, while snippets of her conversation with Del danced excitedly in her mind. Eric Mannering described two additions to their range of gardening books while Fran recalled the look in Del Farrar's grey eyes and the way Del's mouth had felt, pressed briefly against her own. There had been nothing secretive about that kiss. It was for all the world to see . . .

Briefly, Eric Mannering explained why the book on flower arranging had been abandoned. Fran, her mind elsewhere, gathered that the author, an elderly spinster, had been taken ill and was never likely to be well enough to finish the illustrations. Marjory suggested that someone else might finish it but, after a short discussion, the idea was rejected as impracticable.

Stuart in his turn rose to his feet, waving a copy of *How's That*! The sales force leafed through their folders.

'This book is going to be our lead non-fiction for February,' he told them, a touch of pride in his voice. 'There is a reasonable publicity budget and we are taking space in the Sunday nationals. The BBC is going to feature an interview with the author – date to be fixed, but within two days of publication.'

One of the representatives raised his hand. 'It's a bit expensive, isn't it? Three shillings and sixpence!'

'It is and it isn't –' Stuart began, and as he started to justify the price Fran allowed herself to drift away again. Del had said he thought it would be 'OK'. What had he meant exactly, she wondered. That eventually they might be together? Was he really thinking that far ahead? Was he as crazy as she was?

'Miss Massey!'

Fran realized with a start that they were all looking at her. Stuart said, 'I'm just saying that it compares favourably with the book you did last year on tennis. That did very well, didn't it?'

'Oh, yes!' Guiltily she racked her brain for details of the book. 'It did very well, although it was expensive – but we had a lot of photographs in it. We brought it out the week before Wimbledon; the timing was good and the libraries loved it.'

Stuart said, 'They're going to like this one, too. I can assure you of that.' He turned to Eric Mannering. 'I think we're doing a run of three thousand.'

'You think?'

'I mean, the last time I heard anything it was three.'

Marjory said 'Three. Yes – with another thousand if it's warranted.'

Stuart sat down and Marjory looked enquiringly at Derek Starr, who after a quick glance at his agenda stood up and cleared his throat.

'*This Sceptred Isle* is going to be the first of many,' he told them. 'Diane Hammel has proved herself to be a major storyteller.' Marjory whispered something to the man next to her and Derek gave her a sharp look. 'Yes, I know it was overdue, but that's to the author's credit. She wanted to be completely satisfied that she had written the best book she could manage and I, for one, am delighted with the results. Diane Hammel, as you probably already know, is distantly related to Priestwell—'

Stuart called out, 'How distant, exactly?' Everyone laughed.

'We've asked him if he'll read it and maybe give us a quote.'

Fran relaxed a little. These meetings could be, and often

were, difficult occasions, and it needed something to break the ice. She took a mouthful of water from her glass and her stomach rumbled. Too late, she wished she had eaten more of her lunch, but the conversation had been too engrossing. They had bared their souls, she reflected, and that was good although some of the things she had learned had left her feeling slightly uneasy. Del was still married. At any moment his wife could change her mind and decide to give their relationship another try. It sounded unlikely if she was now expecting another man's child, but suppose she did? Would Del feel under any obligation to her? She might lose the baby . . .

'Miss Massey? Are you with us?'

She rose hastily to her feet, fumbling for her notes, aware of the amused looks that were being exchanged by her colleagues. Fran prided herself on her efficiency, and they must all be wondering about her obvious confusion. Well, let them wonder, she thought rebelliously, but she tried hard to put Del Farrar out of her mind. She owed that to her author.

'Mr Lucas has given us a worthy successor to his two earlier novels in this series,' she began and launched into a résumé of the plot. As she went on, her enthusiasm grew. James Lucas was a scholarly man, an ex-professor of history, a gentleman. His novels were set in the early part of the century when most of the English were settling in the north of Portugal alongside the wine trade. The Fenwicks, Mr Lucas's fictitious family, lived in Oporto and ran a small horse farm.

'Are we holding down the price?'

Kenneth Starr's usual query. Fran smiled sympathetically. A few pennies on the price of a book sent the booksellers into a spin.

'Exactly the same as last year,' she assured him.

After a few more questions she sat down, aware that

she had done a good job. Almost immediately, Kenneth Starr began to talk about plans for the following autumn and specifically the International Book Fair held annually in Leipzig. Fran thought about Matt and what Del had said about him. Was he unstable? She tried to be fair. Possibly he always had been. A loose cannon – liable to roll around the deck and blast off indiscriminately? She wanted to give him the benefit of the doubt, but she frowned unhappily. There *was* a doubt. Guiltily she admitted to herself that since Mary's death there would always be a doubt, no matter how unfair that was. If only he had come to the funeral ... What else had Del said? Oh, yes! 'All that repressed anger'. Poor Matt! She tried to envisage a happy future for him, with a loving wife and children. She was still trying when the meeting came to an end and, as she made her way back to her office, the picture remained determinedly elusive.

*

When Fran reached home that evening, she found Dot in a state of great exhilaration.

'I answered the telephone,' she told Fran, her eyes wide with excitement. 'It rang and it rang and I waited for Annie, and then she didn't answer it and then it stopped, and then she still didn't come and it rang again and I answered it!'

Fran smiled. 'Well done, you!'

Dot beamed. 'Fritz wanted me to answer it.'

'He's a very knowing dog.'

'Yes, he is.' She danced ahead of Fran into the lounge. 'When Annie came back I told her and she said she was in the garden, trying to find a decent cabbage—'

'Who was it?' asked Fran, sinking on to the sofa and reaching for *The Times*.

Dot faltered in her account. 'Who was what?'

'Who was it on the telephone?'

'Oh!' Dot clapped a hand to her mouth. 'I forget.'

Just then Annie came in with a tray of tea. 'You're early,' she remarked, setting down the tray.

'I couldn't settle after the sales meeting, so I brought some work home with me. Dot says she took a telephone call but she can't remember who it was.'

Annie's expression changed. 'Oh, she did. While I was out. She insists it was about birds. I couldn't make head nor tale of it.'

Fran paused, the cup half-way to her lips, looking at Dot.

'That's right,' said Dot. 'It *was* about birds. I remember now.'

'And?' Fran prompted gently.

'And . . .' Dot screwed up her eyes.

Annie said, 'You've been told to write things down if you answer the phone.'

'I forgot.' Dot looked stricken.

'Never mind,' said Fran. 'Try to remember what it was about.'

Slowly Dot sat down, her face screwed up with the effort of recall. 'About the bird-watcher,' she said at last. 'The man watching the birds. He saw something; he saw the car and – oh, dear!'

'Which car, Dot?' Fran's heart had quickened its beat. 'Take your time, now. Nobody's cross with you.'

Finally Dot said, 'It was the police.'

Fran and Annie exchanged startled looks. 'Was this the police at Hastings, Dot?'

'Yes!' Dot's expression cleared magically. 'That's right! At Hastings. It was a man watching the birds.'

Fran rose to her feet. 'I'd better ring them,' she said.

Annie was trying to hide her alarm as she sipped her tea, blowing on it because it was still too hot.

Fran said to Dot, 'Wait here, with Annie. Drink your tea.'

'But Fritz wants to know about the bird man.'

Annie shook her head. 'Fritz is fast asleep,' she said, 'so let's leave him out of this.'

Fran hurried out into the hallway and looked up the number. The sergeant to whom she spoke was reassuringly casual.

'We just thought you might like to know that we had a follow-up on the accident. A man came forward yesterday. A Mr Albert Grainger; a bird-watcher. You know the type – beard and binoculars. Spends a lot of time at Fairlight, apparently. He's been away and only just heard about the accident. He saw a young couple in a car and then a bit later saw them walking down towards the Lovers' Seat. Grainger was lying down amongst the gorse bushes, out of sight of the birds. He doesn't think they saw him. They were laughing, he said, and the man had his arm round her. That's all really. But it confirms what we thought – an accident and a man panicking.'

Fran took a deep breath and let it out slowly. Stay calm, she told herself.

'Are you still there?' he asked.

'Yes. I'm just thinking. Did he give a description of the man?'

'Only that he was dark-haired and a bit taller than her – your sister. This chap was quite a way off when he saw them.'

'What was he wearing? Did he say?'

'Didn't notice.'

'But he was using binoculars.'

'True. But remember, he wasn't particularly interested. Not the sort that spies on courting couples; not the peeping Tom type. You get a nose for these things. He was looking for our fine, feathered friends. He's not a suspect if that's

227

what you're thinking. Not by a long chalk. Why should he risk his neck by coming forward since it's all over bar the shouting?'

'Did he describe the car?'

'Only to say it had yellow wheels and it was dark. Blue or black or brown, maybe, but darkish.'

'Did he know the make?'

'Sorry, no. You know these scientists! They're only interested in one thing, and in his case it's birds. He could tell you the difference between a robin and a blackbird, but not between a Jowitt and a Ford! So – just thought you'd like to know. Set your mind at ease. No quarrels. No fights. Just happy.'

'So you're not going to try and find the man – the one who was with Mary?'

'We haven't got enough to go on, I'm afraid. It's not as though it's a murder investigation. Accidental death, that's it. If I were you, Miss, I'd try to accept it. Nothing can bring her back. Don't dwell on the pros and cons. Believe me, it's easier in the long run. I've been in the force a long time, Miss. You can cause yourself a lot of unnecessary suffering, one way and another. Best let it go.'

'Well, maybe you're right. I'll try. And thank you.' She hung up, staring into space.

Annie looked up as she went back into the lounge, and Dot said eagerly, 'What *about* the birds?'

'It was a bird-watcher; a Mr Grainger. He saw Mary with the man in the car and again walking together.' She sat down. 'He had his arm round her apparently. The policeman said they looked happy.' She looked at Annie. 'They'll never find this man. We'll never really know, will we?'

Annie considered this. 'Even if they find him, we'll only know what he tells us. He might not tell us the truth. Is that all they had to say?'

'He had dark hair and was taller than Mary. The car was a dark colour with yellow wheels.'

Annie sighed. 'At least this man Grainger was an honest citizen. He came forward. Lots of people in his position would have decided to say nothing.'

Dot said, 'So it *wasn't* about birds.'

'Not exactly.' Fran shrugged. 'I daresay he's right. The policeman says it's best to accept the accident theory rather than go on harbouring suspicions.' She shrugged. 'Nothing will bring Mary back.'

Annie said slowly, 'At least she is at peace in the hereafter, wherever that may be. She's at rest. Whatever happens here, nothing can touch her now.'

'If only she could talk to us!' Fran studied her hands. 'I keep willing her to come to me in my dreams. It can happen that way, that people are told things. Stranger things have been known.' She was thinking of Del's little boy and the birthday parties. Suddenly she stood up. 'I think I'll drop this man a note to thank him for coming forward. I'll send it care of the police.' Seeing Dot's downcast face, she forced a smile. 'And then, if you like, we'll take Fritz for a walk.'

'He'd like that,' said Dot.

Chapter Eleven

S COTTIE WAS MAKING HIS WAY home with a
little difficulty. It was nearly eight o'clock and already
dark, with heavy rain and a nasty wind. He knew from
bitter experience that by the time he had cycled the three
miles to his home, he would be wet through. He'd drunk
several pints of The Feathers' best stout and was feeling a
bit under the weather. Well, maybe he'd drunk four or five,
but who was counting? As the bike wobbled from side to
side Scottie cursed. He wished he'd never set eyes on Wally
Street, who always talked him into 'just one more'.

'Whoa!' he cried in alarm as the bike ran on to the
grass verge and threatened to tip him off into the ditch.
The trouble with bikes was that they weren't horses and
couldn't find their own way home. You knew where you
were with horses – at least Scottie did. He'd worked with
them most of his life until the farmer had bought himself
a tractor. 'Don't expect me to drive that ruddy thing,' he'd
said, and he'd refused point-blank. Noisy, smelly things! He'd
sat on it once and it had scared him to bits, shaking his liver
and God knows what else. He'd like to meet the man who
invented tractors. He'd tell him where to shove it!

'Not long now,' he told himself. 'Just hang on a bit and
you'll be home and dry.'

Alfred Scott was cycling to his home just outside Cambridge. He was cycling without lights because he had coins jingling in his pocket and three rabbits in a bag slung over his shoulder. That is to say, three *poached* rabbits, caught on the old colonel's land. Not that the old boy would miss them – he had hundreds, mean old skinflint. But Norris had been warned to look out for him. 'A thieving bastard' – that's what the colonel had called Scottie. Nice language for a so-called gentleman. Scottie had bagged five rabbits altogether which was a decent haul for a night's work. Two of the rabbits had already found a home. May Berry, the landlord's missus, was always willing. Her old father loved rabbit pie and May knew better than to ask questions. Especially if Norris, the gamekeeper, was in the snug. May was smart, she was. 'Got a couple of *marrows* for me?' she'd say, with a wink behind Norris's back.

'Marrows!' He laughed throatily. Old Norris would have to spark up his ideas if he wanted to get the better of Alfred Scott.

The seven o'clock bus from Cambridge passed him, throwing muddy water all over the right leg of his corduroys.

'Road-hog!' Scottie shouted, but the effort made the bike wobble and he watched in a resentful silence as the bus slowed to a halt at the stop, a few hundred yards further on. Wiping the rain from his face, Scottie peered through the gloom suspiciously and wobbled to a standstill. It never was wise to meet folk when you had three rabbits about your person.

'Now who's that when he's at home?' he muttered, seeing a man alight from the bus and stand indecisively, as though unsure which way to go. For a moment the lights from the vehicle illuminated him, just long enough for Scottie to see that he was a stranger. Then the bus disappeared into the night, leaving it darker than before. Dismounting, Scottie wheeled his bike slowly towards the man who, on closer inspection, proved to be young-ish.

'Oh, aye,' he said, seeing the brightly coloured scarf. 'One of them bally students!'

Reassured he went towards him, intending to offer his help if the young man was lost. He'd never understood why they'd put the bus stop there. Nobody lived within a mile of it in either direction. Daft, really, but that was the council for you. Or the government. They all liked to waste taxpayers' money.

He was within hailing distance of the stranger when he became aware of a car approaching from behind him, driving at a reckless speed towards them. The headlights dazzled him and he shouted, 'Hey!' but the car kept coming.

'What the blazes—!'

Scottie's instinct for self-preservation was a strong one and without thinking twice about it he threw himself into the hedge, abandoning his bike to its fate. As he fought off the brambles he heard a brisk crunch of metal and then the squeal of wheels as the car swerved. It regained direction and swept on. There was a shout and a thud, but by the time Scottie had crawled from the ditch the noise of the car's engine had faded and the road was silent again.

Badly shaken, Scottie stood up, relieved that his legs still functioned and that he seemed to be in one piece.

'Well, damn that for a ruddy lark!' he said, but the trembling voice sounded unfamiliar and he felt worse instead of better. He put a shaking hand to his face, aware for the first time of the scratches inflicted by the hedge. He was wet and cold and horribly sober. After a search he found his bike, its rear wheel mangled.

'Bloody hell!' he muttered and shook his fist in the direction the car had taken. 'Maniac!' The man who had invented the motor car ought to be shot, he reflected sourly.

Abruptly he remembered the young student. 'Did you see that lunatic?' he cried, but there was no reply and Scottie remembered the thud he had heard. 'Oh, no!' he muttered and shouted, 'You there, old lad?' The ensuing silence was broken by a faint sound, a groan of pain.

Scottie said, 'Christ! He's hurt!'

Stumbling cautiously forward in the darkness, he finally located a crumpled figure at the roadside and rushed to kneel beside him. The man's leg was bent awkwardly and he was face down in the muddy grass.

'Are you hurt?' he asked. Bloody silly question, but it was all he could think of. 'Speak to me. Say something, for Pete's sake!'

He ought to do something, but nothing in his life had prepared him for this moment. Vague ideas about first aid entered Scottie's head and, clumsily, he tried to straighten the twisted leg. An anguished groan rewarded his efforts and he hastily decided to leave well alone.

'Jesus!' Scottie looked at him helplessly. Then he had a small brainwave which momentarily restored his self-confidence. He ran back to his bike, detached the light and hurried back to the victim.

'Now let's take a look-see,' he muttered.

In the light from the torch the blood showed up quite clearly as it ran from a large gash in the young man's head. Scottie gave a yelp of fright. He must get an ambulance or a doctor – or maybe a policeman. But on this quiet stretch of road there was never much traffic. He leaned forward. 'Don't worry, old son. I'll get you some help. Couple of ticks and you'll be tucked up in the hospital, right as ninepence!'

He stood up and then his face brightened as he heard a car approaching from the direction taken by the bus. Stepping into the middle of the road Scottie waved his arms frantically and yelled 'Stop!'

To his relief the car slowed obediently to a halt. A man wound down the window and asked, 'What's wrong?'

'This lad's been knocked down. Some crazy, bloody fool—'

'Is he dead?'

Scottie shrugged. 'Pretty near,' he told him. 'He soon will be if we don't get him to a doctor—'

The driver ducked his head back inside the car and revved the engine.

'Oi!' Scottie stared in disbelief. 'What's your game? Come back here!'

But the car had driven off at speed.

'Jesus O'Riley! Of all the—' Scottie shook his head. 'Some people!'

He knelt once more beside the injured man and very gently turned him over so that he faced upwards. 'You just keep your pecker up, old son. I'll get some help. Not long now.' There was no reply, not even a groan, and Scottie suddenly felt a cold sweat break out on his skin. This man might be dying, and he felt somehow responsible for him. Ignoring the cold rain, he took off his coat, folded it clumsily into a pillow and gently laid it under the young man's head. 'Just you lie there and take it easy.' Jesus! What else could the poor blighter do? He felt ashamed of his lack of imagination.

'You're going to be OK.'

But would he be? He might have broken bones. He might be bleeding to death. Scottie stepped out into the road once more and waited, shivering and unhappy, for the arrival of a motorist with more heart than the last one.

*

Twenty minutes later the young student was being wheeled into the X-ray department in Addenbrooke's Hospital and the operating theatre was being prepared for immediate surgery. A houseman and a nurse were anxiously awaiting the arrival of a surgeon who an hour earlier had left the hospital, intending to attend his brother's stag night. A policeman with a notebook was writing down everything Scottie could tell him about the accident, and three rabbits lay sodden and forgotten in a muddy ditch.

*

The next day was Thursday, February the ninth. Fran was working at home, so she had allowed herself the luxury of a late start and was still in her dressing gown when the taxi arrived. Tutting with annoyance, she went to the window.

'It's *Connie!*' she muttered and her irritation was tempered by unease. She hesitated, wondering whether to rush upstairs and dress. But if Connie was ringing her doorbell at nine thirty-five in the morning it must be urgent. She tightened her dressing-gown cord and went to open the door, thankful that Annie and Dot had gone to Canterbury for a day's shopping. One look at Connie's face told her the news was not something she would welcome.

Connie pulled off her coat and removed her hat. She was very pale and Fran could sense her agitation.

'Something has happened!' she began breathlessly, hurrying into the lounge without waiting to be invited, and Fran followed her in. Connie gave a nervous glance round the room and then sat down heavily on the sofa. 'It's Henry. It's awful and—' She broke off. 'Is Dot likely to come barging in?'

'No. She and Annie have gone to Canterbury.'

'Good. There's been an accident, although—'

'An accident? Another one?'

'Yes.' She looked at Fran with an expression of desperation.

'Oh, God, Fran! I've got to tell you something.' She put a hand to her head. 'I feel ill with worry. I'm beginning to think . . .'

Fran sat down on an adjacent chair and told herself not to panic. 'Did you say Henry? What kind of accident?'

'A road accident. He's still alive but –' She began to tremble. 'I can hardly breathe, my chest feels so tight.' She began to gasp for air and Fran's panic returned.

'Would you like a drink? You look terrible.'

'Yes, please. A large brandy.'

'I meant tea but . . .' Her own heart was beginning to beat erratically. 'Is Henry – oh Connie, you're sure he's not—'

'No, he's not dead. Yet.' Connie covered her face with her hands and took several deep breaths.

Fran hurried to pour them each a drink. 'Here – sip it slowly. Take your time.' She counted to ten then could wait no longer. 'Now tell me what's happened.' She took a gulp of her own brandy and waited apprehensively. First Mary and now Henry?

Connie took a deep breath and drained her brandy in one gulp. Fumbling in her pocket for a handkerchief, she failed to find one and uncharacteristically wiped her mouth with the back of her hand. 'The police came this morning. A detective inspector. It seems they've put two and two together and they're worried.'

'But Henry? How bad is it?'

'I'm coming to that. Let me tell it my own way, Fran. You always do butt in.'

'Sorry.' Fran tried to restrain her impatience.

'Henry was knocked down by a car yesterday evening. There was a witness who saw it happen. I forget his name, but he saw it all; he says the car's headlights were blazing and he *must* have seen the man. It was deliberate, in other words.'

Fran met her glance and saw her own suspicions mirrored

in Connie's eyes. Knocked down deliberately? She could not trust herself to speak and waited for Connie to continue.

'Henry is very ill. He's in the neurosurgical ward with serious head injuries, and he's also got a fractured pelvis and a broken leg.'

'Oh, my God! Poor Henry!'

Connie held out her glass for a refill.

'Connie! Is this going to help?'

'Let me worry about that.' While she watched Fran pour another brandy Connie said, 'After what happened to Mary I'm sure they're suspicious. The policeman as good as said so. It's a bit of a coincidence, and if you count in Mother that's three of us!' She took the glass, gulped a large mouthful and then clutched the glass to her with both hands. 'The detective inspector – his name's Bruce, by the way – said they are in discussion with the police at Hastings. He asked me if I knew of anyone with a reason to . . . to hate us.'

There was a silence which lengthened uncomfortably. Then Fran said, 'And do we?'

Connie took another mouthful of brandy. 'I couldn't answer that but – oh, Fran, I'm scared.'

Fran frowned. 'But why? Who are you scared of? Nobody *hates* us, do they? Hate is a very strong word.' She tried not to think what she *was* thinking.

Connie said, 'I have to tell you something; something awful.'

'Oh, no!' Fran felt a chill sweep through her.

'Mother told me something about Matt and said I was never to repeat it; she made me promise. It was when Matt and I were together. She told me about his mother. Aunt Violet – she's his mother. That's one of the reasons why I left him. We're cousins.'

'Aunt Violet?' Fran was stunned by the revelation. 'And his father?'

237

'She didn't mention his father.'

'Do you think it was *our* father?'

Connie shrugged. 'She wouldn't say. She said it was enough to know about Violet and that – oh Fran! I'm so ashamed.' Her mouth trembled and Fran was astonished to see that she was on the brink of tears. So Matt was a cousin! They could never have married. If she and not Connie had run away . . .

Connie said, 'The thing is that I *told* him, Fran. I told Matt. I was so angry and upset after Mother's funeral. He was so cruel to me, humiliating me that way in front of Del, and then you and Del – I couldn't bear it.' She began to cry. 'I wrote to him and told him. A really hateful letter. I wanted to hurt him—'

'And you did, presumably.' Fran's earlier apprehension was turning to fear. If . . . *if* Matt had pushed Mary off the cliff, it was perfectly possible that he had also tried to kill Henry. But of course that was impossible, because they knew Matt and he was one of the family, and yet . . . 'What did he say?'

'He didn't answer the letter but – he went to France and met her.'

'Good heavens!' Fran finished her own brandy in one gulp. She tried to imagine Matt and crazy Aunt Violet together, but the image remained elusive. 'And *was* she crazy?'

'No. Apparently she was very nice. Or so he said. You can never be sure with Matt, can you? He came down to Maidstone a few days ago to try and make up – to say that he didn't bear a grudge because he likes his mother. He was very nice, actually; he can be charming when he tries. He wanted to take me out to dinner at The Star and he brought me some flowers.'

Fran tried not to feel slighted at this evidence of Matt's feelings towards Connie. Immediately conquering her unworthy thoughts, she considered this. After a moment's pause she said, 'But if he likes her and if he wants to be friends with you – surely he could have no reason to hate the family? He doesn't know about the tontine.' She saw Connie's expression and gasped, 'Oh, no!'

Connie nodded. 'Yes. I told him that too. You can call me a bitch if you like but—'

'You're a bitch!'

Connie shrugged. 'Maybe. But I did it. It can't be undone. If I could turn back the clock I wouldn't tell him, but the strange thing is that he didn't even mention it.' She leaned forward eagerly. 'I think he's so pleased to have found his mother. He was very protective towards her, doesn't want any of us to bother her. Apparently she and Alice live a very quiet life and hate visitors. And yesterday this—' she fumbled with the catch of her bag '—came in the post with a letter from Matt.'

She produced a small box and handed it to Fran. 'Fran, he was so sweet about it. It made me feel very guilty for all the bad things I've said and thought about him.'

Recognizing the box for what it was, Fran felt the familiar twinge of envy. Opening it she found a gold ring set with five opals. She could not meet Connie's eyes, knowing how smug she would look, but managed to mumble something complimentary.

Connie continued. 'It was his mother's, given to her by his father. She sent it to Matt, and he said he wanted me to have it because I had brought them together. He says he'll never marry; he'll always be alone. Honestly, Fran, I don't know what to think. I must admit I wondered about him when Mary died. I wondered if it could possibly be that he was punishing us because of the letter I wrote. You can't imagine how terrible I felt – if it *was* him! And yet I couldn't quite believe it. Matt is a strange person, but he wouldn't . . . he wouldn't kill someone. Would he?'

239

Fran hesitated, turning the ring over and over in her fingers, reluctant to put her own disloyal thoughts into words. At last she said, 'I didn't think he could do anything violent until you told me about your letter to him. But if he's forgiven you and wants to forget the past, as you say he does, then – oh, damn! I still don't know what to think. And with Henry being attacked . . . isn't that rather a long coincidence?'

Connie shook her head. 'Could he be trying to lull our suspicions, you mean? Pretending to be happy so that we don't think he has a grudge? He can be devious, he always was. But even if we thought he was somehow responsible, could we tell the police? Suppose they arrest him? Suppose they found him guilty and it wasn't him? We couldn't do it.'

Fran handed back the ring. 'It's beautiful. Aren't you going to wear it?'

Connie hesitated. 'I wanted to, but somehow I couldn't. Aren't opals supposed to be unlucky? Or is that moonstones?' She slipped the ring on to her finger and held out her hand for inspection.

'It suits your hand. Lucky you!'

'I shan't keep it. I shall send it back with a kind note.'

Fran hid her relief. It hardly seemed fair that Connie had been the one to hurt Matt, yet she was the one who got the ring. She held out her hand. 'Let me try it.'

She slipped it on to her finger, but it was too small and wouldn't pass her knuckle. She tried it on a smaller finger and admired it.

'Maybe I *will* wear it,' said Connie.

Fran pretended indifference. 'Well, I don't think we'd better drink any more brandy,' she said, and was pleased to see Connie return the ring to its box. 'I'll make some tea. Thank goodness Dot and Annie aren't here.' She stood

240

up and Connie followed her into the kitchen and propped herself against the jamb of the door while Fran reached for tea, sugar and milk.

'So, Connie, tell me about Henry. Is he conscious? Does he remember anything? Do they know anything about the car – or the driver?'

'Only that it was deliberate. Also they suspect that the blighter who ran Henry down turned the car round and drove back to see if he had been successful.'

'That's unbelievable!' Fran was shocked.

'Well, it seems that a man pulled up in a car and asked, "Is he dead?" Not "What's happened?" or "Can I help?" but "Is he dead?" As though he knew that the person on the ground was the victim of an accident. The natural thing to think would be that maybe the man lying in the road was drunk, especially around closing time. When the old chap said that Henry wasn't dead, he drove off without offering to help. They haven't got a description because the old man – his name is Scott – was three sheets to the wind and didn't take too much notice. All he remembered about the driver was that he was wearing a scarf with white stripes. He couldn't tell what other colours there were. Oh, and a motoring cap. It could have been anybody.'

Fran carried the tray back into the lounge and set it down on the coffee table. There was a sick feeling in her stomach.

Connie trailed after her, then crossed to the window and stared out. 'It seems impossible that we're having this conversation,' she said. 'You and me discussing the possibility of someone trying to murder us. Quite impossible. But the police don't think so. They're treating it as suspicious circumstances.'

Fran put her hands around the tea-cosy, eager for a little extra warmth. She felt chilled in spite of the brandy. 'Henry *can't* die!' she said. 'Not Henry. He's always been so full of life. Is the head injury serious?'

'They're still doing tests. Too early to say. You know what hospitals are like; they never think you are able to cope with the truth so they hide behind comforting phrases.' She turned to Fran. 'To be honest, Fran, I'm scared. If someone is trying to kill us—'

'If someone is trying to *scare* us, he's succeeding. Who will be next?'

'If Henry dies it will—'

'Don't even think it!' cried Fran.

'But if he does die it will be murder or manslaughter. Either way there'll be an investigation.'

Fran stirred her tea, staring into the swirling liquid. 'What on earth can I tell Dot?' But even as she voiced the question she knew the answer. 'I shall tell her the truth. She has to be warned. She's terribly vulnerable. Maybe she ought to stay in until we know just how far all this is going. She adores Henry. It'll break her heart.'

'Do you think you should tell her? I'm sure Mother would have kept it from her.'

'Maybe, but Mother wasn't infallible.'

'Fran! What a spiteful thing to say.'

'It's not spiteful, Connie. It's my honest opinion. None of us are fallible, and I think it best to treat Dot as an adult wherever possible. How do we know what she can deal with if we don't give her a chance to show us? Mother was too protective, in my view.'

Connie bridled, as Fran had known she would. 'So what makes you the expert?' she demanded.

'I'm not an expert. I just have to follow my instincts. Mother is dead and now we have to manage without her.'

Connie turned from the window. 'Mother is dead and Mary is dead and Henry might die. Someone out there wants us all dead. I know it.'

'Stop it, Connie. Come and sit down.' Fran poured the tea – anything to distract her thoughts from the unpleasant realities which Connie had expressed. 'Will you be all right on your own?'

Connie smiled faintly. 'Before I called the taxi I bought a new lock. For the front door. The maintenance man from the library is going to put it on for me. I shall keep all the curtains drawn once it gets dark, and I shan't answer the door to anyone unless the chain is on. I'll be all right.'

'Should we have some sort of weapon, do you think?'

'I've got a heavy torch. I shall keep it beside my bed.'

Fran shook her head helplessly. 'You were right. This is impossible. We can't be talking like this.'

Connie looked at her fearfully. 'But it *is* possible, Fran, and we *are*!'

*

Connie had only managed to take the morning off, so she returned to Maidstone after a snack lunch with Fran. It had been decided that Fran should go to Cambridge to be with Henry and this meant several telephone calls. One of these was to Del Farrar, and he at once volunteered to drive her up to Cambridge. After much heart-searching she turned down the offer, knowing that there was nothing he could usefully do up there except keep her company. Not that she didn't want his company – she most certainly did – and the thought of being so far away added to her unhappiness. It seemed selfish, however, to take up so much of his time, and at last common sense prevailed. She suggested that while she was away he should carry on with the revisions to his novel.

'Are you sure?' he asked. 'I'm going to miss you.'

'Ditto!' she told him, 'but your time in Britain is running

243

out and I would like to get a decision on the manuscript before you go home. Then we'll have something to celebrate.'

'Or commiserate about!'

'Think positive thoughts, Del. I really do think we're going to see you in print before another year is out.'

'But you'll take good care of yourself and keep in touch, Fran? It's going to be lonesome without you.'

'I'll be counting the days,' she said. Counting the hours and the minutes, too, she thought. Circumstances had brought them together and now they were tearing them apart. It was what Annie called 'Sod's Law'!

'Poor Henry. I hope they can do something for him.'

Fran's mouth trembled at this reminder that they might lose their brother. 'They *must* save him,' she said shakily. 'They say he's in a very bad way, but Addenbrooke's has a very good reputation. If anyone can pull him through, *they* will.'

'My poor little Fran. You mustn't lose hope. You have to believe in miracles, Fran.'

'I know. I'm trying to do just that.' A miracle might be all that could save Henry's life, she thought fearfully, but blinked back tears and steadied herself. There was so much to think about that she dare not weaken or she would be lost. Although she longed to see Del, the sight of him would release all her pent-up emotion and grief. She would throw herself into his arms and surrender to her tears and that would be disastrous. This crisis was one that she must cope with alone. As brightly as she could she said, 'Give me your telephone number, Del, and I'll ring you. I promise.'

*

That evening, when Annie and Dot returned from Canterbury, Fran broke the news about Henry's accident as gently as she could.

244

Dot's face paled. 'Henry? In an accident? I want to see him.'

Fran put an arm round her. 'As soon as he is a little better you can visit him. I promise.'

Annie was staring open-mouthed. 'Another one?' she whispered. '*Another accident*? What's going on, for God's sake?'

Fran shook her head helplessly.

Dot picked up Fritz and hugged him until he squealed a protest. 'Fritz wants to see Henry and so do I.'

Annie said, 'You heard what Fran said – as soon as Henry is well enough.' She turned to Fran. 'Are you going to see him?'

'Of course. I'm already packed and the taxi is coming in about an hour. I've booked myself into a small hotel, and I've told the hospital I shall be there for visiting hour in the morning.'

'It's not fair!' cried Dot. 'Why can't I go? He's my brother too.'

Crossing her fingers, Fran produced the lie she had prepared. 'There is a slight problem, Dot. The man in the art department at Starr Massey is very pleased with your watercolours, but he wants you to do a few more.' She saw that she had caught her sister's interest. 'He wants you to do four still-life paintings before the end of the week.'

Dot wavered and Annie said quickly, 'You could do them, Dot, if you work hard.'

'Could I?' She looked dubious. 'What *are* still-lifes?'

'A still-life is an arrangement. Pottery, fruit, flowers – that sort of thing. Annie could help you think of an arrangement.'

'It would be fun,' said Annie.

Before Dot could change her mind, Fran said, 'That's settled, then. I told them I thought you would do it. If not, I would ring them.'

'Well, Dot!' Annie smiled. 'Four still-lifes! Things are getting very exciting, aren't they?'

Dot's smile broadened. She hugged Fritz so hard that he tried to bite her wrist and she put him down with a token slap for his impudence, but Fran knew she could go to Cambridge with an easy mind.

It was one thing less to worry about and she told herself to be grateful for small mercies.

*

In Ward B, the neurosurgical ward, Henry lay in bed, hovering somewhere in a grey limbo between life and death. At times he sank gratefully into oblivion, at other times shadowy images and random thoughts filled his mind and these brought with them an overwhelming sense of dread. From time to time he gained consciousness, but these occasions were rare and fleeting. When he was conscious, he understood where he was but he had no idea why he was there. Nor did he know how long he had been there. He could remember nothing, not even his name. His world was reduced to a dark place with voices, none of which he recognized. He drifted in and out of consciousness, occasionally suffering an agonising pain in his head. Then he would cry out and a merciful needle would slide into his arm. His right leg refused to function and he knew that his bed sheet was being changed frequently. He ate nothing and took only an occasional drink when a nurse held a feeding cup to his mouth and said, 'Come along, Mr Massey.' Mr Massey? Was that who he was? 'Take a little sip of barley water, just to please me.' Then he felt like a child again, wanting to oblige. He wanted to smile at the nurse but he seemed to have lost control of the muscles of his face. He would have said 'Thank you' but he could not speak. On the one occasion when he managed to open his eyes he saw that the sides of the bed had been raised and were padded like those of a perambulator.

At times he heard the doctors conferring about him and caught the odd word ... 'base fracture ... epistaxis ... cerebrospinal fluid ...' The words themselves were meaningless jargon but the voices were hushed and anxious. He sensed their concern, but he was too tired to care whether he lived or died. Time passed erratically and he soon stopped trying to work out how long he had been there. The effort to make sense of the confusion left him exhausted.

Once, in a brief period of clarity, he heard a voice he knew.

'How are you, Henry? This is a dreadful business.'

So, now he was Henry. But which Henry? And what was the dreadful business? He struggled to identify the speaker's voice but quickly gave up, exhausted by the effort.

The man went on, 'We're all praying for you.' Henry thought the voice was familiar. It evoked tantalizing memories which slithered away when he tried to grasp them. He heard the visitor ask about his chances of recovery and a woman's voice answered.

'Well, we've managed to stabilize his condition and he's as comfortable as we can make him.'

'Will he live, sister?'

'Well, we're still hopeful, Mr Ryan, but I must emphasize that it's early days yet. There's every chance that he may not make a full recovery. There is considerable damage to the base of the skull and there has been extensive internal bleeding ...'

'But *will he live*?'

'We can't promise anything, Mr Ryan. It would be best not to hope for too much ...'

Ryan ... Ryan ... Henry tried to think about the name but the effort set up a throbbing in his head. This in turn accelerated into pain, and he allowed himself to drift gratefully into another merciful blackness.

When he came to again he felt hands busy about his body. Through his closed eyelids he sensed that the room was brighter and suddenly he remembered sunshine. Sunlight glinting on water and glancing through the leaves of a tree ... A word floated into his mind and he wanted to say 'Matt' but his lips remained stubbornly uncooperative ... He was being sponged down, but the slightest movement caused him acute discomfort and he was glad when they finally smoothed the bedlinen around his neck and left him ... The room seemed to be full of the groans and coughs of his fellow patients and the click, click of the nurses' heels on the floor ... 'Matt' he thought. 'It was Matt.' But the small triumph of memory lasted for only a moment before he slid once more into the chaos of his dreams.

*

When Fran arrived at Ward B she was greeted briefly by the ward sister. She was busy with another of the visitors, but told Fran that Mr Fraser was the consultant she needed to speak to. He would be along within ten minutes – and that, she said, pointing, was Mr Massey's bed. Fran thanked her and then made her way across the ward, steeling herself for what she would see, willing herself to stay calm. Her first glimpse of Henry left her shocked and cold with fear. Her brother's hair was hidden by a heavy bandage and his face was unnaturally flushed and swollen. His eyes were closed, the beautiful dark lashes resting against his cheeks. His lips were grey.

'Oh, Henry,' she whispered. 'Dearest Henry!'

There was a long graze down his right cheek and around the right eye the flesh was discoloured. His breathing was slow and laboured as though each breath might be his last. Fran took hold of his right hand and kissed it.

With tears threatening, she leaned over and gently kissed his face.

'It's me, Fran,' she told him urgently. 'Can you hear me? It's Fran.'

The man in the next bed said, 'Pull up a chair, missus. Make yourself at 'ome, like.'

Fran turned to him, dazedly. 'What? I'm sorry—?'

'I said "Sit down 'fore you fall down".' He smiled, a small, elderly man dwarfed by the expanse of hospital bed.

'Oh, yes. Thank you.' Obediently, Fran drew up the nearby chair and sank down on it with relief. She realized that she was trembling and took several deep breaths.

'I'm Thomas Hatter,' the old man went on eagerly, 'but everyone calls me Tom.'

She made no answer, unwilling to be sidetracked. Tentatively she pulled the curtain across a little to give her slightly more privacy; then she took hold of Henry's hand and rubbed it gently between her own. 'I'm here now, Henry,' she told him. 'I'm here and . . . and it's going to be all right. Do you hear me, Henry? You'll be fine. I won't let anything happen to you, I promise. You hear me, Henry? Oh, God, Henry!' Her voice broke and she bent her head, daring the tears to fall. She could not help him if she gave way to her emotions. What was she saying? She could not help him at all. She was helpless to solve his problem; unable to intercede on his behalf. With startling detail an image rose before her of Henry aged seven, clambering on to the breakwater at Hastings. He slipped and fell and scraped his ankle on some barnacles. He had come running up the beach, screaming with fright and pain and Fran had 'kissed it better'. She had taken him on her lap and comforted him while Mother produced a bandage from her capacious beach-bag. Mother had called him her 'brave little soldier' and he had finally recovered his equilibrium. Now he was indeed a 'brave little soldier', but Fran knew deep in her heart that it would take more than kisses to restore her brother to his usual cheerful self. It would take more than all the surgeon's skills. It would take that miracle.

From behind the curtain Tom tried again. 'Family, is he?'

She half turned. 'My brother.'

'Student?'

She said sharply, 'Yes.' She wished he would stop talking, but then felt a little mean. Perhaps he had no visitors and craved a little conversation.

'I thought so.' His tone was mildly triumphant. 'His professor come earlier. From the university. Nice chap. A Mr Ryan. Very upset he was. Asking all about him. Was he going to pull through. All that.'

'That was nice of him.'

Fran glanced round the ward which was to be Henry's home for the next – for as long as he—. She pressed agitated fingers against her eyelids. Through the blur of unshed tears she saw the twin rows of beds, some hidden by drawn curtains, others revealing their hapless occupants to the curious eyes of strangers. She noted the large uncurtained windows, outside which grey clouds did their best to obscure the wintry sun. There was a nurses' station midway along the polished floor with a nurse in attendance, her head bent over the paper on which she was writing. At the bottom of Henry's bed a medical chart was clipped to the rail, but Fran made no attempt to read it. Medical phrases would mean nothing to her and would almost certainly frighten her.

Silently she watched him while she uttered a prayer for his recovery. God must surely be willing to help him, she assured herself. Henry was one of the nicer members of His flock. She kissed Henry's hand and leaned a little closer. 'It's me, Henry. It's Fran. You hold on. They can save you if only you hold on.' He gave a small groan and his fingers twitched convulsively. Fran looked at him intently. Was that a groan of pain or an attempt to speak? Was he trying to make contact? He turned his head slightly on the pillow and his lips moved, but the mumbled words were incomprehensible.

Tom said, 'He's been doing that for the last couple of hours. Muttering and suchlike. Once he got hold of the bed rail. "Hang on!" I told him. "You stay where you are!"'

Fran fought down her impatience. Where was the consultant? She looked at the clock on the wall. Had she only been sitting there for twenty minutes? It seemed like a lifetime. Her thoughts drifted and she allowed Del back into her mind. She tried to imagine him in his hotel room, his lean fingers darting over the keyboard of his typewriter. Had he any real idea how much he meant to her, she wondered? And was it really possible that they would find a way to stay together? He had talked about taking her back to America with him. Would that be feasible? Would Dot ever be able to manage her own affairs? That seemed less likely, although already she was showing encouraging and unexpected signs of maturity. When asked to stay behind and do the watercolours she had agreed without any fuss. Maybe, with Annie's support . . .

Tom said, 'Here comes Maid Marian!' He chuckled throatily and Fran returned to the present. 'I call her that because her name's Marian and she ministers to all us men, you see.'

Fran laughed dutifully as a plump nurse headed towards them. She was almost cut in two by her stiff webbing belt, and Fran felt momentarily comforted by the familiar blue uniform with its starched white cap and apron.

The nurse took Henry's pulse, standing on the other side of the bed, smiling briskly without speaking. Fran saw that she frowned a little as she took up his chart and wrote on it.

'Is it – as it should be?' Fran asked, unable to hold back the question but dreading the answer.

'It's falling,' said the nurse, reclipping the chart to the bed rail.

'Falling? Is that good or bad?'

The nurse avoided her eyes. 'Mr Fraser will answer all your questions,' she said.

'Is it a good idea for me to speak to – to my brother? I don't want to tire him.'

'Talk away. Who knows? He might hear you.' She bustled away to the next bed where she took Tom's wrist and checked his pulse.

Tom laughed. 'Going up, is it? That's you, nurse. *Marian*! You do things to me. Make the old ticker go pitter-pat!'

The nurse said, 'Stop it, you old devil,' but she was obviously pleased by the compliment. As she moved on he called out, 'Just call me Robin!' and laughed uproariously at his own joke.

Fran turned back to Henry and tried again. 'Connie sends her love, Henry, and so does Dot. And Annie, of course. We're all so terribly sorry . . .' Her voice faltered.

A young man in pyjamas and dressing gown was making his way slowly back to his bed, leaning heavily on a nurse for support. Was he recovering? Fran watched him hopefully. Perhaps he had once been as helpless as Henry and was making a full recovery? She smiled at him as he passed and he winked at her without speaking. Fran felt slightly comforted. Addenbrooke's was one of the best hospitals in the country, with an international reputation. Her hopes rose marginally. Suddenly Henry fluttered the fingers of his right hand. Then he groaned.

Tom said, 'The police was 'ere. Asking questions. Not getting many answers!' He chuckled. 'Did he see who done it? Did he think it was done deliberate? That sort of thing. Course, poor bloke can't tell them anything, can 'e. Could you answer questions if your head was all bashed in?'

Fran, doing her best not to think along these lines, was inordinately pleased to see that Mr Fraser had finally put in an appearance. The consultant surgeon was a tall, stooped man with spectacles and a weary manner. He leaned over Henry, examining him carefully, and then consulted the chart. In reply to her request for the unvarnished truth he was blunt and to the point.

'Your brother's condition is extremely serious. I might even say precarious.'

Fran felt a shiver of apprehension. Not Henry, she thought desperately. Not Henry as well as Mary. Please, God!

'Is he in a coma?' she asked.

'A stupor, actually. There is a difference. We have done what we can to relieve the pressure on his brain, but the damage is to the base of the skull. He has what we call a cerebral compression and the prognosis is not good. You see how restless he is becoming. That is a bad sign, I'm afraid. I suspect haemorrhage into the meningeal artery but I daren't operate again while he is so weak.' He drew a long breath. 'I'm so sorry, Miss Massey. I wish I could be more positive, but you asked me to be frank.'

'Yes, I did, and I appreciate that you have been honest.' In fact, with a terrible coldness growing within her, she was regretting her request for frankness. She glanced down at her brother. 'He's rather special.'

His smile was entirely impersonal. 'We're all rather special to someone, hopefully.'

'The nurse said his pulse was falling.'

A spasm of annoyance crossed his face. 'She had no right to tell you that.'

'I insisted – and surely a patient's relatives have a right to know what is happening.'

He shrugged. 'Sometimes it's important that they *don't* know. Everyone asks, but many cannot deal with the truth when they hear it. A hysterical parent, husband or wife can cause a patient a great deal of stress and lessen their chances of recovery.'

For some reason she persisted. 'So what *does* a falling pulse rate mean?'

'It means a higher than normal blood pressure, for a start. It's an intermediate stage in a downward spiral. Often it speeds up again, becomes erratic. This normally means that death is inevitable.'

Fran clung to the bed-rail for support and cursed her own stupidity. Stop *asking*, she told herself.

'And you can't do anything? You can't operate?' Her voice shook slightly.

'Not at present. If you could see his eyes, you would see that one of the pupils is dilated, and if I were to shine a light into it, it would not react. That plus his fluctuating consciousness tells me that he is not fit to withstand the rigours of surgery. I'm sorry, Miss Massey, but at the moment there is nothing more we can do. Please excuse me as I have my rounds to complete.'

Fran watched him stride away across the ward. Tom spoke to her, but she had no idea what he said. She sat down heavily, hiding her face in her hands, and shortly afterwards a ward orderly brought her a cup of tea. There were three tea-leaves floating on the surface and Fran stirred and stirred her tea, watching the tea-leaves as they were sucked down into the middle of the liquid. That was exactly how she felt, she thought. Helpless. Drowning.

Her kindly, innocent brother was going to die and beyond these caring walls, in the outside world, someone would be glad.

Chapter Twelve

F RAN STARED AT THE LETTER she was writing. Twenty-four hours had passed since she had spoken to Mr Fraser. She had spent the day at the hospital, waiting in vain for a sign that Henry's condition might improve. Instead he had shown signs of increasing restlessness, and his pulse had speeded up. Refused permission to stay with her brother, Fran had spent the night at the hotel. When she returned to the hospital at nine o'clock she was greeted by a police sergeant who told her that Henry was dead. There would be another inquest, he explained, and the police were now treating both deaths as suspicious. After the various formalities at the hospital, she returned to the hotel in a state of shock bordering on hysteria. With Henry's few belongings in a brown paper parcel, she called a taxi and made her way to the station. There she sat on a bench and waited for the train that would take her back to London. The journey passed in a daze. Henry was dead. Murdered 'by person or persons unknown'. That night she went to bed at ten o'clock and woke in the early hours of the morning. Wide awake, she found pen and paper and wrote to Matt:

Dear Matt,

  I'm sure this will come as a terrible shock, but Henry is dead. He was knocked down by a motorist and died in Addenbrooke's Hospital early this morning. We are all deeply shocked and grieving as you will be . . .

Or would he? Again and again the thought returned that perhaps he would *not* be surprised; that Matt might, in fact, be the one person in the world who wanted Henry to die. The thought made her physically sick.

  Dot is in a great state, but fortunately we still have young Amy staying with us who is cheerful company for her. Poor Annie almost collapsed when I broke the news of Henry's death. I was terrified that it was her heart. The doctor sent her straight to bed and gave her a sleeping draught, but it didn't work for long and now she is agitating to get up again. She has aged ten years; she is really too old to withstand all these shocks.
  I have to tell you, also, that the police are treating Henry's death as either murder or manslaughter, as the witness insists that the 'accident' was in fact quite deliberate. An act of malice. Bearing in mind Mary's death, they seem to think it likely that our family is the target of some kind of hate campaign, and they have warned us all to be careful. The idea is like something out of a nightmare but they say the coincidences are too great . . .

She was writing this letter because she had to carry on as though Matt was still the Matt they had grown up with and not a monster. The police suspected him, but did not want him to be alerted to this fact. 'Write to him,' they had told her. 'Pretend everything is normal between you. Don't let him think he is under suspicion.' And of course he might be innocent, she reminded herself. She wanted him to be innocent, but something deep within her subconscious hinted to the contrary. It could be that circumstances had been stacked against him – or that

257

someone was deliberately trying to frame him for the murders. She brightened momentarily. Was that a genuine possibility? Only the tontine might have triggered thoughts of murder, but somehow this did not seem quite enough. She continued writing:

> ... They are going to re-interview the bird-watcher who saw Mary on the cliffs with a man. Also they have a witness to Henry's so-called accident. They believe the inquest will bring in a verdict of death by person or persons unknown. I think that's the phrase they used, but I am in such despair, Matt, I don't know if I'm on my head or my heels.

She had thought long and hard about the tone and intention of the letter. What should she try to get across? One of her motives was a vague sense of family preservation. She was going to let Matt know indirectly that, if he *did* have any designs on the rest of the family he would find it difficult.

> ... The police are talking about giving us some protection and I shall ask Del Farrar if he would like to move in with us for a few days. He can bring his typewriter and press on with his manuscript. I'll give him Mary's room ...

Or Henry's room, she thought bitterly. At this rate there would soon be a house *full* of vacant rooms! Damn him! Or whoever it was. She went on with the letter but her hand was shaking with anger. If Matt noticed a change in her handwriting he would no doubt put it down to fear and he wouldn't be so far from the truth.

> ... When I have to be in London it will be wonderful to know that Annie and Dot are in safe hands. The police will probably put a man on guard somewhere outside Connie's flat – a detective in plain clothes ...

She frowned. Perhaps she ought to mention Matt's own safety.

> ... You will be harder to protect, Matt, because you are on the move a lot for your job. Perhaps you could warn your landlady to keep an eye open for suspicious characters. Without frightening her, of course ...

Fran re-read the letter with some satisfaction. That should allay his suspicions and might deter him from making an attempt on anyone else's life. If it *was* him. Suppose it was someone else? The idea confused her. She didn't want Matt to be a murderer, but if it wasn't him then the police had no leads at all.

Just then Dot came into the room. Her eyes were red and puffy and her hair, usually so neat, was a little dishevelled. She was clutching Fritz in her arms and the dog was wriggling indignantly.

'Fritz wants to go and sit with Annie,' she announced. 'Shall we both go?'

'Annie may be asleep.'

'If she's not asleep can we go?' Dot came closer. 'Who are you writing to?'

'To Matt, to tell him about Henry.'

Dot knew about Henry's death, but Fran had not yet told her that Matt might be involved. If Matt was innocent, Dot would be able to feel happy about him. If she knew he was under suspicion, she might never trust him again. Annie and Connie had been consulted on this point and they had joined forces against her. Reluctantly Fran had bowed to a majority verdict. Later, if the police found proof of his implication, they would tell Dot.

'Poor Matt. He'll be so sad!' Dot frowned at Fritz, who was still making desperate attempts to escape. 'Don't do that!' she told him. 'Stop fidgeting!' Fritz, however, slid suddenly to the floor with a yelp of pain. Dot's hands went to her face and her voice rose shrilly. 'Serves you right, you horrid dog!' She watched him scuttle out of the room, her mouth trembling, then she looked at Fran. 'I'm glad!' She gulped convulsively. 'I don't love Fritz any more!'

Fran, understanding the cry within the cry, held out her arms. 'It doesn't matter, Dot,' she said soothingly but it was too late. For the third time that day Dot burst into passionate tears and flung herself into Fran's arms. Fran found tears coursing down her own face and the two sisters clung together, sharing their loss and making clumsy efforts to comfort each other. They were still crying when the door opened and Annie came into the room in her dressing gown.

'Annie!' cried Fran, struggling to stem the flow of her tears. 'What are you doing out of bed? You go straight back upstairs and stay in bed. The doctor said—'

Annie's eyes flashed. 'And what happens when I do?' she demanded. 'You two break your hearts.' Her voice shook. 'I'm no use to anyone stuck up there, so don't argue with me.' She tightened the cord round her waist. 'We are now going to have a cup of tea with a dash of whisky in it.'

Dot's eyes widened as she wiped her eyes on her handkerchief. 'Whisky? In tea?'

'My mother swore by it,' said Annie.

Dot blew her nose. '*I'll* make it!' she told them. 'You and Fran can sit in here and *I'll* make it.'

Annie opened her mouth to protest but Fran said, 'Oh, if you *would*, Dot. That would be marvellous.'

Annie, catching her eye, quickly sank on to the sofa. 'Dot, you're an angel. I'm so weak and wobbly I don't think I'd get as far as the kitchen.'

'How much whisky?' Dot asked eagerly.

Fran hid a smile. 'We'll add it in here,' she suggested.

'It doesn't need much,' said Annie. 'A dash or a splash!'

Dot thought it over. 'A teaspoonful each?'

'Make it a dessertspoon!' advised Annie.

Stuffing her damp handkerchief back in her pocket, Dot smiled. 'And some biscuits?'

'Please.'

Dot rushed to the door. There she paused and looked at Fran. 'I *do* love him.'

Fran hesitated. 'We all love Matt, Dot. But maybe—'

'Not Matt. Fritz. I do love him really. I didn't mean it.'

'Of course you didn't.'

Annie said, 'There's a mutton bone for him in the meat safe. You could give it to him.'

'He adores mutton bones!' The door banged behind her and they were silent, listening to her eager footsteps in the hall.

Annie said, 'She's happy again.'

Fran looked at her soberly. 'But for how long?' she asked.

*

Poppy was emptying the carpet sweeper when she heard the front door-bell.

'Blast!' The scullery smelled of the cat's fish and she was still wearing her curlers tucked inside a headscarf wound turban fashion around her head. She considered who it might be at this time in the morning. The postman always came before nine, and it was now twenty to ten. The butcher had stopped calling since she had complained about that piece of salt beef, and it was too early for the divvy man from the Co-op. Anyway, whoever it was, there was no time for her to pull out the curlers and arrange her hair. With a bad grace she put away the sweeper and made her way along the passage.

'I'm coming!' she called in case it was someone she might want to see. As she neared the front door, however, her face fell. Through the coloured glass panes she could see the outline of a policeman's helmet.

Pulling the door open, she asked, 'What's happened? Is it my Mum?' Her eighty-year-old mother was her only relative.

'Mrs Parfitt?' He was tall and slim, with a neat moustache and brown eyes.

She cursed her curlers. 'I'm Brenda Parfitt. Yes, that's me. What's the matter?'

'May I come in?'

'But why?' She gave him a coy smile. 'You're not going to arrest me, are you, officer?'

He was rather handsome, she thought, or would pass for handsome in a dim light. The small mouth spoiled his face, making him look babyish.

'It's not about your mother,' he told her. 'We are just making a few routine enquiries. May I come in?'

She held the door open wide. 'Please do.' She would sit him down and then on the pretext of making him a cup of tea she would take out the curlers.

He removed his helmet – a real gentleman – and sat down at the kitchen table. Poppy rushed into the scullery and half filled the kettle so that it would boil quickly. She clattered the crockery while she pulled out the curlers and, using the scullery mirror, hastily coaxed her hair into what she hoped was a becoming cluster of waves and curls and stuck in a few hair grips. With relief, she saw a distinct improvement; it was amazing what a few curls did for a woman. When she went back into the kitchen she saw him glance at her hair.

'I was a bit late getting up this morning,' she said. 'Late night. A party.' She hoped she looked the type who went to parties. 'You caught me on the hop. I don't always sleep well. You don't when you're alone.' That last word would let him know that there was no Mr Parfitt. She was feeling rather pleased with herself. A few little lies wouldn't matter. The kettle whistled and she rushed out into the scullery again. She found a lipstick in the dresser drawer and hastily outlined her lips, then she carried the tray back into the kitchen. He smiled and she thought she saw admiration in his eyes.

'Mrs Parfitt, we are investigating an accident which happened recently. Can you tell us whether or not your lodger, Matthew Massey, was at home on the twenty-ninth of January? That is, whether you can vouch for him being here.'

She shook her head immediately. 'My birthday,' she told him. 'Twenty-one again!'

He laughed politely.

'I was on my own that day,' she said. 'He wasn't here; he was in Birmingham. He's a rep for a big stationery firm. I especially remember because—' She stopped suddenly. The twenty-ninth was the day when her lodger's sister had fallen over the cliff. She had seen it in the cutting. So why were they asking about his whereabouts? 'Why do you ask?'

'Just routine. We always check up on the relatives first and then—'

'But that was an accident. He told me all about it, poor man. He was so upset. She fell!'

This time his smile was short-lived. 'So he wasn't here on that day?' He pulled a notebook and pencil from his pocket and began to write.

Poppy looked at him uneasily. 'Did he say he *was* here? Because I might have got the day wrong.'

'But you said it was your birthday on the twenty-ninth.'

'Oh, yes. So I did, but—' She thought frantically. 'He's away such a lot with his job.'

'What about February the ninth? That is, Wednesday of this week. Do you recollect where he was on that date?'

'Wednesday? Er – let me think ... Today's Friday. Wednesday?' Had he told them he was at home? *Was* he at home? 'He came home quite late,' she said. 'No, he was at work. On the road. I told you he's a rep. They go all over the place. Why? What happened on Wednesday?'

'I didn't say anything happened, madam.'

He seemed to be eyeing her suspiciously, and for some reason she felt herself blush.

'No, that's right. You didn't.'

'Do you think anything happened that night?'

'No.' She was beginning to feel trapped by these strange questions. Had Matt done something? No, that was impossible. Anyway, what could he have done? 'Matt is a very nice person,' she stammered. 'Respectable. A respectable working man. Goes to work. Comes home again. Keeps his wireless down low. He's no trouble. He's got standards, if you know what I mean. Takes a pride in himself. Never leaves the house looking scruffy – and he looks after that little car of his. The other day he gave it a good old wash and then a polish. Ever so upset he was because one of the back lights was broken. Hooligans, most likely, he reckoned. He has to leave it in all sorts of places and there's always someone who wants to spoil things. Poor Matt. I sometimes wonder what the world's coming to.'

He glanced up. 'Call him Matt, do you?'

'Yes. No law against that, is there?'

'Friendly, are you?'

She swallowed. This was tricky. Were they trying to blame *her* for something?

'Yes, we are. So what?' At once she wished she hadn't sounded quite so cheeky. The police were a funny lot; she mustn't get on the wrong side of him. 'I mean, we're both adults and we live in the same house. Not that there's any of *that*, if that's what you're thinking.' Blast! She was making it worse although there wasn't any of that, more's the pity. Still, Matt had squeezed her arm yesterday in a romantic sort of way and had hinted that they might go to the pictures together one evening. So some of *that* might be on the cards; she certainly hoped so. She also hoped that this meddling policeman wasn't going to spoil everything. 'We're just friends,' she insisted.

He gave her an odd look. 'Did you know that Mr Massey's brother had died?'

She stared at him. 'It was his sister that died. Not his brother.'

'His brother died on Wednesday. Didn't you know? Didn't he tell you? I thought you said you were friends.'

Poppy opened and closed her mouth, at a loss for words. Two members of his family had died, then. Her eyes widened. 'Poor man! That's terrible.' She stared at the policeman wide-eyed. 'He must be half out of his mind with worry!'

'I suppose so.'

'Well,' she said helplessly, while her mind spun. Two of Matt's family had died and now the police were making enquiries. 'You don't mean somebody *killed* them? His brother and sister?' Her cup was poised half-way to her mouth. 'Not—!'

'We aren't jumping to conclusions, Mrs Parfitt. Just making routine enquiries.'

'His brother? How did he die?'

'Knocked down by a motor car.'

'Oh, no!' She frowned. 'Another accident?'

He shrugged. 'We can't say at this stage. Early days in this sort of enquiry. Could be an unfortunate coincidence.' He flipped back through the previous pages of his notebook and said, 'He didn't go to his sister's funeral.'

'Well, how could he? He'd hurt his leg – his leg and his back. He was limping, I remember. And he asked me to post a letter for him because he couldn't walk. He had to rest his leg.'

The policeman stood up, made a final note and closed

265

the notebook. 'You've been very helpful, Mrs Parfitt, and thanks for the cuppa.'

She followed him to the door and showed him out. In daylight he looked a bit pasty and hardly handsome at all. 'Goodbye,' she said and watched him go down the path to his bicycle which was propped against the inside of her hedge, out of sight of the road.

'Can't be too careful!' he joked as he wheeled it out of the gate.

When he had gone, Poppy's neighbour on her right side came out into the garden, on the pretext of shaking a small rug. She smiled at Poppy. 'Stolen the Crown Jewels, have you?'

Poppy groaned inwardly. If Ivy Potter ever knew anything, it was soon all over the street.

'Just routine enquiries,' she said and shut the door with more force than was necessary, then made her way slowly back to the kitchen. On the way a sudden thought came to her. The opal ring, the one she had found in Matt's drawer. One day it had been there and the next time she'd looked for it, it was gone. Had he stolen it? And then sold it? Her mouth fell open. Was he a whatever-they-called-it? A *fence*? Was her lodger a receiver of stolen goods? If so, then all those other questions had been a blind.

'Gordon Highlanders!'

Oh, they were crafty, the police. She poured herself another cup of tea and slowly her anxiety faded. So what if he was, she asked herself defiantly. She still fancied him. Perhaps that was why he'd asked her out to the pictures. Maybe now he had a bit of extra cash.

'Why should I care?' she asked the cat. 'It's nothing to do with me. What I don't know can't hurt me. Why shouldn't I help him spend it?'

The cat wound itself round her legs and she said, 'Want your din-dins then?' She busied herself for a few minutes, mashing the boiled whiting with a slice of stale bread and adding a little liquid from the saucepan. Putting down the plate, she watched the cat crouch to eat, the long ginger tail flicking from side to side as he settled down.

So, her desirable lodger was a small-time crook! Well, 'Bully for him!' as her Dad used to say. She patted her curls. 'What a lark!' she said softly, and a broad smile lit up her face and made her almost pretty.

*

The next morning Matt dressed early and went down to collect his post before nosey Poppy could get a look at it. He found Fran's letter and, reading it, his sigh of relief was heartfelt. So the brat *was* dead! No more worries over whether or not he had been recognized in the hospital or at the scene of the accident. Still, he had been a little careless. Henry might just have survived, which would have counted as a failure. In his mind's eye he saw Henry standing at the roadside, shielding his eyes from the glare of the headlights. He felt again the satisfying impact as the car hit him and threw him to the ground. He had felt strong then. Untouchable. The way he had felt when Mary fell away from him, her mouth open in a scream of horror. A pity it had been dark when Henry went down but that had been necessary. Still, he had seen him in the hospital and that had been a triumph. Professor Ryan, the caring tutor! A lovely touch. And they had all believed him. The nurse had rather fancied him; he had seen it in her eyes. And Henry had not survived. He, Matt Massey, had finally wiped the smile from that handsome face. The world was well rid of him. Students! They were nothing but parasites, fooling about in boats and climbing in and out of windows after dark. Stupid good-for-nothing louts!

But now there was one less. He grinned. Suddenly, instead of a victim in a hospital bed, Matt saw Henry as he was at his mother's funeral. Henry was laughing, that eager, boyish laugh of his. Telling a story about one of their student pranks. 'One night he shinned up the flagpole . . . put a jerry on the top!' Pathetic! Idiots, all of them. Well, at least he had put a stop to Henry's little games. Then his smile faded as a thought occurred to him. With hindsight it had been rather foolish to stop beside the body and ask, 'Is he dead?' Fortunately the man seemed a bit tipsy and had probably not registered the question. Even if he had, he might not remember exactly what had been said. But he must be more careful in future; must take no more chances. He had been very wise not to kill Connie that evening after Del Farrar had turned up. A pity about that; he had wanted to get rid of a third before the police started to regard the deaths as suspicious. And Connie had been putty in his hand. Still, better safe than sorry. Her turn would come. He was softening her up and then he would decide how to kill her. No point now in trying to make it look like an accident. Might as well go the whole hog – and strangle her, maybe. He could still remember how his hands had felt near Poppy's scrawny little neck. Connie's was fatter, but he could still do it. But somehow he had to coax her out of her flat first. And where to take her? She would be on her guard now.

'Two down, three to go!' he said softly.

He re-read the letter. So they were going to protect themselves? That was laughable. And Fran, *dear* Fran, wanted *him* to be careful. He snorted faintly with amusement. Then he raised his eyebrows enquiringly, as a wonderful idea struck him. Perhaps he should arrange an attempt on his *own* life, to lull any suspicions anyone might have about him. Presumably the police would contact him some time, and if they did he must be ready for them. Not that he expected much trouble there. His opinion of the police force was pretty low. He'd got away with Mary's murder

268

for long enough to kill again – that made them a bit slow on the uptake.

'But don't underestimate them,' he warned himself. He must keep one jump ahead of them if he was going to carry out his plan. They were now treating the deaths as suspicious and he was going to need an ally; someone to provide an alibi when necessary.

As though reading his mind, Poppy came up the stairs and knocked on his door. 'Mr – I mean Matt. Are you there?'

Where did she think he was?

'Coming!' He opened the door and hid a smile.

She was wearing her dressing gown and had already combed out her curls and added a smear of lipstick to her mouth. Was he really supposed to think that she looked like that in bed, he thought, amused by her transparency.

'Who was late home last night, eh?' She wagged an admonitory finger. 'Naughty boy! I was waiting up for you all on my tod.' She pouted and Matt bit back a scathing remark as she went on, 'But then I fell asleep listening to the boring old wireless and when I woke it was nearly twelve so I went to bed.'

He felt some comment was called for. 'I'm sorry.'

'Can I come in? Just for a mo.'

'I have to go out shortly,' he began.

'The police came for you yesterday,' she said.

His stomach tightened instantly. 'For me?' It wasn't fear, he told himself, but excitement.

'For *you*!' she repeated. 'A big, burly policeman. Quite a ladies' man actually. Took quite a shine to me really, but I wasn't having any. I'll wait for my gentleman lodger, I thought.'

'Come in,' he said.

As he held open the door, he wished he had tidied up. There was a dirty milk bottle on the top of the chest of drawers and yesterday's pants and socks were still on the floor.

But to his relief she showed no interest in the state of the room. 'He said that they want to interview you. Routine enquiries, he called it.' She sat down uninvited, making a great show of covering her legs. 'Asking me where you were on this day and that.'

Matt's smile wavered. 'What did you tell them?'

'I told them what I thought you'd want them to know.' She tapped the side of her nose and grinned. 'I'm not daft, Matt.'

His stomach churned. What the hell did she mean? What could she possibly know? 'I don't quite understand—' he began, assuming a puzzled expression.

She shrugged. 'I just mean that I don't set much store by the police. I don't suppose you do, either. Nosey clodhoppers! I act dumb, I don't tell them anything. Whatever you say's OK with me. Know what I mean?'

He thought that perhaps he did and felt he might be getting into rather deep water. 'They've nothing on me,' he said. 'Nothing at all.'

'Then let's keep it that way.' She put her head on one side and seemed to be sizing him up. 'They said they'd be back, Matt. I told them you were often away for your work, which you are. I said you were a real gentleman.'

She was eyeing him in a strange way, he thought uneasily. As though she knew something and wasn't saying.

'Thanks, Poppy.' He was thinking rapidly. 'You were great. Really.' He hesitated. What had the police actually been told? 'Look, Poppy, you'll have to excuse me. I'm in a bit of a daze at the moment.' He waved the letter. 'I've had a terrible shock. My brother Henry—'

'He's dead. I know. He told me.'

'I've only just heard. Letter from my sister. A road accident. Poor Henry! I can hardly believe it. He had all his life ahead of him; he was only eighteen.'

'You're having terrible luck, Matt, at the moment but

270

– well, maybe tonight I could cheer you up. I mean, *you* know. You and me.'

He was taken off guard by the speed with which this relationship was moving. Him and Poppy? To buy a little time he said, 'I'm shattered. We were very close, me and Henry. Losing a brother—' He brushed away imaginary tears and swallowed hard.

She stood up and came closer and he could smell cheap perfume as she walked her fingers up his tie until her hand brushed his chin. 'I could make you forget your troubles, Matt. I'm no silly young thing. I've been married.' Her fingers walked down the tie until they were below his belt and Matt was surprised to find himself responding to the crude caress. 'I *know* what men like done to them, Matt, and what they like to do.' She lowered her eyelids slowly and then stared up into his eyes. 'I could make you really happy. Tonight, Matt. What d'you say?'

Matt tossed up in his mind. If he said 'No' she might turn against him, and God knows what she knew or had guessed. He certainly needed to keep her on his side. If he said 'Yes' he'd have to go through with it. 'I'm tempted,' he said in a low voice.

'You won't regret it, Matt. We could do it *now* if you like.' She reached up and kissed him on the mouth and to his surprise it wasn't as bad as he had expected. 'I bet you're the sort of man who doesn't need asking twice.' She slid her tongue over his lips and kissed him again. He found himself kissing her in return and suddenly her arms were round his neck and she was pressing her body up against him.

'I have to go to work!' he protested, but she clung on as he tried gently to disentangle himself.

'Matt! You know you want it as much as I do! Let me show you. Here. Feel this.' She drew his hand down the top of her nightdress to her breast and Matt found himself fondling it with a growing sense of excitement.

271

'They're for you, Matt,' she whispered breathlessly. 'All for you.'

He could see by her face that she, too, was becoming aroused. 'Poppy, I—' He was beginning to weaken; beginning to want her. But something held him back. This was going at her pace, not his; he was losing control. He grabbed her arms and held her away from him. 'When *I'm* ready,' he said. 'Not before.'

To his surprise she smiled delightedly. 'Matt! I didn't know you could be like this!' She pretended to struggle. 'You're so strong, Matt!'

Matt's heart pounded and he pulled her close again. 'You'll do what *I* say when *I* say it!' he hissed. His breathing was ragged and he released her arms and grabbed her by the shoulders, pulling her roughly towards him and kissing her as hard as he could on the mouth. She cried out, wincing with pain as his teeth ground into her lips. He forced her slowly to her knees and then down on to the floor. She put up a token resistance and suddenly there was no going back. He was on top of her and inside her and she was groaning and gasping.

'Yes! Yes!' she cried. 'Yes, Matt! Oh, God!'

*

Afterwards he helped her up and she sat on the bed breathing deeply, watching him tidy his clothes. Glancing at her surreptitiously, he was surprised to see how much better she looked. Her eyes shone and her skin was flushed; she looked years younger. Funny. Some women thrived on a bit of rough stuff. He had slammed into her, regardless of her feelings, almost wanting to punish her. She hadn't once complained or tried to direct him the way Connie had done all those years ago. Fortunately she had suffered everything without a sound because he had been in no mood for reproaches. One wrong word and he knew he'd have silenced her for ever. Sweat broke out on his forehead as he thought how easily it could have happened. One false move and his hands would have been round that throat. She was *that* close to death, and she had absolutely no idea. Stupid cow! He could have killed her. No trouble at all. The thought pleased him – but he must watch himself. Must keep control. He knew she was wanting to catch his eye, but he wouldn't look at her. If she was hoping for sweet nothings she'd be disappointed. But who'd have thought it? Poppy, of all people. He'd lived here for years and never known. She must have been dying for it. *Dying* for it! The choice of words made him laugh.

She asked, 'What's the joke?'

'Nothing!'

It had felt good, he wouldn't deny that. A long time since he'd had a woman, and he'd nearly forgotten how good it was. And it was there all the time, waiting for him. He pulled up his braces and bent down to tie his shoelaces. Then at last he looked at her. She looked like the cat that had got the cream, he thought, surprised. Tough as old boots.

'So?' he asked.

She put a hand to her mouth and then felt her neck. 'I'll be all bruises,' she said, half accusing. 'You don't know your own strength.'

'You loved it!'

She smiled. 'Did I say I didn't?'

He took his tie from the back of the chair, put it round his neck and knotted it in front of the mirror. 'Make us a cup of tea,' he suggested.

She stood up carefully. 'We going to the pictures tonight?'

'If I get back in time.'

She went to the door and out on to the landing, but at that moment the doorbell rang. Poppy leaned forward to look over the banisters. 'It's the police,' she said.

273

Matt smoothed his hair. He felt a tremendous glow of well-being, of being on the winning side. So the police were here. So what? He was supremely confident that he could field any of their questions. He went out to join Poppy on the landing and to his surprise he gave her a kiss. Then he patted her bottom. 'Make us all a cup of tea, there's a love,' he said and went downstairs to do battle with the law.

*

In Ward B the sister glanced up with annoyance as the tall man made his way towards her, hat in hand. The police again – as if she didn't have enough to do with one nurse off sick and every bed spoken for. The policeman was watched eagerly by the patients who would, she knew, listen avidly to anything that was said. Hospital life was very dull for them, a matter of routine, and they loved a bit of excitement. She tightened her mouth impatiently. More questions about poor Mr Massey. What could they need to know now? The poor boy was dead, wasn't he? She glanced briefly at the identification which he showed her and gave him a half-smile. 'Please make it as brief as possible. I'm rushed off my feet. I have eleven seriously ill patients on this ward, sergeant, one in theatre, seven on the way to recovery and three due in during the course of the afternoon. I appreciate that—'

He interrupted her. 'It's Detective Chief Inspector, sister – Detective Chief Inspector Bruce – and I also have work to do. A man's been killed – one of your patients – and I have to find the killer. So let's try to help each other, shall we?'

They eyed each other like dogs squaring up for a fight. The sister gave ground first.

'What is it exactly that you need to know?'

'It's about this fellow Ryan.'

'The professor from the university?'

274

'The same.'

She shrugged. 'He was a kindly man, apparently.' Actually Nurse Heywood had waxed lyrical about him, she remembered, but there was no need to say that. 'He was charming. He—'

'We have reason to believe that he was not a professor at all. Nothing to do with the university, in fact. He might even have been the killer. Probably was.'

She stared at him, open-mouthed. 'The professor a killer? What on earth are you talking about? He *taught* the boy. I didn't actually speak to him, but Nurse Heywood did. He was very concerned. Why should a professor try to kill one of his own students?'

'I've just told you, sister, that he *wasn't* a professor. That's my point: he was an imposter and that was simply a way to get in to see his victim. He wanted to know whether his victim was going to die or not. I'm sorry.'

'I don't believe – I mean, I can't – a *killer*? In this very ward?' She could hardly take it in.

'I'm afraid it looks that way. We've checked with the university and there is no tutor by that name.'

The sister sat down on the edge of the desk. 'He came here – he had the gall to knock down that poor boy and then come here and . . .' She took a deep breath. 'Sorry, Inspector. But that's horrible. We should have known . . .'

'How could you?'

'I don't know, but—' She felt shaken by the knowledge that such a thing could happen, and her thoughts whirled. 'Good heavens! He might have done the boy some harm! Tampered with the drip-feed or – or something.'

'I imagine the nurse confided that he was close to death. Maybe that satisfied him. I need a full description of the man, sister.'

'But Nurse Heywood is off duty. She doesn't come back on until six. Oh, dear.'

'Don't worry. I'll send a sergeant down around that time to take a statement from her. Please ask her to remember everything she can about the man. We do have a suspect, but no evidence as yet. Anything she can recall – his clothes, his appearance, his accent.'

She nodded. 'I'll brief her,' she said. 'And I'm sorry if I was a bit hasty. I had no idea.'

'Understandable in the circumstances.' He held out his hand.

She watched him go. Professor Ryan an imposter? A *killer*? Well! Her mother used to say fact was stranger than fiction . . .

*

Alfred Scott put his head out of the window and said, 'Come round the back.'

The front door hadn't been opened in years because if it was, the draught made the fire smoke. He opened the back door to the policeman and wondered if it was about the rabbits. He had gone back for them the following day but they'd gone. Pinched, most like. You couldn't trust anybody these days. Unless a fox had come across 'em and thought it was his birthday! 'So what is it this time?' he asked.

'The chappie in the car, Scottie. We need a decent description of him, and you're the only one who saw him. The young man has died from his injuries, so we're looking at a manslaughter charge.'

'Died? Cor lumme!' Scottie sat down and rubbed his chin. So it wasn't about the rabbits. 'Well now, I did tell all I know 'cos it was dark and I couldn't see what with them headlights and all, right in me face, dazzling me.'

'We'd like to know what he sounded like, Scottie. Was he Irish, maybe?'

'Not Irish. Nope.'

'Scottish?'

'Nope. Not that, neither.'

'Welsh?'

Scottie shook his head.

'A foreigner, perhaps?'

Another shake of the head.

'Local maybe.'

'Local? No.'

'North Country?'

'What's that when it's at home?'

'What's it like?' The sergeant considered. 'You know. "Oop North". They don't say "barth", they say "bath". And "hur" for "hair". You must have heard them on the wireless.'

'Well, I haven't.'

The sergeant grinned. 'They eat jam butties, so I'm told, whatever they may be. They say things like "our Harold" and "our Edna". They put the word 'our' in front of folks' names.'

'Our Edna?' Scottie shook his head. 'Never heard anything like, that. All he said was "Is he dead?" Nothing about jam butties. Then he roared off again.'

'Was it a sporty car?'

'I wouldn't know. Don't care for motor cars.'

The policeman wrote in his notebook. 'What's wrong with motor cars, then? Scare away your rabbits, do they, and your pheasants?'

'Pheasants?' Scottie adopted an air of great innocence. 'I don't know nothing about any pheasants.' He frowned suddenly.

'What is it?'

'London, maybe. His accent.'

'A southerner . . .'

'Yes, maybe a southerner. A bit posh, too. Know what I mean?' He adopted what he assumed to be a "posh"

277

accent and said, '"His 'e dead?" Posh like. That sort of thing.'

The policeman scribbled furiously. 'And you're sure he didn't say anything else?'

'Not another word. He had a stripey scarf and a cap, but I told 'em that already. And he might have been tallish, because when I looked in at him his head was just about touching the roof of the car.'

'And you said dark hair. No beard. No moustache.'

Scottie thought for a bit. 'No.'

'About how old? An old man?'

'Not old. Not quite middle-aged. Maybe thirty, thirty-five.' He shrugged. 'Is there a reward?'

'Not that I know of.' The policeman put away his notebook. 'If there is, you'll be the first to know!'

Scottie closed the door behind him and stared after him through the grimy lace curtain. 'Jam butties,' he said wonderingly. 'Some sort of biscuit, I dare say.'

Chapter Thirteen

FRAN WENT IN TO BREAKFAST just after seven-thirty and found Annie finishing a bowl of porridge. 'Dot's having a lie-in,' Annie told her. 'She didn't sleep well last night and it's such a miserable day. Best stay in the warm, I told her.' She swallowed the last of her cup of tea and stood up. 'I must say I slept better for knowing Mr Farrar was in the house. I hope he slept well in Mary's room.' She sighed. 'I can't get used to the idea that we'll never see her again or poor Henry, either. I never thought I'd see such calamities fall on this family.'

Fran nodded. 'I'm glad Mother isn't here to see it.'

'She'd cry herself to sleep every night.'

Just like the rest of us, thought Fran, as Annie hurried out of the room. In a thoughtful silence, she helped herself to porridge and had just finished it when Del joined her. At the sight of him her spirits lifted a little. Annie had found Del's presence reassuring, but Fran had found it exciting. She had been looking forward to seeing him at the breakfast table and now greeted him with a happy smile. To her surprise he leaned forward and kissed her lightly on top of her head.

'You're looking very smart this morning,' he told her. 'I like the blouse. It suits you.'

Her smile broadened. 'Office clothes,' she explained with a smile. 'It's supposed to make me look efficient. I can be a little more relaxed when I'm working at home.' He was wearing dark slacks and pullover over a white shirt and Fran hoped her admiration wasn't too obvious. 'Forgive me for starting without you,' she said, 'but I have to be at Starr Masseys later this morning. A literary agent from your neck of the woods is coming at ten-thirty and I've been chosen to wine and dine him over lunch.'

'Lucky man!'

'I'm not so lucky. You may know him – his name's Jorge Markowitz and he's terribly overbearing—'

'Markowitz? I've heard of him.'

'Nobody actually likes him, but he's sold us some successful books and his client list is pretty impressive. The trouble is he fell out with Derek Starr on his last visit and Stuart is tied up with another visitor. Marjory is at a librarians' conference in Dudley so it has to be me, unfortunately. In view of what's been happening to this family I'd rather be at home, but beggars can't be choosers.'

Del surveyed the table which had been set for four. 'Do I sit anywhere?'

Fran was all contrition. 'Of course. Forgive me. Leaving you standing like that.'

'I find it easy to forgive you!' He smiled. 'You have a lot on your mind right now.'

Fran said, 'Annie has already eaten and Dot is having a lie-in.' She waved a hand towards the sideboard. 'Do help yourself, Del. I'm afraid it's a very English breakfast – porridge, scrambled eggs, toast and Annie's cherry jam – it's a bit runny but otherwise very good. Or marmalade. I regret to tell you that we have no orange juice, no muffins and no "shortstack." '

Amused, he said, 'I bet you don't even know what a shortstack *is*!'

'I don't, but I know it's what Americans eat for breakfast. I read a lot of American manuscripts.'

He helped himself to scrambled eggs which he piled generously on to a slice of toast. As he sat down at the table he explained the term. 'It's a pile of small waffles or pancakes, with maybe bacon or an egg. We put maple syrup over it.'

'Good heavens!'

'It's delicious!'

'I'll take your word for it!'

Del smiled. 'Things are looking up!' he said. 'Together over breakfast!'

Her answering smile was short-lived. 'Del, I had a phone call from the police just before I sat down.'

He was instantly serious. 'Bad news?'

'I'm afraid so. It seems that the kindly professor by the name of Ryan, who went to the hospital to enquire after Henry, wasn't a professor at all. They think it was whoever killed him. As soon as the nurse hinted that Henry's chances weren't good, he left . . . as though satisfied.'

'Jeez, Fran! That is something else!' His shocked eyes looked into hers.

'Isn't it! And someone has come forward in Cambridge. A man who was walking his dog. I forget his name. It seems he saw a car suddenly turn round at great speed in the road – the road where Henry was knocked down. He saw it swing round and back into someone's gatepost and then jerk forward. Then it drove back the way it had come and disappeared round a corner. The police think it was *the* car.'

'Did he get a good look at it? I know it was dark.'

Fran shook her head. 'There was a street-lamp nearby. He said it was a dark colour, probably brown—'

'Ah!' He looked at her soberly.

'I know,' she said. 'It had light wheels, possibly yellow.'

She sighed. 'I don't want it to be Matt for all sorts of reasons, but if it's not him, then someone else is trying to kill us.'

'I'm glad you asked me to move in. I had thought of suggesting it, but I thought you'd take it the wrong way.'

'I wouldn't, Del. I know you too well. At least—' She floundered a little, not wishing to sound presumptuous. 'At least, I don't know you at all well, but I *feel* as though I do. And I know I can trust you.'

'That's good to hear.' His grey eyes regarded hers steadily.

'There's coffee as well as tea,' she told him quickly. 'We have managed some concessions to your American roots!'

His nearness was a tremendous comfort but it was also unsettling. Fran found it hard to concentrate and, to hide her confusion, she buttered a slice of toast which she didn't want and spread it with marmalade which she didn't like. 'I was talking to Annie, and she thinks we should tell Dot what we suspect. I don't know what to do – about naming Matt, I mean. She's so highly-strung and I don't want to frighten her. There's also the point that if Matt should turn up here before we know anything for certain – and he might – Dot would almost certainly give the game away. That thought scares me.'

For a moment he was silent, considering what she had said. Then he said, 'It can't be long before they at least take him in for questioning. Or search his flat. Something. Maybe that would be the right time to tell Dot? You'd have something definite and it wouldn't be supposition.'

'Maybe you're right. At least she knows she mustn't go out alone, or let strangers into the house. The trouble is that Matt *isn't* a stranger. Still, you're here now.'

He put a hand over hers. 'I'm so glad you need me, Fran, even though it's for the worst possible reasons. I'm beginning to feel pretty good around you, you know that?'

'I know. I'm glad you're here. I feel so much safer – and when I go up to the office I shan't have to worry about Dot and Annie. Oh, dear! This is such a crazy situation. I have to keep pinching myself to be sure it's not some kind of nightmare.'

'You're not eating your toast, Fran.'

She stared at it. 'I don't like marmalade,' she told him shakily. 'I don't know why I took it. I'm probably going quietly mad.'

'No, you're not, Fran. Don't be so hard on yourself.'

'You're right, I know, but I feel so hemmed in. And responsible, somehow.'

'Fran, you're not responsible. How could you be?'

'Not responsible in that way; responsible for Dot and Annie and Connie. If Mother were still alive . . .'

Del regarded her earnestly. 'She couldn't do any better than you, Fran. And you can't be mother hen – no, not even to Dot. Oh, sure, you can try to help each other out, but you each have to stand alone some time. We all do. It's the way of the world, Fran.' He reached out and took hold of her hand. 'It's how people grow, Fran.'

'If they live long enough!'

He sighed ruefully. 'I take your point.'

'And I understand what you're saying, Del, and I know you're right.'

Sighing, he withdrew his hand. 'I'm interfering. It's a bad habit. I'm sorry, I'm just so worried about you.'

His kindly concern was undermining Fran's fragile composure and to disguise this she poured herself another cup of tea and began to stir it. 'If only we knew for certain. One minute I'm sure it's Matt, and the next I can't believe it. I can't imagine him going into that ward to look at Henry – to *gloat*. Seeing him there so helpless, in all those bandages and with that awful drip thing in his arm. And to ask how near to death he was! That is so horrible.'

'Whoever it was he was taking one hell of a chance!' Del took a couple of mouthfuls of coffee and then put the cup down. 'You know I'm supposed to be in Scotland? They're expecting me late tomorrow. I must get out of it somehow; I just can't leave you here unprotected—'

'Tomorrow? Oh, Del! I'd quite forgotten.' She shook her head vigorously. 'Of course you must go. You're the best man! It would spoil the whole wedding. Please, Del. Don't give it another thought. You'll only be gone for a few days. The police will keep an eye on us until you come back.'

'I'm not happy about it, Fran.'

'Just pretend we had never met. Then you wouldn't be here to watch over us.'

He smiled but he was obviously worried. 'That's a very illogical argument, Fran! I appreciate what you're doing but I am still not happy. I feel as though I'm deserting you when you need me most.'

Fran resisted the urge to say that she would always need him, but this was neither the time nor the place. 'But they need you too. We're not so selfish, I hope, as to keep you from your duties. Go to Scotland, Del, and enjoy yourself,' she urged. The idea that he must leave them filled her with dread, but she reminded herself that she was not the only star in his firmament. He had family commitments which he must honour, and it would be unfair to persuade him otherwise. 'Go with a clear conscience. We'll still be here when you get back.' As soon as the words were out she wished them unsaid. They sounded like a challenge to Fate and might bring bad luck.

He stared into her eyes. 'Is that a promise, Fran? I don't want to lose you.'

'It's a promise, Del.' Hiding her uneasiness, she nodded as cheerfully as she could and then glanced at her watch. 'Heavens! I should be on my way by now.' She stood up.

'Annie has my number. If anything happens which I should know about, you'll ring me?'

'I'll do that.' He stood up as she moved from the table. 'And take care, Fran.'

*

Jorge Markowitz, the American agent, was tiring company. From the moment he walked into the office, Fran felt overwhelmed by his loud voice and confident manner. He was a bearlike man who smoked large, pungent cigars and peered at her over rimless spectacles. His accent was broad (Fran suspected the Bronx), and he seemed to fill her tiny office. Once again she found herself wishing that Stuart or Derek had been able to deal with him. He had brought two novels and a manuscript to discuss with her, hoping to persuade her that Starr Massey should publish them in England. The first novel was set in Alaska and the blurb sounded intriguing – but then they always did.

'I think I shall like this one,' she told him. '*White Wolf.* Good title. Tell me about the author.'

He explained that James Dubarr was a French-Canadian who had lived in Alaska for eleven years and knew what he was writing about. He understood and respected the Eskimos, and had endured the hardships which featured in his novel. He had based the main character on a real person, a friend of his, who was now dead.

'This guy writes from the heart,' Jorge told her. 'He really cared for this friend, and he blamed himself for his death. Don't ask me why; I forget the details. I don't know how much of the novel is true and how much fiction, but it makes one hell of a read!'

'Has it sold in Europe?'

'Not yet. D'you want the rights?'

'I don't know yet, but we have been very successful recently in Holland. Maybe France, too.'

285

'Your offer would reflect that?'

'Of course.'

'Hmm.' He tossed a second book into her lap. 'Anne Bly. *The Winds of Morning*. You've had her first two, but she's been slow to produce the third. Two kids in three years – that'd slow even me down!' His booming laugh rang out. 'You're getting first bite, but if we can't do a deal I shall probably put it up for auction. Have a look at it, it's good.'

The telephone on Fran's desk rang and she picked it up. 'I said I didn't want to be disturbed . . .'

'I'm sorry, Miss Massey, but it's your brother. He says he must see you.'

Fran almost dropped the telephone. She felt suddenly cold. 'My – you mean *Matt*?'

'Matt Massey. Yes.'

Fran's hand went up to her mouth. Matt was downstairs! Oh, God! 'Did you tell him I was with a client?'

'He says he must see you. He insisted.'

'Tell him "No", will you? I'm tied up all day.'

She felt breathless, as though someone had punched her in the stomach. *Please* let him take 'No' for an answer. She couldn't face him.

'I'm sorry, Miss Massey, but he – hey!'

Matt had obviously snatched the phone from her. Now he said, 'You can spare me a minute or two, Fran, surely. I'm your brother, remember? I shan't leave until you speak to me. If you prefer, I can create a scene.' The phone went dead and Fran stared at it as though hypnotized. She became aware that Markowitz was giving her a strange look.

He said, 'Trouble?'

She nodded, then quickly shook her head. 'It's my brother – I don't know . . .'

'Go ahead. I'll wait,' he told her.

Still she hesitated, unwilling to be brought face to

face with Matt. She was totally unprepared; at a loss to know how to react. She was also afraid, although her common sense told her that Matt could hardly do her any physical harm in the reception area with other people looking on.

'Please excuse me,' she said.

He looked at her. 'You OK?'

'Yes, thank you. I won't be long.'

She was most certainly not OK, she told herself, but she hurried to the lift and pressed the ground-floor button with a trembling finger.

*

She saw him at once, standing by the front desk, his hands thrust into his pockets, his collar turned up around his face. Her first thought was how *ordinary* he looked, how like the Matt she had always known. Somehow, after the events of the last few weeks, she had expected him to have changed. If he had killed Mary and Henry he *couldn't* look this normal, she told herself.

'Matt!' She crossed the foyer towards him, a stiff smile on her face.

The receptionist said indignantly, 'He just snatched the phone from my hand!'

Fran said, 'I'm sorry.'

Matt was smiling and something in his smile told her that he understood her inner turmoil and was *enjoying* her discomfiture.

'Fran, how are you?' He kissed her before she could draw back and somehow she resisted the urge to wipe the kiss from her lips with the back of her hand. It was important that she shouldn't antagonize him.

'I'm fine, Matt.' She had never felt worse in her life. 'What is all this? I'm desperately busy.'

'I thought I'd stay over with you at Maidhurst for a few

days,' he said. 'I have some calls to make in the Kent area and I—'

'No!' It was almost a shout and hastily she modified her voice. 'I'm afraid not, Matt. I wrote to you. I told you that Del would be staying with us; he's having Mary's room.' Thank goodness he didn't know about the wedding in Scotland!

'Then I could have my old room.'

'No, Matt.'

'But why not?'

Fran searched desperately for a reason that might convince him. 'It's too much for Annie,' she began.

'Rot!' His gaze was challenging. 'Annie would love to have me there to fuss over.'

'No, Matt. It's my decision and—'

'But there's plenty of room.'

The thought of Matt sharing the same house terrified her. It was just like him to challenge her this way. He must know what everyone was thinking; must realize that he was under suspicion. 'I don't want you there, Matt. I'm terribly busy and—'

He said, 'Look, I don't mind Del being there; I quite like him. Does Connie know, though?' He lowered his voice. 'Stolen her thunder, haven't you! Stolen her chap, too, by all accounts.'

'I don't have time for this,' she told him, controlling her voice with an effort. 'You ask if you can stay and the answer's "No". That's an end to it.'

'Is it, Fran? Do you really think it's as easy as that? You think you can brush me off and I'll just creep away?' The expression in his eyes sent a sudden shiver down her spine. He was playing with her, tormenting her. 'I might not be as soft as you hope I am – as I used to be.'

She said, 'You were never soft, Matt. You were devious and . . . and sometimes cruel. You were only nice when you wanted something!' He was threatening her, she thought furiously. 'I won't be bullied, Matt,' she said and hoped she sounded convincing.

'So I'm a bully now, am I, as well as everything else?'

His eyes were cold and Fran regretted the outburst immediately, cursing her lack of control. This was what Matt wanted; this was what he was good at – arousing people's anger, probing their weaknesses, reaching the emotions they preferred to keep hidden. His eyes narrowed and she saw, fleetingly, the hatred he felt for her. It was there, naked and blazing from the depths of his soul.

'Dear me!' he mocked, his voice low. 'We are in a paddy, aren't we? Now that wasn't nice, was it, Fran? Not nice at all. Bully, indeed! You may live to regret that little outburst.' He lowered his voice. 'Or rather, you may not!' His lips curved into a deadly smile, full of menace.

Fran felt a tightness in her chest as though unseen hands had gripped her. She was finding it hard to draw breath as fear paralysed her. Because now she *knew*. There was a roaring in her ears. This was why he had come to the office. He didn't really want to stay with her, that was merely an excuse. Matt *wanted* her to know, to be afraid, to feel helpless. He wanted them all to know that he had killed Mary and Henry. The evil deep within his eyes said it all. Her doubts fled and she was left weak and trembling. 'Why are you doing this, Matt?' she whispered. 'Why?'

'Doing what, Fran?' His expression was at once innocent and mocking.

Fran was vaguely aware that other people were coming and going through the reception area and yet she felt completely alone. Alone with a man who had killed and who would kill again. Soon it would be her turn, or Dot – or maybe Connie would be next. Matt could and *would* do it. She wanted to scream out, 'Catch him! Take him! While he's still around and before he strikes again!' But she knew how ridiculous that would sound. Matt would smile and be charming and everyone would be embarrassed, and she would feel an absolute idiot. It was impossible and he knew it. Matt was no fool.

'Please go, Matt,' she whispered. 'Just go. Leave us alone.'

He smiled. 'But why, Fran? Don't you love me any more?'

She thought of Mary falling on to the rocks below and of Henry being hurled to the ground by Matt's car. She hated the smiling face, the mask that hid the murderous hatred.

She drew a deep breath. It was too late now for pretences. 'No, I don't,' she said. 'I don't love you, Matt. I don't love you because I don't even know you any more. Whoever you are now, you are not the Matt I loved.'

'Harsh words!' he said with a short laugh.

'I don't want to see you ever again,' she told him.

To her relief he gave her a mocking bow. 'Your wish is my command!' he said. 'But you will see me again, Fran. You can count on it!'

The threat was blatant and Fran almost reeled back.

Turning on his heel, Matt walked to the swing doors and pushed his way through without a backward glance. Desperately, weak with relief for the momentary reprieve, Fran grabbed at the desk to prevent herself from falling.

The receptionist asked, 'Are you all right?'

Fran stammered, 'Could you get me a chair, please . . .' She felt herself sway and her legs were no longer holding her up. The face of the receptionist faded. 'I think I'm going to . . .'

Blackness engulfed her.

*

When she came to she was sitting on the floor and the receptionist was offering her a glass of cold water.

'You gave me a real turn!' she told Fran. 'You were as

white as death! What happened? Was it that man? He said he was your brother. What did he say to you?'

'Nothing. I can't explain.' She gulped down the water. 'Would you like a cup of tea?'

'Not just now.' Fran put a hand to her face and felt the perspiration. She felt dizzy and shocked.

At that moment the lift door opened and Stuart stepped out, accompanied by his visitor.

'Fran! What on earth's happening?'

The receptionist said, 'She fainted clean away, Mr Starr. Frightened the life out of me. Her eyes rolled up and she was gone. She banged her forehead when she fell, poor thing. Bit of a bruise coming there.'

Stuart crouched awkwardly beside Fran, his kindly face drawn into a look of concern.

'You do look terrible. Do you think you can walk to the lift, Fran? You could go in to my room. I've got a comfortable chair there and you could rest.'

Fran shook her head. 'I'll be all right. I've got Markowitz in my office, and he'll be wondering where I am.'

'He can wait.' He stood up and said to the receptionist, 'Give Marjory Evans a ring, and ask her—'

Fran said, 'Marjory's in Dudley, Stuart, but I'm OK now. If you could just help me up? I feel such an idiot.'

He pulled her gently to her feet. 'You don't look all right.'

She managed a smile. 'I'll survive. Don't worry about me.' She smiled apologetically at Stuart's visitor. 'Truly, I'm over the worst.'

When Stuart had reluctantly shepherded his visitor into the waiting taxi, Fran turned to the receptionist. 'May I make a quick phone call from here?' she asked. 'Mr Markowitz is in my room.'

'Certainly.'

Fran dialled the operator and asked for Maidstone library.

While she waited she breathed deeply, trying to restore her shattered nerves. She must warn her sister without frightening her, if that was at all possible.

'I need to speak to Miss Massey,' she said. 'It's urgent.'

After what seemed an eternity Connie came on the line. 'Fran? What's happened? It's not Dot . . .'

'No, she's all right. But Matt's been here. I'm in London in the office. He says he's going to make some calls in our area. He wanted to *stay* with us!' She heard Connie's sharp intake of breath.

'I said no as nicely as I could, but he insisted. Then I had to refuse him point-blank – and, Connie, listen to me. I mean this. *Matt did it*! I know he did, it was written in his eyes.'

'God in heaven, Fran! You can't know that for—'

'I haven't got time to talk, Connie. Just listen and trust me. The point is he might contact you. Does he know you've got a spare room?'

'Yes, but—'

'Oh, God! Well, whatever he says remember *he did it*.'

'You can't be a hundred per cent—'

Fran drew a sharp breath of exasperation. She was going to have to spell it out in words of one syllable. Cupping a hand round the mouthpiece of the telephone, she said, 'Connie, he killed Mary and he killed Henry. I can't prove it, but I know he did. He wanted me to know, to frighten me.'

'Oh, God, Fran! You shouldn't have antagonized him!'

'Connie! That's rich, coming from you! But I haven't got time to argue. I'm just warning you. For God's sake keep him out of your flat, Connie. He's dangerous. Before, I wasn't sure, but now there's no doubt in my mind. Are the police keeping an eye on you?'

'I suppose so. I haven't seen any, but they might be in plain clothes.'

'For heaven's sake be careful. If you'd seen the look in

292

his eyes, Connie! I can't describe it but I was terrified, I don't mind admitting it.'

'I will. But you, Fran. Are you all right?'

'Not really, but what matters is that we all stay safe until the police can arrest him. I'll speak to them later, but right now I've got an agent waiting for me upstairs in my office. I'll have to go.'

'Right, then. I'll be in touch.'

Fran replaced the telephone. The receptionist was staring at her. Had she heard?

'That man was your brother?' the girl said.

Yes, she had heard! Fran hesitated. How could she possibly explain? Instead, she nodded briefly and made her way back to the lift. Suddenly Jorge Markowitz seemed the least of her worries.

*

The two policemen waited in the car a few doors down from No. 25. Bayfield Road, at four in the afternoon, was suddenly full of schoolboys in red and grey caps, making their way home. Book-filled satchels were draped carelessly over shoulders, strapped to a back or dragged along the pavement with glorious disrespect. The two men watched, amused, as the boys, released from the discipline of school, let off steam in their various ways. Some ran shouting along the street, whirling their caps. Others pushed and shoved each other off the pavement into the road which fortunately was free of traffic. A few shuffled along as though exhausted by all the day had had to offer. One boy, egged on by his friends, tried to climb a lamp-post.

'Watch it, lad!' said Sergeant Hollis.

His companion smiled. 'Were we ever that young?' he asked rhetorically. 'God, it seems years ago. I seem to have been old and careworn for ever!'

The sergeant chuckled. 'I went to Allandale Boys, for

my sins. Hated it. Played truant whenever I could. The attendance officer hated me, and my poor mother was always making excuses for me.'

They had been sitting in the unmarked police car for over two hours. They had eaten all the fish-paste sandwiches which the sergeant's wife had prepared for him and had drunk all the tea in the detective chief inspector's flask. They had discussed the latest film, the state of first-division football, the likelihood of another war in Europe and the contrariness of women. The sergeant was married with two children, Detective Chief Inspector Bruce was single.

A group of boys crossed the road in front of them, lurching excitedly, shouting and joking. A cap was snatched off and tossed about, ending in the gutter.

Sergeant Hollis groaned. 'Those caps cost money!' he said. 'Two and ninepence for my eldest boy's. It's so expensive, school uniform. You've got to have it, but they charge the earth. Two and ninepence! And that's what the kids do. Chuck them about!'

A plump, elderly woman came out of the house next to No. 25 and stared at their car. After a moment's hesitation, she made her way across the road towards them, her arms crossed belligerently across her chest.

Hollis said, 'Oh, no! Here comes trouble.'

Bruce muttered, 'Go away, woman!'

She stood in the road and rapped on the window of the car and the sergeant wound it down. 'You two!' she said. 'What are you up to? Hanging round the school, spying on the boys. I've been watching you.'

'Mind your own business, madam!' said the sergeant. 'We're minding ours.'

She stared hard at each man in turn. 'Well, I'm taking a good look at the pair of you. My sister's boy goes to this school, and I'm not taking any chances. If you don't move on I shall tell the headmaster, and he'll send for the police.'

294

Bruce said, 'And your name is?' He produced a notebook and she looked startled.

'Ivy Potter. Mrs. But what's it to you?'

Bruce said, 'We *are* the police, madam.'

Her mouth fell open. 'The police? Why . . . What . . .' Confused, she glanced around her as though deciding she had missed something. Seeing nothing untoward, she asked, 'You after one of the boys, then? Up to no good, is he?'

Bruce said, 'We appreciate your vigilance, Mrs Potter, but you're interrupting us in the execution of our duties. Please go away.'

She opened her mouth to argue, then thought better of it and retreated to No. 27.

Hollis said, 'Do we look like dirty old men?'

Bruce grinned. 'I suppose we do look a bit suspicious.'

'God preserve us from the righteous citizen!'

The curtain moved in the front window of No. 27 and their accuser peered out inquisitively.

But Bruce was leaning forward. 'Could this be our man?' he muttered.

A dark-haired man was walking along the street. He moved with confidence, his gait almost jaunty. He was of average height, his hands were thrust into the pockets of his overcoat and he wore a brightly striped scarf wound round his neck.

'That's him!' said Bruce.

'Cocky-looking bastard!'

'But where's the car?'

'Tucked away in a garage somewhere, no doubt, while the damaged rear light is replaced.'

'Not if I can help it!' Bruce opened the door. 'Let's get him!'

The two men raced across the street. The man at No. 25 hesitated as he put his key in the lock, turning to watch them.

Bruce flashed his warrant card and so did the sergeant. Massey looked at the cards and then at the policemen. 'Well?'

Bruce said, 'Mr Massey? Matthew Massey?'

'That's right.'

'I am Detective Chief Inspector Bruce and this is Sergeant Hollis. We are making enquiries into the death of Mary Ann Massey and her brother Henry Massey. I have reason to believe that you may be able to assist in those enquiries, and we are taking you in for questioning, Mr Massey.'

'You'll never make it stick! This is ridiculous!'

Bruce's eyes narrowed. It was always a giveaway, that first reaction to the caution. Massey had not denied the murder; instead he had insisted that they would never 'make it stick'. No denial of guilt, just a confident assurance that it could never be proved. Interesting.

He finished the caution. '. . . but anything you do say will be taken down in writing and may be used in evidence.'

'Me? Murder my own sister?'

He was trying to correct that first impression, thought Bruce. The man knew that his first careless words had been a giveaway. The indignation was well done, with just the right amount of vehemence: innocence personified. Bruce was under no misapprehension. This man was clever; he was now playing 'wrongly accused' – but weren't they all, he thought wearily. The reaction they had all practised for just such an eventuality. The false surprise, the indignation, the 'how-could-you-think-I'd-do-a-thing-like-that?' expression.

'We'd like you to accompany us to the station, sir,' he said.

Massey looked at him. 'Assisting you with your enquiries? Is that it?'

'It's a little more than that, sir.' Bruce allowed a sinister note to creep into the words. He'd put the fear of God into him right from the start.

Ivy Potter, abandoning her observation post in the front window, rushed from her doorway and leaned over the hedge, her round face almost comical with excitement. She said nothing but looked from one to the other, open-mouthed.

The door of No. 25 opened and a woman appeared in the doorway. She wore an apron over her dress and was still in her slippers. Her hair was tied up in a scarf. She clutched a tin of polish and a cloth. 'What's this?' she demanded, her voice shrill. 'He's my lodger. Honest as the day. He'd never pinch anything.' She turned to the suspect. 'Matt! What on earth's happening?'

On the pavement a group of schoolboys watched the little drama with interest. Other boys joined them. Marvellous, thought Bruce. If Massey was to make a run for it through that lot, it would be damned awkward. Kids flying in all directions. To the landlady he said, 'And you are?'

'Mrs Parfitt. That is, Brenda, but everyone calls me Poppy.'

Bruce watched her closely. 'Mrs Parfitt, we're arresting your lodger on suspicion of murder. We—'

'Murder?' Her shock was genuine. '*Murder*? Mr Massey?'

Bruce continued, 'We shall be asking him a few questions. If the answers are satisfactory he will be released.'

'If? *If*?' Her eyes widened. 'Of course they'll be satisfactory. Mr Massey wouldn't hurt a fly. I'm sure of that.' She gave Massey a quick look and years of interpreting such glances told Bruce that the pair were slightly more than landlady and lodger. So, no good relying on her as a hostile witness. Pity.

Bruce said, 'Put him in the car, sergeant.'

Hollis said, 'Come along, sir – and don't give me any trouble.'

'Why should I? You're making a mistake, that's all.'

To the suspect, Mrs Parfitt called, 'What does he mean, murder?'

Massey said, 'It's nothing. A mistake. Don't worry.'

She stared as he was pushed into the rear seat of the police car. 'Don't worry?' she muttered. 'How do I "not worry", eh?' Nobody answered.

In a low voice Bruce asked her, 'Where does Mr Massey garage his car? Do you know?'

She frowned. 'He doesn't. Leastways, not that I know of. It's always standing right here.'

'But not today?'

'No.' She looked up and down the street, puzzled. 'It's usually here.'

'And you don't know where it might be?'

'No, I don't ...'. She made an effort to pull herself together. 'And I don't know why I should stand here answering daft questions about a car. I don't know anything about anything.'

He looked at her coldly. 'Mrs Parfitt, I'd like you to understand something. A crime has been committed, and if you don't answer my questions you might be considered an accessory to that crime.'

He was pleased to see the abrupt collapse of her defiance. It always worked, he reflected grimly.

Mrs Potter found her voice at last. 'What's he done?'

'Nothing, you nosey old cow!'

Bruce raised his eyebrows. 'Ladies! Please!' To Massey's landlady he said, 'I shall be back later with a search warrant and we shall search your lodger's room, Mrs Parfitt. We shall need to see everything exactly as he left it. We shall dust the room for prints, so I advise you to stay well away unless you wish to become implicated. I have to remind you that we are investigating a very serious crime.'

She nodded speechlessly, obviously shaken. He felt almost sorry for her.

Mrs Potter said, 'Well, I never did!'

Brenda Parfitt said faintly, 'I'll be in all day.'

'I'll be back.'

He walked briskly back to the car, his mind already on the interview ahead. He was looking forward to it, scenting blood. The cockiest bastards were sometimes the easiest to crack.

Chapter Fourteen

WHEN FRAN ARRIVED HOME THAT evening she was greeted by Annie, who had obviously been crying.

'Annie! What is it?' Her spirits, already low, plunged further at the prospect of another disaster.

'It's Matt. They've arrested him. That poor boy!' Annie's eyes filled with tears again as she stood, twisting her hands with misery, watching Fran take off her coat and hat.

'Arrested?' Fran's heart lifted a little. At least they would be safe now. 'But, Annie, how can you think like that? Think of Mary and Henry—'

'I know. I know.' Fresh tears poured down the wrinkled cheeks. 'But I can't help remembering him when he was little. Such a funny little lad. Such funny ways. And now they'll hang him.'

'We don't know that yet.' Fran put a comforting arm round her. 'But I'm glad, Annie. *Glad!* He came to see me today, and he was utterly hateful. He killed them, Annie, and he doesn't feel the slightest remorse. I could see it in his face.' She drew the old lady to her, patting her back the way someone comforts a child. 'Don't feel too bad for him, Annie. He's not the Matt you once loved, believe me.' Gently she tilted Annie's face towards her own. 'He frightened me today,'

'Frightened you? Oh, Fran!'

'I was so frightened I fainted. That's what he did to me, Annie. Think of Mary and Henry whenever you feel sorry for Matt. And remember that if they hadn't arrested him, he would have killed again.'

But Annie shook her head and, pulling away, stumbled back towards the kitchen. Fran watched her go with mixed feelings. She understood how betrayed Annie felt, but she would have been grateful for a little comfort herself. The lunch with Markowitz had seemed interminable, his ebullience exhausting. She had only partially recovered from the faint and had felt nauseous throughout the meal. Markowitz's loud voice had dominated the restaurant, embarrassing her and obviously annoying other diners. She was so thankful when, just before three, he had taken himself off to his hotel. Her journey home on the slow, jolting train had further depleted her energies, but the thought that Del would be waiting for her had given her strength.

She stood alone in the hallway, clutching her hat, coat and gloves, gathering what resources she had. Del's well-meant advice occurred to her. He would probably send her straight to bed if she would allow it, but she knew she could not ignore everyone else's needs. It was not that easy; people depended on her and she would not willingly let them down. She drew a deep breath as she put both hands over her face and heard Fritz's scampering feet as he hurried to greet her, barking a greeting. That meant that Dot would not be far behind. She wasn't.

'Fran! What's the matter?'

Hastily Fran lowered her hands. 'Hullo, Dot. It's nothing, just a headache.'

Dot was smiling cheerfully, so Fran realized she could not have been told of Matt's arrest or the reason for it.

Just for the moment Fran hoped they could keep it that way. There was really no reason to shock her with yet more dreadful news, and it might be months before Matt came to trial. That would give Fran time to break it to her gently. How, she had no idea, but she knew it must be done with care. Not for the first time, she wished her mother alive again. Mother would have known what to do – or would she? This heretical thought surprised her. Her mother might well have kept the news from Dot indefinitely, pretending that Matt had gone to live abroad. That was Mother's way, the way she had hidden the truth about Matt's parents. Yet if Matt had grown up with the knowledge, he might have found it easier to accept. But it was easy to be wise after the event and Fran was ashamed of her disloyal thoughts. Her parents had done what they thought best, which was all Fran could do now.

She smiled at Dot. 'A bad headache,' she repeated. 'Nothing to worry about. I had an awful man with me in the office. He had a loud voice and he gave me a headache.'

'Poor old you!'

'Yes.' She bent to pat the dog.

Dot said, 'Fritz is upset because Annie keeps crying. The telephone rang and she talked to someone and then she started crying.' She looked at Fran anxiously. 'Poor old Annie and poor old you.'

Fran's heart sank. Dot was so shrewd – Mother had never given her credit for that. She wondered uneasily exactly what Dot had heard. Crouching to tickle Fritz she said, 'Don't be upset, Fritz. I'll talk to Annie. I'm sure it was nothing too terrible. Perhaps it was about Amy's mother.' She stood up. 'Where's Del?'

'He's finishing his packing. I—'

'Packing?' The day's events had driven from her mind Del's imminent departure. Now, despairingly, she remembered.

'I helped him, Fran. While Annie was crying. I wanted to help Annie, but she didn't want me there. I wanted her to stop crying, but she wouldn't and she said, "For God's sake leave me alone," and Del said would I help him pack. I folded his shirts, a blue one and a white one with frills down the front, and then I rolled his ties. He said I was the best helper he's ever known. Really, Fran, he did.'

Fran nodded. Still, at least he need not worry about their safety while he was away. Now that Matt was in custody the threat was removed and they could relax again.

'He's going to Scotland, Fran.'

'Yes, I know.'

'Someone's getting married and he has to be there. He's got the ring; he showed it to me. And I polished his shoes for him. I didn't make any mess.'

'I'm sure you did a good job on them.' She would miss Del, but it was only for a few days and in the meantime they could all sleep easily. She wondered whether Connie knew. She would have to talk to Annie and find out exactly what had happened. Matt had been with her in the morning, so he must have been arrested later in the afternoon. Not that she cared when or how. All that mattered was that they were safe. The horrors of the trial were still to come and would somehow have to be borne, but for the moment all they could do was carry on with their lives.

From somewhere above a door opened and closed and Del came down the stairs towards her. He took one look at her face and held out his hands. Fran ran towards him and sighed with pleasure as his arms went round her. Into her hair he whispered, 'I know about Matt's arrest. Annie told me. We've got to be thankful.' She nodded, not trusting herself to speak, aware that Dot was close. Suddenly she looked up and held out her left arm and Dot moved into the little circle and was hugged by both of them. Dot would take it the hardest, she reflected sadly. She would never understand the intricacies of the human heart or the eternal struggle between good and evil. A wicked Matt would be difficult for her to accept. They might have to try another approach. A misguided Matt, perhaps?

Del released them, smiling cheerfully, willing her to do the same. She tried, but her mouth quivered and she was afraid she would cry.

'A stiff drink!' he said quickly, 'for all of us. It's been a tough day.'

Dot nodded. 'All that packing!' she said.

They went into the lounge and Fran sank on to the sofa with Dot beside her. Fritz watched them, his head on one side, his tail wagging uncertainly. He senses the tension, Fran thought.

'I think Fritz wants a cuddle,' she suggested, and at once Dot scooped him up and put him on her lap where he settled with a little snuffle of satisfaction.

Fran knew that she ought to go in search of Annie and do what she could to reassure her, but for the moment she felt drained and vulnerable herself. A drop of brandy wouldn't go amiss, she thought wearily. She would miss Del, but he would only be gone for a few days and then they would be together again. She tried to think about his return but her mind focused stubbornly on Matt. She had very little knowledge about prisons, but in her imagination she saw him in a cell with bare, whitewashed walls, a bunk bed, a bucket with a lid on it. It was a chilling and degrading picture and yet he deserved nothing better. He had brutally cut short the lives of two young people who had trusted him. She must never forget that. Eventually even Dot would have to understand.

Del handed her a brandy and she sipped it eagerly. 'Now I can go away with an easy mind,' he said, raising his glass.

Dot asked, 'Why can you?'

Fran saw Del's rueful expression and knew that, too late,

he regretted the small indiscretion. Thinking rapidly she said, 'The man who knocked Henry down has been caught. We thought he might escape and maybe knock down someone else. Now the police have locked him up.'

'Locked him up? Oh!' She looked down at the dog in her lap. 'Fritz is pleased, aren't you, Fritz?' She peered into his face. 'He's not quite sure.'

Del mouthed 'Sorry' and Fran smiled her forgiveness. She asked, 'Which train are you taking tomorrow?'

'The two-fifteen, but I said I'd pop in and see Peter Westrop before I go. He's keen to see the revisions I've done so far. I'll take him the first seven chapters.'

'So many? You have worked hard. Last time we spoke of it I seem to remember you were working on chapter five.'

'I'm a fast worker!' he grinned and raised his eyes a little.

Yes, you are, Fran thought. And I'm no slowcoach. The attraction had been there for both of them, right from the beginning – from the day of her mother's funeral, in fact. Had Mother somehow brought them together? It was a nice idea, but Fran was forced to reject it as too fanciful. A firm belief in fate was an easy way to reject responsibility.

Dot looked up, suddenly hopeful. 'So may I take Fritz for a walk now that the bad man's been caught? Me and Amy, I mean. When she's done her homework. She has to draw a map of Africa and mark in all the important towns. She hates geography. I said I would draw the map for her, but Annie said that was cheating and that Amy must do it herself.'

Fran caught Del's eye. 'Why not?' she asked.

He shrugged. 'Exactly.'

Fran glanced out of the window. 'It will soon be dark,' she said. 'Don't go too far. Ten minutes there and back; just a breather.'

It was difficult to relax the vigilance, she noted with

surprise. And yet, for the first time since she had heard of Matt's arrest, Fran began to feel a lightening of the burden she had carried. There was nothing more to fear and they could resume their normal lives, unshadowed by doubts. Maybe, eventually, she and Del could make a new life together. Maybe not. She mustn't raise her hopes. There was Dot to be considered. Del's home was in America and he, too, had responsibilities. There were problems in his life that needed to be resolved. A happy ending was hardly certain. But at least the danger – the *physical* danger – was at an end. The future had to look a little brighter, surely, and for the present she would be satisfied with that. She watched as Dot rose to her feet, tucking Fritz under her arm, and departed in search of her young friend.

Del said, 'That was stupid of me. Sorry.'

'Don't be. She is sharp, but I don't think she connects Matt with any of the other troubles.' 'She leaned forward and touched his hand. 'Sit next to me, Del. I shall miss you so much.'

'But at least I know you will still be here when I get back!' He moved to sit beside her and slid an arm round her shoulders. 'Annie took the news about the arrest very badly. I didn't know what to do, so I lured Dot away with the idea of helping me pack. I was afraid Annie would say too much.'

'I must go to her . . .' Fran began guiltily. 'Poor Annie! She loved Matt more than any of us. Always making excuses for him.'

As she made to rise, Del held her back. 'Not yet,' he said. 'You've had a terrible day. Just relax, be nice to yourself for a moment. You give too much, Fran. You'll make yourself ill.'

He was stroking her arm with his free hand and she leaned closer, letting her head rest on his shoulder. 'Five minutes, then,' she agreed. 'I could put up with a lot of this!'

He grinned. 'I promise you, you'll have to!' He kissed her lightly. 'It's so good to see you smile. You've had a rotten deal these last few weeks. When I get back from Scotland I'm going to take you to the theatre, and the ballet, and the movies. Your feet won't touch the ground.'

'Sounds wonderful!'

'And I'll finish the novel and it will be a tremendous hit—'

'And we'll all live happily ever after?' She turned her head slightly so that she could press a kiss into his shoulder.

'Something like that!' he said.

She rested against him, drawing strength from his nearness, feeling the warmth of his body through the rough wool of his pullover.

'You will marry me, Fran, won't you?' He pulled back, looking anxiously into her face. 'I mean, we're talking like this. I'm not fooling. I want to be with you always.'

Her heart leaped. 'Del!' She stared at him, unable to believe that this was actually happening. 'Are you – are you asking me to marry you?'

'I guess so. Yes, I am. Are you accepting me?'

'Of course I am!'

For a moment they stared at one another as though a word or an action out of place would break the spell.

'Fran!'

'Is it possible?' she whispered. She would have said more, but Del swung himself on to his knees and seized her hands. 'You won't regret it, dear, sweet Fran! I swear to God you won't.'

'Nor you, Del.'

The suddenness of his proposal had taken her breath away and the immediacy of her answer astonished her. She, Fran, had agreed to marry! Without a moment's hesitation she had said 'Yes,' to a man she hardly knew – and she wanted to shout for joy. There was no room for doubts. 'I *love* you,' she said.

'Fran! Darling!' He couldn't stop staring at her, a wide smile illuminating his features.

Suddenly he was on his feet, pulling her upright. When she stood facing him his smile faltered. 'I may not deserve you, Fran Massey – I'm not the greatest catch in the world – but I shall love you with all my heart, as long as we both shall live. My dearest Fran!'

She was in his arms and returning his kiss when the door opened and Annie stood with a tray of tea in her hands. Her mouth fell open in surprise.

Fran recovered first. 'Annie,' she said, going forward and taking the tray before it fell. 'I think it's about time you heard some good news . . .'

*

The interview room in Maidstone police station was no better than any other – a gloomy area with dark green walls and a single overhead light. The small window, high in the wall, was barred. A battered metal filing cabinet stood against one wall, with a withered pot plant on top of it. There was a large wooden table covered with brown lino-cloth and on it was a bakelite ashtray and a small brass bell; there was a pencil but no paper. Around the table were four bentwood chairs and on one of these sat Matt Massey, his hands resting easily on the table in front of him. He appeared unruffled and there was a hint of arrogance in his expression. Detective Chief Inspector Bruce intended to change all that before he was through with him. Since the 'missing person' file had been abandoned in favour of a 'suspicious death' enquiry, a full murder investigation had begun into the two deaths. Because of this, there had been several developments that Massey could not know about, and with these D.C.I. Bruce would begin the process of demoralizing the suspect.

Another witness had come forward in the Fairlight area, a woman who had seen the car with only a single occupant, driving back towards the main Rye-Hastings road. She would vouch for the fact that the car's driver was 'smiling'. They were going to bring her in for a line-up. They had a team of policemen searching the area around Bayfield Road, checking all the garages, looking for a car fitting the description that was in for repair, or a respray. If they could find the car, the lab boys could match up the paint with the scrapings from a gatepost in Cambridge.

But most of all Bruce wanted a confession. He wanted to rattle this smug devil's composure, he longed to see him crack. He wasn't a brutal man by nature, but the job had hardened him and the sight of countless victims had toughened his will.

He sat down opposite Massey and nodded to his sergeant to join them.

Bruce regarded his suspect coldly, a long stare intended to unnerve, and Massey raised an eyebrow. 'If you're hoping for a confession, you'll be disappointed. I've done nothing and you can't prove that I have.'

'And you don't want a solicitor?'

'I don't need one.'

'That's a matter of opinion, Mr Massey.' Bruce leaned back, tilting his chair slightly. 'You are being accused of the murder of Henry John Massey. That's the most serious charge we could make against you, and it carries the death penalty if proven. Doesn't that cause you the slightest unease?'

'It would if I'd done anything. I've already told you, Inspector. You've—'

'Detective Chief Inspector!' Bruce snapped.

Massey gave a little shrug. 'You've got the wrong man. I was not in Fairlight at the time of my sister's death; I was in Birmingham, making calls on a number of stationer's shops. Ask my landlady. She'll corroborate—'

'We've asked your boss, Mr Massey. He thinks you're lying.' Did he imagine a flicker of disquiet in the dark eyes? 'Mr Eddington, your area manager, claims that you had no calls to make in that area on that day.'

'Dave Eddington is a fool. He doesn't know his arse from his elbow!'

Inwardly Bruce rejoiced. The tone of the suspect's voice had risen marginally, a sure sign that he was not quite as cool as he pretended.

'I would like you to write down the names and addresses of the people you called on that day. Assuming that you *did* make the calls?'

'I can't remember. It was some time back.'

'But you would have paperwork to that effect?'

'Not necessarily.'

'Your boss says you would.'

'I've told you what I think of him.'

Hollis took out a packet of tobacco and some papers and rolled a cigarette with painstaking attention to detail, tucking in every last strand of tobacco and licking the paper carefully. Bruce remained silent, giving the suspect time to ponder his plight. Sometimes the silences were more effective than words.

Hollis patted his pockets and frowned. 'Got a light, sir?'

All part of their strategy. Show the humanitarian side. Demonstrate the friendship between the two officers. Make the suspect feel isolated. Bruce fished a lighter from his pocket and flicked it into flame.

Massey said, 'You can't keep me here without arresting me.'

'That so?' Hollis blew smoke into the cold air. 'Studied the law, have you, Mr Massey? I wonder why that might be?'

Bruce studied the nails of his right hand as Hollis took over the questioning.

'Know your rights, do you? Think you're clever?' He leaned forward. 'They all do, Mr Massey. They all do.'

Massey said, 'I don't always report on my calls, especially if I don't get an order. It looks bad. Better not to report a blank order form. Get the idea?'

'Oh, I get the idea, all right. I get the idea perfectly. Nice little alibi that can't be broken – or that's what you think. Suppose I tell you that you were seen in Fairlight near the scene of the crime ...'

'My sister fell to her death, Sergeant.'

'We beg to differ.'

Massey shrugged.

'We have a witness who saw your car near Fairlight cliffs, and another witness who saw you and a young lady—'

'Not me, Sergeant. I was in Birmingham.'

'Your car was seen ...'

'A car *resembling* mine.'

'Was seen driving away with you at the wheel ...'

'With someone *resembling* me at the wheel!'

'Smiling!'

'I beg your pardon?'

Bruce wanted to knock the polite smile from his face. Instead he fiddled with the brass bell, his lips pursed, saying nothing.

'I said you were smiling, Mr Massey. You had just pushed your sister to her death and you were *smiling*.' He stiffened suddenly. 'You were smiling because that's the sort of man you are, Mr Massey. A cold-hearted, calculating bastard. You could kill your sister and then smile about it!'

Hollis looked at Bruce. 'That's murder, sir.'

'Yes, Sergeant. It's murder.' He turned back to the suspect. 'You'll hang, Mr Massey. You may think you can get away with this, they all do, but in the end they *hang*!'

Massey was keeping remarkably cool, he thought. Not as rattled as he should be.

'Even the innocent ones?' Massey asked.

Bruce slammed his fist on the table, catching the edge of the ashtray and sending it flying across the room.

'Don't you come the smart-alec with me!' he shouted. 'You little creep! Unless you want to find out just how far I'll go to prove your guilt. Oh, yes! I know you did it. *I* know. Mr Massey. I *know*. Here!' He pressed the knuckles of his right hand against his chest. 'I get a feel for it, see? I've been in this business for nearly twenty years. Twenty bloody years of dealing with scum like you. I've spent the best years of my life with the worst kind of people. Liars, thieves, con-men, bigamists, embezzlers – you name it, I've met them. And I've put most of them where they belonged: behind bars. I've sat here with rapists and arsonists, listening to their false alibis and their phoney excuses. I've heard them whining – oh yes! The world owes them a living. Nobody understands them. And, d'you know what? I've *smelled* them when they finally realize that I've got them!' He swallowed hard, his hands on the desk white with tension. 'And murderers, Mr Massey. You're not the first and you won't be the last, because I'm paid to put away people like you – *and I love my work*. I've listened and watched and waited – and then I've pounced. You see, Mr Massey, I get a gut reaction to people like you. And I'm getting that reaction right now! You killed them, you lying bastard, and I'll see that you go down for it!'

He stood up and pushed back his chair so that it fell to the ground with a crash. Then he strode the few paces to the door and leaned his head against it.

The silence lengthened.

Eventually Hollis said, 'Now look what you've done, Mr Massey. You've upset the Detective Chief Inspector. Not very clever of you.' He folded his arms. 'You'll live to regret that. Upsetting Detective Chief Inspector Bruce is your first mistake.' He shook his head. 'Oh, dearie me!'

Bruce was pleased to see the beginnings of dismay on the suspect's face. They were getting to him at last.

'I want a solicitor,' said Massey. 'I'm entitled to one. I've changed my mind – I want one.'

They both ignored him.

'I said I want a solicitor.'

Bruce turned from the door. 'Did you hear anything, Sergeant?'

'Nothing, sir.'

Bruce sat down again, then he said, 'Pick up the ashtray, Massey.'

'Pick it up yourself!'

Hollis said, 'Oh, dearie me!' again.

They both stared at the suspect. Again they allowed a protracted silence to develop, then finally Bruce said, 'Pick it up, Massey.'

'I want a lawyer.'

'First things first.'

As Massey stared at the table, obviously wavering, Bruce resisted a glance at his sergeant. When the suspect remained in his seat Bruce decided the time had come for scare tactics. He was rather good at this. Practice makes perfect, he reflected, keeping his face impassive. Should have been an actor. He allowed another minute to pass and then, without warning, he sprang from his seat and rushed round the table. He yanked Massey from his chair and hurled him across the room in the direction of the ashtray. 'Pick the bloody thing up!' he roared. 'Or I'll kick the living daylights out of you! And don't think I won't! It would be a pleasure!'

Massey stumbled but somehow remained upright, his face red with anger. After a moment's hesitation he slowly picked up the ashtray. Bruce watched him narrowly. Massey was red with anger, not white with fear. This man was hard.

He expected Massey to place the ashtray on the table, but he held on to it.

'Put it on the table, you murdering little swine!'

Massey turned to look at him. 'I want a lawyer,' he said, his voice flat.

'All in good time.' Bruce felt genuine anger rising within him and counted to ten. Never let the suspect rile you; always stay in control.

Massey gave him a look full of loathing. Then he dropped the ashtray on to the floor and stamped on it. It cracked and fell apart.

'Right!' cried Bruce. 'You've had your chance.' He took several deep breaths. Play it cool, he reminded himself. Like a fish on a line. He turned to Hollis and said, 'Bring Mr Massey the names of three solicitors who might be prepared to act as his brief. Arnold Catton might be available.' To the suspect he said, 'While we're waiting, you can write out that list – the calls you say you made on the stationers in Birmingham. When Catton or whoever gets here, we'll start all over again. From the very beginning. And I'll ask you about the moment when you pushed your sister over the cliff. And the moment when you ran down your brother. I'll ask you how it felt, to take an innocent life. To kill two of the people you grew up with – family, people who loved you. Oh, yes, your lawyer will be sitting beside you and you'll think you're safe. They all do.' He smiled thinly. 'You know what that is? It's an illusion. An illusion of safety. So don't get any funny ideas, Mr Massey. You killed them and I know it . . . With or without a brief you're going down for this!'

*

When Massey had been taken to a cell to await the lawyer, Bruce looked at his sergeant.

'What d'you think?'

'He's a bloody hard nut, sir.'

314

'Yes, he is. Cold, callous, hard as nails.'

'We rattled him a bit though, sir.'

'I hope so. Smug bastard!' He sat down heavily. 'I hope to God they find the car before it's too late. If they can match the glass we've got him. That's our best hope, except for the line-up.' He glanced at his watch. 'I'll set it up for first thing tomorrow morning. Let him know he's got that to look forward to. Make him sweat. A sleepless night would do him good.'

'Fingers crossed then, sir.'

Bruce took several sheets of paper from the top drawer of the filing cabinet and gave one to his sergeant. He pulled a fountain pen from his pocket, leaving Hollis to pick up the pencil.

'Reports!' muttered Hollis. 'I love 'em!'

'Paperwork, laddie!' Bruce grinned mirthlessly. 'It's what makes the world go round. I bet you thought it was love.'

They both wrote the date and then stopped. Bruce said, 'We'll see how that list checks out. He can't have been there.'

'The landlady will say he wasn't at home, so he *could* have been at Fairlight.'

'*Could* have been almost anywhere!' said Bruce gloomily.

'We could bring her in, sir – the landlady. Frighten her. She'd crack easily enough.'

'There was something between them. She might lie.'

'Not for long. She's hardly on to a winner. If he's guilty, then she's sharing a house with a murderer. If I was in her shoes that thought would make me very nervous.'

For just over five minutes both men pored over their reports, trying to recall exactly what had been said and what denied.

Bruce suddenly put down his pen. 'I keep looking for a motive and I can't find one. According to his sister Constance, he and his natural mother had been reconciled, so was it only the money? This tontine business? All the money going to the others?'

'Men have murdered for less,' the sergeant shrugged. 'Though it would only come to him if he married one of the sisters.'

Bruce sighed. 'Matthew Massey . . . I can't quite get under his skin. I want to know what makes him tick.' He picked up the pen and twirled it aimlessly, somehow managing to get ink on his fingers. 'Damn things!' He glared at Hollis.

Hollis waved his pencil. 'Mine's not leaking.'

'Fountain pens, Hollis. It's called progress.'

'Yes, sir.' Grinning, he bent once more over his report. 'How many f's in preferred?'

'Preferred? What on earth are you writing?'

'"He preferred to remain silent," sir.'

'For God's sake! Use "He said nothing." Don't try to be clever, Hollis. It doesn't suit you.' He wiped the ink on some blotting paper and said, 'I might go over to France to see the mother. Just to check that they really are reconciled.'

'Nice little trip, that. South of France.'

'In February? Do me a favour.' He stared at the pen, his eyes unfocused. 'That could be it, Sergeant. The mother-son relationship . . .' He sighed again. 'Motive . . . motive . . . There has to be a motive.' He brightened suddenly. 'And they should be through with searching his room by now. That might be interesting.' He pursed his lips. 'We've got to nail this bastard. If he's killed two of the family, he might be planning to do in the rest. He could, you know. I felt it.'

The sergeant put one fist against his chest. '*Here*!'

Bruce said, 'Too bloody right!'

Chapter Fifteen

THE NEXT MORNING MATT FOLLOWED the sergeant along the passage towards the room where the identification parade would be held. He walked with a trace of swagger. Mustn't let them think he was nervous. The lawyer, that prat Catton, had proved worse than useless when he finally turned up the previous day – fat, balding, bespectacled. Matt hadn't even wanted to sit next to him. The man was a loser, anyone could see that. Earlier this morning, over a breakfast of cornflakes and a bacon sandwich, Matt had rejected the offer of his presence at this morning's farce. Nobody was going to identify him and he was going to be bailed – at least Catton had insisted on that.

He was glad he had moved the car before anyone reported it as abandoned. He had finally left it in a pub car park in Muswell Hill, next to a broken-down Ford and half-hidden by brambles. As soon as he was released he would put it somewhere else. Too early still to get the rear-light fixed; the police would have alerted all the garages and repair shops. Unless he took it further afield, somewhere like Bournemouth. He might take Poppy along for the ride . . .

'In there!'

He was pushed into a room where a group of men were arranging themselves into a straight line along one wall. Matt looked at them curiously. So these men were supposed to resemble him! He almost laughed at the motley collection who had been invited in off the street to take part in the line-up. The first one was too tall, the next was too tubby, the man on the end must be nearly fifty. At least he was better-looking than any of them, he reflected with satisfaction – and probably a whole lot smarter.

'Hardly flattering!' he remarked.

'Shut up and do what you're told.'

Charmless twerp, thought Matt. They were just bullies in blue uniforms. He would be glad to be shot of them.

A man came into the room and announced himself as the Station Inspector. He explained that it was his job to set up the identity parade for the CID who were investigating the murder.

'You,' he said to Matt. 'Any objection to any of these men?'

'Yes. I object to all of them.'

'Don't try to be funny. I'll ask you again. Any objection to—'

'No.'

'Then find a place in the line.'

'Anywhere?'

'Yes.'

Matt hesitated, aware that the rest of the men were watching him with unabashed curiosity. He wanted to say, 'What's up? Never seen a murderer before?' But that would never do.

He placed himself third from the left, making the ten men into eleven.

A woman came into the room, carrying a handbag and gloves. She was well dressed in tweeds, around sixty at a guess, he thought. As soon as she opened her

318

mouth, Matt knew she was not the sort to be intimidated.

'I'm ready when you are,' she announced in a clear voice.

'One moment, madam, please.'

'I have an appointment at ten.'

'We're almost there . . . Right you are.'

Matt tried not to catch her eye. He did vaguely recall that as he drove back from Fairlight he had passed a woman walking a dog. A big dog, Labrador or maybe a retriever. This could be her. Of all the rotten luck!

'Now then, madam.' The Station Inspector cleared his throat. 'I'd like you to walk along this line of men and look carefully at each one. Take your time, there's no hurry. If you see anyone you recognize, I want you to touch him on the shoulder and say, "This is the man." All right?'

She bridled. 'What do you mean, "All right?"'

'I mean, do you understand, madam?'

'Well of course I do.'

Without further ado she began to walk along the line, looking fixedly into each face. She stopped almost immediately and Matt prepared to congratulate himself.

'He was smiling,' she told the Inspector. 'The man I saw that day was smiling. That's the only reason I remember him. I remember thinking, "How can one be that happy on one's own? Don't you think these men should be smiling, Inspector?'

'Right!' said the Inspector. 'Do as the lady says, please, gentlemen.'

The woman went back to the beginning of the line. 'No . . . No . . .' Matt decided to play it cool. He would look her straight in the eyes, as though he had nothing to hide. He would try to give the impression that he found it all rather amusing. A suitable topic for dinner-table chat and nothing more. As he stared straight ahead he was aware that she

319

was moving to stand in front of him. He could smell her expensive face powder. She stared into Matt's face and he felt a prickle of doubt, but he kept the smile fixed to his face and looked directly into her eyes. Think innocent, he told himself. Think bloody innocent!

'No-o ...' she said, after a very long pause.

'Then move on, you stupid cow!' he thought. '*Move on*!'

She moved on. 'No ... No ...'

Matt breathed a sigh of relief. He was free to go. He was sweating profusely, but you couldn't be arrested for that. He drew a shaky breath. It had been worse than he expected. One word from her, a well-manicured finger pressed against his shoulder and ... Christ! That had been close!

She reached the end of the line and turned away from the men. 'He's not here,' she said.

The Station Inspector thanked her politely and led her away. The men relaxed, laughing among themselves, and began to make their way out of the room. Matt felt the sergeant's hand on his shoulder.

'You're free to go, sir,' he said, his face giving nothing away.

Matt could sense his disappointment. 'I should damn well think so!' he snapped. 'A waste of everybody's time.'

'We've got our job to do.'

Matt noticed the non-committal tone and smiled, wondering how many other abortive parades had been held in similar circumstances. His smile broadened as he stepped outside and into the corridor; he was still beaming when he passed the woman who was writing or signing something at the desk. As he passed he heard her say, 'For a moment I thought it was the man third from the left—'

'Why didn't you say so?'

Matt, grinning, recognized the frustration in the Station Inspector's voice.

'I wasn't sure. One really cannot incriminate the wrong man, Inspector.'

'It doesn't work like that, madam.'

Matt quickened his step, elbowing his way past the other ten men who were clustered inside the entrance, comparing notes on the experience like excited schoolboys after an exam. He pushed open the door and stepped thankfully outside, breathing in gulps of cold air. He must get himself home and see what Poppy had to tell him. No doubt she had never expected to see him again, the stupid cow. Well, she *would* see him, and what's more she could do other things for him. His triumph had left him feeling excited in more ways than one. Funny what fear could do to a man! As far as he knew there was nothing in his room to incriminate him in any way. He went down the steps and turned left, then walked along with head down, unconsciously avoiding all eye contact. When he had put about a hundred yards between himself and the police station, the thought of Poppy quickened his step and in no time at all he was running.

*

The next day Fran settled herself into her office with a sense of relief. The nightmare was over, and their lives could return to something approaching normality. She had insisted on coming into work, rejecting Annie's suggestion that she give herself at least a day to recover from the traumatic events of the past week. Del had gone to Scotland and she was missing him dreadfully. She thought that at the office she could concentrate on work, and that way the time would pass more quickly. Del Farrar – the man she was going to marry! He was the only good thing to come from the past few weeks, she reflected with a smile of pleasure. If Mother hadn't died when she did ... Fate played strange tricks. If Mother hadn't died, then Connie wouldn't have brought Del to the funeral and they would never have met. But, ever fickle, Fate had played a further trick. If Mother hadn't died, Connie would never have met Matt again and would never have been provoked into writing that terrible letter. She sighed, trying to wrench her thoughts in a more positive direction. Today she would work so hard that she would not be able to think about anything else.

But first she must make a few telephone calls, to organize Henry's funeral. The coroner's findings had been unequivocal — assault by person or persons unknown resulting in death. She tried to keep the word 'murder' from her thoughts because the anger she felt towards Matt frightened her. He had killed her sister and brother; had wilfully caused them unimaginable fear and pain, and she could never forgive him for that. She wanted him locked up for the rest of his life to dwell on his dreadful crimes. Hopefully he would eventually suffer the anguish of remorse, perhaps the most suitable punishment of all. Deeply regretting something that could never be undone must be the greatest torture a man could endure. And serve him right! For all she cared, the warders could throw away the key.

'Let him rot!' she whispered.

But he might hang. She had never been a vengeful person and the idea of capital punishment had always appalled her. There were people who were trying to change the law and, until now, Fran had felt a good deal of sympathy for them. Even now she was unsure how she would feel if the worst happened and Matt were hanged. Hanged by the neck until he was dead! It sounded grotesque, and the thought of him dangling from the end of the rope disgusted her. But so did the thought of Mary fighting for her life on a cliff-edge, suddenly aware that the man she loved as a brother was going to kill her. And Henry, lying in the hospital, hovering in a confused darkness somewhere between life and death, broken by someone dear to him.

322

Hopefully he hadn't known that it was Matt who was responsible for his horrific injuries.

'Stop it, Fran!' she told herself urgently. She *must* stop these morbid thoughts. Matt had done enough harm, and the family must somehow find the strength to withstand the damage he had inflicted. They must thank God that three of them remained alive, and they must comfort and help each other.

The ringing of the telephone made her jump and she reached for the receiver with a rapidly beating heart.

'Oh, you're in. I'll pop along.'

It was Stuart, and she suddenly wondered what he would say if she told him that she was going to marry Del Farrar. The thought of Del cheered her and she made a hurried attempt to look businesslike, tidying her hair and dabbing on a little extra lipstick. By the time Stuart reached her office she had assumed what she hoped was a brisk smile.

He sat himself down and looked at her with concern. 'You look awful!'

So much for her efforts. 'I don't feel too wonderful.'

'You must have taken a hammering, Fran. All of you. You really shouldn't push yourself too far.'

'I'm managing. I had to come in, to get away from it all.'

'At least it's over. I heard it on the nine o'clock news. Thank God for that, Fran.'

'It's been fairly dreadful—'

'It must have been pure hell. And your own brother!'

'I don't want to think about it, Stuart.'

'Of course not. I'm an idiot. Forgive me.' He regarded her soberly. 'Come and have lunch with me – to celebrate. I thought we were going to lose you.'

Fran hesitated, tempted by the idea. Food was a universal comforter and she felt frayed and vulnerable. But there was Del. She would have to tell Stuart about him. 'Stuart,

I have something to tell you. The one piece of good news ...'

He waited.

'Del Farrar – that is, Paul Hallam ...'

He looked puzzled. 'The American?'

'Yes. We're going to be married.'

His expression was comical. 'You and – but for God's sake, Fran. You hardly know the man!' He rolled his eyes. 'I mean, congratulations and all that but ... are you sure, Fran? Isn't a bit sudden?'

She smiled. 'Very sudden, but I *do* know him and I *am* sure. Please wish me luck, Stuart.'

'Of course I wish you luck,' he said. 'You deserve a break. It was just – well, a bit of a shock.' He reached across the desk and shook her hand. 'Jolly good luck to the pair of you. He's a very lucky man!' His smile was genuine. 'All the more reason to have lunch with me. Or have you got a prior engagement? Is he taking you—'

'He's in Scotland for his godson's wedding.'

'That's settled then. Lunch it is.' He sat back, folding his arms. 'Hallam, eh? A coincidence, really, because I've had Westrop on the phone. Seems you and he have been in cahoots over this chap's manuscript. Westrop wants us to take a second look. He's very excited, and he's not often wrong.'

Fran leaned forward eagerly. 'It's going to be good, Stuart. All he needed was a few pointers. He accepted them without a quibble, really keen to learn.'

'That makes a change. Most of them squeal to high heaven when you ask them to make changes. Remember the trouble we had with Sarah Watts? God, she really went to town. Sobs and reproaches and "I-stand-by-every-word!" Talk about histrionics, she should have been an actress. I was glad to see the back of her.' He shook his head at the memory, whistling softly. 'Took herself off to Schumann's

324

in the end, but they never did much with her. Two or three mediocre novels and then nothing. Pity. She had something to say.'

'She was her own worst enemy.'

Stuart grinned suddenly. 'You and Hallam! That's incredible!'

'But you will read his manuscript?'

'I certainly will. But Marjory's not going to be too pleased; she'll accuse you of dirty dealings!'

Fran laughed. 'After what I've just been through, it'll take more than Marjory Evans to frighten me!'

'You're a great girl, Fran. I envy Hallam. My father used to say, "Never trust a Yank!" And look what he's done. Sneaked in and pinched my best girl!'

'Your best girl? I was never that, Stuart, and you know it. I was one of many strings to your bow.'

'Oh, God! Is that how it seemed? I'm covered in confusion!'

'No, you're not. You're just not the marrying type.'

He looked at her thoughtfully. 'But who will love me when I'm old and grey?'

'You'll survive, Stuart. You'll have all the elderly widows baking you pies and bringing you casseroles. They'll be beating a path to your door.' She smiled. 'You have *charm*, Stuart, and you always will.'

He shrugged humorously and stood up. 'Thanks for those few kind words. I think I'll go while I'm ahead! Twelve-thirty OK for lunch?'

'Make it one.'

'Right you are!'

She watched him go with affection and wondered if she could bear to leave all this and go to live in America. If that was what Del really wanted . . .

'Concentrate, Fran!' she told herself sharply. 'You've got things to do.'

First things first. Henry's funeral. She had already arranged for the hospital to release his body; the undertakers who had buried her mother and sister would collect it and bring it back from Cambridge.

She telephoned the vicar.

'My dear Miss Massey!' he cried, before she could say more than her name. 'What can I say? Of course I know what has happened. The whole parish is talking about it, but that's human nature, I'm afraid. This is unbelievable. So very, very wicked! How can I even start to comfort you? I feel so very helpless. First your dear mother . . .'

Fran thought, 'If he pretends this is God's will, I shall scream obscenities at him.'

'. . . then your sister and now poor, dear Henry. A family torn apart – and to think that Matt . . . I remember him as a boy, you see, in the choir. Those large grey eyes! So soulful, I used to think. I remember him taking communion, his face uplifted. I said to my wife on more than one occasion, that boy's eyes are the saving of him. Not handsome, but those large eyes. To think that he could have become so – so *monstrous*! I can't believe it, you see. I pray that before too long we shall hear that—'

Fran took a deep breath. 'I'm afraid your prayers will be wasted, reverend. Matt did it. Matt-with-the-large-grey-eyes did it! He killed his sister and his brother. He's in custody, I'm pleased to say. Helping the police with their enquiries – Isn't that the phrase?'

There was a short, startled silence. 'My dear, I shall pray for him. I shall ask God to forgive him . . .'

'*I* shall thank God that some of us have been spared!'

'My dear lady!'

'That silenced him for a while,' Fran muttered with a flash of irritability. Blast him! Their hearts were broken, their lives shattered and he had nothing to offer but platitudes. She said carefully, 'I'm ringing to ask when you could bury Henry. The undertakers are collecting his body some time today. I'll let you have the details of hymns and psalms later. I'd like the bell to be tolled, and the choir as before – very much as before, in fact.' She was surprised at the sharpness in her voice. Perhaps she was not coping as well as she imagined. The vicar was a mild-mannered, well-meaning man, and she had not meant to snap at him. Was she becoming hysterical, she wondered? Cracking under the strain? With an effort she softened her tone. 'I think we may need to choose another plot for the rest of the family. I could call in at the vicarage on my way home, if that helps.'

'That might make things easier. We can take a quick walk round the churchyard. As to the funeral – what about the day after tomorrow, early evening, or is that too short notice? Far be it from me to hurry poor Henry into his grave, but I'm already booked up for a few days ahead.'

'What about next week?'

'If you don't mind risking the weather. I keep thinking we're going to have snow; it's late this year, but I don't think we shall escape it.'

Fran thought quickly. The family were all close by and local friends could be notified. 'The day after tomorrow, then,' she said and they quickly agreed four-thirty.

She then rang the undertaker and ordered a mahogany casket with brass handles similar to the one in which they had buried Mary. She made a call to a local florist and ordered a wreath from the family. Add a few ribbons to brighten it, she told them. Henry had been a young man, full of the joys of life, and she wanted nothing sombre. She rang Addenbrooke's Hospital to make sure that the death certificate was in the post, then phoned home to pass the news on to Annie.

'Don't worry about the catering,' she told her, anticipating her reaction. 'I think we've had quite enough to contend with these last few weeks. I shall ask the Star Hotel to provide a

buffet meal and we'll hire some of their staff to serve it
... No, Annie, I won't change my mind. I don't want you
slaving away for the next two days when what we really all
need is a little peace and quiet ... I know you did it for
Mother and Mary, but this is getting too much. We are all
at our wits end, dear, and I won't have you making yourself
ill. Enough is enough. If Henry were here he'd agree, I'm
sure. He'd understand what we've been through ... Now
please, Annie, don't start to cry. We have to learn to live
with what's happened, to come to terms with our losses.
Annie, dear. *Please!*' She rolled her eyes in exasperation.
'Make yourself some tea or something. Or take a nip of
brandy. Annie, please don't cry. Annie? *Annie* ...'

But Annie had hung up and Fran stared at the receiver,
her heart aching. Would they ever feel human again, she
wondered? Would they ever be able to put all this grief and
horror behind them, or would they always be vulnerable to
the odd word or a snatch of music that brought back the
memories? It was hard to envisage a time when they would
not be grieving for their lost loved ones. Perhaps there would
always be a shadow over this generation of the Massey family.
And they had Matt to thank for it. At the thought of him her
mouth twisted with bitterness and her hands clenched.

'No, Fran! Don't!' she told herself. She must keep her
anger under control.

Making a determined effort to banish such sad thoughts,
she opened her mail, made a few business calls and then
went along to see Marjory and ask about the conference
she had attended. Suddenly, to her great relief, it was one
o'clock and she surrendered herself to the idea of a good
lunch and some cheerful company. Anything was better than
the slow recognition of the growing anger within her, a dark,
consuming anger that was gradually turning into rage.

*

Amy watched the hands of the school clock on the wall behind the teacher's head. Two more minutes! Idly she chewed the end of her pencil, spat the pieces into her hand and wiped them on her skirt. Outside lay freedom, and Dot and Fritz and a chat with the station-master.

'Amy! Are you listening to me?'

'Yes, Miss.'

'What did I say?'

'About the Romans.'

'Roman what?'

Amy trawled through hazy fragments of memory. 'Legions.'

'What about the Roman legions?' The teacher's gaze lingered triumphantly. 'You weren't listening, Amy.'

'I was, Miss.' A quick glance at the clock. One minute and this nagging would be over. Saved by the bell. Her mouth twitched.

'I see nothing to laugh at.'

'No, Miss.'

Behind her Barry Hogg whispered something and she caught the word 'hundred'. Amy lifted her head. 'A hundred,' she ventured hopefully.

'A hundred *what*, Amy?'

Amy didn't know. From the corner of her eye she saw the bell monitor slide from his seat, take the brass bell from its place on top of the cupboard and sidle out of the room.

The teacher sighed. 'Barry will tell us.'

Barry said, 'There were a hundred soldiers in—'

The rest of the sentence was drowned out by the noise of the bell being rung. All eyes were on the teacher.

'Stand!'

They rose to their feet as one.

'Class dismiss!'

The silence gave way to uproar as desk lids banged and seats were pushed up on squeaking hinges. Shrill voices rang with relief as the children tumbled out into the hallway and rushed for the cloakroom. Amy found her peg, changed out of her plimsolls, and pulled on her coat. She pulled a knitted pixie hat on to her head and tied the strings under her chin. On the far side of the cloakroom Barry taunted, 'A hundred *what*, Amy?' He grinned.

'Sausages!' said Amy, who knew that a sausage was vaguely rude.

She left a ripple of laughter behind her and dived out into the frosty playground.

'A hundred soldiers?' she muttered, 'in something.' She would probably never know and cared less. The Romans were all dead anyway. As she skipped and hopped through the playground, her satchel bumping against her side, she murmured the words of the song which all the girls were singing at playtimes as they bounced two tennis balls against the school wall in a kind of juggling game:

> One, two, three a lairy,
> My ball's down the airey,
> Don't forget to give it to Mary –
> Not to Father Christmas.

Her own attempts at the game had come to a temporary halt since one of her balls had been thrown over the railings into a bunch of stinging nettles by Steven Hallett, one of the boys in the top class. Amy didn't mind too much, because she took the boy's action to be an indication that he was interested in her. She understood things like that. Boys like Steven Hallett were like gods and would be moving on to the Senior School at the end of the summer.

Outside in the lane she saw no sign of her great-aunt, and for that Amy was thankful. Sometimes, if she had been to the village shops, Annie would wait for her outside the school. Amy hated it because her great-aunt always found fault. 'Look at the state of you!' she would say. 'Pull up your socks, for goodness sake!' And then Amy would have to carry the smaller of the two shopping baskets. She much preferred to walk home alone.

Seeing that today she was in luck she dawdled, running her hand along the railings, singing, 'One, two, three a lairy . . .'

Joan Croft rushed past, her plaits flying.

Amy shouted, 'Pigtails! Pigtails! Piggy piggy pigtails!'

Joan put her tongue out and yelled, 'Townie! Townie!'

Amy ran after her, screaming with laughter. Then she stopped abruptly in mid-scream as a heavy hand descended on her shoulder.

'Amy?'

She turned to see a tall man with dark hair. His collar was turned up, a scarf concealed the lower part of his face and a hat hid most of the rest. His hand was firmly clamped to her shoulder.

'What if I am?' she demanded.

'You're Dot's friend, aren't you?'

'So?' She wriggled free.

'She's told me all about you, Amy. What good friends you are. How you can keep a secret.'

She was flattered to discover that Dot had been talking about her to the grown-ups.

'I'm one of Dot's admirers,' he went on. 'She said you know all about it; about flirting.'

'I do.'

He put a finger to the spot where his lips would be and glanced round cautiously. Then he lowered his voice. 'I want to marry her.'

Amy gasped with excitement. 'Marry her?' Dot's gentleman friend was confiding in her. 'Do you really?'

He nodded. 'But it's a secret. The trouble is they are all so mean to Dot. They don't want her to marry anyone. I want us to to be married, and you know what that means.'

'Do I?' She looked at him doubtfully. For all her brave words to Dot, she didn't know *that* much about flirting.

'It means we shall need a bridesmaid.'

Amy stared at him, relief overshadowed by thrilled anticipation as she saw herself floating down the aisle behind Dot, dressed in a wonderful pink dress. She would have roses in her hair, and pink satin shoes with a buttoned strap, and she would carry . . . Reluctantly she forced herself to concentrate on what he was saying.

'I want you to do something for me, because you're her best friend in all the world. It's something very important. I don't feel I can trust anyone else. I want you to give her a very special, very romantic letter. Can you do that?'

It was her turn to nod. So this was the man who would be Dot's husband! She wondered if he was handsome, but probably Dot wouldn't mind. Maybe their children would take after Dot. 'I'll take it,' she promised.

'And you won't tell a soul? Not another living soul? Cross your heart and hope to die?'

'I do,' she said. 'I mean, I won't.'

'Say it properly.'

Amy put her right hand across her chest and said solemnly, 'Cross my heart and hope to die!'

'Here you are.'

She took the letter and stuffed it into her pocket. 'What's your name?' she asked.

He tapped the side of his nose. 'You'll know soon enough. Mustn't spoil the secret.'

'Oh! No!' She tried to hide her disappointment.

'You promise me you won't let anyone know about the letter and you'll keep this—' he laid a finger on her mouth '—buttoned? You've taken the vow, Amy, and you don't want to die, do you?'

'No.' Just for a moment she thought that perhaps she didn't like him, but then she thought she did.

He said, 'If you tell anyone, then I won't marry her and you won't be a bridesmaid, will you?'

'No-o.'

'So?'

'I'll give it to her when no one else is looking.'

'Good girl.' He slipped something into her pocket and then walked quickly away.

She stared after him. Lucky Dot! It was all so romantic. She stuck her hand into her pocket and brought out – *a shilling*! Amy had never had a shilling in her whole life! She set off slowly in the direction of home, scuffing her feet thoughtfully through the frosty leaves that had blown into drifts below the hedges. Unusually she resisted the urge to stand on the second rung of Perkins' gate and watch the cows, and she passed the Beddows' big Shire horse without pulling him a handful of grass. Amy walked with her head down, her brow furrowed, burdened with responsibility. She had been entrusted with a secret and she must guard that at all costs. It was also obvious to her that sudden wealth brought its own problems. She would have to spend it a little at a time; that way no one would ask any awkward questions . . .

*

At home, Dot also watched the clock, awaiting Amy's return from school. She was alone and she always felt a little anxious without someone else in the house. Annie was at the hairdresser's, having her hair set. If she could not cook Henry's farewell supper, she had told Dot, she could at least make herself look presentable for his funeral. Dot stood at the window with Fritz in her arms and wondered why Amy was so late. Of course, she might have been kept in after school. It wouldn't be the first time. Once she had made a noise like a raspberry and once she had flicked ink at one of the boys. On both occasions she had stayed behind, writing something called 'lines'.

Dot stared out at the bleak garden, hating the winter. Christmas was fun, and New Year's Day, but after that there was only Valentine's Day and nobody ever sent her a valentine. There was nothing to look forward to unless the snowdrops came through early.

'Come on, Amy!' she muttered impatiently.

She had a sudden vision of a younger Mary presenting Mother with a bunch of snowdrops. Poor Mother! Poor Mary! She wondered if they could possibly be looking down from heaven, watching her. It made her a little uneasy to think so. And Father, of course; she felt a little guilty for forgetting Father. With a sigh she turned from the window and moved to sit beside the fire. Thank goodness she had Fritz to keep her company! The quiet of the house weighed on her spirits, especially as the overcast sky made the rooms dull and grey. She looked around her. Was Mother with her in spirit? Was Mary nearby? She shivered. Mother, Father and Mary. And now Henry. There were more of the Masseys in heaven than on earth, she thought with a shiver.

Fritz woke suddenly and slithered to the floor. He set off purposefully for the door.

'No, Fritz!' she called. 'Not yet.'

He wanted to go out, but she was unwilling to move from the reassuring warmth of the fire. She would take him out as soon as Amy returned.

He began to bark at the front door. 'Not yet!' she called. She went into the hall. Standing on the mat, his nose thrust towards the edge of the door, Fritz barked again.

'Stop it!' she cried.

The high-pitched trill of the telephone made her jump and she stared at it. Normally, she liked to answer it, but today she felt a strange reluctance. Last time she had got the message all wrong and Annie had muttered under her breath ... Perhaps it would stop ringing.

To add to the noise, Fritz now switched his attention to the ringing telephone, barking excitedly and making ineffectual jumps.

'No, Fritz!' she shouted, becoming flustered.

He scrabbled at the legs of the table on which the telephone stood and Dot leaned down to smack him.

'Naughty boy, Fritz!'

The smack was harder than she had intended and he ran away, whimpering reproachfully. At once she was stricken with remorse, but the telephone would not stop. She snatched it from its hook and said, 'Stop it! I mean—'

A man's voice said, 'I'm afraid we have some bad news ...'

She stared after Fritz, who was retreating towards the kitchen and the safety of his basket.

'Fritz! Come back. I'm sorry, Fritz.'

'I beg your pardon? Who am I speaking to?'

'It's me.'

There was a baffled silence. 'Is that Miss Massey?'

She hesitated. Was she 'Miss Massey'? Yes, of course she was. 'Yes?'

'This is Detective Chief Inspector Bruce. I'm afraid ...'

Putting two fingers in her mouth, she tried to whistle for Fritz the way Amy did but no sound came out. Frustrated, she called 'Fritz!' The prospect of a walk down the gloomy hallway was something to be avoided; she must persuade the dog to come back to her. She realized that the voice on the telephone was still talking.

'... unfortunately had to release him ...'

Guiltily, she reached for the pencil and notepad. Always make a note, Fran had told her. She wrote 'unfortunate' but could not remember the rest of it.

'What else?' she asked. Fritz's slim snout appeared round

335

the kitchen door and she called, 'Good boy, then!' Hopefully she patted her thigh, but the dog immediately ducked out of sight once more.

'. . . the witness was unable to identify him . . .'

She wrote 'unable' and then added 'him'. It didn't look quite right. Blast and bother the silly man! She peered along the passage.

'Fritz! Come back here! I'm sorry!'

Suppose he wouldn't forgive her that hasty smack? Suppose she had hurt his feelings and he wasn't going to love her any more? Her throat felt dry with misery.

The man was still talking. '. . . at least we have found the car and the evidence we need. We can can match the glass from the . . .'

She wrote down 'car' and glared at the telephone. Was there no end to his jabbering?

'. . . gatepost in Cambridge. The lab boys are very hopeful as the Refractive Index Test is a hundred per cent reliable . . .'

She wondered vaguely what a lab boy was, and why they were hopeful. Dutifully she wrote down 'hopeful' and stared after Fritz. Poor little dog, he would be feeling so miserable. Unable to bear it any longer, she said, 'Wait a minute,' and put down the telephone. Gathering her courage, she ran down the dark passage and into the kitchen. As she suspected, the little dachshund was in his basket. He stared at her, his brown eyes reproachful.

'Darling, I'm sorry!' she cried, close to tears. 'Poor Fritz. Come on!' She picked him up and kissed the top of his head. 'We're still friends, aren't we?' Hugging him, she ran back to the lounge and pushed him in at the door. Where was Amy, for heaven's sake? She shut the door and rushed back to the telephone.

'Miss Massey?'

'Yes.'

'Is anything wrong?'

'No.' She and Fritz were still friends.

'You will be on your guard, won't you? And you'll pass on this information to your sister in Maidstone. We'll let you know the moment we make an arrest.'

An arrest? Dot frowned, worried. Had she missed anything, she wondered? At that moment she heard the back door open and Amy's voice called out a greeting. With a sigh of relief she realized she was no longer alone.

'Thank you,' she said to whoever was calling. 'Thank you very much.' She hung up and stared at the notepad. Whatever did it mean? Unfortunate car? Anxiety flooded through her. Annie and Fran would want to know what the man had said; they would badger her with questions which she couldn't answer. She remembered what had happened about that bird-watcher man. Unfortunate car? Which car would that be? They'd go on and on.

'Dot! There you are!' Amy hurtled along the passage. 'Are we on our own?'

'On our own? Yes.' She stared again at the words she had written on the pad.

'What's the matter? What are you staring at?' Amy picked up the pad and read the few words Dot had written. 'Who was it?' she asked. 'You're supposed to say who it was from. Annie'll moan like anything.'

'It was somebody,' Dot told her. 'A man.'

'Oh, never mind that,' Amy urged. 'Listen, Dot. I've got the most wonderful, delicious surprise for you. No, really, I have!'

Her eyes were shining with excitement. For a moment Dot eyed the message she had written. Better to say nothing, she decided and with a quick movement she tore the page from the pad and crumpled it into a ball. She would throw it on the fire. Whoever it was would ring back – that's what Fran always said when they didn't reach the telephone in time.

'What is it?' she demanded. A wonderful delicious surprise?

'You're sure there's just us, because this is a *secret*!'

'No. Just you, me and Fritz.'

Slowly Annie pulled something from her pocket. 'I've brought you a letter,' she said.

Chapter Sixteen

FRAN AWOKE EARLY ON THE day before the funeral and found that she was shivering. One glance at the window confirmed her worst fears. The snow had finally reached England! Unable to resist the sight, she pulled on a dressing gown and rushed to the window. As always the sight of the swirling flakes inspired in her a sense of awe. Look down and the flakes were white, look up and they were dark against a leaden sky. Magical. Already the landscape had changed and the garden had vanished. The shrubs were capped with a froth of white and the branches of the trees were similarly outlined. She opened the window a fraction, listening to the absence of sound. No cars on the road. At a guess she calculated the snow to be a couple of inches deep already, and it was coming down fast.

Poor Henry. A sad way to be laid to rest. The thought of the freezing earth made her shiver and she closed the window. Moving to the fireplace, she saw that a small patch of red was all that remained of last night's fire, but it might be possible to rekindle it. She opened the lid of the box by the hearth and threw a twist of paper and a few pieces of wood on to the embers.

'Burn!' she told it. Seeing nothing but a sullen gleam, she unfolded a sheet of brown paper and covered the small grate so that only a sliver of space remained at the bottom. The draught thus created had the desired effect and she was soon warming her hands at the small but cheerful blaze.

'Dear Henry!' she whispered. 'Are you anywhere? Can you hear me?' She wondered, not for the first time, whether in fact there *was* a hereafter. Perhaps it was all a story invented by the Church to comfort the bereaved. 'We shall miss you dreadfully.' Tears filled her eyes as she thought of the coming funeral. How desolate the churchyard would be, and how hurried the service. Suddenly she recalled that Del would be attending a wedding in this same weather. It might be worse in Scotland.

'Oh, no!' she cried as a new thought struck her. If they had heavy snow, the train services would be disrupted and he might be snowed in. When would she see him again? The thought of an extended parting was agony to her.

'Del! *Del*!' she said, her heart full of yearning. If only he would walk through the door and hold out his arms. She would rush into them and stay there for ever! The thought that he returned her love was a small spark of hope. To her absent brother she whispered, 'I'm going to marry Del, Henry. Do you wish me happiness?'

What a question, she reproached herself. Of course he did. Henry would be delighted for her. He never grudged anyone their good fortune. In fact, he had probably never had an unkind thought in the whole of his short life. Losing his parents and then his sister had undoubtedly cast a huge shadow over an otherwise enjoyable existence. Snow . . . She wondered if the caterers would reach them. And the undertakers? Would they be able to bring their precious cargo to the church? And what about the florist? A funeral without a few wreaths would be a sad affair. She put a guard against the fire and made a dash to the bathroom. The water was just warm enough for a hasty bath and then she was back in her room, dressing hurriedly. There was so much to do.

Downstairs she noticed that the daily paper wasn't on the mat. No doubt that too would be late, if it came at all. There was already a fire in the lounge and the dining room.

'Morning, Annie.' She crossed the kitchen to put an arm round the old woman's shoulders. 'What time did you get up? I thought I was early, but you beat me to it.'

Annie's eyes were red-rimmed. 'Don't "Good morning" me!' she said irritably. 'It's not a good morning. The way I feel, it will *never* be a good morning again. Snow! That's all we need! Poor Connie will be getting herself into a tizzwaz! I suppose she will come?'

'She'd better!'

Fran switched on the wireless. 'No paper today,' she said.

'Not surprised, are you?'

Fran looked at the clock. 'We're just in time for the eight o'clock news.'

Annie poured some tea and they both sat at the table, hands round the steaming cups, waiting for the radio pips which would herald the news broadcast.

The sounds of Big Ben died away and the voice of the announcer crackled over the airwaves.

'This is the BBC Home Service on February 11th, 1938 . . . Snow has fallen over most of Britain, and roads in the north and east of the country have been disrupted over a wide area. Scotland has also suffered a severe blizzard and many trains have been cancelled. Attempts are being made to keep open roads leading to hospitals and other emergency services, and volunteers are coming forward to help the police . . .'

Annie said, 'Poor Henry! A snowy funeral – although he will be past caring. Strange to realize that nothing, absolutely *nothing*, can hurt him now. No harsh words, no illnesses, no bad luck—'

341

Abruptly Fran held up a hand, interrupting her. 'Annie! Listen!'

The announcer went on, '. . . has been discovered in a house in Bayfield Road. She was found in the bedroom, and first reports suggest that she had been strangled with her own stocking. She has been identified as Mrs Brenda Parfitt of the same address. The next-of-kin have been informed. The police are searching for a man already wanted for another murder which took place near Hastings recently.'

Fran heard her own voice, thin and high. 'Bayfield Road?'

Annie said, 'What about it?'

'I think . . .' Fran stared at the wireless as though hypnotized. Not another one! No! *No!* She must have been mistaken; Matt was in prison.

From the wireless the calm voice continued impassively, impervious to the horrors of which he spoke. 'A description has been circulated to all police stations. He is of average height, clean-shaven, with dark hair. He is twenty-six years old and is considered dangerous. Members of the public who may know of his whereabouts are warned not to approach him but to pass on any information they may have to the police . . .' There was a brief pause. '. . . In Germany there have been more dismissals among high-ranking officers in the army. Adolf Hitler has now declared himself Supreme Commander . . . King Carol of Rumania—'

'Matt lives in Bayfield Road!'

Annie and Fran exchanged horrified glances, but for a moment neither of them spoke. With a trembling hand, Fran reached out and switched off the radio.

Annie broke the silence. 'Bayfield Road? Are you sure?'

'Yes. Yes!'

'You don't mean that Matt has – that he's killed someone else?'

Fran nodded. 'It sounds like it.'

Annie's hands shook so violently that tea spilled over on to the tablecloth and abruptly she set down her cup. 'Maybe it just *sounded* like Bayfield. Could have been Mayfield.'

Neither of them believed this for a moment. Fran was white with shock. 'A man who is already wanted for murder – but that can't be Matt; he's already in custody.'

'Strangled with her own stocking!'

'Why should Matt . . . No, it *can't* have been him. He's got no grudge against anyone else. He only kills *us*!' She saw her own fear reflected in Annie's eyes. 'Doesn't he?'

Annie shrugged. 'So far! But it's a bit of a coincidence, isn't it? Two murderers in the same street.'

'But he's locked up! How could it – unless he's escaped.'

Annie covered her face with her hands. 'Please God, no!' she cried. 'Don't let it be him. Oh, Matt! Matt! You haven't, have you?' Tears swam in her eyes. 'When I think of the time I lavished on that boy! How I tried to help him. Where did we go wrong, Fran?'

'Don't blame yourself, Annie. He's the way he is.'

Fran swallowed. Running her fingers through her hair, she stood up, surprised to discover how weak she felt. 'There's only one way to find out what's happening. I'll ring the police inspector – the one in charge. Bruce.'

Annie followed her along the passage and stood nervously beside her, hands clasped, while Fran looked up the number and dialled the operator. For Fran, with a thousand worries clamouring for attention, it seemed an age before she was connected and Bruce listened to her stammered request for information.

'Yes, Miss Massey, I'm afraid it was your brother. You knew he had been released, surely?'

'No. We had no idea.'

'I rang yesterday and spoke to you myself. You were obviously . . .'

343

'You didn't speak to *me*, Inspector. I was in the office all day, in London.' She realized suddenly what had happened. 'It must have been Dot, my sister, although she didn't give us a message of any kind.'

'That explains it, then. I did think you were rather confused. Something about Fritz—'

'Oh, heavens! That was definitely Dot.' Panic gripped her. Matt was free and had killed a woman in London. She kept her voice level with an effort. 'What should Dot have told us?'

'That the witness couldn't identify him, and at that time we had not found the car. We had to let him go. About two hours later we traced the car, which he had sold to a garage in Muswell Hill – for cash.'

'So – are you saying that Matt's free again?'

Annie's face paled and she stumbled to the stairs and sat down, clutching the banister for support.

'Inspector, we were listening to the news. The woman in Bayfield Road. Was it . . . ?' She could not finish the sentence.

'She was his landlady. We assume it was your brother. I'm so sorry.'

Fran turned to Annie and nodded her head.

He continued, 'There's a big man-hunt under way, and we *will* find him. But for the moment, yes, he's still free. We went to the house to arrest him and found the body of his landlady. We think – no, never mind.'

'Tell me.'

'It appears she may have been sexually assaulted.'

Fran gasped. 'That's horrible! Disgusting!' Bile rose in her throat. 'Where will it all end?' She drew a shuddering breath. 'Why the landlady? What had she done, for God's sake, to deserve to be strangled?'

'We shall probably never know.' He paused. 'Possibly she had taken the opportunity to steal from his room, imagining that he was never coming back. They're dusting a box for prints. It may have been your brother's, in which case it would support the light-fingered theory. There were signs of a struggle. Excuse me . . .' There was a pause while he spoke to someone else. 'Miss Massey? There was a box alongside the body; a butterfly box. Does that mean anything to you?'

Fran frowned. 'A butterfly box? No. I don't remember one.' She glanced enquiringly at Annie.

Annie said dully, 'Of course you do. Your father used to collect butterflies. He took you all out one day. Matt was very interested and for once your father was pleased with him. Showed him how to kill them and pin them on to . . . to . . . Oh, Matt! How could it end like this?' She began to sob and her distress had an effect on Fran, who now felt her own voice quivering.

'I don't think I can talk any more, Chief Inspector. Not just now!'

'I understand. But one more thing – a piece of good news. We sent a man to interview the students in Cambridge and it seems Henry had a girl-friend. Nothing too serious, but she told us about a note. She says Henry received a note asking him to meet "a friend" at the bus stop – the bus stop where he was run down. Seems they all thought it was some kind of hoax. Students go in for that sort of thing.'

Fran sat down on the nearest chair, her legs weak. 'You mean Matt lured Henry to that particular spot and then deliberately ran him down?'

'That's the way it looks. She, that is the girl-friend, wanted him to ignore it, but he thought it a "bit of a lark". He had to go alone and the girl wanted to go with him. They had a bit of an argument and then they tossed for it. He won, so he went alone.' After a few moments, he asked, 'Are you still there?'

'Yes. I was wondering what she's like?' It pleased Fran

to know that Henry had had a girl-friend. It helped to know that his last few days had been happy.

'Small, pretty, a bubbly sort of girl. Elizabeth Martin, known as Lizzie. More importantly, she still had the note so we can match the handwriting.'

'Was it signed?'

'With an "M" followed by a question mark.' When she made no reply Bruce said, 'I'm sorry.'

'Don't be. You're doing your job.'

'When we get him we'll have the evidence to nail him. There'll be no way his solicitor can ask for bail.'

Fran didn't want to think about it. 'I have to go now.' She cut him off in mid-sentence, hung up and moved to kneel beside Annie. 'Cry away, dear!' she told her gently. 'You can't keep all this grief bottled up inside you. It's all right, Annie. I'm here.'

Angrily she fought back her own tears. She had cried for Mother and Mary and Henry. She would not cry for Matt. Hating was easier. She would allow herself to hate Matt for what he had become. She would shed no tears for the boy he had once been. She could and would hate him, but she could and did *fear* him. He had killed his landlady for no apparent reason. What could she have done – unless she knew too much. Or suspected what was going on. Had he simply silenced her? Was he so far along the path of destruction that there was no point in holding back? What did one more victim mean to a man like Matt?

Annie was struggling to overcome her hysteria. She wiped her eyes, blew her nose and took several deep breaths. 'Suppose he comes to the funeral!' she cried. 'What on earth shall we do?'

Fran's expression hardened. 'They'll arrest him,' she said. 'There'll be police all over the place. A big man-hunt – that's what the chief inspector said. But he won't dare show his face. If he did I'd . . . I think I'd go for him myself! I'd like to punish him for what he's done. I'd like to *hurt* him. Is that so dreadful of me?'

Annie was silent.

'It is then,' Fran said. 'Not at all Christian of me. But I can't pretend to forgive him. I'm beyond that, Annie. I'm hurting for Mary and Henry – and now this other poor soul. I may look all right on the outside, Annie, but I'm screaming inside.' She put her hands over her face.

'He won't get away with it. The police will deal with him.' Annie put a trembling hand on Fran's knee. 'You stay out of it, Fran, there's a love. I know how you feel but—'

'No, you don't! Nobody knows how I feel except me. I don't know how you feel.'

Annie shook her head. 'If only Mr Farrar was still here.'

Fran's face softened at once. 'He'll come as soon as he can. I'm sure of that.'

Annie sniffed and sighed. 'Well, this won't do. There's a million and one things to do for tomorrow. I thought I'd use the cream damask cloth on the table, and the white one on the sideboard.'

Fran nodded. 'We'd better make a start.' Struggling to her feet, she helped Annie up and gave her a kiss and a quick hug. 'Now we're over the worst,' she said, with an attempt at cheerfulness.

'What about Dot?'

Fran hesitated. 'Perhaps we should warn her – although we aren't going anywhere, not with all this snow. She's quite safe here with us. Is it worth upsetting her before we have to?'

'I say leave the poor girl in blissful ignorance,' said Annie. 'Her poor mind must be going round in circles already. I know mine is.'

'Then we won't. Later, if it's necessary. We'll see how things turn out. But we'll stay together as much as possible.

347

Eat with us, Annie. I know you prefer the comfort of the kitchen, but just until all this is over? And we'll keep a special eye on Dot. She doesn't miss much.'

Annie gave a half-hearted smile. 'Right then. Let's get a move on. But first I could do with another drop of tea. Then I'll be as good as new!'

'I'll join you!' said Fran.

*

They were sitting down to dinner just after seven when the sound of wheels on the gravel outside alerted them to a visitor. Dot leaped from the table and rushed to the window.

'It's Connie!' she said.

Fran glanced at her in surprise. 'Well, don't sound so disappointed! Who did you think it was?'

She went to the front door and had opened it before Connie had paid off the taxi driver.

'What's happening?' she asked as Connie, hatless and dishevelled, struggled up the steps with a suitcase.

'What's happening?' Connie hissed. 'Matt is free, that's what's *happening*! You must have heard the news. He has killed his landlady, for God's sake, and I'm not staying at the flat on my own, waiting for my turn to come.' Inside the door she dropped the suitcase and her face crumpled. 'I can't stay there, Fran. I can't be alone. I'm going to stay with you until he's caught. And don't say I can't, because I *have* to.' She blinked furiously.

'Of course you can stay.' Fran was ashamed of her initial dismay and put an arm protectively round her sister's shoulder. Connie looked ill, she thought, but then none of them were at their best.

Connie kicked off her wellington boots, avoiding Fran's eyes. 'That damned taxi driver cheated me. Drove so slowly. Blamed it on the snowy conditions, but I knew what he was doing. Bumping up the fare.' She suddenly raised her eyes and Fran saw the desperation. 'I know we don't always see eye to eye, but I won't get on your nerves, Fran, truly I won't. I was all right until I woke and saw the snow. I thought, "That's it! That's the last straw". You know how I am about the snow.' She glanced round, apparently surprised. 'Where's Dot?'

'In the dining room.' Fran lowered her voice. 'She's in a funny mood at the moment.'

'Aren't we all!'

'We still haven't told her about Matt. I thought it best, for the moment.'

'She'll have to know eventually, but I agree. Better later. I won't say anything.' As Annie came into the hall she said, 'Oh, Annie, it's so good to see you. I was so fed up.' She accepted Annie's kiss. 'Do be a dear and try to rustle me up something to eat. It doesn't matter what it is. I'm starving. I might feel better when I've eaten. I couldn't eat at the flat. I couldn't even think about food.' She lowered her voice. 'I'm so scared. I've never felt like this before. Never in my whole life.'

The admission shocked Fran. Her sister had always boasted of her strength of mind. The fact that Connie was frightened somehow increased her own fear.

Connie laughed shakily. 'That rotten so-and-so has finally got to me! I'm not too proud to admit it.' She dumped her coat on the hall table and without a 'by your leave' went through into the dining room. To Dot she said, 'No welcome for me, then?'

Dot said, 'Hullo, Connie.'

Amy echoed, 'Hullo, Connie.'

Fran pulled an extra chair up to the table and fetched another set of cutlery from the sideboard drawer. As Connie sat down, Fran noted her pallor and the dark shadows under her eyes. No better and no worse than the rest of us, she thought, but in one way she was pleased her sister had come. Now at least they were all together under one roof. What's left of us, she thought, and anger flared again.

Annie ladled soup into Connie's bowl, and Connie smiled her thanks. 'I thought,' she said with a pathetic attempt at brightness, 'that, what with the funeral being tomorrow and the snow starting – well, I might not have been able to get here, so it seemed sensible to make the trip while I still could.'

Fran watched her. Perhaps her sister was in worse shape than she had at first thought? Connie's voice shook and there was a small muscle twitching in her right eyelid. She had been coping with all this alone, Fran reflected, and additionally she carried the burden of guilt because of the letter she had written to Matt. Blaming herself for the entire disaster, no doubt. Poor Connie who was always in the right, or believed so. Now she was definitely in the wrong, and that must be a particularly bitter pill.

Connie was looking at Dot, her eyes narrowed suspiciously. 'What's so funny?' she demanded.

'Nothing.'

Amy giggled, and Annie gave her a sharp look. 'Mind your manners, girl!' she told her.

Dot said, 'She didn't say anything!'

'She giggled. That's enough.'

Amy gave Dot a sly look. 'One day I'm going to be a bridesmaid, aren't I, Dot?'

It was Dot's turn to giggle, and Connie looked at Fran. 'What's the matter with these two?'

'I've no idea,' said Fran. She thought about it. Dot did seem to be in a strange mood, but she had put that down to the strain they were all under. She had considered Amy's presence a stroke of good fortune, but maybe she was wrong. Dot could be very childish when it suited her, and being with Amy might be exaggerating that trait. Perhaps, after all, it would be a good thing when the girl went back to her mother.

Connie finished her soup and wiped her mouth with her serviette. 'Snow!' she remarked. 'How I hate it. Cold, slushy stuff! Goodness knows what it will be like tomorrow in the churchyard if it goes on like this. It's already eight or nine inches. Deeper in places, and if the wind gets up it will form drifts.'

Fran nodded. 'The whole country will grind to a halt, the way it always does.'

Amy rolled her eyes. 'Footprints in the snow. They're ever so spooky.'

Dot threw her a quick glance and Fran thought she caught the hint of a smile. She felt a moment's irritation, followed by something deeper. These two seemed to be sharing some private joke, and for some reason it made her feel nervous. As if she didn't have enough to contend with, she reflected irritably.

Dot said, 'Amy's saving up to buy a bicycle. She's got *lots* of money in her piggy-bank. Haven't you, Amy?'

'Yes, I have.'

Annie looked at her suspiciously 'Lots of money? That's news to me.'

Amy said, 'Is it? Well, I have, so there!'

Another of those conspiratorial glances, thought Fran. She was watching them closely now.

Annie said to Amy, 'You come with me, young lady. You can make yourself useful and bring in the parsnips.'

When they had gone Fran looked across at Dot. 'Don't encourage Amy, Dot. She's only a child and she can be rather silly at times.'

'Amy's my best friend.' Dot looked sullen.

'Oh, is she? I thought that honour was reserved for Fritz!'

'*And* Fritz. Amy and Fritz are my best friends. I tell them all my secrets. Nobody else.'

She was positively glaring now and Fran's uneasiness doubled. There was something in Dot's voice that she didn't recognize. 'I didn't know you had any secrets.'

'Well, I do.'

Connie said, 'Oh, leave her, Fran. Secrets! What does it matter? I'll be glad when tomorrow is over.' She rubbed her eyes tiredly. 'I have to take this a day at a time, Fran. I wake up in the morning and think, "If only I can get through one more day!" I've hardly eaten for days. That soup was good. I wish Annie lived with me. Yesterday I lived on cheese and biscuits. Simply couldn't be bothered to cook for one. You've no idea.'

Amy came in with a tureen of vegetables and put them on the table. Annie followed with a casserole dish.

Fran watched for a moment as the food was served and passed along the table. She was so desperately tired of tension, doubts and fears. It seemed light years away since they had enjoyed a relaxed meal. To lighten the mood she smiled at Connie. 'How are things at the library?'

'Quiet. The snow puts people off, especially the older folk. They don't want to risk a fall, and it's understandable. I hate it when we're slack; the day goes so slowly.'

Fran nodded, feigning interest. She was wondering whether to take the coward's way out and break the news about Del in front of the family. Hopefully, Connie would behave better with an audience. However, it would be kinder to tell her when they were alone. Connie appeared to be at breaking point already, but the news could not be delayed indefinitely.

'Of course,' Connie was saying, 'the snow brings in more of the undeserving poor – the poor wretches who only come in to the library to keep warm. They sit there, pretending to read.' She shrugged. 'I try to turn a blind eye, but sometimes

352

they have to go. There was an old man in this morning who stank to high heaven, and people began to complain. What made it worse was that he was sitting close to the fire – and then he started to eat something revolting that must have come from somebody's dustbin! He didn't want to be moved, but when we mentioned the police he finally ambled out.'

Annie shook her head. 'Dregs of humanity!' she said. 'You can't help wondering what brought them so low.'

Fran, grateful for the turn the conversation was taking, was still considering her dilemma when Dot's next words solved the problem for her.

She said, 'I'm going to have a brother-in-law, Connie. I'll be a sister-in-law.'

Connie froze in mid-sentence as she stared at Dot. 'But that means . . .'

Fran and Annie exchanged a brief but frantic glance.

Dot went on, 'For Del. I shall be Del's sister-in-law.' She frowned. 'And so will you, Connie. At least I think so.' She turned to Fran. 'Will Connie be a sister-in-law too?'

Slowly the colour mounted in Connie's face. 'Does she mean what I think she means?' She stared at Fran, shocked.

Fran stammered, 'I was going to tell you myself, Connie, but . . .'

Connie swallowed. 'You and Del Farrar? Well!' She was struggling to hide her displeasure. 'How long has this been going on?'

Annie said hurriedly, 'Aren't you going to congratulate her, Connie? It's good to have something to cheer about, the way things are at the moment.'

Amy and Dot, sensing drama, had fallen silent, watching.

Connie laid down her knife and fork and wiped her mouth carefully. 'Something to cheer about?' Her gaze remained fixed on Annie's face. 'Fran gets herself engaged to a man she hardly knows, a virtual stranger, and you want to *cheer* about it? That takes some beating.'

Fran said, 'He's hardly a stranger, Connie. Over the past few weeks . . .'

'Weeks? *Weeks*? That's my point exactly. You hardly know the wretched man. It's ridiculous.'

'Isn't that for me to decide?' Somehow Fran kept her voice steady. 'I didn't expect you to be such a bad loser, Connie.'

'Bad loser?' Connie's hands crumpled her serviette. 'So that's how you see it. You think I'm jealous! Well, I'm not; not in the least. I'm just sorry for you both for being such fools. The poor man has hardly set foot in England—'

'He's gone to Scotland,' said Dot.

'Keep out of this, Dot!' snapped Connie. 'I can't believe that Fran would just throw herself at the first man who . . .'

Annie turned quickly to Amy and said, 'Go into the kitchen and wait for me there. Do you hear me, Amy? Scoot!'

Amy slid from her chair. 'Why do *I* have to go? It's not fair.'

Annie raised a warning finger. 'No arguments. Just go!'

In silence, everyone watched Amy's departure.

Dot inched her chair back. 'I think I'll go to my room,' she muttered. 'Fritz wants me to.'

Connie glared at her. 'Go where the hell you like. Who cares?'

As Dot rushed from the room Fran turned on Connie. 'There's no need to take it out on her. She didn't mean any harm.'

Annie stood up, then thought better of it and sat again. 'Please!' she said. 'Must we have a scene? Haven't we got enough to contend with without quarrelling amongst ourselves?'

Fran forced back an angry retort, closed her eyes and counted to ten. But when she looked again at her sister's furious face she knew that Annie's plea would go unregarded. Well, let Connie have her say. Maybe when it was all said she would calm down.

Connie turned towards Annie, her face flushing angrily. 'Well, thank you for those few comments on my behaviour, Annie. When I want your advice I'll bloody well ask for it.'

'Connie! Watch your language!' gasped Annie.

'I'll say and I'll do whatever I please, so mind your own damned business. This is between me and Fran.'

Annie's expression hardened. 'You are so jealous of Fran, Connie! You always have been.'

'And Fran hasn't been? Jealous of me, I mean? What about that doll then? The one at the photographer's. He gave that doll to me, Annie. To *me*! But who ends up with it?' She pointed an accusing finger at Fran. '*She* does. She whines and screams and kicks her legs until they give it to *her*!'

Annie cried, 'But that was years ago when you were children. You're supposed to have a bit more sense now. You shouldn't begrudge her a little happiness— If Fran and Del love each other . . .'

Connie snorted with disbelief. '*Love each other*?' she echoed. 'They don't even know each other. That's not love, that's indecent haste and it's pathetic.' She turned to Fran. 'Oh, don't think I don't know what this is all about. It's revenge for what happened all those years ago between me and Matt. It's Fran getting even in her own small-minded way!'

Fran stood up slowly. 'I've listened to enough of your raving, Connie. Annie's right: you are a small-minded bitch, and I'd like to throw you out right now. But in the circumstances I can't, because for the next few days we are all prisoners here. So since you must stay, I suggest you try to come to terms with the facts, Connie. Del and I love each other and we intend to get married as soon as we can. You may not like it, but you'll have to put up with it – and for God's sake, do try to have a bit more dignity.'

She stalked furiously out of the door, and as she did so she heard Connie burst into tears, and Annie saying, 'Now Fran's right, Connie. You're not a child now. Just pull yourself together, for heaven's sake.'

Fran made her way up the stairs to her bedroom, her heart pounding. 'Wonderful!' she told herself bitterly. 'Henry is lying in his coffin, Matt is trying to kill us and Connie is in one of her rages. It can't get much worse than this!'

But as she closed the bedroom door behind her, she wasn't prepared to bet on it.

*

Upstairs in her room, Dot sat on the edge of the bed and hugged Fritz to her. 'They're all hateful!' she told him tearfully. 'I hate them all – except Fran. And Amy, of course; she's going to be my bridesmaid.' She kissed the sleek head. 'I'm sorry you can't come with me, but I *will* come back to fetch you. Matt said I can and I will.'

She stared out of the window where large snowflakes swirled inexorably. She would go with Matt – of course she would. He had promised to take care of her for ever, and they would travel to exciting places and do wonderful things. They were going to Italy and they would eat spaghetti and see a coliseum and all the other places Matt had told her about in his letter. She put Fritz down and went over to the window. Footsteps in the snow – that's what Amy had said, and she had made it sound quite funny. Now, alone, Dot thought it sounded rather frightening. She wished it would stop snowing.

She glanced down at the dog. 'You mustn't pine for me, Fritz. Some dogs do, you see. They stop eating and mope and then they die. You *must* keep eating your dinner!'

She knew exactly what she must do and if she *did* forget, she would simply re-read Matt's letter. But she had learned it by heart. She would slip out of the house tomorrow night, after Henry's funeral. She would meet him at the station, and they would be miles away before anyone missed her. Matt had told her not to worry because he would explain everything to Fran and nobody would be cross with her.

She knelt down and pulled a small attaché case from its hiding-place under the bed. 'This is the secret, Fritz,' she told him in a whisper, 'between you and me and Matt. Nobody else knows about it – except Amy, of course.'

She opened the case and stared at the contents. Had she thought of everything, she wondered anxiously? Matt had told her not to bring anything at all because he was going to buy her lots of new things, but she had decided to take a few of her treasures. There was the ballerina musical box that Mother and Father had given her when she was seven, the scrapbook of wild flowers she had pressed over the years, her best lace handkerchief and her fur-lined slippers. She touched each item reverently. She had also packed her comb and brush set with the silver handles, a nightdress, dressing-gown and a few of her paints. As an afterthought, Dot plucked the blue knitted rabbit from her bed and stuffed him in as well.

'Oh, dear!' She picked the rabbit up again and frowned. If she packed him now, she couldn't cuddle him in bed tonight. 'I'll pack you in the morning – first thing,' she told him and put him back beneath her pillow. It was going to be strange sleeping somewhere else, but she supposed Matt would find them a very nice bed. It wouldn't be the same, though. She sighed. The case wouldn't shut and she tried to rearrange the contents without much success. Somehow she closed the lid and refastened it. She knew she would be happy with Matt, but she wished it could happen *now*. The waiting depressed her. And tomorrow was Henry's funeral, and that would make her even more miserable. She really would have preferred to stay with Fran and Annie until she felt happier, but Matt's letter was so sweet and he had promised to give her a ring to show that they were engaged. He would be waiting for her at the station and she couldn't bear to disappoint him.

'One more day, Fritz,' she told him. 'Then as soon as I can I'll come back for you.' Her fingers shook as she stroked the long, smooth back. 'You'll like Italy, Fritz. Italian people live in Italy and they love dogs. At least I'm sure they do. Everyone does. And you'll get to know some other dogs.' Matt hadn't actually mentioned this, but she was sure he had thought of it. He had said, 'Leave everything to me. Don't worry about a thing,' so she was trying not to. If only she could take Fritz tomorrow night . . . but Matt had been quite stern about that . . . 'And you promise me you won't pine, Fritz. You must eat your dinners. Whatever you do, remember that.' She wagged an earnest finger. 'Eat – your – dinners!'

Chapter Seventeen

T HE FOLLOWING DAY, IN A subdued silence,
Fran, Connie and Annie helped each other through
knee-deep snow while Amy and Dot insisted on
bringing up the rear. Annie and Fran made desultory conversation but Connie, still sulking after the previous night's
quarrel, spoke only when spoken to and then as briefly
as possible. It was still snowing, large lazy flakes which
occasionally swirled in the breeze. Overhead the sky was
heavy with more snow and the news bulletin had warned
that the severe blizzard affecting Scotland was moving south
and would affect most of the country before the end of the
day. When they finally reached the church they were ten
minutes late. As a reminder of the danger they all faced, they
found two constables keeping a discreet watch from beneath
a large cypress tree. They all exchanged polite nods.

Dot asked, 'Why are the policemen here? Did they know
Henry?'

'I suppose so,' said Fran, unwilling to expand on
the subject.

In the porch the vicar waited fretfully, a coat flung over
his dark robes.

'The undertakers aren't here,' he told them, blowing on
his bare fingers. 'I tried to telephone them, but the line

359

must be down. I couldn't get the operator. They'll be making slow progress through this snow.' He led them into the church, where Fran saw that all the pews were empty. She was not surprised that nobody else had come to the funeral; she could hardly blame them.

'If the undertakers can't get here, what will happen?' asked Connie and Fran read her mind immediately. Connie would hate the idea of another journey through the snow.

'We'll have to postpone the service,' the vicar told them. 'But I think we must give them another half an hour.' He stamped his feet and Fran resisted the urge to feel guilty on his behalf. Del was right – she must not take responsibility for everyone else.

'We'll wait,' she said. 'If they do manage to get through, it would be rather dreadful if the church was empty and the mourners fled!'

She smiled, to show that this mildly humorous remark was intended to lighten the mood and showed no disrespect. Connie ignored the remark and pulled her collar up closer around her face. She walked to the rear of the church where she pretended to be interested in the font, which she had seen hundreds of times before.

Fran's feet were cold in spite of her boots and thick socks and she was worried about Annie.

'I'm perfectly all right,' Annie insisted. 'I'm cold but I've been colder!'

There was nothing to do but wait. The church was unheated and the family, with the exception of Connie, huddled together in the front pew. From the corner of her eye, Fran watched Dot with growing concern. Her sister had woken that morning with feverish eyes and a tendency to burst into tears at the slightest provocation. She had moped around the house, hugging Fritz fiercely to her for such long periods that he had become resentful and snappy. She had resisted all Fran's attempts to draw her into conversation, and even

Amy's presence had done little to improve her mood. Could it all be related to Henry's funeral or was the strain of the past weeks beginning to affect her? Fran suddenly decided that, as soon as the snow melted and the roads were fit for traffic again, she would insist that the doctor called to see her. Now Dot was deep in a whispered conversation with Amy, her head bent forward, her shoulders hunched defensively.

Annie looked years older and Fran worried about her too. She was no longer young and therefore less resilient. Fran hoped she was not going to find herself with a household full of invalids by the time this wretched business with Matt was at an end. At once she felt a wave of guilt for her selfishness. They all had their problems and she had her fair share – but she also had Del. That knowledge gave her hope and strength. Somehow they must find a way through the confusion and pain to happier times. They should be helping each other, she thought, with a glance at Connie. They had lost a sister and a brother, and what was left of the family should close ranks against the world.

Her reflections were interrupted by Annie who cried, 'Here they are!'

The vicar hurried forward thankfully and they followed him outside. After a few minor difficulties, Henry's coffin was carried into the church, and Fran made a mental note to pay the undertakers a little extra for persevering under such extreme conditions.

Five minutes later the funeral service began. The coffin, resting on the oak trestle, was devoid of flowers or wreaths since these had not arrived. Offered a last glimpse of her beloved brother, Fran had accepted and had been comforted to see how peaceful he looked in death. Annie, too, had joined her, patting Henry's cold hand and blinking away her tears with a determined effort. Connie had refused, saying that she preferred to remember him as he had been in life. Dot had simply shaken her head.

The choir had been cancelled since many of them lived too far away to even think of attending but the vicar's wife, bundled up against the cold, arrived towards the end of the service, just in time to play the organ while they carried the coffin ouside into the churchyard. The family watched while the coffin was lowered into the inhospitable earth and wept helplessly. The gravedigger would come later in the day to do what he could with the frozen earth.

When they returned to the house, chilled and grieving, Dot was first inside the front door and she pounced excitedly on an envelope which had been put through the letter-box while they were away. It was addressed simply to 'The Massey family'.

Forgetting her self-imposed silence, Connie said, 'I'll open that, thank you!' and snatched it from Dot's hand.

Annie said, 'It isn't your place to open it! It was sent here and—'

Fran said, 'Oh, let her. What does it matter?'

'Why can't I read it? I *found* it!' Dot's voice was high with indignation.

Amy said, 'Yes, let her read it!' and received a sharp cuff from Annie for her cheek.

Meanwhile, Connie had slit the envelope and was reading the enclosed note. Her face paled. 'It's from Matt!'

Shaken, she surrendered it to Fran who read it reluctantly. It seemed that even though he could not be there to witness his victim's interment, Matt felt it necessary to make his presence known.

Annie asked, 'But how? I mean, there's been no post today. How did it get here?'

Dot peered over Fran's shoulder. 'What does it say?'

Fran read aloud '. . . Regret I cannot be with you at this sad time. I shall be thinking of you. Matt . . .'

Amy cried, 'Oh, isn't that *kind* of him!' She looked at Dot, who nodded belatedly.

Fran, deeply disturbed, stared at the note which shook slightly in her fingers. She was filled with a terrible suspicion – that Matt had come *in person*, to the house, to deliver this note, which was in effect a warning. And 'I shall be thinking of you . . .' Was that a veiled threat?

Connie, abandoning her position of martyred isolation, glanced from Fran to Annie for moral support. 'Let's shut and bolt the door,' she suggested and, without waiting for anyone to agree, slammed the front door and slid the bolts home. For a moment they said nothing, exchanging frightened looks. The threat which had once appeared distant was closing in on them. It had reached into the place where they should have felt most secure.

Fran said, 'Do you think he brought the note himself? Could he have paid someone else to bring it – to scare us?'

Connie swallowed nervously. 'If that was his idea, he's damn well succeeded. I feel sick!'

Annie said, 'Ring the police. Tell them what's happened.'

'The lines are down, remember?'

'Oh, Lordy!' Annie was very pale.

Fran began to take off her coat, boots and hat. Outwardly she remained calm but inwardly she was struggling to avoid panic. 'Look,' she said, 'Matt wants us to know that he can come and go as he pleases. He wants to scare us; he wants us to feel helpless. To panic. So we mustn't. We must stay calm.'

Connie hissed, 'Calm? Are you mad? How can we be calm? I thought the police were supposed to be keeping a watch on the house? You said they said they—'

Fran's patience was wearing dangerously thin. 'Oh, for heaven's sake, Connie! They said they'd do what they could, but they didn't anticipate all this snow. It can't be easy to hide yourself in a white landscape. Chief Inspector Bruce knows the situation better than we do. He'll do whatever he thinks necessary.'

'They were at the church,' Annie said.

'Yes, but they didn't stay; they left while the coffin was being lowered. I suppose they thought he might show up, but it was a long shot. They wouldn't really be expecting him to take such a risk.'

Connie's voice rose fearfully. 'So we're not protected here?'

Dot looked round from petting Fritz. 'Protected from what?'

'Nothing,' said Fran, after a moment's hesitation. With Dot in such a hysterical state, she dared not add to her anxieties.

Connie looked at Fran. 'I came here because I thought we'd be safe. I thought . . .' She bit her lip.

'Well, you thought wrong!' Fran snapped. 'And don't take that attitude. It's nobody's fault the snow is so deep. Nobody asked you to come, so maybe you made the wrong decision. Maybe you should have stayed in Maidstone. Maybe we should all have moved in with you!'

Annie said, 'Please! *Please!* Both of you! Don't let's make matters worse than they are. There's not much we can do about it. We're in a rather . . . well, a rather difficult situation and squabbling won't help. We've just got to try and help each other through it.' She tried to smile but failed abysmally. 'I suggest we get some hot food inside us. I'll see to it.'

The last thing Fran wanted to think about was food, but she said, 'Thank you, Annie.' Anything to keep people occupied. She turned to Connie. 'I'm sorry.' She put a hand briefly on her sister's shoulder in a small gesture of conciliation. 'This is no time to be at loggerheads. You're right about the food, too, Annie. We're all cold and miserable. But don't go to the kitchen alone.' Seeing

Annie's expression change, she added hastily, 'I think maybe we should try to – well, to think sensibly and not take risks.'

Annie said, 'Yes, I agree. Dot'll come with me, won't you, Dot? Give me a hand with the food? And Amy, of course.'

They went off in the direction of the kitchen, leaving Fran and Connie regarding each other nervously.

'I never thought I'd hate him,' said Fran sadly.

Connie's face sagged with misery. 'I'm sorry about yesterday,' she began. 'What I said about you and Del.'

'It doesn't matter,' Fran told her. 'Let's worry about Matt. If the police aren't around, all we can do is pray – and take a few precautions.' Lowering her voice, she said, 'I suggest we have a good look round the house. To make sure he's not in here.'

'*In here*! My God, Fran!' Connie's hand went to her mouth.

'I don't think he is, but just to be certain? He got as far as the front door, remember? Who knows where he is now? We could go round together and have a quick look in all the rooms while it's still daylight, without alarming the others.'

They spent ten minutes searching the house, opening all the cupboards and looking under all the beds. They even looked in the attic. Finally, a little sheepishly, they regarded each other with satisfaction. Matt was not in the house.

'Now what?' Connie asked. 'Is there anything else we can do?'

'We can turn the place into a fortress,' said Fran. 'Check and double-check all the windows and doors. Not just at night, but *now*. I'll see to it.'

'It's me he must hate most,' Connie stammered. 'You do see that, don't you? It's me he'll kill next!'

The words chilled Fran. 'Don't talk like that! He won't kill anybody because now we're wise to him. It was easy for him before because Henry and Mary still believed in him; they trusted him. We don't. If he got into the house . . .' What could he do, she wondered, and what would defeat him? She shook her head wearily. 'Perhaps we should all sleep together tonight, in one room.'

Connie frowned. 'What a dreadful idea!'

Fran shrugged. 'Safety in numbers.'

'I'm not sleeping anywhere with that dreadful Amy! And how would you explain it to Dot?'

'We could say it was for warmth, to save fuel. Pretend we are short of coal or something.'

Connie shook her head. 'We could leave Fritz downstairs. He'd bark if anyone tried to break in.'

Fran hesitated. 'Yes, he would. But that would upset Dot. You know Fritz sleeps in her room. He always has done, and she's in such a state at the moment.'

But Connie was not to be deterred. 'State or no state, she'll have to put up with it. It makes a lot of sense for the dog to stay downstairs. Dot may not like it, but we know it's for the best. I'll tell her if you don't want to.'

'Right. Do, then.'

Connie clasped her hands in front of her chest. 'I keep wondering how he would do it – I mean now that he doesn't have to pretend. He doesn't have a gun, presumably, and he surely wouldn't stab us . . . would he? Or strangle us? Like that Parfitt woman.'

'Oh, God, Connie! I can't listen to this!'

'I wake up in the night and think, "Thank God Mother isn't here to know what's happening."'

Just then Dot and Amy appeared carrying platters and dishes and Annie followed, shooing everyone into the dining room and telling Connie to hurry and take off her outdoor things. Connie meekly obeyed as Fran threw some more coal on to the dining-room fire and pulled the curtains to shut out the wintry view.

'We'll all feel better when we've eaten,' Annie insisted, 'so I don't want anyone saying they're not hungry.'

Coaxing and bullying, she persuaded the family to eat and Fran realized that she was right. Her appetite returned, and she certainly felt better with a full stomach.

After the meal they all helped with the washing-up and then Fran suggested a game of Monopoly which would keep them all together. She and Connie had checked the doors and windows and Fran felt reasonably safe. It was hard to imagine Matt breaking in and trying to kill them. She tried to convince herself that the letter had been a ruse to frighten them, delivered by someone else. Matt was probably miles away, laughing to himself at their plight.

After Monopoly they played 'I Spy', then Amy recounted a rambling story which her guide mistress had told them at camp. It was nearly midnight when Fran finally plucked up courage to suggest they go their separate ways to bed. Hot-water bottles were already in the beds and the bedroom fires had been lit at seven o'clock. They all had a drink of Ovaltine and then made their way to their rooms. Dot, separated from Fritz, went under sufferance, but by twelve-thirty they had all settled down. Fran heard the house fall quiet and decided to stay awake all night. She propped herself up in bed with a book, but the day's alarms had taken their toll. She was desperately tired, and around two the book slid from her grasp and fell unheeded to the floor. Her eyes flickered, opened briefly and then closed again. When, half an hour later, Fritz began to bark, there was no one awake to hear him.

Except Dot.

*

As soon as Annie went into the kitchen next morning she sensed that something was wrong. Instead of rushing to greet her with a wildly wagging tail, Fritz remained in his basket, his head on his paws, a mournful look in his soft brown eyes.

'Fritz!' She patted her thigh encouragingly, but the dog managed only a few flips of his tail and made no attempt to get out of his basket. She opened the back door. 'Out you go, then!' He snuggled deeper into his blanket. 'What's the matter with you this morning?' Apprehensively she looked round the kitchen but saw nothing untoward; nothing that might account for the dog's lethargy. 'Are you ill? Poor old boy.' She broke some stale brown bread into a dish and added some milk – his usual breakfast – but Fritz ignored it.

Sighing, Annie turned her attention to the range, raking out yesterday's clinker and relighting it with screws of paper and a handful of kindling wood. Meanwhile the kettle began to whistle and she made the first tea of the day. The longing for this sweet, hot brew was the only thing that persuaded her to leave her warm bed at this time of the year. With hands clasped around her cup, she regarded Fritz with concern. Perhaps he was ill. If anything happened to him it would break Dot's heart. Or maybe he was just moping because he had been made to sleep in the kitchen instead of with his mistress.

'Don't sulk, boy,' she told him. 'Dot will be down soon.'

His only response was a reproachful look, and Annie had more important things on her mind. Matt was somewhere nearby, that much was obvious, and the only reason for that was a determination to . . . to *hurt* them. Annie could not bring herself to think the word 'kill'. Not that he had a grudge against *her*, but if he harmed the others she would know; she would be a witness. Then he would have to get rid of her too. Her night had been a jumble of confused fears, alternating with a few snatches of restless sleep. She had prayed to see the dawn come up and God had granted her that much, so she was thankful. It was just before seven

368

and still dark outside, although there was a glimmer of light in the east. It was impossible to see whether or not any more snow had fallen. The high winds had already reached the south, a little earlier than expected, the sash windows rattled in their frames and the wind howled in the chimney.

During the night, the house had been full of terrifying creaks and murmurs. Once she thought she heard Fritz whining and scratching at the back door, but she had lacked the courage to come downstairs and investigate. If he made a puddle on the kitchen floor, it could easily be wiped up. Like a child afraid of the dark, she had kept a night-light beside her bed, comforted by the small glow, and had slipped a heavy brass candlestick beneath her pillow. Whether or not she would have been able to wield it against an intruder she had no idea – she would probably faint with fright if she saw anyone – but it made her feel better to know it was there. And if the intruder were Matt? Could she strike Matt with a brass candlestick? Only if she could think of him as a stranger. A dangerous stranger! If the worst happened she must cling to that thought.

She glanced up as Connie came into the room, rubbing her eyes. She was wearing a flannelette nightdress beneath a wool dressing-gown, but she still shivered.

'I'd forgotten how cold this house can be,' she grumbled, sinking on to a chair and pouring herself some tea. 'My fire went out. Damned thing!' She pulled the dressing-gown closer around her legs. 'There's a terrible draught. Can't you feel it?'

Annie held out her legs, which were encased in long woollen socks.

Connie rolled her eyes. 'My little flat gets really cosy.'

Annie bit back a suggestion that Connie should return there as soon as possible. This was no time for wrangles. 'I'm worried about Fritz,' she said instead. 'He looks a bit off-colour.'

Connie gave him a casual glance. 'I know exactly how he feels! If I had a nice warm basket *I'd* crawl into it!' She sipped her tea noisily because it was hot.

Slurping it, Annie called it, and it irritated her. She bit her tongue, however, and said nothing.

Connie asked, 'Fran not down yet?'

Annie looked around the bare kitchen. 'It doesn't look like it.'

'Very funny!'

'The longer she can sleep in, the better,' said Annie. 'We've nowhere to go, so she's better off asleep.'

'I couldn't sleep. I came down just before three to check that the front door was still bolted. I was a nervous wreck, to tell you the truth.'

Annie sighed. 'Poor Dot was crying in the night. I went in to see what was wrong, but she's in such a funny mood. Wouldn't even talk to me. Just kept saying, "Leave me alone, why can't you?" So in the end I did.'

'Missing Fritz, I expect.'

Annie shrugged. 'Or suspects something is wrong. She can hardly miss the fact that we're all scared out of our wits. She must wonder what's going on. I'm not so sure . . .' She broke off as Fritz slithered from his basket and padded towards the coal cellar. 'What's the matter with him?'

'Perhaps he wants to go out.'

'By way of the coal cellar?'

Annie got up slowly and moved towards the cellar. 'That draught!' she said. 'It's coming from the cellar. I wonder if . . .' She turned wide eyes towards Connie. 'The coal chute! Those outside doors never did close properly. Oh, God, Connie! You don't think—'

Connie gasped. 'That Matt has come into the house through the coal cellar . . .' She jumped to her feet, spilling her tea. 'We'd better wake Fran.'

But there was no need, for at that moment they heard

a strangled cry from above and then frantic footsteps on the stairs. Fran burst into the kitchen.

'Where's Dot?' she cried. 'She's not in her room or the bathroom or anywhere. Her bed's made and her blue rabbit's gone!'

There was a stricken silence, then Connie put a hand to her mouth. 'The coal cellar!' she whispered. 'That's why Fritz—'

Annie said sharply, 'Sit down, Fran. There's something we have to tell you.'

Fran swayed and Connie rushed to steady her. 'Do as Annie says!' she told her. 'Sit down and drink some tea.'

Taking the hint, Annie filled another cup with tea and added milk and three spoons of sugar. 'Drink this, Fran, and don't argue. We've got a lot to talk about, and God knows what to do! We'll need all our strength.'

While Fran, under Connie's eagle eye, forced down the tea, Annie took her courage in both hands and made another search of the house. As Connie had suspected, the wooden flaps to the outside of the coal chute were wide open and, just discernible beneath the fresh snow, a set of footprints led away from the chute towards the lane leading to the station. Annie stood irresolutely in the hallway while her mind pieced together the jigsaw . . . Dot's strange mood . . . Dot and Amy whispering together . . . She rushed upstairs and shook the child awake. In no time at all she had forced the truth from her and knew the worst. Dot had received a letter from Matt and had gone to the station to meet him! Threatening Amy with dire punishment to be decided later, Annie went downstairs with a heavy heart to break the news to Fran and Connie.

*

Fifteen minutes later Fran was dressed as warmly as she could, with wellington boots, a felt hat tied on with a

371

scarf and fleecy-lined leather gloves. Diagonally across her chest she wore a large tartan wrap which was intended for Dot, should she be found. Nobody added the word 'alive', but the thought was there nonetheless. Annie handed her a heavy metal torch and a sturdy walking-stick.

'Are you sure you'll be all right, Fran?' she asked for the fourth time.

Fran nodded. She was not at all sure, but there was no point in saying so.

Annie said shakily, 'I could cheerfully kill Connie! There's no excuse. She's just a coward!'

Fran shrugged. Speech was difficult because fear had overridden all her senses. She felt unable to see properly, and Annie's voice came to her as though from a great distance. Her throat was tight and her limbs ached with tension. The effort to prepare herself for whatever lay ahead was sapping her energy and she felt frail and vulnerable. It was all she could do to fasten the buttons at the wrists of her gloves, and she did this as slowly as possible. But then at last she was ready and could think of no further excuses. Somehow, alone, she must force herself along in Dot's footsteps and, if possible, bring her home before she met Matt. They had no idea how long she had been gone. Hopefully she had never reached the station – maybe *he* hadn't – but had stopped along the way, unable to navigate the deep drifts. If only Fran could find her, she could persuade her to come home. If she had to tell her about the murders, so be it.

From the sitting room she heard the sound of Connie's frenzied weeping – a Connie she had never known before, bowed and humbled by her terror of the blizzard which was now developing outside. The dawn had revealed snow up to three feet deep and more was falling, swept into dangerous drifts by the gale-force winds. Ashamed of her lack of courage but hysterically refusing to accompany Fran in her perilous search for Dot, the prospect of the journey to the station terrified Connie and nothing Fran or Annie could say would persuade her to leave the house.

Suddenly Connie staggered into the hall, her face blotched and swollen with tears. 'I'm sorry!' she wept. 'I'm sorry! I know what you think of me but I can't – I just can't!'

Annie looked at her dispassionately. 'Get out of my sight!'

'Oh, Annie! Don't!' Fresh tears coursed down her face. 'I can't help it. I'd go if I could. Oh, Fran, forgive me!'

Annie said, 'You'll be a damn sight sorrier if you lose another sister!'

Fran took a deep breath, trying to ignore the exchange. She wanted to leave the house with as much determination as she could muster, and Connie's weeping was demoralizing her.

'Go back to the fire!' she told her, 'and keep quiet!'

'I don't want you to die!' Connie cried.

'That makes two of us!' snapped Fran, who was finding that a little anger had a bracing effect. 'I'll come back and I'll bring Dot with me!' The little phrase sounded melodramatic, but Fran was past caring.

'Oh, Fran! *Dear* Fran!'

Annie turned impatiently, pushed Connie back into the sitting room and slammed the door. 'We can do without all that!' she told Fran. 'Now, is there anything else you might need? You've got the flask of soup—'

Fran patted her bulging coat pocket.

'—and the torch and the tartan blanket.'

'I've got everything.'

'And if she's not at the station, you'll come straight back. You promise? Please, Fran. If you don't come back I shan't know what to do next. You will be careful, won't you?'

'I will.' Fran gave her a quick hug, not trusting herself to say more. It would do neither of them any good to voice her fears — that if the snow didn't kill her, Matt probably would.

She opened the front door and plunged down the steps, leaving Annie to close and bolt the door behind her. At once the wind sucked her breath away and she quickly closed her mouth, drawing the collar and scarf around her face so that only her eyes remained uncovered. Clumsily, with the snowflakes stinging her eyes, she made her way down the steps and began the long trek along the drive to the gate. She made the mistake of glancing back towards the house and was startled to see Connie's face pressed to the window, watching her progress.

'Selfish bitch!' she muttered, but there was no real venom behind the word. Since first learning of the contents of Matt's letter to Dot, Fran had always known that she would have to make this rescue bid alone. Connie's phobia was too deep-rooted, her abhorrence of the snow too well established.

Stumbling, relying heavily on the walking-stick, she forced one leg and then the other through the deep snow which in places came over the tops of her boots. By the time she reached the gate into the lane, the melting snow which had fallen inside her boots added to her discomfort. The freezing wind numbed her face and forced its way into every crevice of her clothing. The gate wouldn't open, so she had to climb over it, which was not as easy as it seemed. She dropped thankfully to the other side and immediately set out along the lane towards the station. Dot's footsteps were still visible, but in places the snow had been compacted which suggested that, alone in the pitch-dark, she had frequently stumbled. Imagining Dot staggering along in the snow and the dark, she was amazed by her sister's courage. If Matt laid a finger on her . . . .

'Oh, Dot!' she murmured helplessly. 'Hang on! Just hang on!'

If she didn't, he would kill them both. It was so simple. Simple but devastating. She stopped about twenty yards away and stared at the station as it stood starkly against the snow. 'Silent as the grave,' she thought and shivered. Dare she call out to Dot? If Matt was there the call would alert him to her presence. Yet surely he must know that someone would come in search of Dot? Was he waiting for her to fall into the trap he had set? Her heart lurched uncomfortably. Had that been his intention all along? Had he used Dot as bait? If so, it had worked, for here was Fran like a lamb to the slaughter.

No, she wouldn't call out. In all probability he was waiting for her, had been watching her unsteady progress along the lane, smiling to himself. No, he couldn't have seen her through the blizzard. At least it would have hidden her approach.

'Please!' she whispered, hoping God would understand the abbreviated prayer.

She went forward, watching for signs of movement, then climbed down on to the track and up the other side. Still no sign of life. She had a sudden vision of Dot lying stretched out on the waiting-room floor, dead. Was that what she would find?

'Fran!'

It was Dot's voice!

'Dot! I'm coming!' Tears of relief filled her eyes as a wild hope suddenly flared within her. Maybe Dot was alone. Maybe Matt had been unable to reach the station. Maybe it was going to be all right.

She pushed open the waiting-room door and gave a scream that was part relief, part horror. Dot sat in one corner with her back to the wall, her face haggard, her eyes wild. In her hands she clutched her blue rabbit. Beside her was a small attaché case.

'Dot! Oh, my love!' Momentarily forgetting the need for

caution, Fran dropped the walking-stick and rushed forward to embrace her sister. As she did so a small movement caught her eye, and it took only a split second to realize that Matt was behind the door. As she whirled to face him she saw that he carried a piece of metal piping raised in his hands.

'Matt!' she screamed. This was it. This was the end . . .

She screamed again. 'No, Matt!' Stumbling backwards, her legs came into contact with something hard, something she immediately recognized. It was the brass coal-scuttle, and it was all she had. Snatching it up and summoning all her remaining energy, she somehow swung it up in a huge arc between herself and Matt. She had intended to use it to ward off the iron pipe, but instead it struck Matt a resounding blow on the side of his head. At the same moment the iron pipe descended on her hands, and she uttered an agonized cry and dropped the scuttle.

'Fran!' cried Dot, but Fran was in too much pain to be aware of anything else. Matt had stumbled back and now swayed sideways, clutching his head in both hands.

'Christ!' he muttered. 'Jesus Christ, Fran!'

Through a blur of pain Fran saw him fall, a look of surprise on his face. As he went down he struck his head on the fire grate, and then lay still.

'Oh, God!' she muttered. 'My hands!' She felt a wave of faintness and hastily sat down before she fell down. She and Dot watched Matt, who now lay very still.

'Get the pipe, Dot!' she gasped. 'He might come to.'

Slowly, fearfully, Dot reached forward until she had taken hold of the pipe. 'Have you killed him, Fran? Have you killed Matt?' Her tone was reproachful and Fran fought back hysteria.

'I don't know. I shouldn't think so.' She crept forward and touched Matt's hand but there was no response. She leaned over him cautiously. His eyes were wide open and staring, his jaw slack. She turned her attention to Dot. 'Did he hurt you, Dot? Did he do anything to you? Anything bad?'

'No.' Dot stared at the crumpled body. 'We were going to Italy.'

Fran looked at her. 'No, Dot, you weren't. It was a horrid lie – a trick to get us here so he could kill us.'

Dot's mouth trembled. 'To *kill* us?'

'Yes. Matt isn't a nice person any more, Dot. He's changed.'

'Did he kill Mary? And Henry?'

'Yes, he did.'

'Then I hate him!' She burst into ragged sobs and Fran put her arm around her, still watching Matt for any signs of a return to consciousness. Surely she hadn't killed him? And yet that lethal length of pipe was to have killed *her* and then, presumably, Dot. So had he kept Dot alive to witness Fran's death? The idea was obscene. 'We have to go home, Dot,' she said, 'before he wakes up.'

They both looked at the crumpled figure on the floor. Dot continued to sob and finally Fran's own tears flowed. Together, they cried for what they had lost – a brother they had once loved but who would never again be anything but a memory best forgotten.

A few minutes later, when they had both recovered, Matt still lay on the floor and Fran knew they must leave him there. If he was not already dead, he would probably die of exposure, but there was no way she and Dot could carry him back to the house, even if they wanted to take such a calculated risk. The decision was made for them, Fran thought gratefully as she struggled to her feet. The journey back would exact every ounce of energy they possessed and the sooner they started, the sooner they would reach the safety of home. Fran was aware that they had a long way to go before they could consider themselves safe.

She made Dot drink some soup and was relieved to see a little colour return to her sister's face. The night's adventure had left its mark, however, and Fran knew that Dot was in no condition to make the return journey unaided. Somehow, with her damaged hands, Fran would have to help her. In Fran's present state she doubted that they could do it, but staying where they were, with Matt's body to reproach them, was impossible.

'Heads you win, tails I lose!' she muttered as she knelt to take a final look at their tormentor. Waves of pain from her hands brought tears of weakness to her eyes. The bones of her fingers must be broken, but she dared not remove her gloves to take a look. She would rather not know.

The edge of the scuttle had carved a deep and jagged cut in Matt's left temple just on the hairline, and a thin trickle of blood ran from one ear. When, greatly daring, she pressed her ear to his chest, she could detect no heartbeat. She sat back on her heels, staring in disbelief. Had she killed him? The thought made her tremble. Had she and Dot really been that close to death themselves? There was a terrible irony about it which had not escaped her.

'Is Fritz all right?'

'What's that?' She dragged her thoughts back to the present.

'Fritz? Is he pining?'

'Dot! For God's sake!' Tentatively she shook Matt by the shoulder and was rewarded by a faint groan. 'He's still alive – but only just.'

Dot begged, 'Don't wake him up, Fran!'

Fran prayed for guidance. If he was, in fact, coming round he might regain his senses, might stagger after them and attack them again. It would be foolish to put themselves at risk. She hardened her heart. If they reached home safely, she would try to telephone the police. The lines might have been repaired by now. She didn't really think it likely, but in

380

her present mood she clutched at straws. They would come and get him; they would save his life. She didn't want to be Matt's murderer.

Dot touched Fran's hand, a gentle touch but enough to produce waves of pain. She felt an uncharacteristic rush of anger towards her sister. 'Of course Fritz is pining. What did you expect? He wouldn't eat his breakfast and he keeps on whining. Now get up, Dot. We have to go home.'

Dot stood up with difficulty, her limbs cramped with cold. 'What about Matt?'

'We'll tell the police.'

'Will he die?'

'I don't know.'

Dot looked at her case. Fran said, 'No! You must leave it for now. Just the rabbit; stuff him in your pocket. And take up the walking-stick.'

'But it's yours,' she protested.

'I can't hold it. Matt hurt my hands.' Fran leaned back against the table as her legs threatened to buckle beneath her. 'Leave the flask, everything. They don't matter.'

Ignoring Dot's half-hearted protests, Fran made her go outside into the blizzard. Somehow she climbed down and up the track and back across the station entrance to the lane. Dot trailed behind her, scared and tired but grumbling about her abandoned possessions. However, anything was better than hysterical tears, Fran thought, and for a while they struggled on, making slight progress but hindered by the snow which blinded them. The contours of the lane were disappearing and Fran was increasingly unsure which way was the right one. Her hands throbbed excruciatingly, but the pain kept her conscious when the cold threatened to numb her mind as well as her body. Dot was in a bad way; her ordeal of the previous night had exhausted her, and the effort now required was more than she could manage. She was simply at the end of her resources, and Fran wondered desperately if she herself would have enough strength for both of them.

Somehow they plunged on, stumbling erratically, trying to keep together. Then disaster struck when, with a faint cry, Dot disappeared from view and through the flurry of heavy snow Fran could see no trace of her. Dropping to her knees, she felt around in the snow and discovered a deep drift. Losing her balance she tumbled into it, landing on top of Dot who lay groaning, her head against a tangle of hawthorn roots.

'Dot! Speak to me!'

'Fran!' Her voice was very weak.

'We've got to get out of here. Come on. Move yourself!' Wincing at the pain in her hands, she tried to chivvy Dot to her feet.

'Can't we have a rest?' Dot pleaded.

'No! Not even for one minute!' Fran tugged and pushed her. 'Get up, Dot. I can't help you, but you must get up.'

After what seemed an age, both she and Dot regained what Fran hoped was the middle of the lane. They looked like two snow maidens. Snow clung tenaciously to their clothes and there was ice along their brows.

Dot gave a little cry of alarm. 'My boot! I've lost my boot!' she wailed. Trying to hop, she almost tumbled back into the drift. 'It's down there!'

Fran brushed away tears of frustration before they could freeze on her cheeks. Without the boot Dot's foot might well become frostbitten. But dare she go back into that drift and search for it? Desperately she looked around for inspiration.

'We're nearly home now,' she suggested. 'Look, I can

see the lights.' It was true! Less than two hundred yards separated them from the welcoming gleam of the house lights. 'You can walk that far without your boot.'

But Dot wouldn't hear of it; she flatly refused to move another step without two boots. 'I want it, Fran!'

Fran stared at her and the last of her patience deserted her. Leaning forward, she punched her sister hard on the shoulder. 'Damn your boot and damn you!' she cried furiously. 'Stop behaving like a child, Dot. If you carry on like this we'll both die. Is that what you want?'

'Fran!'

'Well, is it?'

Fran returned Dot's stare, half hoping that the surprise tactics might jerk a little sense into her sister, but unfortunately it had the opposite effect. Dot's eyes rolled upwards in her head and she slumped forward. Her full weight fell on to Fran, sending her face first into the snow. Fran lay there, weak with pain and an overwhelming sense of failure. The shock of her encounter with Matt was finally telling on her. She shivered uncontrollably, but not from the cold. There was suddenly no way she could make another move.

Dot was on top of her, murmuring incomprehensibly, but occasionally Fran caught the name Fritz. She was full of compunction now but it was too late. Her concentration was slipping away. She knew vaguely what needed to be done, but she could no longer do it. Aware of a merciful drowsiness creeping over her, she finally surrendered to it and, closing her eyes, allowed herself to drift into sleep.

*

'Fran! Wake up, Fran! Dot! D'you hear me! Wake up, damn you!'

The voice came from far away and Fran wanted to ignore

383

it. It persisted, however, and with a tremendous effort of will she opened her eyes. Dimly she caught a glimpse of Dot's face as she was hauled to her feet by someone. It was all too much ... Closing her eyes, she drifted once more until she was rudely shaken by the arm and slapped around the face.

'Fran, open your eyes! Help me, for God's sake!'

It sounded like Connie and she frowned in confusion as slowly and painfully she struggled to her knees.

'Connie?' she muttered drowsily. 'Is that you?'

'Yes, it's me. Pull yourself together, Fran. Wake *up*!'

Blinking in disbelief, she felt a strong arm go round her waist and somehow she was on her feet and Dot was standing too, both leaning against Connie for support, staggering desperately slowly towards the lights of home. Dazed and barely conscious, Fran recognized the front steps and then Annie was rushing out to gather them all in. The sudden warmth of the house restored her wits and slowly Fran turned her head. She bit back a gasp of surprise as tears of gratitude filled her eyes.

'Connie!' she whispered. 'It was you – out there in the snow!'

Connie nodded. 'I didn't have much option!' she said with a faint smile.

'You were wonderful!' Fran told her.

Her sister's arms, still in their snow-covered sleeves, went round her in a clumsy but tearful hug, and Fran knew that the animosity which had existed between them for so long was finally at an end.

*

While Dot was bundled upstairs to bed, Fran and Connie changed into warm, dry clothes and huddled by the fire. They tried the telephone but the lines were still down. A thoroughly chastened Amy had brought them scrambled eggs on toast before returning to temporary banishment in her bedroom.

Fran's hands were blue and swollen and Annie had to feed her. In between mouthfuls, Fran told her and Connie of the encounter with Matt and its terrible end.

'You think he'll die by morning?' Annie whispered. 'Matt will *die*?'

Fran recognized the anguish in her voice. 'I don't know, Annie. Maybe. And maybe it will be for the best. Do you want to see him hanged?' She wiped away a large tear. 'I had to leave him. He would have killed me and then Dot. I wasn't trying to kill him, Annie. It was self-defence.'

Annie shook her head speechlessly.

'It just happened. I had to protect myself and Dot. I was so lucky the scuttle was there; he would have beaten us both to death with that iron pipe.' She held out her hands. 'He did this with just one blow. Can you imagine the force behind it? He would have split my skull!'

Annie tutted. 'As soon as the roads are passable we'll get the doctor out here to see you and Dot.' She set down the plate of eggs and, producing a handkerchief, wiped her eyes. 'You must think I'm a very foolish old woman. You must forgive me. Of course you did what you had to, Fran. I see that. It's just like a nightmare that never ends.'

Connie shrugged. 'It's ended now, Annie. Whatever happens to Matt, we've got to put it all behind us and get on with our lives.'

Annie patted her hand. 'You were so brave, Connie. I know exactly what that cost you, and I'm sorry for all the bad things I thought about you.' She turned to Fran. 'And don't think I bullied her into coming after you; she made up her own mind and just did it. You've all been so brave. Even poor, misguided Dot. Fancy crawling out through the coal shute in the middle of the night and setting off for the station – without telling a soul except that wretched Amy.' She scowled. 'I've given that young madam a piece of my mind. A *large* piece! Silly little scatterbrain. She's going home to her mother as soon as it's humanly possible. Filling poor Dot's head with all that nonsense about boyfriends!' She shook her head incredulously.

Connie pushed her plate away and stood up wearily. 'That was wonderful, but now I'm going to bed.'

Fran nodded. 'I'll do the same,' she said. 'But what about you, Annie? You've been through a terrible time. It must have been dreadful, waiting here alone, not knowing if you would ever see any of us alive again.'

'I'll stay here by the fire for a while,' Annie told her. 'I hate to waste a nice blaze. I'll be fine now I know you're all safe.'

Fran glanced back as she and Connie left the room and thought how much Annie had aged. But then the dreadful events of the last few days must have left their mark on all of them – with the exception of Matt who, in all probability, would never be a day older than he was today.

*

Ten days later, when the snow had been cleared from the railway tracks, Connie was able to return to Maidstone and Fran finally managed to get up to London to Starr Masseys. As soon as word spread that she was back, everyone gathered in her office to congratulate her on her survival. Matt's abduction of Dot, and Fran and Connie's rescue, had made the headlines, and her colleagues were eager to hear the story from her own lips. Promising herself that this would be the very last time, Fran told the story once again.

'When the police finally reached the station Matt was dead. From exposure to the freezing temperature.'

Marjory said, 'I'm so glad you didn't kill him. I know he deserved it, but you would have had to live with it. It was better the way it happened.'

Fran nodded. 'The most amazing thing is the way Dot has behaved. She rallied round and was quite sensible about it. After what she endured that night I expected problems, but she understands. She even apologized to us for the trouble she caused.'

Derek smiled. 'And she'll be receiving her first cheque soon! That'll be a thrill for her.'

At that moment the telephone rang and the receptionist said she had a Mr Farrar on the line. Fran felt weak with excitement: he was back from Scotland at last!

'Fran! My dearest! Oh, God! It's so good to hear your voice again. I'm in London. I rang you at home and Annie said you'd be here. Can I come over and see you?'

'Of course you can.' Her smile was radiant. 'And Mr Starr senior has some good news for you.'

'I'm on my way.'

Fran hung up, aware that Stuart's eyes were on her. 'That was Del Farrar,' she said, somewhat unnecessarily. While she had been talking most of her colleagues had slipped out of the room, unwilling to intrude upon what was obviously a private call.

Stuart smiled. 'He must be counting his blessings. He almost lost you.'

'I expect he is.'

'And our offer for the novel? Is that your news?'

'Yes. Peter Westrop has advised him to accept. It was very fair for a first novel.'

'And all thanks to you.'

Fran shrugged. 'He wrote it,' she said.

387

'You made it happen, Fran. He's a lucky man. I'm jealous as hell, but you'll make a splendid team.'

'Thank you.' She looked at the pile of unopened mail. 'I think I'd better make a start on these!'

As he made his way out, the telephone rang again. This time it was the police.

'Detective Chief Inspector Bruce here. I thought you'd appreciate an update. I've just come back from St Maxime. I was trapped over there by the snow.'

'St Maxime? Oh! Then you saw Violet?'

'Yes. It seems they did not have a very happy encounter. She had some news for him – bad news – about his father. It seems his father was Alex Massey, Violet's brother.'

Fran frowned. 'Her *brother*! But isn't that . . . well, it's incest, isn't it?'

'Exactly. My guess is that that information was what finally turned him against you all. The knowledge that he was the result of an incestuous relationship, plus the fact that maybe all the tontine money should have been his.'

'Good heavens! Poor Matt!'

'Must have been a blow – a double blow in fact. But I shouldn't waste too much sympathy on him. Other people suffer similar misfortunes and they don't all turn to murder. They certainly don't set out to revenge themselves on an entire family.' Fran said nothing, trying to come to terms with the information, and he asked, 'Are you still there?'

'Yes. I'm sorry. I was thinking . . .'

'I also want to say how sorry I am that we weren't on hand when you needed us.'

'It's nobody's fault and water under the bridge.' She was thinking of Del, wondering how long it would be before he arrived at the office. 'When can we bury Matt?'

'As soon as you like after the inquest, which is set for this coming Friday. You'll all have to be there, and you and your sister Dorothy will have to give evidence. Do you think she'll be able to do that?'

'Yes, she will.'

There was a short pause, then Bruce said, 'You won't want to bury him in the family grave, surely?'

'No. We've talked it over and we'll buy another plot, just for him.' She hesitated. 'Are any charges being brought against me, Inspector? I did abandon him, and indirectly that caused his death.'

'None. Firstly, you struck him in self-defence. Secondly, you didn't know how serious his injury was, so you couldn't tell whether or not he would recover. You and your sister had to get away. You phoned us as soon as you could. It was the weather that killed him, in a way. But we'd have had him, you know. We had all the evidence we needed and he'd have faced the death penalty.'

Fran thought she detected a note of regret in his voice. 'Well, that's a weight off my mind,' she said.

'It's been tremendously rough on you. I'm glad it's all over – as much as it ever can be. If I can be of any further help, don't hesitate to call me.'

'Thank you.' She hung up.

At that moment one of the secretaries put her head round the door. There was a mischievous look in her eyes. 'There's a very nice-looking author on his way up to see you. Hallam, I believe!'

She withdrew and her place was taken by Del Farrar. For a long moment they stood looking at each other, and Fran knew without a doubt that she had made the right decision. This was the man, God willing, with whom she would spend the rest of her life. She hurled herself into his waiting arms and, as she did so, the horrors of the past few weeks began to fade. Nothing would bring back

389

Mary or Henry, and the survivors would never be entirely free of the shadow Matt had cast over their lives. But Fran, Connie and Dot had drawn closer together, and for them life would go on. For Fran and Del, the future was full of promise.

LONG DARK SUMMER

Pamela Oldfield

Life seems full of promise for Sophie Devine, young wife and mother of two. But it is 1665 and, as spring gives way to summer, the shadow of plague hangs over London.

When the city is finally stricken, Sophie is offered a safe haven for herself and the children on her brother's farm in Woolwich. Fanny, their maid, is left behind in London to care for her master, but discovers that Matthew is in love with someone else.

Stunned by the knowledge of his infidelity, Sophie is forced to return to a London now ravaged by sickness and death to try to win back his love – and finds herself also fighting for his health, and her own feelings for Luke Meredith, one of the few dedicated doctors to remain in the belcaguered city . . .

FICTION
0 7515 0137 9

SWEET SALLY LUNN

Pamela Oldfield

Fleeing from Louis XIV's persecution of the Huguenots,
young Solange Luyon arrives with her family in England.
They know no-one there, except the one person most
important to Solange – her father, Pierre, who
mysteriously deserted his family years ago. But unable to
locate him, the Luyons are forced to struggle on alone
through the harsh realities of a new life.

Solange, inheriting her family's traditional baking skills,
and taking the English name of Sally Lunn, moves to Bath
and becomes the celebrated owner of Sally Lunn's
Coffee-House. With her bright eyes and golden-yellow
curls, she attracts a stream of admirers. But the path of
true love is not a smooth one; it is strewn with the torment
of fierce passion, voices from the past, the hurt or rejection,
and the ardent attentions of Beau Nash, the handsomest
dandy in England . . .

GENERAL FICTION
0 7474 0873 4

A DUTIFUL WIFE

Pamela Oldfield

Marion is one of the lucky ones. Married to Dr Gilbert Reid, she has everything she could possibly want – except love. And then she meets Ralph . . .

It is Ralph's mother, the philanthropist Amelia Gaunt, who unwittingly brings her adored son and the doctor's wife together. Eager to alleviate the terrible plight of London's poor, her charity also leads to an encounter between Gilbert Reid and Meg, a cheerful Cockney streetwalker. It is a meeting that sets in motion an extraordinary series of events that she is powerless to control . . .

While Marion tries dutifully to deny her growing love for Ralph, her husband battles against the darker side of his nature that he has suppressed for so long. Losing the battle will drag him relentlessly down into an alien world, the brutal world where a faceless murderer of prostitutes stalks the courts and alleyways . . .

GENERAL FICTION
0 7474 0495 X

☐ Long Dark Summer	Pamela Oldfield	£4.99
☐ Sweet Sally Lunn	Pamela Oldfield	£5.99
☐ A Dutiful Wife	Pamela Oldfield	£3.99
☐ The Halliday Girls	Pamela Oldfield	£4.99
☐ The Passionate Exile	Pamela Oldfield	£4.99
☐ String of Blue Beads	Pamela Oldfield	£5.99
☐ Falling From Grace	Pamela Oldfield	£5.99

Warner Books now offers an exciting range of quality titles by both established and new authors. All of the books in this series are available from:

Little, Brown and Company (UK),
P.O. Box 11,
Falmouth,
Cornwall TR10 9EN.
Telephone No: 01326 372400
Fax No: 01326 317444
E-mail: books@barni.avel.co.uk

Payments can be made as follows: cheque, postal order (payable to Little, Brown and Company) or by credit cards, Visa/Access. Do not send cash or currency. UK customers and B.F.P.O. please allow £1.00 for postage and packing for the first book, plus 50p for the second book, plus 30p for each additional book up to a maximum charge of £3.00 (7 books plus).

Overseas customers including Ireland, please allow £2.00 for the first book plus £1.00 for the second book, plus 50p for each additional book.

NAME (Block Letters) ....

....

ADDRESS ....

....

....

☐ I enclose my remittance for ....
☐ I wish to pay by Access/Visa Card

Number ☐☐☐☐☐☐☐☐☐☐☐☐☐☐☐☐

Card Expiry Date ☐☐☐☐